FIREBORN

SERAPHIM: BOOK TWO

DAVID DALGLISH

www.orbitbooks.net

Copyright © 2016 by David Dalglish
Excerpt from *Shadowborn* copyright © 2016 by David Dalglish
Excerpt from *Hope and Red* copyright © 2016 by Jon Skovron

Cover design by Kirk Benshoff
Cover illustration by Tommy Arnold
Cover copyright © 2016 by Hachette Book Group, Inc.

Orbit
Hachette Book Group
1290 Avenue of the Americas
New York, NY 10104
orbitbooks.net

First Edition: November 2016

Orbit is an imprint of Hachette Book Group.
The Orbit name and logo are trademarks of Little, Brown Book Group Limited.

The publisher is not responsible for websites (or their content) that are not owned by the publisher.

The Hachette Speakers Bureau provides a wide range of authors for speaking events. To find out more, go to www.hachettespeakersbureau.com or call (866) 376-6591.

ISBNs: 978-0-316-30273-9 (paperback), 978-0-316-30272-2 (ebook)

Printed in the United States of America

LSC-C

10 9 8 7 6 5 4 3 2 1

To my wife, for everything

PROLOGUE

The letter lay before Jay Simmons on his desk. When the army of Center had invaded their home and declared sanctions against their island, he'd hoped that would be the end of the aggressive measures. That letter dashed those hopes to dust.

"You'd have us shut down our academy and disband our Seraphim?" Jay asked the messenger, a balding man wearing the red robes of Center's theotechs. His name was Eyan, and Jay hated him from the moment the man had stepped into his office and sniffed as if he'd entered a pigsty.

"Is the wording not clear enough?"

Jay's upper lip twitched.

"The desire is clear, but not the reasons for it. The Speaker has already burdened us with sanctions against purchasing any new elements. Now he'd leave us without a single harness or elemental prism to protect ourselves from the other three islands?"

Eyan scratched at his bulbous nose, seemingly more fascinated with that itch than the dismantling of Weshern's last semblance of independence.

"For the duration of our occupation we will deny any requests for duels or battles from the other minor islands. Weshern is under Center's care. You and your people will not be in any danger."

"For the duration." Jay rose from his seat, his fist rapping against the top of his hardwood desk. "And how long might that be?"

Eyan shrugged.

"Until the Speaker decides the danger is passed. What happened to Galen will not happen here, no matter the cost."

"So days? Months? Years?"

The theotech finally met his eye. The acknowledgment worsened Jay's mood further. This was not the look of a man addressing an equal, but of a master berating a dog for ceaselessly barking.

"Decades, if that is what it takes," Eyan said. "You grumble as if you have a say in this matter, Headmaster. Weshern's carelessness cost tens of thousands of innocent lives. Do you think your petty grumblings mean anything compared to that?"

He held up a wooden board in his left hand, along with several sheets of thick paper.

"Soldiers are on their way with wagons to load up your wings and elements. We'll ship them back to Center, for safekeeping until the sanctions end. If you wouldn't mind, I'd like to get started cataloging your total inventory."

Jay swallowed down what felt like a razor blade in his throat.

"Not at all," he said. "Follow me."

He stepped around his desk, past the theotech, and out of his office. The outside hall was empty but for his over-secretary, Rebecca Waller. Ever since the Speaker arrived two weeks ago accompanied by his army of knights and ground troops, Jay had sent home the vast majority of students from the academy,

Jay told himself he'd done his best. The game was over. Weshern's freedom would now be in the hands of others.

Jaina walked alongside the wagon, and she gestured for him to follow her. He thought to disobey, but every second he played along might be the difference between life and death for the Sky-born twins. Keeping to the grass, they walked beside the wagons on the dirt road. Jaina's gaze remained on him at all times.

"You're a brave man," she said, suddenly interrupting the monotony of the rolling wagon wheels. "It is not too late to repent and confess your sins."

For decades Jay had lived his life as a soldier, and then as a teacher of students. That experience allowed him to keep his face passive when he answered.

"I do not understand."

"I think you do," she said as she stared at the armory. "My knight's delay tells me all I need to know."

Jay was about to plead further ignorance when Loramere and Aisha burst from the armory, remaining dangerously close to the ground as they streaked in opposite directions. Wings thrummed as knights immediately gave chase. Jay watched, trying to judge the separation between them and the knights. They had surprise on their side, but the knights' wings were faster, and they had the height advantage. Perhaps if either could make it to a forest, and hide amid the trees...

From the corner of his eye Jay spotted Jaina moving. He felt pain in his stomach, felt warmth flowing down his abdomen. Jaina held him close with one arm around his neck, the other clutching the jeweled dagger pierced up to the hilt in his belly.

"It's not lethal," she whispered into his ear. "Not yet. If you behave, and do not struggle, you might survive this."

By David Dalglish

Seraphim

Skyborn

Fireborn

Shadowborn

Shadowdance

A Dance of Cloaks

A Dance of Blades

A Dance of Mirrors

A Dance of Shadows

A Dance of Ghosts

A Dance of Chaos

Cloak and Spider (e-only novella)

leaving the fields and halls quiet and dull. Every single prism was precious, for the flow from Center had ceased completely. They didn't have any to spare on training students. And now what they had left was to be taken . . .

"Rebecca, could you carry a message for me?" he asked the woman as she sprang from her seat.

"Of course," Rebecca said. Jay felt a pang of regret in his chest, and he fought to keep his voice calm.

"The academy is shutting down, and we're moving out our gear and elements. This ends it all."

Rebecca's slender face didn't crack in the slightest.

"I will inform the remaining Seraphim," she said, dipping her head in respect.

"Such dour attitudes," Eyan said as Jay led him down the hall, Rebecca hustling in the opposite direction. "I'm sure there will be other cushy jobs for a man of your age and reputation. Your standing in Weshern won't be diminished significantly."

That Eyan would believe Jay's most pressing concern was his reputation made him loathe the man all the more. All Eyan cared about was status and position. Dismantling the Weshern Academy was just another assignment, a bothersome one that would eat up too many hours of his day.

"Perhaps," Jay said, opening the door and holding it for Eyan. "But this is the job I'm best at, and the one I expected to hold until my last days."

A golden-winged and -armored man waited at the entrance, two swords sheathed to his wide waist. He was an angelic knight, Center's elite version of the outer islands' Seraphim. The knights were generally considered to be of far greater skill, not that such claims had been challenged in decades. To rebel against Center was considered suicide. The knight scanned over Jay as if analyzing a threat, then dismissed him, eyes returning to the skies.

"Herding little brats into apartments and classrooms, all in the hopes that a few will accomplish something to make the effort worthwhile?" Eyan asked. The theotech shook his head. "I'm not sure why you'd miss it at all, Headmaster. I'd think working the fields with the cattle would be more rewarding. At least the bovines won't talk back to you when you give them an order."

Jay chuckled, the good humor faked in an effort to keep Eyan and his bodyguard at ease while they crossed the academy grounds toward the nearby armory.

"Too true," he said. "And you can whip a cow without fear of their parents' displeasure."

Eyan laughed.

"Now you're seeing the brighter side of things. Perhaps I misjudged you, Headmaster. You seem like a man with a good enough head on your shoulders. Even if your Archon is reinstated, there will be significant administrative changes in the way Weshern's government works. I daresay we might find you a suitable position. If you can handle the entitled whelps here, then the rest of Weshern's ilk shouldn't prove any more difficult."

They arrived at the squat building. Jay pulled out a key and unlocked the wide front door. Normally one of the mechanics would be lurking nearby, but they'd all been dismissed as Jay shrank the staff in anticipation of Center's complete takeover. Besides, there was somewhere far more important for the mechanics to be.

"Do you want to start with the wing harnesses, the swords, or the stash of elements?" Jay asked.

"The harnesses," Eyan said. "They'll be the most difficult to transport. If we need more wagons, I'd like to know immediately."

"Smart thinking," Jay said, and he pushed open the door.

Eyan led the way, eyeing the dozens of harnesses hanging from thick iron pegs nailed to the wall. As before, the knight hung back, keeping watch outside.

"Not a bad collection," Eyan said. "And well cared for, surprisingly enough. I'd expected them to be more weathered, given all the use by trainees."

"The trainees' equipment is in the gear sheds at the center of the academy grounds," Jay said. Beside the door rested the long pole used to remove the harnesses from the wall, and Jay casually took it into his left hand. "And even those are in fine condition. We take good care of what is ours here in Weshern."

Eyan pulled out his pad, steadily adding marks to his paper with a piece of charcoal as he counted row after row. Jay followed after him a few feet behind.

"How long until the wagons arrive?" Jay asked when Eyan was deep into his counting.

"We flew ahead, so maybe thirty minutes or so. Why?"

"No reason."

Jay swung the pole with both hands. It cracked against Eyan's neck, striking with the metal just beneath the hook. The theotech let out a cry as he dropped to the ground, body flopping limply. Jay hoisted the pole, bottom pointed toward Eyan's temple, and thrust it down with a grunt. The metal crunched through bone, ending Eyan's pathetic cries. Jay pulled the pole free and shook it in a futile attempt to clean off the gore and blood, frustrated by the racing of his heart. He should be calmer than this, more clearheaded.

A thud at the door turned Jay about. Argus Summers, the legendary commander, stood in the doorway, uniform crisp and clean as always. He held a bloody blade in his right hand. At his feet lay the body of the dead knight, unceremoniously dumped onto the armory floor.

"How much time?" the commander asked.

"The theotech said thirty," Jay said. "So act as if we've got twenty and get this stuff moving, now."

Argus motioned to someone outside, and a dozen men and women rushed into the armory. They were Seraphim, and they'd been stationed in the barracks waiting for just this possibility. Rebecca's summons had brought them here for removal of all useful equipment. *This ends it all,* he'd told the over-secretary. The academy was finished, thought Jay with a heavy heart, but it was also a new beginning. There was no turning back now, no hoping for peace. Weshern's resistance would officially begin here, in his academy, before his very eyes.

"We can't get a tenth of this out in time," Argus said as Seraphim grabbed spare sets and exited. "I told you we should have done this days ago."

"Once the Speaker discovers their absence, there is no going back," Jay said. "Forgive me for holding off signing our own death warrants until we had no other choice." He crossed his arms. "Are you clearing out the gear sheds as well?"

"Another ten are there taking what they can," Argus said.

"Focus on the elements. You only need enough wings for our Seraphim. The elements, though, may one day run out."

"I've already told them," Rebecca said, the over-secretary's demeanor still calm as ever as she strode into the building. Seeing the dead theotech, she walked closer and took the pad from his limp hand. Her eyes flitted over what few scribblings there were before she pocketed the pad.

"At least Center won't know the number of our supplies," she said. "Every bit of information is precious."

"What of our own records?" Jay asked.

Rebecca smiled at him, just the tiniest of curls at the edges of her mouth.

"Already burned. Some of us did not wait until the very last moment to make our move, Headmaster."

Another stab to Jay's heart. Another reminder that their academy was at an end, and that he'd been foolish to delay so long.

"You were always better than I deserved," he said.

"Yes, but you were aware of it," Rebecca said. "That helped more than you might believe."

Jay caught a glimpse of a particular Seraph from the corner of his eye, and he turned to see Breanna Skyborn strapping on her own pair of wings.

"Make sure you get plenty of fire element for that one," Jay said, projecting his voice. Bree glanced up from her buckles, and she blushed when she realized others were staring at her.

"I'll try not to be wasteful with it," she said.

"There is no waste," Argus said. "Not when the flame covers your blades."

The commander patted Jay on the shoulder, grabbed a set from off the wall, and hurried out. Jay glanced at Rebecca, who was busy jotting down numbers on a sheet she'd stolen from the dead theotech.

"It's time for you to leave," he told her.

The over-secretary lowered her pad.

"Excuse me?"

"You may walk, or have a Seraph carry you. Either way, it's time for you to go. Center's people will be here soon, and when they discover what's happened they'll scour the nearby countryside to catch whoever's responsible. I refuse to let you be found when they do."

When it looked like she'd still argue, Jay straightened up to his full height.

"Miss Waller, this is my last order as headmaster of this academy," he said. "I expect you to follow it. Is that understood?"

Rebecca sighed.

"Don't linger too long yourself," she said. "You may be old, but you're still useful."

Jay chuckled.

"I'm one of those two," he said. "Now go."

She left, and Jay wished he could shake the feeling that he'd never see her again. The minutes raced by as the Seraphs loaded up what they could and then flew off, leaving him alone. Jay walked the armory, staring at the gaps on the wall. Each missing set represented a soldier to fight against Center's invasion. Each one might mean the difference between slavery to the Speaker, and freedom.

The Seraphs returned in groups, having stashed their supplies at several nearby safe holds Jay and Argus had prepared in advance.

"Hurry it up," Jay barked at them. "Time's almost out."

The last group of four returned, led by the gray giant that was Loramere.

"Knights are swarming like bees beyond the academy," Loramere said as he slammed open the door. The other three followed, Kael, Bree, and a veteran Seraph that had graduated from Jay's academy more than a decade earlier, Aisha. "Had to fly us low and slow to get back here."

"If it's that bad, you shouldn't have come back at all," Jay said, stepping past them to the door. "Now grab a set of wings and go, all of you."

The other remaining Seraphs hurried out as the last four pulled harnesses from the wall and began strapping them to their own to carry during flight. Jay kept his head out the door, watching for a sign of the wagons' arrival. It came far too soon, a dozen angelic knights suddenly racing overhead in tight formation.

"Damn!" Jay shouted, and he hit the door with his fist. "They're here already. Damn!"

Loramere yanked loose one of the belts holding the second harness to his own and let it drop to the ground.

"How do you know?" he asked.

"They're already scouting overhead."

"Do they know what we're doing?" Kael asked, unhinging his own spare set.

"They don't seem alarmed. This is only standard procedure, I'd wager. But the others will be here soon." Jay glanced at the two older Seraphim, then the twins. Mind racing, he bit his lip as a plan formed in his mind. "Bree, Kael, take off your wings."

Bree frowned.

"Sir, I don't think…"

"I said do it!"

The twins obeyed, rapidly undoing the buckles to their harnesses. Jay turned to the others, and he lowered his voice.

"Two unarmed students may go unnoticed, but not you," he said. "If you flee now, you might have a chance to outrace the knights. The other option is that you stay and ensure Kael and Bree escape."

Loramere frowned at the two young Seraphim.

"Two experienced for two learners," he said. "Are they worth it?"

Jay lowered his voice even further.

"I don't know," he said. "But who Bree is, and what she represents, might be worth a dozen Seraphim."

Aisha shared a look with Loramere, then thudded a fist against her breast.

"If we're flying, it's with a purpose, and not as cowards," she said. "What do you need us to do?"

"Loramere, go north; Aisha, go south," he said. "Wait until

the last possible moment, then keep all eyes on you. And... and thank you."

Jay returned to the twins, and he knelt before them, a hand on each of their shoulders. Their silver wings lay on the floor behind them.

"Listen carefully," he said. "I want you to walk, not run, *walk* to the eastern wall. Anything else might spark the interest of the knights overhead. Argus should have already seen their arrival, and he'll be keeping low, watching for any signs of you. Climb over the wall the moment you think you'll go unnoticed. If you don't think that's possible, return to your apartments and pray you aren't taken for questioning."

"But what about Aisha and Loramere?" Kael asked.

"Don't you worry about us," Loramere said, putting on a brave face. "Me and Aisha here have our own plan."

Jay squeezed their shoulders, then stood.

"You've done your island proud, and me most of all." He smiled at Bree. "I told you I'd make a fine Seraph out of you. I just wish I deserved more of the credit. Both of you have your greatest moments ahead of you, so do not despair, do not give up, and do not give in. We are the sword in the sky. We shall not be slaves. Make Center and her theotechs regret the day they set foot on our sovereign soil."

Kael and Bree saluted him, fists against their breasts. Both fought back tears.

"We fly unchained," they said, the rallying cry of the newborn rebellion.

They walked for the door, but before exiting, Bree broke from her brother's side and flung her arms around Loramere's broad waist.

"Thank you," Jay heard her whisper.

Kael followed up her hug with one of his own. Jay saw the big man's calm veneer threatening to break.

"You're good kids," he said, rubbing the tops of their dark hair with his hands. "Now get the hell out of here."

They stepped out, leaving Jay alone with the two Seraphs.

"Surprise must be on your side if you're to have a chance to live," Jay said. "I'll stall as long as I can, but once you see anyone nearing the armory or the gear sheds, it's time to move."

"Let's not fool ourselves," Aisha said, and she patted a sword strapped to her waist. "There's no outrunning them. We'll fly as far as we can, and then we'll die taking as many knights with us as we can. No one will capture us, or torture us for names. We'll fall from the sky like soldiers."

Jay bit his tongue. He would not argue, nor pretend there was any other realistic outcome. Saluting them both, he wished to God he'd vacated the contents of the academy days ago.

"The best of luck to the both of you," he said, and he exited the armory before he might lose his calm. Once on the path, he hurried toward the western entrance. A pair of wagons approached along the dirt road, each pulled by a team of donkeys. Several knights hovered just overhead, while high above, four more circled like vultures over a battlefield. Once he knew they saw him he slowed his walk and put his hands into his pockets as if he were in no hurry.

"Who is in charge?" Jay shouted once they were within earshot. He stood directly in the center of the road, leaving them with no choice but to run him over if they didn't stop. Stop they did.

"I am," said a red-robed woman hopping out the back of the first wagon. Gold and silver chains rattled about her neck. Most notable was the gold dagger buckled to her waist, its hilt encrusted with five gems, each of a different color. Such daggers belonged to the Erelim, the highest-ranking members of the theotechs. Only the Speaker himself carried more power and authority. It took some effort for Jay to hide his surprise at someone of such importance coming to oversee the removal of their equipment.

"And you are...?" he asked.

She stopped just shy of him, arms crossed over her chest. No hint of cosmetics upon her face, just pale skin creased with lines about her lips and eyes. She'd spent her lifetime frowning, and they had left their mark. Her blonde hair was tightly braided, held together by thin gold ribbons. Though she still looked young, her voice was one of age and authority. Her red robes were smooth and vibrant, her silver-buckled black boots immaculately clean.

"Er'el Jaina Cenborn. I assume you are this academy's headmaster?"

"I am," he said. "And Eyan told me to find you when you entered. You'll need a third wagon to cart everything out. He insisted that you send for another immediately, lest, and these are his words, 'we be forced to sit on our asses all day waiting for it to arrive.'"

Jaina eyed him carefully, a gaze Jay didn't like one bit. A sharp mind was hidden behind those blue eyes, of that he had no doubt.

"Where is Eyan right now?" she asked, cool voice revealing none of her inner debate.

"In the armory," Jay said.

Jaina snapped her fingers above her head. One of the flying knights landed in a kneel beside her.

"Tomas, go confirm the request," she said. She pointed past him. "The squat rectangle there, just beside the barracks."

The knight thudded a gauntleted fist against his chest. His gold wings shimmered, and with a deep hum he shot into the air, straight for the armory.

"You know the layout of our academy?" Jay asked her. "I don't remember you having been here before."

"I haven't," she said. "But I have come here with a task to complete, and I did not do so blind and dumb. Given past experience, I'd argue those are more Weshern traits. Now step aside, Headmaster, before I have my wagons run you over."

Jay did so, telling himself he'd done his best. The game was over. Weshern's freedom would now be in the hands of others. Jaina walked alongside the wagon, and she gestured for him to follow her. He thought to disobey, but every second he played along might be the difference between life and death for the Skyborn twins. Keeping to the grass, they walked beside the wagons on the dirt road. Jaina's gaze remained on him at all times.

"You're a brave man," she said, suddenly interrupting the monotony of the rolling wagon wheels. "It is not too late to repent and confess your sins."

For decades Jay had lived his life as a soldier, and then as a teacher of students. That experience allowed him to keep his face passive when he answered.

"I do not understand."

"I think you do," she said as she stared at the armory. "My knight's delay tells me all I need to know."

Jay was about to plead further ignorance when Loramere and Aisha burst from the armory, remaining dangerously close to the ground as they streaked in opposite directions. Wings thrummed as knights immediately gave chase. Jay watched, trying to judge the separation between them and the knights. They had surprise on their side, but the knights' wings were faster, and they had the height advantage. Perhaps if either could make it to a forest, and hide amid the trees...

From the corner of his eye Jay spotted Jaina moving. He felt pain in his stomach, felt warmth flowing down his abdomen. Jaina held him close with one arm around his neck, the other clutching the jeweled dagger pierced up to the hilt in his belly.

"It's not lethal," she whispered into his ear. "Not yet. If you behave, and do not struggle, you might survive this." Then, louder, "Garesh, check the armory. Find Eyan and Tomas."

Jay tried to strike at the theotech with his shaking hands, but she was too close, her grip too tight. The dagger was always twisting and shifting, sending unending waves of pain up his spine. His blood flowed, steadily draining him of strength. A long moment passed, Jay clenching his jaw against the increasing pain.

A knight landed beside them, and he looked in a foul mood.

"They're both dead," he said.

"The gear?" Jaina asked.

"Some taken, but not all. Looks like they didn't have enough time."

Jaina pressed her cheek against Jay's.

"Time you were meant to buy them," she said, her voice a seductive whisper in his ear. "You still have this chance. Plead to God for mercy, and tell me where they're taking the harnesses. Tell me, and you will die quickly, and your soul will pass on to the golden hereafter without the stain of sin. Tell me, and I will give you absolution."

The dagger slid upward, tearing flesh on its way to his rib cage. Jay tilted his lips to her ear, whispered back as if she were his lover.

"I'd rather burn."

Jaina shoved him free. Too surprised to react, Jay staggered a few steps, mouth hanging open as a fresh spurt of blood poured down the front of his shirt. In that brief moment, he met Jaina's gaze. He saw no anger, no frustration, just mild disappointment as the Er'el stretched her arm to the fullest, jamming that jeweled dagger of hers deep into his throat.

"A brave man," she said as he dropped to his knees, upper body hitching in a hopeless attempt to draw breath. "Such a shame. Cowardice would have spared a great many lives."

The dagger denied him speech as Jay collapsed to his knees, his vision turning white from pain. In one last act of defiance, he lurched forward, ensuring he bled all over those clean black boots of hers. Despite the blood, she did not shy away. Her next order echoed in his ears, the last words he'd ever hear.

"Weshern needs to learn the price of rebellion. Take all that's left, then burn the academy to the ground. Leave them nothing but ash."

Ash, thought Jay as he watched his blood trickle across the smooth leather. *Is that my legacy of twenty years? Ash...*

The boots pulled out from beneath his head. He dropped limp, felt something push him over. His eyes saw only blurry shadows. When the dagger yanked out from his throat, he felt nothing, for death had finally come to take him away.

CHAPTER

1

On their first-ever visit to the Academy, Kael and Bree had walked to the academy with nothing but the clothes on their backs, and now they left its smoldering ruin carrying only the same. Argus had offered to have his knights fly them home after rescuing them outside the academy wall, but Kael refused.

"We'll be fine," he'd said. "Get yourselves to safety instead."

The long walk offered the two plenty of time to talk, not that either felt like doing so. The growing smoke behind them was a giant pyre, burning whatever peaceful life they'd known.

"They must be more frightened than they let on," Bree said after an hour of walking. She glanced over her shoulder at the smoke that blotted the sky. "They wouldn't have torched the academy if they didn't fear rebellion."

"Or maybe they're just spiteful," Kael said.

"Spiteful?" Bree shook her head. "They've invaded our home. They've imprisoned our Archon. They don't get to be spiteful."

"Tell them that."

The two wore their Seraphim uniforms, earning themselves many guarded looks from the few men and women on the road. With it only midday, most would be out in the fields, and Kael wondered what the people would make of the smoke. Would they think it a battle? Would they even know Center was responsible? If they didn't at first, they soon would. Word would spread like wildfire in the many taverns. Lately there were only two topics of conversation: Center's invasion, and New Galen.

"They burning our homes?" an elderly woman shouted at them from the open window of her home. Kael looked to her, torn as to how to answer. In the end, it didn't matter. The woman understood his look, and she spat. "You'll make them pay, won't you?"

"We will," Bree answered. "I promise."

That gave the woman satisfaction, and she ducked back into her home.

"Shouldn't make promises you can't keep," Kael said.

"I'll keep it or I'll die trying," Bree said. "If I fail, I won't be around to care."

"I will. What if that old lady comes to call you a liar at your funeral?"

"Let her holler until she feels better. It's the least I can do."

Kael almost felt guilty for laughing. Jay Simmons was likely dead, the same for the veteran Seraphs Loramere and Aisha, and now the academy was burning. But he was alive, as was his sister, and if dark humor could counter the ever-present feeling of dread that hovered over their shoulders, was that really so terrible?

They reached the junction of Winged and Fountain Roads, and they turned south, toward home. More than halfway there, the eight miles between Aunt Bethy's place and the academy felt painfully long. Perhaps having spent the past year soaring through the skies made traveling such a distance on foot feel that much longer. Sadly, flying anything faster than the sets the fishermen used would instantly earn the attention of the angelic knights. The golden-armored men were a constant presence now, as common as clouds in the blue sky. Bree resigned herself to spending a great many future days with her feet planted on the ground.

As they traveled south, they passed by several streets whose junction with Fountain Road was marked with a pole pounded into the ground, then topped with a red ribbon or cloth. Kael caught his sister staring at each one from the corner of her eye, her displeasure as obvious as it was intense.

"I know," Kael said at the fourth one. "I don't like it, either."

The poles marked the farthest extent the members of New Galen were allowed to travel beyond their newly established town in the far southwest of Weshern. The boundary wasn't official, and certainly not endorsed by Center, but any red rags or ribbons the knights yanked down were quickly replaced. Similar vigilante tactics forced all former citizens of Galen to wear red loops of cloth around their arms or wrists, a reminder of their fallen home. Anyone wearing such a cloth beyond the accepted limits invited robbery, beatings, or far worse. Over the past two weeks, Kael and Bree had heard of the Speaker's growing dissatisfaction at Weshern's treatment of New Galen's residents.

"They shouldn't be here," Bree said. "The punishment doesn't make any sense."

"We're the ones they claim caused Galen to crash into the ocean."

Bree shook her head.

"Not us. Galen's people. Putting them here, among us, is a cruelty to those who've suffered enough already."

Kael shrugged.

"Maybe the Speaker's hoping to teach us to get along?"

"Then he's doing a piss-poor job of it."

Another fluttering piece of red cloth. Kael's mood sank even further.

"Where else were they to go?" he asked. "Whose land should have been given to them instead?"

"I don't know," Bree said. "The only easy answer's at the bottom of the ocean."

The hour passed, and with bittersweet relief Kael stepped into his hometown of Lowville. The main road ran through their quaint market, and Kael debated circling around it to avoid the growing crowd. With the afternoon approaching evening, people were beginning to filter in from the fields, clothes soaked with sweat, hands worn and caked with dirt. Kael swallowed his nerves and kept his head held high as they walked through the stone booths covered with thick cloth tarps held aloft by wooden poles. Passing through the market unnoticed would have been fine with him, but there was no chance of that, not with his sister at his side.

"Phoenix!"

Two little boys came dashing over, weaving through the crowd like Seraphim avoiding blasts of ice and fire. They each wielded a pair of thin sticks, undoubtedly the sharpest of blades in their minds. When they jolted to a halt before Bree, they smiled up at her with unabashed awe.

"Can we see your swords?" the first asked.

"Yeah, your fire swords? Where are they?" asked the second.

Bree blushed, and she glanced at Kael as if expecting him to rescue her.

"Well, Phoenix?" Kael asked. "Where are they?"

"I don't have them with me," Bree said, kneeling down before the two. "I only carry them when I'm in danger, but I'm not in danger here, am I? Not with you two here to protect me."

They beamed, and they thrust out their chests and pulled back their shoulders.

"That's right we will!"

Bree laughed as she poked one in the stomach, then rose to her feet. Her smile vanished upon seeing a woman, apparently the boys' mother, rushing over.

"Don't mind them," she said, grabbing each by the wrist and pulling them away despite their protests. "They're just so proud knowing you came from our town."

"They're no bother," Bree said, tilting her head in a vain attempt to hide her face with her short dark hair.

"None at all," Kael added, and he put a hand on Bree's shoulder to guide her forward. More people were gathering, forming a loose ring of onlookers, and he wanted to get his sister moving before she locked up completely. The two boys shouted "Bye!" waving the sticks in their free hands as their mom pulled them back. Kael led the way through the market, the onlookers parting. Murmurs followed their every step, and always amid them was that single word: *Phoenix.*

"They're all staring," Bree muttered, shifting even closer to him. "What are they hoping for?"

"For you to shoot fire out of your fingers, maybe," Kael said. "Just keep moving."

Thankfully pleasant calm greeted them once they reached the market's exit. Picker Street wasn't far, and when they turned south, a lump grew in Kael's throat. How long had it been since he was home? How long since he'd seen his aunt? A year, he guessed, but it felt like a lifetime. He'd left as a student hoping to not fail out of the academy. Now they returned having fought in battle and taken the lives of others. The person he'd been felt so distant and unrecognizable. No, not the person. That wasn't it. Just…that life. Of waking without responsibilities beyond long, tedious hours in a field. Of living without believing anyone's life was in his hands beyond his own. Of sleeping without reliving the same battles over and over.

"So strange coming home," Bree said, and Kael wondered if her thoughts mirrored his.

"You don't have to tell me."

Upon reaching Aunt Bethy's home, they found the door locked, and the inside quiet.

"Think she locked the windows, too?" Bree asked, staring up at the second floor.

"Only one way to find out."

Kael took a running start, jumped, and caught the window-sill. When he pulled himself up, the shutters opened with ease, and he climbed inside. He dropped to the floor with a thud, and just like that, his old life returned to him. He was in his room. There was his bed, still made, as if waiting for him. A trunk of his old belongings sat in the corner, and the half-open closet still contained his civilian clothes. Being there felt so good, so peaceful, he plopped down on his old bed and let out a sigh.

Bree's voice interrupted his relaxation.

"Kael?"

He chuckled.

"Yeah, give me a second."

Grunting, he pushed himself off the bed, hurried down the stairs, and unlocked the front door. Bree stepped in, elbowing him in the side as she passed.

They took turns changing into their old clothes, with Kael

annoyed by how tight the dark pants were about his waist and the pale shirt around the collar. He knew he'd grown, but surely not that much in one year...right? It almost made him want to put on his uniform, but with Weshern's Seraphim disbanded, keeping it on invited potential trouble from Center's knights.

The two sat at the kitchen table, a pot set to boil, when Aunt Bethy stepped inside. She froze in the doorway, clothes dirty from the field.

"You're home," she said, a smile spreading across her face. Kael rose from the table so he might accept her embrace.

"We made you supper," Bree said. "You hungry?"

"Not at all," she said, moving to hug Bree next. "But if you'll sit with me at the table, I'll eat every bite until it is gone."

Given how little time they'd had to prepare, the soup wasn't much of a soup, but the warmed potatoes and carrots still tasted divine on Kael's tongue. They ate while Aunt Bethy rambled, filling them in on everything that had happened over the past year. She told them about who'd married whom, and the elderly who'd passed on, but inevitably she came to the subject of New Galen.

"It seems only the Speaker and his people don't see the obvious," Bethy said as she dabbed at her chin with a napkin. "Galen was full of evil, sinful people who warred against us without reason. God sent their island to the water as punishment, and a warning to the rest of us. To give their people our land, to act as if *we* are guilty, is an insult. That's why the midnight fire burns so much brighter, so much *angrier*."

Kael saw Bree start to respond, and the look in her eye was hardly kind, but a knock on the door interrupted her. Kael's heart leapt into his throat. Had theotechs come to question their involvement with removing the wings and elements from the academy? Or was their involvement already known, and were knights waiting outside to arrest them? Their aunt sensed their worry, and she rose from the table before either could.

"I'll see who it is," she said, careful to keep her voice calm. Kael turned in his seat, watched her open the door. His aunt frowned, glanced to either side of the house, and then bent down to retrieve a small scrap of folded paper.

"There's no one," she said as she shut the door. "Just this."

Aunt Bethy handed him the folded note. The top bore two names: Kael and Bree. With his sister sliding next to him at the table, Kael unfolded the thin sheet of paper. The message inside was simple and quick: *Nightfall. Glensbee. East on Thomas Road, look for the laughing frog. Ask for Milly. Fly unchained.*

"What is it?" Bethy asked.

"Nothing," Kael said, glancing at his sister. "Just some friends from the academy hoping to see us again."

"Oh, how nice. Will you?"

"Of course we will," Bree said, returning to her chair. "Tonight even, isn't that right, Kael?"

"It is," Kael said, wishing he didn't sound so guilty when he answered.

The note requested they wait until nightfall, and so they did, exiting Aunt Bethy's home when the first of the midnight fire burned in the west. The streets were blessedly empty, though the same could not be said for the skies.

"Don't act like you're in a hurry," Kael said as they both spotted an angelic knight flying overhead. "That'll make them more likely to stop us."

The knight dipped lower, and Kael clenched his hands into fists as he forced himself to stare straight ahead. They'd practiced their cover story in case they were stopped: they were on their way to one of Lowville's nearby taverns. Kael ran the words he'd say over and over in his head, trying to get them to sound right, to feel natural, but it proved unnecessary. The knight continued on, the thrumming sound of his wings barely audible.

Bree glanced over her shoulder, confirmed the knight's absence.

"The sooner we're out of here, the better," she said. "Time to run."

They jogged the road, an easy pace Kael could continue for hours after all their morning runs with Brad at the academy. The squat homes ended, grass and farmland surrounding either side of the road as they crossed the mile between Lowville and Glensbee. Kael kept an eye on the sky at all times. If a knight flew overhead, they needed to slow down, if not hide entirely. The grass was tall enough that they could vanish within if need be.

It wasn't long before the midnight fire covered the entirety of the sky. The sight of it made the trip feel all the more ominous. Ever since Galen's fall, a change had come over the fire. It burned brighter, fiercer. Most noticeable of all was how the fire rippled, as if it were a reflection in a pond. Kael had heard plenty of theories, none of which had any scrap of proof to it. The most prevalent was Aunt Bethy's, and how the fire expressed God's displeasure. The people of Galen were evil, wasn't that what Bethy had said? An evil people they now gave shelter to instead of letting be wiped out and forgotten.

"Do you think Aunt Bethy's right?" Kael asked, and he gestured to the sky. "You think that's God's anger up there?"

Bree didn't even bother to look.

"The fire's burned for centuries, and we've never understood why," she said. "To pretend to know why it's changed now is a joke."

Kael watched the curling and pulsing fire. While he couldn't argue with her, neither could he shake the feeling that, like Aunt Bethy had said, the fire appeared angrier somehow, as if it raged against the world below. He let the matter drop, for they'd reached the outskirts of Glensbee, and he needed to pay attention if he were to follow the directions he'd memorized. Neither he nor his sister had been to Glensbee more than a few times while growing up, and getting lost was a distinct possibility.

"We're looking for a road marked Thomas," he said, squinting in the red light.

"It doesn't seem like any roads are marked," Bree said as they walked.

"Well, then let's hope at least Thomas Road is."

Glensbee was larger than their own home, and as they neared its center, Kael saw the first of many signs marking the wider roads. They also were no longer alone. Men and women passed by, usually in pairs or groups. Being recognized by people on the ground worried Kael, but it also meant any angelic knight flying overhead would think nothing strange about Kael and Bree walking the road.

"There," Bree said, stopping and pointing. A rectangular sign nailed to a post read THOMAS, the words carved deep into the wood. "Which way from here?"

"The note said east," Kael said. "So we go east."

They turned onto a road surrounded on either side with tall, multistory buildings made entirely of wood instead of stone. Glensbee was both a newer town compared to Lowville, and nearer to Slender Forest, which allowed that extravagance. Most stores went unmarked, though a few bore hanging signs above their doors with pictures representing whatever merchandise was sold within. They'd entered a trade district of sorts. Kael kept his eyes peeled for a sign marking the place they'd been told to find.

"See any laughing frogs?" Kael asked.

"Not yet. Shouldn't be hard to find."

It turned out it wasn't, and not because of the large sign bearing a crude frog holding a mug in its webbed hand. No, it was the only building with candlelight visible through its windows. Kael and Bree stopped before its steps and listened to the raucous laughter and song coming from inside the tavern.

"I'll go in first in case it's a trap," Kael said.

"So I can, what, go running for my life?"

"Exactly, Bree. We both know when it comes to fighting Center, you're more important than I am."

She frowned at him but didn't argue. Kael winked to let her know he wasn't upset at that fact, then flung open the door. The tavern had about nine people scattered among three tables, the groups lively and well supplied with alcohol. Not a one gave Kael a second glance. Walking up to the tavern keeper, Kael swallowed down his nerves and smiled at the old, gentle-looking man.

"I was hoping Milly was here," he said.

The tavern keeper smiled, but his eyes glanced to his patrons with sudden caution.

"Out back," he said, voice dropping so that Kael had to lean closer. "In the cellar. Milly's waiting for you."

"Thanks," Kael said, and he hurried back out. Bree lifted an eyebrow, and in response, Kael beckoned her to follow. They slid around the tavern, to where a cellar door was built into the base of the building. Kael pulled it open, coughed at the dust, and then led the way down the creaking wood steps.

Thin slits of glass near the top of the cellar allowed what little red light they had. Kael stepped off the stairs and put his back against a wall, with Bree joining him. Three people waited inside: Argus Summers, Rebecca Waller, and most surprisingly to him, the academy's librarian, Devi Winters.

"Devi?" Kael asked, immediately feeling embarrassed by such an outburst. The tiny woman sat with a piece of charcoal and thick sheet of paper covered with her tight handwriting.

"Good to see you two," she said, smiling at him. "And don't act so surprised. Those theotechs took my library from me, damn it. I may not be able to fight, but I'll still do what I can to help."

"Were you spotted?" Argus asked from the other side of the room. He sat atop a crate in the corner, and it was strange seeing him out of uniform. Though his pants were the same, he wore a loose long-sleeved shirt, a pale blue that seemed to glow in the dark light. One of his swords lay across his lap, and his fingers drummed across the hilt.

"Only once, while still in Lowville," Kael said. "Just a flyover by a knight. I doubt he knew who we were."

"Good." Argus's fingers tightened about the hilt. "Good."

"Did Loramere and Aisha escape?" Bree asked, immediately broaching the subject that had been weighing on Kael's mind as well. Argus shook his head, his frustrated frown making his answer almost unnecessary.

"No," he said. "They did not."

"Are you sure?" Bree pressed on. "Maybe they're in hiding. It's only been a day, and—"

"I saw Loramere die with my own eyes," Argus interrupted. "Yes, I am sure."

Kael could only imagine what it would have been like for Argus to watch his fellow Seraph die, and be unable to intervene.

It sounded like hell. Knowing the two died to save him and his sister certainly didn't help the guilt pressing on his own spine.

"So who's Milly?" Kael asked, trying to pierce the awkward silence with anything else at all.

"Milly's my middle name," Rebecca said. "The tavern's owner is my great-uncle, and he'd go to the grave before selling us out to Center. Now, a lot is still scheduled for tonight, so we need to speak quickly."

She stood in the center of the cellar, the only one still wearing her uniform, her black shirt and blue jacket smooth and prim as ever. Stranger was how she had no pad or notes on her, with Devi seemingly having taken over that responsibility. It was as if her hands didn't know what to do now that they were empty, and she kept tapping them against her thighs.

"The academy's shutdown is only a part of Marius Prakt's dismantling of Weshern's infrastructure," she continued. "A dismantling that began the moment they imprisoned our royal family and imposed sanctions against us. Today the Speaker officially disbanded our Seraphim, and he also ordered our ground troops to evacuate Fort Luster and return to their homes. With our entire military scattered, and our Archon imprisoned, we are now at the complete mercy of Center and her theotechs."

Argus shifted on his perch atop the crate.

"I'm thankful for your aid in rescuing supplies from the academy," he told the siblings, "but we'll be needing far more help than that. Center has crossed a line, and it's time we made our stand. Rebecca here has drafted a list of demands for the Speaker. Tomorrow morning we'll deliver the list to the theotechs, as well as post it all throughout Weshern."

"What type of demands?" Kael asked.

"Things any rational man or woman would accept as fair," Rebecca said. "An end to their imposed sanctions, the release of our royal family, and the return of our wings and elements so we might defend ourselves. Most important of all, we need them to acknowledge Weshern's independence and vow never to repeat such an invasion of our territory."

For the most part, it was a return to the way things were prior to Galen's fall, but Kael knew in his gut that obtaining such a peace wouldn't be easy, and it was clear Bree agreed.

"Marius won't back down to these demands," she said. "Not without a fight."

"And that's what we're going to give him," Argus said. "We need to rebuild our military, quickly, and in secret." He gestured their way. "Gathering Seraphs such as yourselves and discovering their loyalty is a large part of that."

"But for us to form an army, we need supplies," Rebecca said, nodding in agreement. "We've lost access to all we had in the academy plus Fort Luster. Everything we'll need must come through other means. Kael, that's what you're here for."

Kael failed to hide his surprise. Him? He'd assumed they wanted Bree in some capacity, either for her skills in combat or her growing reputation. What could they want with him?

"Just ask, and I'll do it," Kael said.

"Excellent," Rebecca said. "We need you to go to the holy mansion and speak with Clara Willer. Use your relationship with her to discover what aid the royal family can offer."

Heat built in Kael's neck.

"How did you..."

"You accompanied her to the solstice dance," Devi said, looking up from her notes. "That, and people gossip at the academy. Yes, even we librarians and instructors hear about your doings, and often far more than we'd like."

Kael wasn't entirely sure what his relationship with Clara was, but he'd not seen her since her parents' imprisonment. Glad for any reason to visit, he nodded, and he tried to make his voice sound firm and controlled when he spoke.

"I'll go tomorrow."

"Good," Rebecca said. "With the Archon and his wife imprisoned, his sons have taken over what few administrative duties are left. We must learn where their loyalties lie. If they won't help us, we must view them as traitors to Weshern and adjust our plans accordingly."

"The wealth and influence of the royal family will accomplish much, but not everything," Argus added. "Center controls the trade of all elements. We're looking into underground markets, but we cannot rely on those to be enough. We must obtain all we can, no matter the risk."

Rebecca approached the two, but Kael noticed her eyes were focused only on his sister.

"I've begun building a network of spies, and one such spy monitored the removal of the remaining gear from the academy grounds," she said. "We weren't able to recover all of our elements before our retreat, but what Center's forces took is still on Weshern soil, and we know it's being guarded. In a few hours, we'll launch an attack before they leave our island and are therefore beyond our reach. If we succeed, we'll have the elements we need to resist Center on a far grander scale than we can now. The harder we hit them, the more likely they'll settle for peace."

Argus cleared his throat.

"Bree, we want you to be a part of that attack," he said.

"Just Bree?" Kael asked, trying to mask the hurt in his voice.

"Just Bree," Argus said. "I'm sorry, Kael. Your role is too important. We have no one else who might go in and out of the holy mansion without attracting attention." Argus crossed his arms. "Well, what do you say? Will you fly with us?"

Kael knew the answer she'd give the moment the question was asked.

"Give me my swords and wings, and I will do my best," she said.

"Excellent," Argus said, but he didn't sound relieved just yet. He turned to Kael, met his eye. "Both your roles put your lives in danger, and not just your own. Should either of you be caught, it puts the other in immediate risk. No theotech will believe one of you acting without aid and support from the other. Knowing this, are you both still willing to pledge your allegiance to our resistance?"

Kael exchanged looks with his sister. The fear was there, the worry, but as before, Kael knew the answer without even needing to ask.

"We're in this together," he said, turning back to Argus. "Even if that means sharing the risks as well."

"Excellent," Argus said, hopping down from his crate. "Kael, return home, and try not to be seen. Bree, you're coming with me."

Everyone else prepared to leave. Kael hugged his sister, burying his fear with a wide grin.

"Make the bastards pay," he told her.

"Don't worry about me," she said, sensing the apprehension hiding behind his grin. "I'll be fine, I promise."

"What'd I say about making promises you can't keep?"

His sister winked at him in the deep red light.

"If I fail, you can join the old lady in yelling at my funeral."

CHAPTER

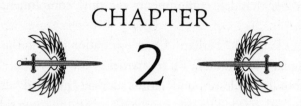

2

"Where are we going?" Bree asked as Argus led her farther north down the road. The trade district was far behind them, the tall wood buildings replaced with the more familiar squat stone homes akin to those in Lowville. They each kept an eye on the sky at all times, painfully aware of how vulnerable they were to any angelic knights flying overhead.

"To a barn just outside town," Argus said. Despite them being alone on the street, he glanced about as if searching for eavesdroppers. "My most trusted Seraphim are already gathered there, waiting for us to arrive so we might begin our surprise assault."

Bree nodded, flattered to be considered one of his trusted few. It should seem silly given all she'd done in her past two battles against Galen, but Argus was still the legendary hero of Weshern's Seraphim, while she... Well, they might be attempting to craft the Phoenix into a similar hero, but she wasn't there yet.

"What do we do when we get the elements?" she asked.

"Then we fly the hell out of there," Argus said. "This is a smash and grab, Bree. It should fit your reckless talents well."

"Are backhanded compliments the only compliments you know?"

Argus laughed. "Perhaps. Once our nation isn't on the verge of complete domination, I'll try harder to use tact."

Before she could respond, Argus suddenly grabbed her wrist and yanked, hard. The two tumbled against the stone side of a house, both backs against it. Bree's startled cry muffled against Argus's palm.

"Quiet," he whispered into her ear.

By then she heard the thrumming of wings. An angelic knight flew overhead, his form a shadow against the rippling midnight fire. He kept closer to ground than the others she'd seen earlier, traveling in a gentle curve about the outskirts of Glensbee. The overhang of the roof was paltry cover, but it seemed enough as the knight continued on. That, or the two didn't appear worthy of notice.

"It's going to get worse," Argus said as he let Bree go. "So far we've only hidden away what is rightfully ours. Once Marius realizes we're organized, and we present him with our demands? Then neither day nor night will be safe for us."

"This is our home," Bree said. "We should never feel unsafe here."

Argus gestured to the sky, where the knight had just flown.

"Then you know who to blame," he said.

They continued on, keeping close to the homes they passed in case another knight flew over. Bree saw up ahead the buildings stopped entirely, meaning they'd soon be traveling in open ground. It was not a prospect she was looking forward to in the slightest. Neither was Argus, by the looks of it, for he stopped at the very last home. He did not meet her gaze, only stared at the road splitting the tall grassland.

"I want to be honest with you," he said. "There's a reason I want you with us tonight. You're our backup plan, our secret weapon in case things go foul. Do you know what that means?"

Bree wasn't sure what she could be missing. It seemed to make sense, but his apprehension gave her pause.

"I'm not sure I do," she said.

Argus turned to face her, his blue eyes shining a deep purple from the midnight fire.

"It means I'm relying on your burning swords to save us. Your burning swords, which no other Seraph of Weshern, if not all the islands, has ever wielded before. In this midnight raid, you could be anyone... until you wield your flame."

A pit grew in Bree's stomach, and she crossed her arms against a sudden chill worming through her.

"If anyone survives, they'll know I participated," she said.

Argus nodded.

"The moment you bathe your swords in flame, and an enemy lives to tell the tale, your involvement will be without doubt."

"Which means I put my entire family in danger," she said.

The older man looked away.

"You heard your brother's words. He's willing to share the risks."

"And my aunt?"

"Theotechs will likely come for her, perhaps for information, perhaps as a hostage. But the risks... these risks are worth it, Bree. If Weshern knows you're resisting Center's unlawful invasion, it'll give confidence to those too frightened to join. War is about more than casualties. It's about morale, and about hope. That's what you can be to us, Bree. You can be that hope." He turned his gaze back to her. "This isn't something I want you doing lightly, nor feeling like you have no choice in the matter. We need you, I won't deny that, but we need you fully committed. The moment you fly afraid is the moment I watch you die."

Bree stood up straight, her bruised ego giving her the strength to meet his gaze.

"I will never fly afraid," she said. "And I'm keeping my fire hidden, at least until I can discuss it with Kael and my aunt."

"So be it." He put a hand on her shoulder. "Surprise will be on our side tonight, so we should endure well enough without your fire." He squeezed, then released. "I merely pray lives aren't lost while we wait for you to make up your mind."

He paused, and she could tell he was waiting for her to make the first move. Swallowing down her nerves, she looked once more to the sky, then back to Argus.

"Time is wasting," she said. "Let's go."

Breaking into a sprint, she raced down the dirt road, the former commander easily keeping up with her. They ran, the tall grass waving on either side of them from the soft breeze. They ran, passing through the red and orange world until Argus finally veered off onto one of several side paths. Up ahead was a barn, and Bree felt relief they'd arrived without being spotted by a patrolling knight. Despite the clear red sky, she maintained her run until reaching the whitewashed wood sides, and the huge doors cracked open a foot. Bree hesitated, waiting until Argus entered first.

At some point the barn would be stocked from floor to high ceiling with hay for the animals in the coming cold season, but for now it was mostly empty, with only a third of the back wall blocked off by tall stacks of hay bundles. The rest of the open space was filled with Seraphs, men and women standing about in uniform, wing harnesses resting on the floor beside them. In the dim crimson light, Bree estimated thirty at most. Their idle conversations dwindled at their commander's entrance, and more than a few eyes stared Bree's way. Bree scanned for familiar faces, vaguely recognizing some from her lengthy drills prior to battle against Galen's Seraphim, particularly those who had been members of Phoenix Squad.

"We're all here," Argus said to them, garnering their attention with a single clearing of his throat. "So suit up. We're taking back what is ours."

Argus turned to her.

"We have a set for you this way," he said.

She followed him to the far side, where atop the hay lay twin pairs of unclaimed wings. One had black lines painted on its silver wings and clearly belonged to Argus. The other was slightly smaller, and a chill swept through Bree as she touched its cool metal. Despite all that had happened, the skies were not yet denied to her. Beside the wings was a thick black jacket, and Bree slowly put it on. Sliding an arm through the harness, she hoisted it onto her back, put her other arm through, and settled it evenly on her shoulders. Immediately she felt more at ease than she had the past several hours.

This was the life she knew. This was where she belonged. The planning, the strategy, the politics: all that belonged to others far more suited to those challenges. For her, she wanted an enemy in the skies before her, and her swords and fire to bring them down. Everything else was unwanted complication. Her hands flew over the buckles, tightening them about her waist, thighs, and arms, a preparatory act she could perform in her sleep.

As she tightened the gauntlet about her right hand, Argus pulled a bag free from a clip on his belt and dipped his fingers inside. He pulled out a single fire prism, which pulsed a soft red. She reached to take it, but when her hand closed around it, Argus did not release immediately. His eyes met hers, and he spoke in a low voice.

"Remember, only if you must, and only if you are truly ready."

"I understand," she said, pulling the prism free, opening the compartment on her gauntlet, and sliding it inside. Element secure, she closed the compartment with a satisfying click. As Argus moved about, checking on others, offering them encouragement, one of the Seraphs came over to join Bree beside the hay.

"We won't be flying in formation tonight," Olivia said. Her dark hair was tied tight behind her head in preparation for battle. The light of the midnight fire coming in through the high windows cast a shadow across her sharp features, adding an edge to her beauty. "We don't expect much aerial opposition at first, so when knights do appear, we'll already be scattered fighting ground troops or loading up the elements. Just stay with me on the way, then break solo when combat begins. Given how few of us there are, we should be safe from potential friendly collisions despite the lack of formations."

"Ground troops?" Bree asked, realizing it was a subject she'd never pondered before. "How do I engage ground troops?"

Olivia gave her a look, then immediately softened.

"Right," she said. "I forget how young you are. If the Speaker had not closed the academy, you'd have studied air-to-ground warfare during your second year. Not much we can do now, so I'll tell you the absolute basics. Arrows are a very real danger, so never fly in a straight line. Veer at all times. Beyond that, a braced soldier bearing a shield will not be deterred by your speed, and should you collide at even half throttle, you'll break both your necks. Everything is hit-and-run. Bombard from above with your element, and rush in to use your swords only when you absolutely must." The woman cracked a rare smile. "Which for you, I assume will be almost immediately."

Bree's cheeks blushed, and she was glad it'd be all but impossible to notice in the barn. Despite her ability to bathe her swords in flame, she still lacked any control over her fire when used as a projectile. Instructor Kime had compared wielding fire to playing an instrument, and her as being tone-deaf. If that were true, her burning blades were a unique bypassing of her disability.

"You're likely right," Bree said, trying to brush off the embarrassment.

Olivia snapped her fingers.

"Oh, and if you do encounter knights, and you try to melee one, be prepared for surprises," she said.

"Surprises?" Bree asked.

"Not all knights wield twin swords. Some have halberds, chains, spears, even shields. They're supposedly blessed by the theotechs, too, giving them strength beyond measure."

Bree frowned. "Is that true?"

Olivia shrugged. "I've never fought a knight," she said. "The only Weshern Seraph who has is Argus. As far as I know, it's the God's truth."

Before Bree could inquire further, Argus called out from the center of the barn, gathering them up. The Seraphs shuffled toward him, and Bree stayed at Olivia's side.

"I'm glad you're here," Bree told her.

"Most everyone from Phoenix Squad showed," Olivia said. "It seems you're the inspiration Argus insists you are."

More nervous blushing. It was bad enough that someone as

skilled and famous as Commander Argus was talking about her, but claiming she was an inspiration? For who? The other Seraphim? The people of Weshern? She didn't know, and she didn't want to know, so she kept her mouth shut and just smiled meekly.

"I'll try to make this quick," Argus began once all were gathered. "From what we can tell, the wagons are making their way toward the western docks. By midday tomorrow, they will be off our island, which means we must attack tonight. My hope is that we catch them unprepared. We've been Center's puppets for a long time, and they may not realize the lengths we will go to achieve true independence. But even with surprise, don't expect an easy fight, nor a short end to this war. The theotechs have held on to power for centuries, and they will not relinquish it kindly. If we want Weshern pried free of their grasp, we'll need to start cutting fingers."

"My swords are ready to do the cutting!" a Seraph near Argus shouted, and the rest laughed. Argus grinned at him, a wolfish gleam in his eye.

"I hope all of you get your chance tonight," he said. "The wagons stopped outside the town of Melisand. For those of you who don't know where that is, it's fifteen miles west of the academy grounds, following Angelic Road. In a fortunate break for us, the Er'el traveling with them rented a room in town, meaning many of the knights will be away from the wagons to act as bodyguards. As for the rest who remained behind, we hit them hard, and slaughter them while they're unaware. After that, we press our numbers advantage, secure a quick victory, and then move out before reinforcements arrive."

Their commander slowly turned, letting his gaze sweep over them.

"Once the battle ends, flee to Aquila Forest. It's there we're building the infrastructure of Weshern's rebellion. Those already there know of tonight's attempt, and they'll be watching for returning Seraphim so they may signal you to safety. Just make sure you're not followed. The moment Center realizes where we are, the Speaker will bring his entire forces to bear against us. We'll all be dead."

Argus pointed to several men and women, listing off their names as he did.

"You will be responsible for obtaining the elements and carrying them to safety," he said when finished. "Everyone else, you're their guards. Clear out any knights you encounter and any ground troops that might be stationed on defense. Do whatever it takes for us to secure the elements. Is that clear?"

A chorus of nervous cheers was his answer, Bree included. Fighting Seraphim of Galen, whom Weshern had a long, storied history of conflict with, was one thing. Battling the elite angelic knights of Center? That carried a hint of fear, of the impossible. Bree was about to engage with the best of the best, and potentially without her fire to aid her. It was terrifying, if she gave it too much thought, which is why she joined the others in cheering instead.

"Very well," Argus said, and he bowed low in respect. "It's time we fly, and we fly unchained."

"We fly unchained!" cried the rest.

Like a stirred nest of hornets, the Seraphim flew from the barn, keeping low to the ground to hide from distant knights. If they were spotted on the way, and their surprise ruined, then the entire assault would be over before it began. Bree flew a few yards to the left of Olivia, treating her like a squad leader even if she wasn't. The land whirled beneath them, just a blur of grass and hills. Argus led the way, and he kept the group dangerously close to the ground, so that they had to rise and fall with every hill. After a few minutes, Bree realized he was guiding them on an indirect route, avoiding any villages between them and Melisand.

Bree's stomach slowly cramped with each passing minute. It was like her first battle all over again, and no matter how much she berated herself, she couldn't remove the growing worry.

This is where you belong, she told herself. *You'll remember that when it starts.*

It'd been the same with the other two engagements. When combat began, a change came over her. The world slowed, and all her tension, all her nerves, eased away. Worrying was impossible with her mind focused on the present, reacting on instinct, dancing a primal killing dance in which she excelled. Pulse pounding in her neck, Bree stared ahead, hands bumping against the hilts of her swords, seeking reassurance from their presence.

Hills became fields of farmland. They flew so close above the rows of corn, Bree could brush the tops of the stalks with her fingertips if she wished. Argus kept the entire pack moving at a blistering pace, throttles pushed nearly to full. Up ahead, a cluster of small squares marked an approaching town. Bree didn't know Weshern well enough to recognize it on sight, but the way they streaked toward it instead of veering told her they'd arrived at their destination.

Hit hard, and slaughter them while they're unaware, Argus had commanded, and all around Bree, the Seraphs activated their gauntlets, eager to do just that. Bree kept her eyes peeled, searching for Center's supply train in the glow of the midnight fire. At such speed, they'd have little time before . . .

And there it was, a circle of three wagons at the outskirts of town. Instead of slowing, Argus's wings shimmered with silver light, and he sped out ahead. Bree pushed her throttle to its maximum and wished she had greater control of her fire so she could attack at range. At such a speed, she could only watch as they made their first pass over the theotechs' camp.

Ice and stone led the way, blasting through the wagons and smashing craters into the ground as if the wrath of God had been unleashed upon the hapless camp. Bree saw no knights, just a dozen or so men in armor standing in a circle about the wagons. They lifted their enormous shields, the overwhelming volley smashing against them and beating them down. Fire followed, wide swaths encircling the camp and setting every wagon aflame. There would be no fleeing, not without enduring the inferno. Those with lightning picked their targets more carefully. Bree saw two soldiers die on their way to their weapons, arcs of lightning tearing through them so that their bodies collapsed unmoving.

That had to have gotten them all, Bree thought as their Seraphim broke in two groups, one veering left, the other right, both looping around for another pass. This approach was slower, each group taking more care to aim, and Bree quickly saw how wrong she'd been. The rest of the troops had awakened, joining those who'd first been on guard. Not nearly as many had fallen against the barrage as she'd expected, and they lifted dented and scratched shields toward the sky. Others beside them lifted bows, and Bree jerked to the right as she saw one aiming her way. The arrow sailed wide, and then a ball of flame crashed down between the two in response, the protector's armor and shield mattering not. Bree pulled higher, seeing no reason to risk her life if she wasn't ready to engage in melee. She climbed above the others, watching them strafe the camp, a barrage of ice from Argus smashing the lone remaining wagon into pieces. Bree winced, hoping the elements they sought could withstand the punishment.

Rotating in air, Bree spotted a hint of gold to the west, the glint locking her body in place. There, between the camp and the town...

A barrage of ice and fire unleashed toward them as two knights suddenly burst into the air, their golden armor gleaming in the night.

Their camp was separate from the others, Bree realized as she angled toward them.

Two Seraphs died, caught unaware by the ambush, one knifed through the stomach by a lance of ice, the other bathed in fire from the waist up. The dying man flew wildly, blind and burning, until crashing into one of Melisand's homes with enough force to crack the stone of its walls. Bree tried to pretend she didn't see, and was glad she could not hear the sound of impact over the roar of battle and wind in her ears. The rest of her group turned about to find their new attackers, but only Bree had seen them coming, so she would reach them first.

Swords drawn, she smiled and pushed the throttle to its maximum, eager to engage. Against ground forces she was of limited use. But here in the air?

In the air, she could dance.

Thin balls of fire flew like comets toward her, and Bree twisted her body with her waist and shoulders, twirling through without slowing in the slightest. They passed so close she felt their heat on her skin. How well the knight had predicted her path cracked her veneer of confidence. Veering hard right, she avoided a thick lance of ice that had meant to cut her in two. Bree veered immediately back, twirling as two more comets burned below her, and then she was close enough to strike.

The knight wielding the ice arced away, as if daring her to chase, but instead she closed in on the one still flinging fire.

He'd hovered in place, left hand holding his right wrist to brace his aim. Bree saw his palm spreading open with fingers stretched, knew what he intended, and banked at the last second. A wide spray of fire shot toward her, covering a great swath of air as it rolled outward, and she just barely skirted its edge. Bree hooked toward him, left hand shooting out to cut with her sword. She almost bathed it in flame. Almost.

The sword hit his chest, but unlike her other battles, it did not slice through the man's armor like cloth. Without her fire, her swords were just swords, deadly but limited. She felt a jolt, followed by a sharp pain in her shoulder as the blade embedded into the knight. Unable to keep hold, Bree released the hilt, and screaming against the pain, she climbed higher. The long stretch of cord attaching her sword to her gauntlet pulled to its limit, then tugged hard. Her body twisted, the strain on her arm intensified, and then the blade yanked free with a spurt of red. Bree searched for the other knight, fearful she'd lost control and was now vulnerable to his attacks, but the rest of the Weshern Seraphim had arrived, preceded by a barrage of ice arrows launched from Argus's gauntlet. The knight dodged the first few, but the awkward movements stole his speed. Avoiding a burst of flame pushed him higher, right into a blast of lightning that ripped through his chest.

Bree lessened the throttle as she spun to find the knight she'd cut. It must have gone in deep, for she saw him drifting east, body limp. Bled out, by her guess. Argus launched a single shard of ice, which caved in his skull, then flew over to the body. He grabbed the left gauntlet, shut off the harness, and let the body fall. The Weshern Seraphim looped up and around, converging on the desolation that had been the theotechs' camp. Bree hovered for a moment, gently pulling on the cord attached to her sword to get the gears inside the gauntlet to start reeling it in. Once it was in her grasp, she sheathed it, then lowered to the ground.

"Get the elements loaded up and out of here!" Argus shouted. "There's not a chance in hell those in town didn't hear that ruckus. Oh, and someone go loot the dead. We can't afford to let a single element go to waste!"

Bree touched down, and she held her aching left arm against her side. Feeling strangely detached, she stared at the charred corpses of Center's soldiers, faces still locked in agony upon death. Most were burned, though a good many had been crushed by ice and stone as well. The ones struck by lightning looked the most peaceful, their hearts having burst inside their chests before they realized they'd been struck. Fire roared in scattered patches all around, the sound of its crackling an accompaniment to the humming of their wings. Bree stared at the corpse of a man lying on his back, a jagged lance of ice protruding from his neck. His bloodstained tabard bore the symbol of Center, a clear circle intersecting five other circles, each bearing the symbol of the respective island. All but Galen, which had been filled in solid black. The sight chilled her, threatening to remove the last of the comfortable numbness that had blanketed her mind since the battle started.

"Bree?"

She turned to see Argus staring at her.

"I'm fine," she said. "It's... it's nothing."

He didn't look convinced, but he let her be, instead supervising the Seraphs shoving aside pieces of the blasted and burned wagons. Amid the wreckage were ornate chests, their stained wood and gold decorations charred by fire. Argus's handpicked gathered about the chests, readying large sacks they'd tied tightly to their waists. The seven opened up the damaged chests and pulled out the elements, their soft velvet cloths barely touched by the fiery barrage that had engulfed the wagons. By two and three they stuffed their bags with prisms, then moved on to the next chest.

Bree glanced about as they waited, eager to be gone. A dead Seraph of their own lay in the center of the camp, neck twisted at an awkward angle, an arrow sticking out from his forehead. Feeling like a scavenger, Bree walked to his side, lifted his right arm, and popped open the elemental compartment of his gauntlet. Inside was an ice element, and she pocketed it to hand in later. Eyes sweeping across the devastation their elements had unleashed, she wondered how much they'd expended to recover what the wagons carried.

I hope it's enough to make up for what we've used, she thought. Part of her thought Argus wouldn't care even if it didn't. He wanted to strike a blow against Center. He wanted to let every citizen of Weshern know resistance wasn't a hopeless endeavor.

"Knights coming in!" a Seraph shouted, turning Bree's attention their way. Sure enough, the gold shimmer of wings rose above the town, three in total.

"Everyone, form up and hit them hard!" Argus shouted in response. "We need to buy time for the element bearers to escape!"

Wings thrumming with silver light, Bree led the way, swords drawn as the Weshern Seraphim flew to engage. With three dead, and seven staying back to loot the chests, it left twenty to face off against the three knights. It should have been overwhelming numbers. It should have been an easy victory.

Then fire and lightning crashed through their formation as three more knights ambushed from high above, lurking so far they were but minuscule dots. Their attacks hit simultaneously with the three at the front, engulfing the battlefield in chaos. Seraphim dropped, bodies burned and scarred, their easy victory now a desperate battle for survival.

CHAPTER

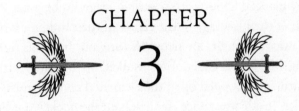

3

Bree pushed her wings to their limits, focusing on the three approaching knights straight ahead. The trio of enemies above would take twenty to thirty seconds to descend from such heights, and during that time their elemental attacks would be inaccurate, relying on luck and guesswork due to the great distance. If they could kill the first three, then engage the others...

Damn it! Bree silently swore as she swerved, lightning blasting to either side of her. Ice, fire, and stone might take time to travel, but one of the three above wielded lightning, and he fired at a frighteningly rapid pace. Enormous boulders flung through the air from above, and she fought her instinct to climb. The knight focusing on her would expect it, and sure enough, when she plunged sharply downward, a bolt of lightning lit the air above.

A fellow Seraph swooped past the stone, and Bree recognized

those black stripes on his silver wings. Twisting to right herself, she pulled upward with her shoulders and back, lifting into a climb. She joined Argus's side, accompanying him as if he were her squad leader. Together they rushed the stone-flinging knight, who'd pulled back into a hover while the other two raced east and west, splitting the Weshern forces into multiple engagements.

A storm of stone exploded toward them, far smaller chunks fired at a pace Bree didn't even know was possible. Argus's hand shot out, two quick symbols with his fingers ordering Bree to split, then converge. Following his command, she rotated her body ninety degrees and shot right while Argus banked hard to the left. Twirling so she faced her foe, Bree arched her back as far as it would go, taking herself on a direct collision course. The knight clearly expected her to attack with her element, whichever it might be, so he flung up a thin wall of stone, again with mastery far beyond any that Bree had witnessed before in battle. The stone also screened her from his sight for the briefest moment until the stone began to plummet.

Fighting off her initial impulse to swerve around, she refused to alter her course. Instead she reduced her speed so that the stone wall would drop just before her arrival. It was a tricky maneuver, but she relied on her instincts to judge it right. Thin, sharp pieces of stone shot around each edge of the falling wall. The top shot streaked through the air mere feet above her, and she flinched involuntarily. The wall continued its drop, she raced over, and then once more she saw the knight. He hovered in place, having spun to bring his gauntlet to defend against Argus knifing in from the opposite direction.

Argus flung a single lance of ice before veering away, dodging a thick piece of stone the size of his head. The ice shot caused the knight to flare his wings, pulling him up and away... and directly toward Bree.

Sword ready, Bree made sure not to make the same mistake twice. This time when she cut, she aimed for the throat. Her arm extended the sword, and its razor edge sliced across the knight's neck. She felt a single tug, but she spun around as she held on, momentum carrying her backward as she looked upon the knight. Blood splashed in a great spray above him, neck cut front to back.

Argus swooped beside her, slowing enough so she might hear his shout.

"At my side, Skyborn!"

She punched the throttle, taking up formation on his right. Argus led her to the nearest engagement. Three Seraphim chased after a knight unleashing burst after burst of flame. Despite being outnumbered three to one, he was on the offensive. Argus flew with his right arm outstretched, as he followed the knight's path. The moment they were close enough, he unleashed a trio of thin lances, each one perfectly aimed. They struck the knight in the chest and shoulder, and though they did not pierce his golden armor, they did knock him off course. Flailing to regain control, he was easy prey for Olivia, who struck him down with a blast of lightning that ripped through his body.

"Retreat!" Argus shouted as he flew past the three. "Retreat to safety, now!"

They did so, flying west as Argus led Bree back to the wrecked camp. The seven there appeared finished loading up the last of the elements, and they soared into the air to join them, heavy bags hanging beneath them off their belts. Bree looked over her shoulder and saw other Seraphim breaking off in wild directions. Only three of the initial six knights remained, but they continued to attack. Bree winced at how few of their own survived. One of the knights chased after a fleeing Seraph, while two others spotted their larger group. Gold light burst about their wings as they soared into chase.

"Can we outrun them?" Bree shouted to Argus beside her.

The commander glanced over his shoulder, then shook his head.

"Their wings are faster than ours," he shouted back. "And ours are burdened."

Then they'd have to fight. Argus fired a single thin piece of ice over the heads of the seven Seraphs to gain their attention, then relayed his order with his hand. They turned around, with Bree and Argus taking the lead of the widening V formation. The Weshern Seraphs raced toward the knights...only to see the two knights spin about to retreat. Bree's worry grew as the knights fled, gaining no distance despite their faster wings, and their heads constantly on a swivel.

Argus motioned an order, sending the V formation banking upward and about to flee toward the Aquila Forest. Immediately the two knights turned as well, following at a steady distance. Bree swore, realizing what they were doing. The knights didn't need to engage. Time was on their side. The longer Argus kept their Seraphim flying, the more likely that additional knights would spot them and join in the attack.

Argus reached the same conclusion, and he drifted close enough to Bree to take her by the wrist. He shouted to be heard over the roar of the wind and the thrum of the wings. Beneath them, the sprawling fields were replaced with a tightly packed forest.

"We'll have to chase them off together," he shouted. "Just you and I."

It was the only way to force the knights to either engage in a battle or lose sight of the other seven bearing the elements.

But two against two? Bree felt a shiver of doubt, but her pride chased it away. She'd show no fear, not to any opponent.

"I understand," she shouted back. "Give the order, and I'll follow."

He smiled at her, icy-blue eyes sparkling in the glow of the midnight fire. It was the happiest she'd ever seen him. Bree wondered how similar they might be, how comfortable they felt in battle as opposed to with their feet on the ground.

"Order given, Seraph. Kill our foes."

Bree arched her back, looping around in a U while rotating her body. Argus maneuvered the same, and side by side, they flew directly toward the chasing knights, wings shimmering silver. Bree jammed her gauntlets against the loops atop the hilts of her swords, locking the safety cord, and then drew them from their sheaths. Eyes wide, she watched for the first sign of attack. Neither side veered, not the knights nor Bree and Argus. Just raw speed on a direct collision course. It was a test of nerves, Bree realized, a game as old as humanity itself. The first to blink, lost.

Argus swung his right hand in a wide arc, and seven shards of ice burst from his palm. The knights barely moved, the shards passing mere inches beneath them. The knights returned fire, the smaller knight shooting bullets of stone from her gauntlet while the far larger on the right formed a thin spray of fire that he weaved side to side. Bree steeled her nerves. Both attacks were too high and low, anticipating dodges that never came. Side by side, Bree and Argus crossed the distance at breakneck speed.

Bree shifted slightly to the right, choosing as her target the giant knight with a strange weapon strapped between his wings on his back. She twisted her body with all her strength, twirling with her arms outstretched. They were so close, and traveling at such speed, she didn't think a man so big could maneuver away in time. She was wrong. The man cut power to his wings, reversed his body so he was traveling feetfirst, and then punched the wings back to life. The pain must have been incredible, but he rose up and away, out of reach of her spinning swords. Bree wondered why he'd perform such a difficult maneuver instead of banking upward like normal, but then realized after a simple twist of his body that he was now chasing her.

Streaks of flame burned the air on either side of her as she weaved, stretching every muscle in her body to change directions, always erratic, always unpredictable. Mostly she fled, but twice she turned about, hoping to catch the knight off guard. He was ready every time. The first attempt nearly bathed her in flame, while the second found her chasing empty air as the knight veered away. Bree's confidence faded fast. His wings were faster than hers, and he used that to consistently stay outside the reach of her swords. She had to do something. If she couldn't win as is, she had to change the rules of the game. If she couldn't beat him in open air, what about in much more enclosed spaces? Moving as fast as she dared, Bree dropped feetfirst through the canopy of leaves, descending into the dark forest below. Upon landing, she raised her swords and spun, searching.

Like a bear crashing through the trees, the angelic knight arrived. He slammed to the ground while striking with an enormous ax, the head leaving a groove half a foot deep in the dirt. That he wielded an ax wasn't surprising. Olivia had warned Bree as much. No, what left Bree's mouth gaping was how the man wielded it with a single hand. It shouldn't have been possible. The head of the ax was almost as big as her.

"The trees won't hide you, little Weshern whelp," the man

said as he towered before her. His pale face looked almost yellow in the faint light that filtered through the leaves. "I'll cut the entire forest down if I must."

"I'm not hiding," Bree said. "Not from you."

Fire burst around her right sword as she tensed her arm and released a flow of power from the prism within her gauntlet. She clanged her swords together, the fire leaping to bathe the other as if it were alive. Bree braced her legs and lifted her burning blades, preparing for a charge. She'd hoped the knight would be intimidated. Instead, he laughed.

"Well, well," he said, lifting his ax in both hands. "Not a whelp. A Phoenix."

He jumped, his wings flaring gold to give him speed as he burst forward. Bree kicked herself backward, using her wings to add to her speed. The knight's ax cleaved in a wide arc, moving impossibly fast for its size. Wind blew past her as the weapon missed. He twirled the ax in his hands as she dashed behind the thick trunk of an oak tree. Without pausing he swung the ax again, blasting it through the trunk in an explosion of splinters.

Bree fled, her bafflement growing. How could he wield that ax with such speed and grace? The knight flew over the collapsing trunk, ax lifted to swing. Bree ran, weaving around trees as he chased. She used her ears to track him, judging distance as he gained on her. When he was painfully close, she did not dodge the next tree but instead ran two steps up it, twisted, and kicked off. Her thumb cranked the throttle, pulling her into a mad collision course with the knight, her burning swords leading.

The smile on his pale face grew.

The head of the knight's ax faced her, wielded like a shield. Bree veered to the side, hoping to strike around it. She'd cut

with ease through the harnesses Seraphim wore, even shattered a sword, but metal this thick made a mockery of her
own thin blades. One sword clanged against the ax head; the
other slashed past it in a failed attempt to cut the knight's neck.
Instead it cut only air as the knight rotated with her passing,
keeping his vulnerable flesh just out of reach. Once she was
past he leapt after her, gold wings roaring. His ax lifted above
his head, its long handle giving him such reach her head start
meant nothing.

Bree cut off her wings, dug her heels into the ground, and
then dove to her right. The knight's ax smashed through overhead branches like they were twigs, then sank deep into the
earth. He laughed as he ripped the ax head free, tearing chunks
of earth with it.

"Look, Phoenix!" he shouted. "I've already dug your grave!"

Deciding that fleeing wasn't an option, Bree faced him down,
using her anger to give her courage. Despite the intimidating
size of the ax, she posed just as much danger to him as he did
to her. A single good hit with her burning blades and she'd
drop him dead. They were on the ground, but nothing else had
changed. The first to make a mistake paid with their lives.

"Give the dirt another whack," she said, grinning at the
knight. "It's your grave you dug, not mine, and it's not near big
enough."

"You're not afraid," the knight said as he lumbered closer.
"Impressive. Maybe you're actually deserving of your reputation."

Instead of swinging like she expected, he extended his right
hand and discharged a wide, thin spray of flame. Bree dove to one
side, punching the throttle as she did. Her body shot out of reach
from the fire, but her path was wild, uncontrolled. Her shoulder
slammed into a tree; she rolled around it, killed her wings, and
then dug in her heels so she might turn about. Her reward was

seeing the giant knight lunging after her, ax raised mid-swing. Sensing an opening, she leapt at him instead of fleeing, blades lashing for his chest.

The knight pulled his ax down as if it weighed nothing, canceling the swing and instead positioning the ax head in the way of her slashes. Burning swords ricocheted off the metal. Bree thrust with her left hand, had her attack parried aside with the ax's handle, and then kicked into the air, throttle pushed to a third. She somersaulted over the knight's head—at least, that was the plan. Before she could slash at his back, he caught her ankle with his free hand, then swung her sideways. Bree flew wild, letting out a panicked cry as she slammed into the trunk of a tree. She heard groaning from her wings, felt the thin metal give and bend.

Bree thumbed the throttle. Her wings shimmered silver, lifting her slightly. Still functioning, but there was nowhere to go. The knight cornered her, so close now, ax at ready. Even flying straight up and away appeared suicidal. The man was ready, his entire body tensed like a feline predator about to pounce. Bree held no delusions as to blocking or withstanding a single hit from that ax. With one swing the knight could fell a tree; her meager flesh and bone wouldn't even slow it down.

"I'll earn great honor when I bring Er'el Jaina your head," he said. "Consider your quick death a show of gratitude."

"Fuck your gratitude," she said, a shadow falling over them both.

The ax lifted, but before he could swing, Argus slammed down atop the knight's back, his sword clutched in both hands as he drove it through the knight's collarbone and into his lungs. Argus guided his body's momentum, swinging about so the skewering sword twisted and tore even farther into the knight. Argus's feet touched ground with him standing face-to-face with the knight, and he ripped the sword out with savage fury.

"There's no honor here," Argus said as his right hand closed around the stunned knight's neck, holding him steady. "Just death."

Ice punched through the knight's throat and out the back of his neck. His body went limp, the ax dropping to the ground with a heavy thud. Bree stepped away from the tree, and she let the fire vanish from her blades.

"Thank you," she said.

"Don't mention it," Argus said as he knelt beside the enormous ax, his back to her. Bree joined him, staring at the weapon in awe. Its pole was thick metal wrapped with leather, the head gilded and carefully crafted with ornate runes and decorations depicting the various elements in battle. The thick steel of its blade looked more like a plow she'd see in a farmer's field, to be pulled by an ox instead of wielded as a weapon.

"How could he lift such a thing?" Bree asked. "Is it theotech magic?"

"No, not magic," Argus said, pulling at part of the head. The metal slid open, revealing a hidden compartment. Argus removed a light element and tossed it to her. She caught it and stared at the prism, which still glowed a soft white.

"Some use light elements to make their weapons easier to wield," Argus explained as he turned the weapon over and revealed a similar compartment on the other side. That prism he kept himself, sliding it into a pocket of his belt. "A toggle here, by the base, activates the light prism. Just as it allows us to fly, inside the weapon, the light element reduces its weight, allowing the knight to wield it with ease. Remember, Bree,

you're fighting the best of the best. While we scrape by on whatever we get our hands on, they'll have every possible resource at
their disposal."

Bree nodded, letting the feeling of helplessness burn into her
memory. She swore never to feel that way again.

"I understand," she said.

"I pray you do," Argus said, rising to his feet. "These enemies
are beyond any you've ever faced. Push yourself beyond your
limits, beyond all reason. It's the only way we have a chance."

He used the dead knight's tunic to clean the blood off his
sword, then slid it into its sheath.

"Follow me," he said, wings shimmering silver. "It's time you
met the rest of the resistance."

CHAPTER

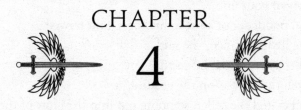

4

After Bree had followed Argus out, Rebecca Waller handed Kael a folded piece of paper.

"On there is all I know about the two Willer brothers," she said. "Read over it before meeting with Clara. The more knowledge you carry in, the more I expect you'll carry out."

Kael took the paper, shoved it into his pocket.

"Thank you," he said, and he caught himself almost calling her over-secretary. "Rebecca," he added at the very end, a hopeless attempt to hide his momentary hesitation.

The left side of her mouth curled in a bitter smile.

"You're right," she said. "I have no title anymore. I guess Rebecca will do for now, until officials from Center give me a new one. Outlaw, perhaps, or rebel?"

"Or give yourself one," Kael said. "Resistance Leader Waller has its own charm."

She smiled at him, this time without any bitterness.

"Time will tell," she said. "Go on home, Kael. Our eyes and ears will be open for you, and for anything you learn. Should you wish a meeting with me, hang two cloths to dry from a window of your home."

Kael nodded, put a fist to his chest, and bowed.

"We fly unchained," he said.

Rebecca returned the gesture.

"Even those of us on the ground."

Kael exited the cellar, stepping out into the glow of the midnight fire. A quick glance north saw Bree and Argus walking side by side on their way to wherever it was the rest of the Seraphim were gathering. Kael suppressed a frown as he turned the other way. Part of him hated the idea of her fighting a battle without him. Worse was the nagging belief that, no matter how important Rebecca insisted his meeting with Clara's family actually was, the reason he was left behind was that his skills weren't good enough. On his own, he was of no use to someone like Argus. It was only who he knew that mattered.

Telling himself it was just nerves over his sister's safety, Kael hurried down Thomas Road and turned toward home. He kept one eye on the sky at all times, watching for the omnipresent knights. The hour was even later, and it'd make his nighttime travel all the more questionable. Seeing someone in the air would be difficult, for the midnight fire rippled and shook, the strange new pattern an easy disguise for anyone flying high enough.

Kael spotted only a single knight prior to leaving Glensbee, which he easily avoided by pressing against the side of a home, hiding beneath the overhang of its long, wide roof. Then came the road between the towns. Kael jogged the path, head on a swivel. Here more than anywhere would be where he was most at risk. His best hope was diving into the grass prior to being spotted, but even then the outline of his body would likely give himself away.

You're just coming home from seeing friends in Glensbee, Kael told himself. *If you're spotted, you'll be fine. Stop panicking.*

Easier said than done, of course, and he pushed himself to run faster. If he was going to be constantly afraid, at least he could use it to urge his body onward. He slowed once reaching Lowville. This close to home, his viable excuses increased tremendously. If he saw a knight, he might not even need to hide. But it wasn't a knight that caught Kael's attention as he passed pole after pole marked with a red ribbon. Instead it was the sound of breaking wood, followed by a scream of pain.

Kael froze, head jerking toward the sound. He heard another scream, and it set his feet into motion. Racing down a thin alley between stone homes, he emerged on the next street over and skidded to a halt in the dirt. Three men stood over a fourth, who'd collapsed to his knees. Behind him was a home, stone pale white, windows covered with dark curtains, and a plain wood door, which was smashed open, hinges broken. Two of the three standing wielded clubs, while the third held a long strip of red cloth in his left hand and a knife in his right. Their backs were to Kael, who froze, confused and unsure as to what had transpired.

"Don't need to be this way," the man with the knife said. He held the cloth out to the kneeling man, the long red material trailing down like a stream of blood in the midnight fire. "Just put it on, Elijah. That's all we're asking."

The man on the ground looked to be in his later years, the top of his head bald and his face covered with a long white beard. In answer to their question, he spat at the feet of the man holding the cloth.

"Three years," he said. "I've been here three—"

One of the men cracked him across the mouth with a club, ending his protest. The cloth holder knelt down, voice gentle, as if still talking to a friend.

"Don't matter how long," he said. "Men and women of Galen wear the cloth. You know that. We know that. That's just how it is, so I'm giving you one last chance. We ain't asking much, are we?" The cloth dangled before him. "It's a small, simple little thing. Surely not worth your life."

Kael had seen enough. Wishing he had a weapon with him, he glanced about for something, anything he could wield.

What I'd give for Bree's broom handle, he thought, nearly laughing at the lunacy of it. He might not have a weapon, but he refused to be a coward. Clenching his hands into fists, he called out to them.

"Let him go."

The three turned, weapons held ready.

"None of your business, kid," said one. "Get out of here."

Kael took a step closer.

"I said let him go."

The looks on their faces made it clear they'd do no such thing. Kael swallowed, shoving down his fear. No going back. No giving in. Before they realized what was happening, he charged the nearest man with a club, fists leading.

He should have surprised them. He should have trained with Bree more at melee combat. He should have kept searching for a weapon. A whole host of things he wished he'd done flashed through his mind as he struck the man on the chin with his fists, then followed it up with another to the gut. Perhaps if he managed to wrestle a weapon free, get a club in hand, and start swinging while they were still surprised...

A hand grabbed his shoulder and flung him back. Before Kael could move, a fist filled his vision, then smashed his nose.

Spots of color replaced his normal sight, and he staggered backward. Something hard cracked his knee, and he crumpled, hitting the ground with his head. Blood splattered. On his stomach, he curled tighter as blows rained down upon his body, sometimes a club, sometimes a fist, sometimes a foot.

"Hey, hold up," Kael heard one of them say. "I think I know this kid."

A foot slid underneath Kael's shoulder and shoved, rolling him onto his back. Blood trickled across his lips as he glared up at the three men. The youngest, thin-framed and with hair growing uneven on his face, peered down at him with his hands on his hips, club tucked underneath his arm.

"Yeah, yeah, I know you," he said, wagging a finger at him. "Liam's son. Kael. Ain't that right, kid?"

The name "kid" made Kael crave his swords and wings. As he flew overhead, assaulting them with ice, would they still insult him so?

"That's right," he said. Opening his mouth allowed the blood in, and he tasted it on his tongue.

"Kael," the man with the cloth said. "As in the Phoenix's brother? Well, I'll be. Tonight just got interesting."

He grabbed Kael by the front of his shirt and lifted him to his feet. Before Kael even realized what was going on, the man had pushed the handle of the knife into his hand.

"Elijah here refuses to obey Weshern law," he said. "So you're going to punish him."

Two held their clubs at ready, the third clearly on edge as well. They watched Kael, reading his face, as he stared back in shock.

"What?" he asked. "No, I won't."

"Yes, you will." The man with the cloth pointed to the injured man. "Aren't you a Seraph, too? A *Weshern* Seraph?

Perhaps you forgot, kid, but we were at war with Galen when that piece-of-shit island crashed into the ocean. Far as I'm concerned, that war never stopped. Everyone likes to act as if we won, but all I see is Galen people living on our land."

He flung the cloth to the dirt.

"An enemy of your nation," he said. "Do your damn duty, Kael. Kill him."

The knife shook in Kael's hand as he looked down at Elijah. The older man had started crying. It left Kael sick to think no one else had stepped out of their home to investigate the matter. No one, if they heard, was interested in putting a stop to this travesty. Kael actually hoped a knight of Center flew over. For once, their presence would make him feel safer than that of his own people.

"Three years," Elijah said, the mantra he clung to, as if in disbelief it would not save him. "I've lived here three years. This is my home." He sat up, screaming louder. "This is my *home!*"

One of the men lifted his club threateningly, but he did not swing. Back to sobbing. Kael wished he could cry with him. This was wrong. All of it, horribly, terribly wrong.

"No," he said.

"You don't have a choice."

Kael opened his mouth as if to answer, and then whirled, dagger slashing at the man's face.

The man dodged in time to avoid the bulk of it, the tip cutting a thin line of blood across his cheek. Kael lunged, thrusting for his stomach. Again the man retreated, arms flinging up to protect himself. The knife cut across his hands, nothing more than a shallow wound that would bleed and hurt, but little else. Before Kael could swing again, a club struck his back. All air blasted from his lungs so only a pathetic whimper could escape his lips as he collapsed to his stomach. A second swing hit his side, and he gasped, fearing his ribs broken. The knife slipped out of his grasp and onto the dirt.

"Enough!" Kael heard one of them shout. "Let him be. Last thing we need is his sister hunting us down."

Kael struggled to stand, something nearly impossible with his lungs still hitching as if they didn't know how to properly breathe. Tears in his eyes, he watched as the leader of the three grabbed the knife and knelt beside Elijah. No more words, no more arguments. Just a long cut across the throat. Kael closed his eyes, hands digging into the hard dirt of the road. He bore enough guilt as it was. He couldn't bear to watch the man die as well.

They left not long after. Kael gingerly rose to his feet, back aching, nose throbbing, chest aflame. His entire face and neck were a mess of blood. Wiping at his mouth in a vain attempt to clean it, he stared down at the body. Gut twisting, he saw they'd tied the strip of crimson cloth around Elijah's arm after he'd died. A message for others, of course. The knot was tight, but Kael ripped at it until it tore free, then stuffed it in his pocket.

"I wish I could have done more," Kael whispered to the dead man. "I'm sorry. This is the best I can do."

Kael limped back through the alley to the main road. He didn't bother hiding from any knights who might fly overhead. He didn't look for the three men who'd committed the murder. He just wanted to be home, to lie down in his bed, close his eyes, and pretend the whole night was an ugly, awful dream that never happened.

Of course, there'd still be the strip of red cloth in his pocket, a very real reminder of the truth.

Kael had thought the hour too late for Aunt Bethy to still be awake, but as he pushed open the door to her home, he found her propped in a rocking chair beside a dormant fire. Red light washed over her, and she smiled in relief, relief that immediately vanished when she realized he was both alone and in pain.

"Are you all right?" she asked, lurching out of her chair.

"I'm fine," Kael said, attempting, and failing, to brush away her worried hands as she tilted his chin so she might have a better look in the dim light. A frown spread across her stretched, oval face.

"Don't lie. You're far from fine," she said. A thought came to her, yet she hesitated to ask. Kael could guess it immediately.

"Bree's safe," he said, gently pushing past her, his eye on her rocking chair. Right now, the thought of settling into it was an overwhelming temptation.

"At least, she was last I saw her," Kael added as he slumped into the chair. Aunt Bethy hovered nearby, fetching a thick cloth from a drawer and dipping it into the bucket of water kept near the fireplace.

"Is she off doing something dangerous?" Bethy asked as she dabbed at his bruised face. Kael winced, then forced himself to relax. He was a Seraph of Weshern, damn it. A few bruises and a busted nose shouldn't overwhelm him so.

"You could say that," Kael answered, glad his aunt was being cautious enough with her questions. Either she sensed he didn't wish to talk, or she understood that the more she knew, the more danger she'd be in if a theotech came questioning. The cloth wiped above his left eye, cleaning blood from his stinging cut. Once done there, she more forcefully rubbed at his cheeks, and the blood that stained them. Kael had thought his injuries mostly superficial, but the blood must have been significant, for twice Bethy had to clean the cloth with the bucket before she moved on to his nose.

"So what happened to you?" she asked as she slowly pressed the cloth against his upper lip.

Kael swallowed hard. The last thing he wanted to discuss was how miserably he'd failed the man from Galen, or how the beating he'd received was from his own people, the people he'd risked his life to protect. Still, he'd have to give his aunt something, because otherwise she'd worry over him nonstop until he finally revealed the reason.

"It was just some men upset about Galen," Kael said, keeping it vague. "I got in the middle of it, that's all."

Aunt Bethy let out a disdainful huff, and she shook her head as if disappointed in a toddler.

"You should have known better," she said. "The men from Galen are ruffians, all of them. You're lucky you didn't get hurt worse."

She pushed the cloth harder against his nose, trying to sop up the blood, and the pain kept Kael from correcting her.

"Weshern suffered from Galen's recklessness for years," Bethy continued. "They fought us tooth and nail for every single privilege Center gave us. When we finally stood up to them, it cost us even more. It cost us the lives of your parents. And now, after God's struck them down for their sins, Center brings the sinners here, to live among us better folk? Damn foolishness is what that is."

Now it wasn't pain holding Kael silent. It was shock. He'd never seen his aunt so angry. Even when she first protested against him and Bree joining the Weshern Seraphim, she'd never been so adamant.

"They've lost their home," Kael said. Such a meager protest, but it was also the most blindingly obvious. "What else should we do?"

"Let them live elsewhere," Bethy said. "That, or drop them to the water, as God intended. Galen fell by their own hands. When a dog dies, you don't rescue its fleas. Claiming the island's fall was our fault is just further proof Speaker Marius's heart doesn't mirror God's."

Kael's eyes narrowed. That final thought sounded far too similar to what he'd heard many others claim before. The disciples of Johan had spread throughout all the islands, and Kael had a feeling that Galen's fall opened many ears once closed to their rhetoric. Kael himself had spoken to two, frightening, determined men convinced of Center's evil. Yet they had also insisted, long before Galen fell, that Marius would send troops over to occupy Weshern. They were the only voices that had cried warning, and Kael wished more had listened before they found themselves in such an awful predicament. Still, the disciples only preached against Marius Prakt's rule over the minor islands. So far as Kael knew, Johan had not spoken out against the people of Galen. Of course, what *anyone* knew of Johan was incredibly limited. Appearances of him were rare, and never in public.

"Me and Bree risked everything to save those *fleas* when the island was falling," Kael said as Aunt Bethy pulled away to give him one more look over. "They're just people, innocent people who were caught in our fight."

"Believe as you wish."

Kael hated it when she did that. A minor acknowledgment of his words, but no real thought. No real belief he could be right. She knew better. Of course she knew better. She was older, wiser, the one who understood how the world truly worked while he was the naïve youngster. Kael's hand dipped inside his pocket, fingering the red cloth hidden there. People of Weshern had murdered a man in cold blood, then beaten Kael for refusing to commit the deed himself, yet it was the people of Galen who were sinners, who were fleas?

Fleas. Parasites. The very words, the very idea of them,

flooded Kael with anger, and he had to bite his tongue to keep from saying things he'd very much regret come morning. What would it matter? What could he possibly say to change a mind so steadfastly decided? The night was too late, his mind too tired, his body too sore. He just wanted to go to bed.

"Your nose should heal without need of a splint or stitch," his aunt said, wringing out the cloth onto the dormant fire while keeping her back to him. Her tone had changed suddenly, something about it off. She was being cautious. Tentative. "I expect you'll be sore but fine." She turned, facing him without looking at him. "So, will your sister be back before tomorrow night?"

An odd question.

"I don't know," Kael said, rising from the rocking chair. "Why tomorrow night?"

She shook her head, quickly turning away.

"No reason," she said, continuing to wring out the cloth despite it being as dry as it could get without time in the sun. "I'd just feel better seeing her alive and well, that's all."

Kael was certain she was lying. He'd spent more than enough years in her household to recognize that tone. Aunt Bethy was a lot of things, but a good liar was not one of them. Curiosity overriding his exhaustion, he crossed his arms and blocked her path from the fireplace.

"Why tomorrow night?" he repeated.

His expression must have made it clear he would not be fooled, so she relented, but only partially.

"There's . . . someone who wants to meet you and your sister," she said.

Not good enough.

"Who?" he asked.

Even in the light of the midnight fire, Kael could tell his aunt was flustered, her neck turning red.

"I can't say," she said.

Kael's heartbeat increased as he thought on who it might be. Not a theotech or soldier of Center, not with his aunt's anger. No one from Galen, either. It couldn't be someone from the resistance, for Rebecca Waller would have surely informed him of such during his rapid debriefing. So who else would seek an audience with him and Bree?

"Is it someone in the royal family?" he asked.

Bethy didn't even flinch. So not close then. Kael stepped closer, met her gaze.

"Why won't you tell me?" he asked.

"For his own safety, I was sworn to secrecy," she said. "But he wants to meet you, both of you, tomorrow night."

Kael's throat suddenly felt very dry, and he feared that despite his awful exhaustion he'd find no sleep when he went to bed. He had one other guess, and he couldn't decide if he hoped it true or not. Keeping close watch on his aunt, to see the truth in her eyes in case lies and deception came to her lips, he asked.

"Is it Johan?"

Her look was answer enough. The most wanted man alive. The man whose very name was a crime to speak. He was coming to their home.

"It's a great honor," his aunt said breathlessly. "Even he sees the promise in you two."

Too much to process. Too much to decide. Kael closed his eyes and slumped against the wall. No more disciples. No more cultish worship and vague promises. Tomorrow night, he'd hear it from the man's own lips.

Johan, thought Kael. *For good or ill, we'll meet at last.*

CHAPTER
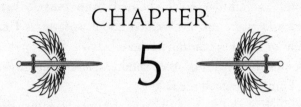
5

Bree awoke with every muscle in her body sore, particularly her back from when the giant knight had flung her into a tree. The thin reed cot she slept upon certainly helped matters none, and she let out a groan as she swung her legs over the side, fighting against the entangling blanket to free herself. Light shone through rips in the thick brown fabric of the tent. Clean light, she realized, not red. Morning, then. She rubbed her eyes, tried to regain her bearings.

After the battle, she'd followed Argus across Weshern to a deep forest, eventually stumbling upon a sprawling camp built in the wide spaces between the trees. Camp Aquila, Argus had called it. It had been too dark for her to see, the leaves blocking much of the midnight fire, and the risk of detection preventing any torches or campfires down below. Argus had brought her to a tent, told her it was hers, and then promised to return in the morning.

Bree tried to stand, felt her back twinge. She glared at the cot, and she briefly wondered if it would have been better to just sleep on the forest floor instead.

"Bree?" a familiar voice shouted from outside her tent. "Hurry and wake up. I've waited about as long as I can, so indecent or not, I'm coming in there."

"Do and you're dead!" Bree shouted back as she rose to her feet. "Think it's worth the risk?"

She opened the flap of the tent, squinted against the sudden light. Standing before her, a grin stretched from ear to ear, was Bradford Macon. Unlike the uniforms she'd seen him in since joining the academy, he wore the plain trousers and heavy white shirts of the fishermen. It somehow made him look bigger, friendlier. Or perhaps it was the dumb grin and the twinkle in his hazel eyes that did that.

Bree's hair was a mess from sleep, she wore the clothes from the night before, and she was certain her face sported a bruise or two from the battle, but she flung her arms around Brad and embraced him anyway. The big guy laughed as he hugged her.

"You look terrible," he said. "Rough night?"

Bree pushed away, and she mussed his curly red hair as she did.

"You know just what to say to a girl in the morning," she said. "Care to tell me how I smell, too?"

"Couldn't say," Brad said. "This whole damn place smells like trees and bird shit."

"And you smell like fish," Bree said. "No wonder you find it all so offensive."

"Once it gets in the clothes, it never leaves," Brad said, tugging on his trousers for emphasis. "Still, less likely to get noticed on the streets wearing this than a Seraphim uniform.

So! Want something to eat? The morning mist is the only time Miss Waller feels it's safe to light the cook fires."

"Miss Waller?" Bree asked as they weaved through the trees. By the looks of it, the camp was spread out across a huge area, with her tent on a far edge. By Bree's best guess, having the tents scattered so far apart instead of concentrated together would reduce the likelihood of them being spotted through the leaves. Nearly every tent she saw was some shade of brown, barring a few with dark green woven into the fabric.

"Camp Aquila is Rebecca's baby," Brad said. "You don't piss somewhere unless you're sure she's approved it first. I think even Argus is scared to defy her. Shouldn't be too surprising, really. She basically ran the academy as over-secretary. Everyone else just played along."

They arrived at the cook fires, and the smell of meat and smoke awoke Bree's empty stomach. Dozens of men and women gathered around the two pits, ringed with stones and piled full with thick logs cut from the nearby trees. A single pig lay slaughtered between them, and four men worked together, carving out pieces and throwing them onto black metal pans, which they constantly turned at the edges of the fire. Brad and Bree took their place in the back of one of the lines.

"So who else is here that I know?" Bree asked as they waited for their turn.

"Couple people," Brad said. "Randy Kime's in charge of training the raw recruits. You should swing by and say hello sometime. I'm sure he'd be happy to see you."

Bree had every intention of doing just that, for she'd be equally happy to see him.

"Who else?" she asked. Their line shuffled forward a step.

"From our class?" Brad thought a moment. "Saul's been

here for at least a few days. I think Ryan Keegan swung by for a bit, but didn't stay. Must not have had the stomach for all this."

"Maybe they just didn't need him?" Bree offered.

"Wait until you see who Instructor Kime's been working with," he said. "Trust me, we needed him."

Their turn. One of the cooks handed Brad a thick white cloth, which he held open across his palms. Then came a single thick slab of meat, from which part of the pig Bree could only guess. Bree accepted a similar cloth, coupled with a piece not quite as big as Brad's. The meat sizzled in her hands, but the cloth was thick, and protected her skin from the heat so long as she consistently shifted her grip.

After thanking the cooks, the two looked for a place to eat.

"Make sure you bring that cloth back to them to be cleaned," Brad said as they sat down on a pair of logs. "I forgot the first day I was here, which earned me the privilege of being the one to wash every single dirty cloth in the entire camp. Not something I'd recommend."

Bree laughed, glad to be around Brad again. She'd forgotten how easily he brightened her mood.

"I'll keep it in mind," she said. She shifted her grip on the slab of pork, fingers seeking a spot where the heat and grease hadn't quite leaked all the way through. After blowing on it, she gestured to the camp, the tents, and the people about them. "So, how'd you become a part of all this?"

Brad scarfed down a piece of the pork, wiped grease from his chin.

"I've actually been here a few days," he said. "Someone from Camp Aquila snuck a note through my bedroom window while I was asleep. Note landed on the floor, the idiot, and I never saw the stupid thing. My mom found it while she was sweeping."

Brad chuckled. "It was a good thing neither of my parents is too fond of Center right now, or they'd never have given it to me. The note requested I join up with the growing resistance, and gave a time and place to go if I wished to accept."

Brad took another bite.

"You should have seen it," he said. "I thought they were proud when I was accepted into the academy. This? This was something else. I'm not sure I could have said no even if I wanted to. They'd have probably dragged me to that meeting place, they were so honored." He cleared his throat, then started to talk in a high-pitched tone. "My little boy's going to fight against the corruption of Center," he said. Then, deeper, "You're not just a Seraph now, son. You're a hero."

Bree smiled at his impressions.

"Did you tell them you wouldn't be fighting, just sitting here getting fat on pork while everyone else did all the work?"

He grinned, proud as could be.

"You kidding?" he said. "When all this is over, and I go back home, I'm going to steal your exploits and claim them as my own. I want every single Macon child for generations to wish they were half as awesome as me."

Bree finally took a bite of her meat, and she was surprised by the taste. It must have been salted at some point, for the flavor was strong, and immediately set her mouth to water. She wasn't even finished chewing the first bite when she took two more, stomach now fully awake and demanding food.

Brad raised an eyebrow as he watched her eat.

"Good thing they won't give you extra rations even if you ask," Brad said. "You seem ready to eat an entire pig. Hoping to look like I did when first entering the academy?"

Bree didn't answer, only took another bite.

When she was finished, and her cloth returned to a basket

near the cook fires, Bree wiped the grease from her fingers on her pants the best she could, then pondered what to do.

"So where is Randy?" she asked.

"Training, I'd wager," Brad said. "Follow me."

Brad led her toward the northern edge of the camp. Just beyond the limits of the scattered tents she found a small clearing made by cutting down a few trees. Light shone bright through the gaps in the leaves, glinting off a dozen sets of silver wings. At the start of the clearing, shouting out corrections and techniques, was Randy Kime.

"I'll leave you two be," Brad said. "I've some business to attend to."

"Business?"

Brad rolled his eyes, and he patted his full belly.

"You know," he said. *"Business."*

Bree blushed despite herself.

"Oh. Right. Uh, hope it all goes well?"

Brad shook his head as he laughed and walked away.

"Great to see you again, Bree."

Bree turned her attention to Randy. His back was to her, so Bree stepped close, then called his name. The man whirled around, eyes widening the moment he saw her.

"There's the girl with the fiery swords," Randy said, and he immediately flung his arms around her. Bree accepted the hug, trying hard not to act awkward.

"Happy to see you, too," she said.

Randy pulled back, and he tapped the stump of his left hand into his right palm.

"I always knew," he said. "I kept saying you'd be amazing at fire, Bree, and now look at you. A legend in the making. I'd bet money on it, if I had any to bet, and anyone foolish enough to take me up on it."

Bree turned her attention to Randy's "students." They were all unmistakably fishermen, and they wore the stubby, clunky wings Bree had first trained in while growing up. She frowned, then tried to hide it, knowing many were watching the pair. Watching her, she realized. *Damn it,* she thought. *Can't people just pretend they don't know who I am?* Proud as she'd been when Argus gave her the nickname Phoenix, sometimes she'd wished he hadn't worked so hard to spread tales of her prowess. With how loudly Randy had greeted her, she had zero chance of anonymity.

"They're wasting light element that could be best served in the hands of others," Bree said, lowering her voice. "Last night we fought knights with trained Seraphim, and still we lost several. What hope do elementless fishers with stunted wings have?"

Randy's smile faded slightly, and he lowered his own voice so his students would not overhear.

"As much chance as our resistance has of toppling the armies of Center," he said. "But we'll still try, won't we? We'll fight, and train, and do all we can to better ourselves while hoping something magical happens to save our nation. Besides, the elements they use were allocated to them for fishing. Bellies will go hungry so they might train."

Bree blushed. It was the gentlest berating she'd ever received in her life, yet because it came from a man as kind as Randy, she still felt embarrassed.

"I'm sorry," she said. "I didn't mean to dismiss them so easily."

Randy put a hand on her shoulder, and together they walked before the line of students, men and women rising and lowering in the exact same drills Adam Dohn had them performing in the earliest days at the academy.

"You're thinking only of engaging Center's knights," he said as he observed the practicing students. "But if war breaks out, there will be a hundred other engagements we must prepare for besides the grand battles most will remember. Marius has placed soldiers throughout the island, and those soldiers will need to be defeated. A man in a fisher suit armed only with a spear and a shield may not mean much to a knight, but they will pose a danger to any archer or foot soldier."

Bree nodded, realizing how much she had underestimated the scope of their conflict. Right now, they'd fought a single fight against a small force of knights and soldiers. If rebellion broke out in full, Marius would begin conquering towns, flooding streets with men in plate and archers eager to shoot down any last Weshern Seraphim. The idea was almost like a dream, something she couldn't believe might actually happen, but the truth was naked before her. Those times were coming. They might even be a single day away.

"You're right," she said. "If there's anything I can do to help, let me know, and I'd be glad to pitch in."

"You should actually meet with Argus about that," Randy said. "He's in charge of our Seraphim. We don't want to be wasteful with our elements, but he also wants to ensure everyone flies as a cohesive unit. He might have a few sessions planned, quick ones just above the forest where we can keep an eye out for spies. When battling knights, there's not much room for error, if any."

"I'll go do that," Bree said. "Do you know where he is?"

Randy pointed back toward the cook fires.

"We've set up a command tent for Argus and Rebecca to share," he said. "Just look for the biggest of the lot."

"Thanks," Bree said. She started to go, then paused. The former instructor's comments jostled loose a memory, one she'd never felt safe asking about before. But now with the academy burned down, and rebellion spreading against Center, what reason was there to remain quiet?

"Speaking of the girl who should have failed out," she said, turning around. "What kept you from having me removed at the six-month evaluation? Theotechs were involved, weren't they?"

A shadow crossed over Randy's gentle face.

"Jay informed me that morning that you would remain enrolled as a student," he said. "He gave no reason, but he did say two theotechs would sit in during your and your brother's evaluations. Whatever they told Jay, I'm sad to say it died with him."

Bree clenched her jaw tight. Another dead end, coupled with a reminder of Jay's death. Their war might only be beginning, but they'd already suffered the loss of good men and women. It pained her to think of just how many they'd lose if the rebellion lasted much longer. Far too many, and odds were high she'd be one of them.

"I understand," she said. "Good luck with your training. I'll be with Argus."

Bree hurried from the training ground as if she could run away from her sadness and unease. The camp stretched out to the south, and as she looped around the cook fires near the heart of it, she saw the largest of the tents, the fabric a dense green, the top covered with a thin layer of leaves. The entire southern half was pulled open, allowing in light. As she neared, she saw Argus standing over a table, leafs of paper spread out before him. Unlike most others, he kept his uniform crisp and clean, a measure of defiance against the forest they resided within. Bree stopped just shy of the tent, and she stood at attention and saluted.

"Reporting for duty," she said.

Argus looked up from his papers, and it took a moment before he realized who she was.

"Glad to see you up and well," Argus said. "How do you like Camp Aquila?"

"It's pleasant," Bree said. "A little rustic, but pleasant."

"We're doing what we can to add more basic utilities, but hiding in a forest has its fair share of limits." He turned back to his papers, frowned at them. "Some things we'll just have to make do without."

Bree stepped closer, glancing over the papers. They listed numbers of elements, she saw, the total haul they'd obtained the night before, plus what she assumed the resistance already possessed.

"I'm using the number of elements we expended last night as a measure," Argus said, sensing her question before she could ask it. "I'm hoping to know just how many engagements we can fight before we're out completely. The number's not near as high as I'd like, in case you're wondering. We might have to shrink the number of Seraphim we send in per battle, at least until Marius starts attacking us at full strength."

Her battle in the forest last night flashed through her mind, and she wondered what it would be like facing not just a pair of knights, but dozens, perhaps even hundreds. The prospect was far from encouraging.

"We'll find a way," Bree said, trying to be hopeful. "Even if it involves scavenging elements from the dead, or taking light from our fishermen."

Argus ran a hand through his short dark hair, and he sighed.

"Truth be told, I'd prefer we run out of element than the alternative," he said. "Better out of elements than out of Seraphim willing to use them, because that's the real threat we're facing right now."

"What do you mean?" Bree asked.

Argus slumped into a wood rocking chair. Bree wondered how he smuggled it into the forest, and the image of him flying with it clutched in his arms almost made her smile. Almost.

"I've sent messages to every one of our Seraphim," he said. "Only a third have come as I've asked. Our ground forces are disbanded, our Seraphim are greatly outnumbered by Center's knights, our Archon and his wife are imprisoned, and we're vastly outmatched when it comes to supplies. Why would they risk their lives in such a hopeless endeavor?"

Bree didn't like the look on the man's face one bit. Argus was their leader, their inspiration. He was also an angel's breath away from cracking.

"We have to convince them to come," she said. "What if you requested their presence personally, or told them of the elements we secured…"

Argus stood, and he leaned against the desk as he met her eye. A fever burned within those blue irises.

"It's not enough," he said. "We're a bee buzzing around Center's head, making demands. Our only hope is to sting so hard and so often Marius would rather make peace than continue swatting at us. But we can't do that if everyone is convinced the slightest confrontation will lead to an unwinnable war."

"We've killed their knights and attacked their theotechs," Bree said, crossing her arms behind her back. "Are you sure war isn't what we've already created?"

"Our demands are fair, and I've ensured the other islands know exactly what they are. We seek a promise of independence and the release of our ruling family, who have been imprisoned without trial or even a single piece of proof offered to justify it. The harder Marius pushes back, the more nervous the other islands will become. We've already managed to bloody Center's nose. Just imagine if all four islands were united in our resistance."

Argus clenched his jaw as he stood to his full height.

"We don't need to win a war," he said. "And it won't come to that, not if we present ourselves as a fearsome enough opponent. But to do that, I need skilled men and women." He put a hand on her shoulder. "I need the Phoenix on the battlefield, and for the whole damn island to know it."

Bree's throat tightened, and she fought back an impulse to pull herself free from his touch.

"You said it'd be my choice."

"And it still is," Argus said. "But you've seen what everyone is enduring, the many lives at risk. You've even seen the danger the knights present, and our need for superior numbers in these rapid engagements. That's why we need you now more than ever. Your swords defy everything we've previously known about aerial combat. People will believe you capable of miracles, because they want to believe. They want to cling to stories no matter how fanciful or exaggerated. Let the entire island know you stand against Center, openly, and without fear. Let your burning blades become the symbol of our resistance. Do that, and I won't have to beg for our soldiers and Seraphim to return. They will come to me, eager to fight at your side."

"Did I disappoint you when I hid my fire at our last battle?" she asked, unable to keep the bitterness from her voice.

Argus stepped away, and his hand left her shoulder. It hurt Bree seeing her beloved commander so exhausted, so stressed and overwhelmed. It hurt worse when he answered.

"Our nation needs you. Yes, if you become our symbol, I understand it puts your family at risk." He pointed out to the camp, and the many Seraphim there. "And every one of those men and women risk their lives, their families, their safety by joining this resistance. You're special, Bree, we all can see that, but the hardships you face, and the risks you endure, *aren't*. Stop letting your cowardice hold you down. Deep inside, I know you're pure, raging fire. Blood is spilling. Lives are perishing. We need an answer, and soon."

Bree stood up tall, and she swallowed her pain down deep.

"If I do this, Kael and my aunt will need to go into hiding," she said. "I need to discuss this with them before I decide."

Argus slumped back down into his chair.

"Then go home," he said. "Spend the night, and talk it over with your family. Maybe that will help clear your head."

The idea of returning home, and sleeping on her far more comfortable bed, appealed to Bree greatly, but before she could go, there was one question she had to have answered first.

"If I say yes, you'll make the Phoenix the symbol of rebellion," she said. "But what happens if I say no?"

Her commander sighed.

"I don't know," he said. "And I pray I never do."

CHAPTER

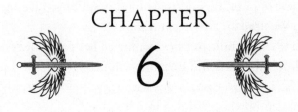

6

Bree wasn't home by the time Kael woke up, but he tried not to let it bother him. His aunt was equally worried as they ate breakfast, and he reassured her as best he could.

"I'm sure she's just fine," he said, pushing away his bowl. "But after her...activities, it might not have been safe for her to come straight home."

There was no way for his aunt to misunderstand his meaning. He watched her expression carefully, but there wasn't much need. Amid her worry, her pride shone through like a beacon.

"I hope she's well," Aunt Bethy said. "And I hope she made a lot of other people pay."

"Knowing her, both are safe assumptions."

He smiled, and his aunt did likewise. He could see her shoulders loosen as her tension eased away.

"You're probably right," she said. "Times are dangerous. I'm sure she'll be back at some point, just hopefully before tonight.

Our guest was eager to meet her. Your sister's reputation has carried all the way to Center, from what the disciple told me. It's a wonder the theotechs didn't arrest her the moment they invaded our island. Did they think she'd sit idly by as they conquered our home?"

"Maybe they underestimated her," Kael said, rising to his feet. "It wouldn't be the first time."

He cleared away the dishes. His aunt watched him from her chair.

"Do you have plans for the day?" she asked.

Kael debated answering, figured there was no harm.

"I do," he said. "I was hoping to visit Clara at her home."

"More friends from the academy? That's nice. Where does she live?"

Kael held back a chuckle.

"She lives in the holy mansion with the rest of her family."

The connection clicked in Aunt Bethy's head, and she let out a soft gasp.

"You're friends with the Archon's daughter?" she said. "That's wonderful, Kael. Good for you."

His sister earned praise for her skill in battle and her swords of flame. Kael earned praise for befriending the Archon's daughter. He tried not to feel too bitter about it. He mostly succeeded.

"We're more than just friends," he said, suddenly compelled to brag.

His aunt's pleased look changed to one of shock and curiosity.

"Is that so?" she said.

Kael immediately regretted saying anything. Sure, he and Clara had been more than friends, but what exactly were they? That particular little detail he didn't have an answer to, and with the academy's shutdown and Clara's parents' imprisonment, he doubted any sort of relationship they did have was on solid ground. Worse, he might find out exactly where he stood, and he might not like it.

"Kind of," Kael said, deciding he didn't want to discuss it further. "So why were you wondering? Did you need me for something?"

Aunt Bethy gestured to the door, and thankfully went along with Kael's sudden change in the topic.

"I haven't seen you for almost a year," she said. "I was hoping you might join me in the fields, assuming you're not too good for that sort of thing now that you're a Seraph."

Kael wrapped his arm around his aunt's shoulder.

"I can visit Clara later this afternoon," he said. "And I'd be happy to spend time with you, even if it's in a field shoveling manure."

She kissed his cheek.

"I'll make sure you pick weeds with me today," she said. "No more manure shoveling for you."

Kael bathed in the lake afterward, emerging from the water feeling reenergized. It had been relaxing spending time with his aunt, catching up on the latest gossip. Turned out, Judy had actually married Raphael instead of the dick Thomas in Glensbee. Kael took pride in knowing he called that one correctly. Besides the gossip, it was nice to bleed out some of his worries with long, tedious work.

His aunt remained in the fields, with many hours left still to kneel and pick. Alone, Kael went home, and he frowned upon realizing his sister was yet to return. Or if she had, she hadn't stayed long, or given any sign of her arrival.

"Hope you're all right, sis," he said walking through the front door. "God knows none of us can afford to lose you now."

"And why would she be in danger?"

Kael fought the instinct to whirl around. It would only make him appear that much guiltier. Instead he calmly turned to address the angelic knight lieutenant at his doorstep.

"A foreign army has occupied our home, and our former enemy lays claim to an entire town," he told Nickolas Flynn. "Why shouldn't I worry for our safety?"

The knight lieutenant crossed his arms. His gold wings shone in the afternoon light, a sharp contrast to the darkness of his skin. Those brown eyes of his narrowed, and they saw far more than Kael preferred.

"You highly exaggerate the circumstances," Nickolas said. "We're no foreign conqueror. We've come here for your protection."

"The ruins of our academy say otherwise."

The knight shook his head.

"Where do you go?" he asked.

"To meet with friends," Kael said, purposely leaving it vague.

"May I walk with you?"

The answer was a resounding no, but Kael dared not speak it.

"Of course," he said, shrugging as if it were no big thing. "Always happy to spend time with a friend of the family."

An edge of sarcasm bled into his words. Kael hoped the knight wouldn't think much of it. The last thing he needed was Nickolas realizing Kael knew the theotechs had assigned the knight to keep an eye on the siblings after their parents' deaths. Kael could only guess if the theotechs were pleased or disappointed in what they saw in him and Bree.

Nickolas walked alongside Kael, easily matching him stride to stride. He kept his arms crossed over his white tunic as he walked, eyes never leaving Kael's.

"Have you heard of last night's attack?"

Kael kept his eyes on the road, his stride perfectly even.

"I haven't," he said. "I thought the Speaker swore we'd fight no battles during the occupation?"

His ignorance was an act, and Nickolas hardly looked amused by it.

"It was no foreign, sanctioned attack," he said. "Argus Summers's rebellious Seraphim assaulted one of our Er'el's caravans. Many good men died, and the retribution will be swift."

"And well deserved, I'm sure," Kael lied.

Nickolas frowned. Kael silently swore. So stupid of him. He wasn't a good enough liar to get away with such remarks.

"Argus appears eager for a war," the knight lieutenant continued. "And if he wants a war, he'll need soldiers like you and your sister. Has he sent anyone to speak with you two yet?"

Kael's heart steadily increased its hammering. He was walking on rotted wood above a very, very high cliff. If Nickolas suspected Bree partook in the nighttime attack, and sought to bring her in for questioning, she'd be forced to flee. Hell, he might even arrest Kael right on the spot.

"Of course he has," Kael said, hoping a bit of truth might aid the rest of his lie. "We turned him away."

Nickolas nodded, feigning relief. None of it reached his eyes.

"Good," he said flatly.

"So was there anything else?" Kael asked as they continued down the road. Nickolas shook his head.

"Only this," the knight lieutenant said. In a blur of motion, he grabbed Kael by the shoulders and slammed him against the wall of the nearby building. Kael cried out, convinced his death was at hand. There'd be no trial. No public execution. Just a sword in his gut as the knight declared him an enemy of Center.

Nickolas leaned closer, the intensity of his eyes so terrifying Kael could not look away.

"Listen carefully," he said. "I am no fool. Argus's rebellion is growing bolder, and they will not leave you be until you've joined their cause, especially not with the reputation your sister carries. Do not listen to them, Kael. Do not believe their fearmongering. All we do, we do for the safety of you and your people. The last thing we want is another Galen."

"Then why not accept the terms Argus offered?" Kael mustered up the courage to ask.

At the mention of the terms, Nickolas looked ready to spit.

"A brute's version of diplomacy, without regard for circumstance or patience to speak prior to bloodshed. No one gives a damn about your royal family. Promises of independence? What does a promise matter if your entire island crashes down to the Endless Ocean? Tens of thousands of lives are at stake. We will do everything, *everything* necessary to keep you safe, even if it means crushing your military into the dirt."

"You'd threaten us?" Kael asked.

"It's not a threat," the knight lieutenant said, gently easing back. His thumb tapped the throttle to his wings, surrounding them with a faint gold aura. "It's a warning. Those who stand against us will perish, without question, without mercy. Don't be a fool and throw your life away, do you understand me? When the recruiters come, refuse their requests."

"I'll keep it in mind."

Nickolas paused just before taking off.

"And, Kael," he said, "if you or your sister has already participated in battle, it's not too late to abandon the cause and turn away. You're only weapons for Argus to use until they break. You don't fight against other Seraphim. You fight against Center's knights. Death is just a matter of time."

Kael clenched his jaw and kept his mouth shut. The knight lieutenant saluted, then flew away. Kael watched him, wondering why he ever used to believe the man had been their friend. His hand disappeared into his pocket, and he touched the rough paper inside. It was the research Rebecca Waller gave him on the two brothers, Lance and Edwin. Kael watched until Nickolas was a speck in the distance, then pulled out the paper. He read it as he walked. He'd met both brothers during the winter solstice celebration, so much of it he already knew. Hair color. Eye color. Estimated height and weight.

When you said "all you knew," you meant it, didn't you? he thought. He couldn't imagine how knowing of Lance's unnatural fear of spiders might help his efforts, but Rebecca had scribbled it along with the rest of the information. He also wondered how she both obtained and remembered such factoids. Brad had once joked that Rebecca could list off the exact amount of forks in the mess hall at any given time. Kael thought there might be far more truth to that offhand statement than Brad realized.

The actual useful stuff was at the very end, and painfully thin.

Lance has spoken repeatedly of his disdain for New Galen's creation. Edwin has said nothing on the matter, though privately he may speak more freely. Both brothers appear to be fully cooperating with the occupation, and have been careful to say nothing disparaging about Center or the Speaker.

Kael read over the note a second time, then tore it up into little strips. When he reached the grasslands just beyond Lowville, he scattered the pieces into the wind. Being searched prior to entering the holy mansion was a distinct possibility, and he wanted to avoid any awkward discussion about how and why he'd have a note containing such information.

The walk was long and boring, but at least it let him calm down from his talk with Nickolas. Kael did his best to focus on any possible interactions with Lance and Edwin, but it never stayed long. Instead he ran a seemingly endless number of meetings with Clara through his head. What she might say. How she might react. What he'd do if she were happy, or mad, or sad, or indifferent. He knew it was stupid, but he found himself far more nervous at how he'd react around her than the two current rulers of Weshern.

At last he saw the stone mansion, protected by a tall fence and bordered with dozens of trees trimmed so their rounded tops flattened at the bottom. The gate through the fence was closed, and two of Center's soldiers stood before it, shields strapped to their backs and long spears held in hand. Kael frowned, quickly banished it while hoping neither soldier saw. No reason to let them know of his unease. The Willer house guards stood by the door farther in, but it was obvious who was considered to have greater authority. No one reached the Willer guards without first passing through Center's.

"Need something?" one of the soldiers asked when Kael stopped before the gate.

"I'm a friend of Clara's," Kael said, purposely not giving his name. He didn't want to know how the two men might react to hearing the name Skyborn. "I was hoping to visit her."

Neither looked ready to believe someone dressed so plainly could be friends with the Archon's daughter. Kael swallowed down a bitter remark, upset at how much that old wound still hurt.

"We're friends from the academy," he added. "Ask her yourself if you must."

"No need for that," said the other soldier. "We'll let the house guards figure that out. You armed?"

Kael lifted his arms and spun in place so they saw he wasn't.

"They'll check you before they let you in," said the soldier.

"Go on ahead. For your sake, I hope you're not lying. We won't stop them if they decide to string you up."

"Understood," Kael said, wishing he could tell them he feared Center's soldiers a million times more than any Willer house guard. The soldiers swung the gate open, and Kael crossed the stone pathway and up the stairs to the next block-ade. One of the guards bore the tattoos swearing him to silence, the other did not.

"Name," asked the tattooless guard.

"Kael Skyborn," he said. "I was hoping to see Clara."

He glanced to the tattooed man, who nodded and gestured inside.

"Wait here," said the first.

Kael nodded, and he stood there, eyes at his feet. The remaining guard did a quick pat search, but he appeared bored with the matter, and finished within a few seconds. Kael crossed and uncrossed his arms as he waited. What might the other guard be doing? Confirming he was who he said? Asking Clara for permission? Would she give it? It seemed stupid to doubt it, given their time at the academy, but it was hard to remain certain as the minutes dragged on, just him and the house guard, who stood completely passive, spear in his left hand, right tapping against his thigh as he hummed a song so quietly only he could hear.

The door opened. Kael's gaze shot upward, panic spiking as a hundred terrible scenarios ran through his mind, but then Clara shot through the opening, flung her arms around him, and kissed his lips. By the time the kiss ended, Kael's face was sunset red. He glanced at the guards, saw that both were pointedly staring off in the distance as if they'd spotted something very, very interesting in the trees that needed their full attention.

Clara crossed her arms, her joy immediately replaced with displeasure.

"What took you so long to visit?" she asked. Clara had been pulled from the academy following the Speaker's announcement that her parents would be imprisoned, and Kael hadn't seen her since.

"I only returned home yesterday," he said. "I would have otherwise, I promise."

"You could have snuck out to spend time with me," she said. "It wouldn't have been the first time."

Kael swore the humming guard choked down a laugh.

"You're right," he said, holding his hands up in surrender. "But I'm here now. Can I come inside, or should we spend our time putting on a show for the guards?"

Clara's mischievous grin made him wonder if she'd do just that to spite him, but then she grabbed his hand and tugged.

"Come inside," she said. "It's a long walk here from Lowville, and I'm sure you could use a drink."

The first thing Kael immediately noticed upon stepping inside was how much darker the mansion had become. Sure, it had its share of windows, but at the winter solstice dance, the entire hallway had been lit with stone torches that burned with fire prisms. Now they were dark, the prisms missing. Kael kept a hold of Clara's hand, letting her guide him as his eyes adjusted to the gloom.

"You're the first to visit since...you know," Clara said.

"Really?" Kael asked. "No one else?"

"Not from the academy. I think everyone's scared to come here. Worried they'll join my parents in some secret theotech dungeon, I guess."

Kael winced at the bitterness and sadness tainting her every word. He squeezed her hand, wishing he could reassure her in some way. Once out of the entryway, they walked the long hall-way, his feet sinking into the thick cerulean carpet.

"A valid worry for me still, given the fun I've had the past few days," Kael said.

Clara froze, and she pulled him close, voice dropping to a whisper.

"Never say anything like that again," she insisted. "My fam-ily's not alone in here, not anymore."

Kael nodded, feeling foolish for speaking so carelessly. Just because the only soldiers from Center he'd seen were at the outer gate didn't mean there weren't more scattered throughout the mansion.

"Understood," Kael whispered back.

Clara kissed him on the cheek, a quick peck.

"You've met the resistance," she whispered, eyes lighting with life.

Kael answered with a nod.

"Once we're in my room," she said, "I want to hear all about it."

They resumed walking down the hallway, then hooked a right toward the interior. The hallway itself was incredibly narrow, with Kael and Clara just barely able to walk side by side. It was a defense against invading Seraphim, he knew. Anyone bearing wings would have to attack single file, and they'd have little room to maneuver against the shields and spears of the house guard. The construction also gave the mansion a claustrophobic feeling, a feeling aided by the dim light and lines of shadows cast by the bars protecting the windows.

After crossing several halls, they passed through an expan-sive set of double doors into what appeared to be a dining hall. A single long table filled the center of the room. The table legs were carved like those of the fabled tiger, darker stripes cut into the sides and long claws sinking into the carpet. Curtains hung

along the walls. The high ceiling was most impressive, covered
with a painting of a sprawling battle between silver-armored
Seraphim and the supposed demons of the old world.

Two servants stood by the doors, and without need of orders
they quickly bowed to Clara and then raced away, fetching
something to eat and drink, Kael assumed. Kael and Clara sat
near the middle of the room in chairs so stuffed and oversized
that Kael felt like a child who'd gotten lost on his way to the
small table.

"Hope you're hungry," Clara said. "Because you're about to
have more food thrown at you than you'll know what to do
with."

A glass of water was delivered first, chunks of ice floating at
the top, and Kael slowly sipped it.

"All this for just us?" Kael asked when the doors opened
again, and more servants arrived carrying trays, bread pans,
and soup bowls.

"My brothers should join us soon," Clara said. "Honestly,
I'm surprised they're not already—"

The doors on the opposite side of the room burst open, and
three men entered at once in a loud, angry procession. Clara's
brothers, both vaguely familiar from the time Kael met them
at the solstice dance. Lance led the way, his face clean-shaven,
while the younger Edwin grew a short, cleanly trimmed beard.
The brothers wore matching dark pants and blue jackets, similar in style to military uniforms, yet softer, more decorated
with silver buttons and black tassels.

Kael's mood soured when he caught a good look at the man
with them: Vyros Longleaf, the bald theotech who'd admin-
istered the seventh-day services. Clara's warning about their
family not being alone was now all too clear. While the brothers looked upset, Vyros appeared as calm as could be.

"You can assign us blame all you want, but it changes nothing," Lance said over his shoulder, his cherubic face red with anger. "We've done everything in our power to quell the riots, and it never seems to help."

"If anything, it makes matters worse," Edwin chipped in.

Kael followed Clara's lead and rose from his seat in respect.

"No matter how hard you protest, both New Galen and the people surrounding it are under your supervision," Vyros said as he took a seat at the long table. Servants flitted about, offering food and drink to the three. The theotech accepted a tall glass of water and nothing else, and he sipped it before continuing. "You may believe you're saying otherwise, but what *I* am hearing is that you are incapable of maintaining the peace."

Lance started to protest, but he realized that Kael and Clara were there, and he nodded toward them in acknowledgment, granting them permission to sit.

"Kael," Lance said. "You live near New Galen. Is the mood as dour as our theotech friend insists?"

This was hardly an argument Kael wanted to be thrust into the middle of, but there didn't seem much hope of escape. Swallowing the last bit of the biscuit he'd eaten, he cleared his throat to stall as he scrambled for an answer. Sure enough, he'd heard plenty of gossip from his aunt about the people of New Galen stirring up trouble, setting fires and threatening to spill violence out beyond the town's borders. Aunt Bethy had insisted it was merely proof of the Galen people's violent tendencies. Having witnessed the death of former Galen man, Elijah, Kael thought differently. But to get into all that, with the brothers watching? No, he wanted to remain unnoticed and ignored as much as possible.

"I don't know how Vyros has described it, so I cannot say whether he is right or wrong," he offered. "But *dour* is a fair word to use to describe the attitude on both sides."

"*Stubborn* is another," Edwin said. His voice was lighter than his older brother's, and more biting. He grabbed a roll from an offered platter, looked at it mistrustfully as if it were diseased. "Though I don't understand why anyone acts surprised. Our most hated enemy has been given a parcel of our own land. Did no one think those who lost their homes might have a few issues with the matter? Our people want their homes back, and their people would rather see our island crash into the ocean than live peacefully among us."

"The people of New Galen are *your* people now," Vyros said, anger leaking into his words. "They are not your enemy. That you continue to think of them as such only shows why you've been so ineffective at disarming the situation."

Edwin waved his hand dismissively. Kael had a feeling this conversation had repeated itself a dozen times over the past week, and no one looked ready to change their position. Vyros was at least right on that last remark, though. Despite the strip of red cloth Kael carried with him still, he did not think of the people of New Galen as fellow citizens. They were strangers, outcasts, displaced and unwanted. As much as he hated their mistreatment, it still felt strange to consider them part of Weshern.

"The people are mistrustful of New Galen because they're afraid," Clara interjected. "And they're afraid because their Archon and his wife are imprisoned in the holy mansion's dungeons for crimes they never committed."

Kael was stunned by her audacity, but it appeared such a display was not uncommon for her, based on the eye roll both brothers gave. Vyros sipped at his water, showing no hurry to respond.

"Weshern's citizens are indeed afraid," he agreed. "But Isaac and Avila's *imprisonment* isn't why they're afraid. The change from one figurehead to another doesn't inspire fear in and of itself among the populace. No, it's the worry that a new figurehead will abuse their power over them. Despite rebellious Seraphim acting against us, have we given the common folk any reason to believe us a danger?" The theotech glared at the brothers. "The people of *New Galen*, on the other hand, have many reasons to fear abuse. Isn't that right?"

Elijah's face flashed before Kael's eyes.

"All hearsay and nonsense," Lance said, a blatant falsehood he put forth no effort in selling. "This whole business will settle down in time. Change is difficult, but people adjust. It's basic human nature. If you'd just be patient with us, Vyros, you'd see this was the case."

Vyros pushed away from the table and rose to his feet.

"I have been patient," he said, smoothing out his red robes. "But now I hear of demands being posted throughout every Weshern tavern and meeting hall. The situation here grows worse with time, not better. We do not desire bloodshed, but your former Seraphim appear all too eager to cross blades. Save your excuses, both of you. Soon you won't be explaining your incompetence to me, but to the Speaker himself. I assure you, he will be far less *patient* than I've been."

The brothers stood as well, bowing in respect. Once Vyros was gone, Edwin sank back into his seat, but not Lance. Lance grabbed Vyros's half-empty glass of water by its long neck, turned, and flung it at the door. The glass shattered, water splashing across the deep-stained oak. Kael winced, the noise startling in the quiet.

"One of these days I'm going to lose it on that bastard," Lance said.

"It wouldn't help any," Edwin said, nibbling on his own biscuit. Crumbs sprinkled across his beard, and he gently wiped them away. "When has a theotech ever admitted they were wrong in the history of existence? Never. Just keep making promises and kiss their asses, and it will all quiet down."

Lance sat back down, and he glared at Clara.

"It would help if a certain member of the family would stop antagonizing Vyros."

Clara flushed but refused to apologize. Kael sank into his chair, wishing they'd sent someone else to handle this task. He felt completely unwanted, a stranger in the midst of family.

"What do you expect?" Edwin asked. "She'd rather fly and throw ice than maintain a civil lifestyle. The academy teaches people how to kill people. I doubt manners is on the curriculum."

Clara was clearly hurt, but she kept her mouth shut, her jaw clenched so tight she looked like she were trying to shatter her own teeth.

"Taught," Kael corrected, unable to keep silent. "It taught us how to kill, but no longer. It was burned to the ground, in case you didn't notice from here in your mansion."

"We're well aware," Lance said. "I signed off on its closure."

"You did?" Kael asked, stunned. "Why?"

"Because the sooner we show the Speaker we're no threat, the sooner we'll have our kingdom back," Edwin said. "Marius wishes no harm for Weshern. If he wanted to, he could have publicly executed our parents and burned the mansion to the ground with a legion of angelic knights, but he didn't. He's here because Galen's fall scared the piss out of him. I doubt he knows who, if anyone, is responsible, so he's making a show of blaming us."

"So meanwhile we play the repentant scapegoat until the matter passes," Lance said. "At least, it would pass, but fucking Argus won't back down. List of demands? Goddamn, what an ignorant ass. We'll never pose a great enough threat for Marius to even consider caving." He glanced at his plate, then pushed it away. "I don't have time for this. I've got shit to do."

Kael stared at his food, not wanting to look at Lance as he left lest he risk saying something that'd get him in trouble. Clearly neither brother sounded willing to aid with the resistance. If anything, they'd turn Argus and Rebecca over to Center. His coming to the mansion was a gigantic waste of time.

He glanced at Clara, immediately felt guilty. No, not a waste at all.

"So what is it you're up to now that the academy's shut down?" Edwin asked, nonplussed by his older brother's abrupt exit.

"Not much," Kael said, glad he didn't have to lie. "Mostly helping my aunt with her work in the fields."

Edwin popped a strawberry into his mouth.

"So no gallivanting off with members of the resistance, then?"

He should have known the question was coming. He should have hid his guilt better. He didn't.

"They've approached me," he said, deciding he'd never get away with a complete lie. His earlier talk with Nickolas proved that well enough.

"I hope you did the sensible thing and told them no," Edwin said. "Getting yourself killed helps no one, and certainly not Weshern."

"Some would argue that working with Center won't help Weshern, either," Kael said.

"So I've heard," Edwin said. "Not from anyone wise, of course." He pointedly looked to Clara. "Just youthful trouble-makers with more fight than sense in their heads."

"It's not hopeless," Clara insisted. "Mom and Dad are

innocent, you know that as well as I do, yet they're imprisoned here in our own dungeon. Is it so wrong to demand their freedom, and to fight for their release if Center refuses?"

Edwin ignored her as a servant took his empty plate and replaced it with one containing a thick slice of cheese drizzled with berries and a dark sauce.

"It's good you're here to keep her company, Kael," he said. "Maybe if she's not so bored she'll stop making things worse for us."

Silverware rattled from Clara's fist smacking the table, and she rose so fast she knocked over her chair.

"I've had enough," she said, voice strained, a dam about to burst. "Let's go, Kael."

Kael stood, and he forced himself to give Edwin a respectful bow. Then he was off, chasing after Clara as she slammed open the tall doors to the dining room and hurried down the hall. Kael followed her through the winding corridors, saying nothing. Clara stopped as abruptly as she'd started, pulling a thin iron key from her pocket and unlocking a wide white door. She yanked it open and stormed inside, and Kael stepped in after.

Clara's bedroom was surprisingly small. He'd thought she'd have a sprawling area for herself, but this was no bigger than his own bedroom back in Lowville. That didn't mean it lacked luxuries, though. Her bed was big, with a thick, soft mattress. Two drawers lined the wall, and he saw a shut door he guessed led to a closet. Most impressive was the view from the window. The holy mansion formed a hollow rectangle, and in the very center grew an expansive garden. The room's curtains were pulled back, revealing a beautiful stretch of roses and tulips growing just outside. Clara sat on her bed, grabbed a pillow, and held it to her face so she could scream.

"I'm sorry," Kael said. Empty words, really, but he didn't know what else to offer.

Clara fell pillow-first onto the bed, face mushed within it. A muffled sigh escaped its confines.

"It's hardly your fault," she said, rolling onto her back. "I've tried being more tactful with them, but they dismissed me as if I'm still five years old. Vyros has my brothers wrapped around his finger. If he told them to strip naked and run through the streets, they'd be out there in a heartbeat, bare asses to the wind."

Kael sat next to her on the bed, and she shifted so she could lean her head in his lap. He gently stroked her short blonde hair, staring at the green of her eyes, the short curls of her eyelashes, and the soft curve of her chin.

"I've missed you," she said, much quieter, her anger draining away. "All of you. It was so much easier to feel like I had friends at the academy. But here? I'm cooped up, alone, and with nothing to do. The worst is knowing my parents are so close, yet I'm not allowed into the dungeon to see them, speak with them, even know they're all right. I may not be in that prison with them, but some days it feels like I am."

"I'll break you out if you'd like," Kael offered. "Shouldn't be too hard. A pickax, a shovel, and a few nights' digging and, *poof,* tunnel to freedom leading right here."

"You don't want to free me. You just want direct access to my bedroom."

Kael felt heat building in his neck, along with certain other awkward places, given the placement of Clara's resting head.

"Either way, it'd be worth the effort," he said.

"It'd piss off my brothers," Clara said. "That alone makes it worth it."

She laughed, and she lifted herself upward while wrapping

her hands about his neck and pulling him toward her for a kiss. Kael was all too happy to oblige.

"You know, the door *is* locked," she whispered when he pulled back for a breath. "And I can think of a few other things that would piss off my brothers."

At first it felt like Kael's heart would stop, and then it hammered at a speed faster than any Seraph could fly.

"Is that so?" he asked.

Her mischievous grin spread ear to ear.

"It is. Now get back down here and kiss me."

"How long until dark, do you think?" Kael asked, glancing out the window above him.

"Why, you have somewhere to be?"

She'd asked it sarcastically, but when he hesitated to answer, she sat up, her entire face narrowing. Her blanket fell to her waist, exposing her chest, and it took a tremendous effort for Kael to meet her gaze instead of letting it linger elsewhere.

"You do," she said. "Is it the resistance?"

Kael shook his head.

"No, not exactly. I'm not supposed to tell anyone..."

Clara crossed her arms and gave him an incredulous look.

"You're going to keep secrets from me?" she asked. "After what we just did?"

He laughed.

"Fine," he said. "I need to be home before the midnight fire begins. I'm, uh, supposed to meet someone."

She gestured a hand, urging him to continue.

"You won't believe who," he said.

"Try me."

Kael shrugged.

"Fine. Johan. I'm to meet with Johan."

Clara's eyes spread wide.

"I'm coming with you."

"Wait, what?"

She was already off the bed, pulling open drawers and grabbing a change of clothes from within.

"I was with you when that disciple, Marrik, predicted Center's invasion, remember?" she said, sliding on a plain brown skirt. "If Johan was right about that, I want to know what else he predicts will happen. Lance and Edwin may not believe it, but I want to protect our nation just as much as they do." She vanished into her closet, then reappeared sliding a plain white shirt over her head. "And to protect it, we're going to need to fight, not whimper and obey. Johan's disciples have been peaceful so far. I want to know if they'll stay that way."

Kael began dressing as well, his mind racing.

"How will you get out?" he asked. "Especially without any of Center's soldiers seeing you? It was risky enough having you visit one of Johan's disciples. Visiting with Johan himself..."

Clara straightened her shirt and gave him a wide grin.

"You know, you weren't too far off when you mentioned tunnels to freedom," she said.

Kael used his fingers to smooth his hair as best he could, knowing it was hopeless after their tumble but trying anyway.

"What happens when someone realizes you're gone?" he asked.

"Assuming anyone thinks to look for me in the first place," Clara said, not hiding the hurt and bitterness in her voice, "they'll assume we've snuck off somewhere on the grounds. There's plenty of places inside the mansion to hide. So long as I'm back before morning, no one will know...or care."

Kael shook his head, once again reminded how he should never, ever underestimate her.

"Well then," he said, "where's this tunnel to freedom?"

They exited and hurried down the hall. A servant passed them by, giving him a look, and Kael blushed. With Clara's change of clothes, and their long absence in her room, everyone would leap to one specific, and correct, conclusion. Kael kept his eyes to the floor, praying they passed no one else.

He'd assumed Clara was leading him to a secret basement somewhere, perhaps a dungeon with a guarded door, but instead they stopped in a quiet hallway on the far-east end of the mansion.

"Where to now?" Kael asked. Clara checked up and down the hallway, ensuring they were alone, and then reached up to grab the bottom of one of the now-dim torches fueled with light element. It slid downward with a rumble, and suddenly a crease appeared along a bare patch of the wall. Releasing the torch, Clara grabbed the crease and pulled, sliding open a secret door on a well-oiled hinge.

"All right," Kael said. "That was neat."

There was no room beyond the door, only deep darkness.

"Go," Clara said. "I'll be right behind you."

Kael bent his head to fit into the entrance, then stooped to continue. Soon he had to drop to his knees as the tunnel they'd entered became smaller. The secret door shut behind him, banishing the last trickle of light shining into the tunnel. Now descending into the pitch black, Kael found himself suddenly fighting off claustrophobia he never knew he had. The sound of Clara following him grew closer, the rustle of clothes and sliding of knees loud in the deep silence.

"So where does this tunnel lead?" Kael asked. Maybe talking

would calm him as he crawled along, touching the wall occasionally to keep himself oriented.

"A small house not far from the mansion," Clara explained. Her voice was weirdly distant, a trick of the tunnel by Kael's guess. "It's been in the royal family for years, and we keep the inside guarded at all times, just in case someone figures out its purpose."

"So we'll pop out from another secret door?"

"Something like that."

"What about the guard? Won't he tell someone you're sneaking out?"

Kael could practically hear the grin spread across her face.

"This is hardly my first time sneaking out, Kael. Galvin's a good friend, and he'll trust me far more than my brothers or any snakes from Center."

The crawl was interminable, but at last he discovered a circle of light in the distance. It appeared at once, suddenly unblocked by the curve of a tunnel Kael had no idea he'd been rounding. To Kael, that circular speck of white was the most beautiful thing he'd ever seen. Only the awkward height of the tunnel kept him from crawling faster toward it.

Silently sighing with relief, Kael stepped out from the tunnel, doing his best to wipe off the dirt from his clothes. He looked for Clara, and laughed when he realized what they'd climbed out of: a fireplace. Before Clara could exit, a cough turned him about. The home was well furnished, and sitting at a round oak table was an older man with a gray mustache. He kept seated, but his hand fell to his side, and the thin sword strapped to his belt.

"I haven't met you before," the man said. He had the voice of a perturbed grandfather addressing a trespasser. Kael's mouth opened, closed. What exactly was the proper response to that?

"I'm Clara's friend," he said.

A bushy eyebrow lifted.

"That so?"

"It is," Clara said as she climbed out from the fireplace. "And you can keep your sword sheathed, Galvin."

The guard's face twitched ever so slightly.

"If you say. Please stay safe, m'lady. Weshern's not what it used to be."

He relaxed back into his chair, and just like that, his eyes glazed over and it seemed Kael and Clara no longer existed to him.

"Door's this way," Clara said, tugging Kael's sleeve. Together they slipped past Galvin, through a short hallway, and out a large wooden door into open air. After the gloom of the mansion and the complete dark of the tunnel, it was a welcome relief.

"Lowville's a good ten miles away," Kael said, offering her his arm. "Are you up for a nice long walk?"

"After weeks cooped up in that stuffy mansion?" she said, sliding her hand around the crook of his elbow. "I'm up for anything."

CHAPTER
7

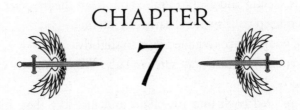

Bree sat in the rocking chair by the fire of Aunt Bethy's home, eyes on the door at all times. The cold, tired look on her face protected her from idle conversation with the other twelve people crammed into the bottom floor of the house, though a few still attempted. A fake smile and a single-word answer usually was enough to convey her desire for solitude. After an hour, only Aunt Bethy spoke to her, and only briefly. The others were neighbors and friends of their aunt. Bree vaguely recognized them, faces and names from her time in the fields. All bore the tanned skin and calloused hands of farmers, and they spoke in hushed, excited tones. No one said his name, but it was on all their minds. Johan. Bree doubted they'd be as excited if the Speaker himself were coming. She wished she could share that excitement. When Bree had come home from Camp Aquila, her aunt had been quick to inform her of Johan's imminent arrival.

He's coming here to meet you, she'd said, already brushing at her tangled hair with her fingers. *We need to get you presentable. This is an honor very few receive.*

Apparently *presentable* meant having Bree bathe in the lake and then change clothes. Aunt Bethy had attempted to pressure her into wearing a dress, but Bree would have none of it. After a year of wearing her uniform, a flimsy dress felt ridiculous. She wore the pants of her uniform, plus a loose white shirt. She almost put on her jacket, which she'd carried back home with her. Bree had no intention of hiding her allegiance to the Weshern Seraphim, disbanded or otherwise. The only reason she kept it off was that she didn't want to attract more attention than she already did. People still kept glancing her way, and the word *Phoenix* was whispered on more than one occasion. The last thing she needed was to put on an even stronger reminder.

Come the rolling dark, more men and women had begun slipping inside the home, one or two at a time. They mingled in the somber light, first from the fireplace in the kitchen, then the rippling glow of the burning skies outside. Each one risked their lives being there. Everything to do with the disciples of Johan had been declared illegal by the Speaker, and after last night's battle, Bree had a feeling Center wouldn't tolerate the slightest hint of rebellion against its authority. There'd be no stocks, no jailing, no forced labor for anyone caught here. Just a long drop into a deep well.

Every time the door opened, heads turned to look, conversations dropping to hushed silence. Talk would resume only upon realizing that, no, Johan was not yet here. It happened again, and Bree's own heart skipped, convinced that he was here at last, but instead Kael and Clara entered, with her brother grinning sheepishly. Bree's eyes narrowed. Clara was dressed in a plain brown dress, and her hair was purposely loose and tou-sled. Aunt Bethy rushed over to embrace Kael, and as she did, he whispered something into her ear. She nodded in return, kissed his forehead, and then let him be, having not said a word to Clara. The two sat side by side on the bottom step of the stairs. Kael said something to Clara, then returned to his feet and made his way through the crowded kitchen.

"I heard Clara's brothers grumbling about the attack on the wagons last night," he said, keeping his voice low. He smiled nervously at her. "I assume things went well?"

Bree thought of the seven Seraphs they lost in the attack, wondered if the elements they'd retrieved were worth it.

"Well enough," she said. "Could have gone better, could have gone far worse."

Kael grabbed her hand resting on the arm of the chair and squeezed.

"I'm glad you're all right," he said.

Bree smiled back.

"Me, too," she said. "So how is Clara handling her parents' imprisonment?"

Kael glanced over his shoulder, his nervous smile faltering.

"Well enough," he said, shrugging. Another squeeze, and then he released her hand. "Try not to say her name again, all right? We're hoping no one recognizes her."

Bree nodded. It was a fair enough request.

"Until we know how Johan would react, that's probably for the best," she said, drumming her fingers upon the wood of the armchair. Aunt Bethy overheard her say Johan's name, eyes flicking her way from across the kitchen table, communicating with a silent glare. Bree shrugged it off.

"You plan on asking any questions?" Kael asked. "You know, when he gets here?"

Bree had been pondering just that over the past hour, and she didn't have any better an idea than when she'd started.

"I'll leave the questions to you and the others," she said. "I'm only here to listen."

"I doubt you'll get away with just listening," Kael said. "But good luck."

He returned to Clara's side. Once again alone by the fire, Bree curled her knees to her chest and rocked the chair back and forth. She wished Johan would get here already. Right now she wanted nothing more than to sleep in a comfortable bed. In a day or two, she expected to return to Camp Aquila, to its hard, rickety facsimiles of beds, its thin blankets, and its military training regimen. Assuming she didn't die in the opening skirmishes, a hard road of conflict lay ahead of her. Was it so wrong to want one good day of relaxation before it?

The door cracked open. Bree glanced at it, immediately sat up. A man in a brown robe, hood hanging loose down his back, glanced about the place. A sword hung naked from his belt. He said nothing, only observed briefly, then pushed the door all the way open and gestured to unseen people behind him. More men in robes entered, and Bethy's neighbors stepped away, pushing their backs against walls to make room. The next two disciples carried a large chest, and they set it down beside the door as three more disciples entered. All were armed with swords, and they kept their hoods off their heads, all but one. He was the last, and Bree felt a twinge in her chest upon seeing him. Johan. It had to be.

His tanned face was bathed in shadow, his hood hanging low over his brow. His cheeks were scarred, thin lines running parallel to his mouth. His jaw was square, firm, his lips showing several pale spots, as if scars from ancient burns. Though his demeanor was like stone, his eyes were vibrant, a blue so deep even the red of the midnight fire was unable to change its hue. Unlike the others, he carried no sword. Its lacking did nothing to remove the palpable feeling of danger Johan exuded. Mere seconds after entering the room, all eyes were upon him, and he'd not said a word.

"Welcome to my home," Aunt Bethy said, pushing through the crowd so she might greet her guest. "Thank you for bestowing such an honor upon me."

Johan turned to her, head tilted slightly.

"This was no honor," he said. His voice was deep, and it bore an accent Bree could not place. Its presence only added mystery and exoticness to the already imposing man. "By bringing me into your home, you risk imprisonment and execution. It is *you* I should thank, Bethy Skyborn. People like you, and the rest of you here tonight, are the reason I feel hope in my heart when I speak my message. People like you, willing to risk everything to hear the truth in a world of lies, are why I believe our cause will echo across the future, forcing change upon those who fear it most."

Aunt Bethy looked ready to explode with pride. She blushed, curtsied clumsily. Bree rested her chin on her fist, eyes never leaving Johan's. Back when she'd witnessed Thane dropping to his death in a well, she'd wondered how someone could be so convinced to die for what he believed in. She was starting to understand that now. When Johan had offered his thanks to her aunt, Bree had felt a spike of jealousy, along with an intense desire for that deep voice to offer gratitude her way as well. That need for approval, for attention, was so strong it frightened her. She'd never felt like this, not even in the presence of her childhood hero, Argus Summers.

"I am sure you have questions," Johan continued. He stood before the door, flanked on all sides by his disciples, as he addressed the inhabitants of the home. "All I desire is that you first let me speak, and see if my words give you your answer without need of asking."

No one would challenge him on this. No one appeared able to speak. Everyone waited to hear his words. Even Bree, if she were being honest with herself. Johan fully understood this, and he let his gaze linger, let his presence build, before he began.

"I was once a theotech," he said. "Considered special by many, but I did my best to work hard and remain humble. I studied, and I read, and I devoted myself to the teachings of prophets collected in the tomes that Center keeps hidden away in their massive libraries. I read, I learned, all under their tutelage, and I was praised for my diligence. But then I started asking questions."

He hesitated a moment, allowing time for his eyes to sweep the room. Bree swore his gaze lingered on her a fraction of a second longer than it did the others.

"Questions," he said. "If the Speaker shares the word of the angels, why can he offer no proof of his connection with the divine? If the Speaker is God's chosen representative for humanity's remnants, why is he elected by a gathering of the Erelim? Wouldn't God's chosen already know long beforehand? Wouldn't the angels tell him of his destiny? Why were these tomes of the prophets hidden, and not distributed among the people? Why was God's word for the elect, and the words of theotechs for the common man?"

Another pause. His hands lifted to the sides of his hood.

"Questions," he said. "I asked questions. And for that, I received my reward."

Off came his hood, and a collective gasp sounded in the room. Bree's chest tightened, and she gripped the arms of her chair instinctively. Johan was completely bald. Where hair should have been were a mess of scars, deep and varied. They crisscrossed like veins, seemingly beyond counting. Some moved in straight lines, others curling about, behind his ears, toward his eyes, only to jerk in a different direction. The thinner scars looked carved by a knife, while much larger, lighter patches bore the unmistakable mark of fire. The revelation made the scars on his cheeks seem less significant, and suddenly carry far more meaning.

"Fire and blade," Johan said, standing to his full height. He bore no shame of his mutilation. Instead it added fuel to his words, an edge to his tone. "They cut, and they burned, all to drive the heresy from my mind. I had my questions, and I tell you now, those long, aching years of torture gave me my answers. The theotechs did not serve God, but themselves. Those who fear questions are those who fear the truth, and the only truth that frightens the theotechs is that they built their power on lies and falsehoods. God is not with them. The Speaker is not a divine prophet. The only right he has to rule is the noose he holds around our necks."

Johan ran a hand over the scars, drawing attention there, as if any could have taken their eyes away.

"I endured, deep in places I pray none of you ever set foot inside," he said. "And one day, I convinced them of my newfound faith in the Speaker. Once free, I fled their watchful eye, fled Center, and started anew on Elern. It was there I met the first of my disciples, and began to preach my message to all with the bravery to listen. And there are brave people out there, so many brave people. Humanity yearns for God's touch, yet you have been denied it by a system void of compassion and devotion, a system that seeks only to establish authority. Your heart matters not, so long as you bend the knee and profess obedience. You are babes suckling on an empty teat, broken dogs returning to abusive masters, orphans eating from an empty bowl. You will always feel hollow. You will always bear a hunger. If you would be sated, listen, and follow me."

Bree was at a loss as to what to believe. She'd never given much thought to the religious lessons they received growing up, nor Vyros's lectures when he came to the academy from the Crystal Cathedral. She glanced to her brother. A look of concern was on his face, poorly hidden. Something troubled him greatly, and she wished she could cross the room and ask him what. It would have to wait. Too many people, and Johan was not yet done. Many looked ready to throw themselves at his feet, others stomping in place, fired up, righteous anger ready to burst from their every pore.

"Some of you care not for what I say," Johan said. His tone changed slightly. It no longer carried a faint hint of sadness and yearning. Now it was hard, definitive. She realized she recognized his tone from Adam Dohn, when the joyless man was about to lecture their class on a subject he held absolute authority in. "Leave the talk of God to the old and the young, you'd say. Then let me speak of something you cannot deny your involvement in: your own slavery." He let the word echo in the room. "Slaves, each and every one of you. Your islands, Elern and Weshern and Candren and Sothren, all one and the same in this regard. Your independence is a lie. Your nations are puppets whose purpose is fast fading. Are you blind to the invasion happening underneath your very nose? Do you not see the golden wings flying overhead, see the red robes of your oppressors walking the streets? Center thrives on the goods we deliver, but their payment of elements in return is too dangerous for them to continue. Soon we will give not in trade, but in tribute to protect us from the sword hanging over our necks."

Bree thought of the wave after wave of soldiers flying over on platforms as the Speaker, Marius Prakt, declared their

Archon and his wife to be imprisoned, and Weshern's rule to be handed over to the theotechs of Center. No warning. No trial. Not even an explanation offered or a scrap of proof given as to how Weshern was responsible for Galen's fall. In light of such events, it was hard to find any fault in Johan's claims.

"Questions," the scarred man said. "They strip away the power of secrets. If we are to have freedom, the secrets of the Beam must be handed over, the safety and power of each island belonging only to the island's people. If we are to have independence, the secrets of the elements must be made public, with each nation able to defend itself with its own resources instead of those bartered from a theocracy seeking domination. Center brands me heretical, but I ask you, can the truth ever be heresy? Only to cowards. Only to the *afraid.*"

Johan drew a knife tucked into his belt, and he held the naked blade before him.

"And they are afraid, for I know the truth. I know who sent Galen tumbling to the ocean, slaughtering thousands upon thousands. It's the only one who benefits. The only one vile enough to do it. *Center* destroyed Galen."

His words were thunder shaking the cramped room. It was an idea that had flitted around the back of Bree's mind, never fully voiced. It was too awful to believe. Too frightening. But the moment Johan spoke the accusation, Bree knew she believed it, knew that many others in that room believed the same.

"*Center* bears the guilt," Johan continued, voice booming. "No one else may investigate. No one else knows how the Beams keep our islands afloat... nor does anyone know how to disable them. Only the theotechs. Only Marius Prakt. The Speaker, so fearful of losing his power over the minor islands, would destroy one of you so he might have reason to enslave the rest. Do you not see it? Do you not feel it in your hearts while he casts blame on your people?"

Johan slammed a fist against the wall, punctuating his words.

"And that is why we must rise up," he said. "I know the demands your burgeoning resistance have given Marius, but do you think such simple measures are enough? Freedom for your royal family, and a promise of independence? A promise, from the man who sent Galen crashing to the Endless Ocean? I ask not for such infantile desires. What does freeing an Archon accomplish if his island crumbles into ruin? There is no greater cause than this, people of Weshern. No stakes are higher. Freedom is bought in blood, and we are many, and we are willing to pay. Center will banish my name, and cry out against my words, but we are the truth armed with a blade, and we will not be beaten. Center's strength is hollow glass. A single crack, and it all shatters. What I ask *you*"—a hesitation, just quick enough so each there believed themselves specifically addressed—"is this... are you willing to take up arms in defense of your family, your nation, and your God? Because the time has come. Your resistance seeks peace, and a return to the old. But the old is gone, and war comes on golden wings. Is that not right, Phoenix?"

Bree froze in her chair. All eyes were upon her now, and she wished she could slink away and hide.

"What do you mean?" she asked, having to clear her throat to talk.

Johan stepped closer. She felt like a hen stalked by a wolf.

"Phoenix of Weshern, hero of her first two battles against Galen," he said. "Resistance blossoms against Center's takeover, and even fools know the value of bringing you into the fold." Johan knelt so he was eye level with her in her chair. Bree struggled to meet his gaze, and to ignore the web of scars across his head. "They've come to you, haven't they? You've spoken to their leaders, seen what they're building?"

Everyone inside Bethy's home was risking their lives by listening to Johan's words. Who there would turn her in to the theotechs? Besides, what she admitted was only what the theotechs would already assume.

"Yes," she said. "I have."

Murmurs throughout the home. Johan grinned wide, and with a sudden jolt of energy he rushed to the door. Two of his disciples parted, granting him access to the enormous chest they'd carried inside.

"Then I ask that you bring them a gift," he said, removing the lock. Bree stood as he lifted the lid so she might see within. Its contents dropped her jaw. Stacked tightly against one another, filling the chest from top to bottom, were elements of every type.

That's more than we recovered from the wagons, Bree thought. And they didn't have to lose a single Seraph in battle to obtain it. Johan stood over the chest, his grin ear to ear. He clearly knew what a treasure his gift was. Pulling the hood back over his head, he returned to Bree. His voice lowered, seemingly just for her.

"We've been preparing for this for many years," he said. "My men have spread throughout all the islands, even Center. This web, this amassing of power and information, I have carefully built in preparation for the inevitable. All I ask is that the leaders of your resistance open their eyes to the truth. Your island will *never* be free without the bloodshed of war. Accept this. Use these elements to wage a true rebellion against Center. Be a spark, and I will ensure a fire blazes throughout every single island, of such size and scope the corruption of the old will burn away into something glorious and new."

He gestured to the chest of elements.

"A spark," he said. "All I seek is a spark."

Bree swallowed, eyes flicking to the elements in the chest. *He offers us war,* she thought. *That's what that chest is, everything we need to wage open warfare.*

Galen's fall flashed before her eyes. The sound of its striking the ocean hammered in her ears. If the Speaker was responsible, then her choice was no choice at all.

"I will inform Argus of your gift," she said to Johan. "And I believe he will accept any aid you and your movement may provide."

Johan clapped his hands, clutching them together tightly.

"Excellent," he said, nodding to the disciple at his right. "Most excellent."

The disciple pulled a bundle of papers out from a deep pocket of his robe, and he began weaving through the home, passing out single sheets to whoever would accept it, which was nearly everyone.

"Read over my demands," Johan said as the disciple worked. "Learn my arguments, and spread this wisdom to any who listen. If you are here, then you came invited, and I assure you we know your names, and will come for you again once the fires of rebellion spread throughout the islands. Once war truly begins. Pray when it does, you have done all that you can to prepare."

A disciple opened the door, and after a moment to check, waved it clear. Johan bowed to them all, and then as quickly as he appeared he vanished out the door, hood pulled over his head to hide the scars. The remaining disciples filed out after him, and with their leaving, the murmur of conversation immediately resumed. Bree stood before the chest, entranced. For Johan to hand over so much, with barely a request made in return, spoke volumes about his trust in Weshern's rebellion.

The hum of voices drifted over her, growing louder until Aunt Bethy shouted over the din.

"Go on home, everyone," Aunt Bethy ordered. "We all have a lot to think on, and truth be told, my house is a mess as it is without you all wrecking it further."

A few laughed politely, others tipped their heads. The men and women filed out in groups, each taking care to scan the skies first. Every time Bree saw that effort at safety it made her feel sick. That they must fear for their lives when in their own home, peacefully meeting other fellow citizens of Weshern . . . it was wrong, so very wrong.

Soon they were gone, and Aunt Bethy let out a long sigh as she scanned the disaster the visitors had made of her kitchen. Only Clara remained, and she and Kael both rose from their seat upon the bottom step of the stairs.

"I need to get back before anyone starts to worry," Clara said, and she kissed Kael on the cheek.

"Stay safe," Kael said. Despite the red midnight glow, Bree could tell he was blushing. Clara dipped her head in respect to Aunt Bethy, then smiled at Bree.

"It's good to see you again," she said. "Try to swing by with Kael sometime, all right? It's lonely up at the mansion."

"I might," Bree said, doubting she ever would. The Phoenix visiting the home of the deposed rulers of Weshern? That would attract attention she couldn't afford, assuming they let her in at all.

Clara opened the door, waved good-bye, and then vanished. As the door shut behind her, Bree sank into her chair, relieved to be off her feet. Her legs felt wooden. She could barely take her eyes off the chest by the door. A veritable fortune, worth more to the rebellion than any amount of coin, just sitting there.

"We have to get that to Argus," she said.

"Tomorrow," Aunt Bethy said before Kael could answer. "It's late, and the both of you look like you've had some long days. Get some rest. The elements will be waiting for you come the morning."

"All right," Kael said, acquiescing. "Sleep doesn't sound so bad right now anyway."

He started up the stairs, but Bree refused to move. Bethy shut the curtains one by one, darkening the room until only a faint red glow shone throughout.

"The chair's fine for now," she said when Bethy headed toward her own bedroom. "It's better than the cot I slept in last night, anyway."

Her aunt paused as if to argue but then relented.

"Good night, Bree," she said, vanishing behind the thick curtain blocking off her room from the kitchen. Bree gently rocked the chair, staring at the chest of elements. Her hands flexed against the armrests, imagining her sword hilts firmly grasped between her fingers.

A spark, she thought, Johan's words echoing in her mind, joined by those of Argus Summers.

That's what you can be to us, Bree. You can be that hope.

Bree did not sleep well, nor for long, and when she did she dreamed of battle, of blood dripping from her bleeding palms, each scarlet drop wreathed in flame.

CHAPTER

8

Kael awoke with the skies still red, a faint crimson flickering before it died off into the morning mist. The light shone through his window, which was wide open. Bree stood over him, and before he could say a word, she dumped a pair of pants and a shirt onto his lap.

"I'm heading downstairs," she said. "Get dressed. We need to talk."

Kael pulled his pillow over his face.

"I'm not going to like this, am I?" he asked as Bree descended the steps.

"Probably not."

He flung his blanket aside and grabbed the shirt, holding it with one hand as he rubbed at his eyes with the other.

Well, at least she's honest, he thought.

Once he was dressed, Kael stumbled down the steps and into the kitchen. Bree sat in a chair waiting for him, chin resting on her palm. Her eyes flicked over him, and her dour mood momentarily brightened.

"Your hair's amazing," she said.

Kael ran his hand through it, felt one half sticking straight up from sleeping on his side.

"I've not exactly had a chance to wash up," he muttered. "So is that what you wanted to talk about? Because if so, I'm going back to bed."

Bree shook her head.

"Not here," she said. "I don't want anyone overhearing."

That "anyone" could only be Aunt Bethy, and Kael nodded.

"All right," he said. "Where to?"

He followed her out the door, then south down the road, passing home after home. At last they curled slightly to the west, and as they reached the end of the road and the stone barricade beyond, Kael realized where they were going.

"Bree," he said, unsure of what else to say.

"Not yet."

Together they climbed over the barricade, and as they crossed the soft grass leading toward Weshern's edge, Kael felt eleven years old again, hoping to catch a glimpse of a star before the battle began. Before the confrontation that took the lives of both their parents. Fearless as she'd always been, Bree walked straight to the edge and then sat, legs dangling. Kael joined her, and he was surprised by his own nonchalant attitude. There was a time when peering over the edge and seeing the gently rolling clouds unnerved him greatly. Now he barely noticed them at all. Side by side they sat, the wind teasing their short hair.

"Well, we're here," Kael said after a long moment of silence, his sister staring to the distant clouds instead of talking with him. "So what's this all about?"

"Kael..." She hesitated. "Is what we're doing right?"

Kael frowned, unsure of what his sister was getting at.

"What do you mean?" he asked. "Fighting against Center?"

She nodded.

"So what if they want to rule us?" she asked. "Does it really matter if we swap the Archon for the Speaker? If we'd never become Seraphim and instead spent our lives in the fields, would we have even noticed?"

Kael picked at the grass that grew all the way to the very last scrap of soil hovering suspended in the air above the Endless Ocean.

"Would we have noticed?" he asked. "Maybe not. But we'd have noticed if another ghost plague happened, hundreds of those we knew and loved taken, never to be returned. And for what? Torture? Experimentation? Execution? We don't even know, and we'd never know, because that's the power they hold over us." He tore another piece of grass, let it drift off the edge of the world. "And what if Johan's right about Galen? What if Marius and his theotechs killed them all, just to solidify power over the rest of us?"

Bree pulled her knees up to her chest, and she wrapped her arms about them as she huddled there, gently rocking. It almost looked like she wanted to fall over every time she tilted toward the edge.

"If he's right, then Marius and all who serve him aren't even human," she said. "They're monsters."

That awful series of moments, of the island crashing, the thousands upon thousands dying, came unbidden to his mind. Kael wiped at his eyes, forcing the memory away. He couldn't comprehend how one could willingly create such a tragedy. He didn't want to.

"Why are we out here?" he asked softly. He knew his sister

carefully circled the edges of the true matter she wished to discuss. "Why are we really?"

Bree sat so still she might have been a statue, eyes locked on a distant cloud.

"Argus wants me to fly as the Phoenix," she blurted out, then immediately fell silent. The words struck Kael like a punch to the gut, but he carefully kept his reaction neutral. It didn't take much thought to figure out what bothered his sister so.

"You're worried about me and Aunt Bethy once you make yourself known."

"If I do this, I'm sentencing you both to death," Bree said, voice muffled by her own knees. "You live only if we win. And I don't know if we can win, Kael. I fought one of their knights, and he treated me like an amusement. I couldn't handle a single knight one-on-one, yet I'm supposed to be Weshern's hero? I'm supposed to be everyone's hope? It's a sick joke, that's all. A sick, stupid joke."

She slumped even further, forehead pressing against her knees as she drew into herself, hiding from all the world.

"I do this, I'm murdering you both, all for nothing."

Kael hated seeing his sister so distraught, and her broken words ignited a fire in his own belly.

"You're not the murderer," he said. "The murderer is the one who sent Galen crashing to the ocean. My life is my own, and if I have to spend it in hiding, then so be it. We already agreed we were in this together, all the way to the end. If I die in the skies, or in a prison, it doesn't matter. I'm dying for what I believe, and what I believe is that we must fight for our freedom, no matter how hopeless it seems. In a single day, the world can change. We've seen it before, and I pray we see it again, only this time for the better."

He reached out to take her hand, forcing her to emerge from within her shell.

"I've seen you fly through the chaos of battle," he said. "When your swords are aflame, and you're dancing through the skies, I truly believe nothing in the world can stop you. Don't you dare let your fear for my safety stop you here on the ground."

Bree squeezed his fingers, and she leaned against him, forehead on his shoulder.

"You're a good brother," she said. "I hope you know that."

"I've always had my suspicions."

The last of the midnight fire burned away, rippling into black mist that thinned as the sun rose in the east. The red hue swapped for blue, and Kael's insides relaxed. A beautiful sight, clouds spread out before them like a painting they could fall into, while high above, the clear blue of the sky grew stronger by the second. If he had his wings, he'd have soared into the tuffs of white, let the wind and speed strip away his worries. It had taken time, but a year in the academy had ignited in him the same love of flight his sister always possessed.

"I'm returning to Camp Aquila," Bree said, the quiet moment passed. "Argus needs to send people to collect those elements. Will you come with?"

Kael thought for a moment, shook his head.

"I promised Clara I'd visit her again today," he said. "Johan's speech shook her up more than she let on."

"His words linger, don't they?" Bree said. "Like a worm that just keeps digging in deeper."

"That's one way to put it."

She was right, though. The whole time he'd tried to fall asleep, Johan's accusations had rang in his ears, his call to action, his prophecy of blood and war. But how could they not? With frightening calm, he'd accused the most powerful and supposedly holiest man alive of destroying Galen and attempting to conquer Weshern. And no matter how many times Kael ran them through his head, there wasn't a single part he could easily dismiss. It made it very hard to believe that Argus's rebellion, and their simple list of demands, had any chance of coming true.

Kael scooted from the edge, then rose to his feet. His sister did likewise.

"Will you tell Argus you'll be his Phoenix?" he asked as he brushed bits of grass from his pants.

"I'm not sure yet," Bree said. "Let's start with moving that heavy chest of elements sitting in our house first, then go on from there." She winked at him. "Have fun at Clara's."

Kael chuckled.

"Surrounded by Center's soldiers and the Willer house guards? I'm sure I'll have loads of fun."

Bree scoffed at him.

"Try harder," she said. "Surely the Archon's daughter can find an unused room or closet somewhere in that giant mansion."

Kael's neck immediately flushed red, as reliable and predictable as if she'd pushed a switch.

"You're awful."

"I know."

She blew him a kiss, then hopped over the stone barricade. Kael followed, stopping in at their home while his sister continued on north. Finding his aunt already out for the fields, he washed his face and hands with the water by the dormant fireplace, ran his fingers through his hair in an attempt to fix the lopsided mess that it was, and then left. The walk to the holy mansion would be a long one, and he jammed his hands into his pockets and whistled to pass the time.

With how early it was, he'd expected to see few people with him on the road. He was wrong. Before he could even leave Lowville he passed two squads of three, armored in heavy plate, tinted gold, their red cloaks and tabards billowing in the morning breeze. Some wielded swords, others spears, but always they carried an enormous shield on their left arm. The sight chilled Kael's blood, and he did his best not to make eye contact as he walked by. He'd known the Speaker's military presence would increase as time went on, and the rebellion made itself known, but it was still strange seeing Center's soldiers marching through the streets of his home.

The first squad ignored him, but a man leading the second called him over with a tone that brooked no argument. Telling himself to remain calm, he crossed the street and stood before the three, arms at his sides.

"Empty your pockets," the man, bushy-bearded and middle-aged, commanded.

"I'm not sure what you think I have," Kael said, doing as he was told. He carried only a handful of coins, and the soldier glanced it over before thrusting his own hands into Kael's pockets. Another patted him from shoulder to ankle. Kael's temper rose by the second, especially as they refused to say a word to him.

"Enough already," he said, stepping back once the pat-search was finished. "You've not even told me what you're looking for."

"Do you possess any materials discussing the beliefs or opinions of Johan Lumens?" the bearded soldier asked.

"No," Kael said, and it wasn't a lie.

"Are you aware of anyone in possession of such materials, or someone with knowledge as to the location of Johan himself?"

Do they know Johan visited last night? Is that why the soldiers are here?

Kael used his annoyance and frustration to hide his nerves, and he stared the soldier in the eye, refusing to flinch in the slightest.

"No, now let me pass."

He tried to push through their center, but the shields locked together, shoving him back.

"You will accept commands, not give them," another of the soldiers, a young woman, said. "Or should we see how brave you are when it's my sword that's pushing you back, not my shield?"

True to her word, she drew the shining steel blade from her sheath. Kael cast his eyes to his feet, and he clenched his fists at his sides and told himself to remain calm.

"Understood," he said. "May I be dismissed?"

The sheer act of asking made his stomach fill with bile. Foreign soldiers, yet they wielded more power than Weshern's own. It wasn't right.

"Get out of here."

The bearded man pushed him with the butt of his spear, the wood shoving into the center of his chest. Kael toppled onto his rear, one arm out to brace against the fall. His hand scraped across the uneven stone of the road. Blood trickled from his palm as he glared up at the three. The woman met his gaze, waiting, eager for him to respond. Knowing it foolish to react, knowing he'd do nothing but get himself hurt worse, if not outright killed, he looked away, head lowered further. The look of the defeated.

The three marched on. Kael returned to his feet, and once he was out of sight of the soldiers of Center, he ran.

Kael knew something was up the moment he saw the row of Center's soldiers blocking the gate to the holy mansion. Just the day before, only two had been on guard, and now there were over a dozen? Fighting down a fresh wave of nerves, Kael strode up to their center and held his head up high.

"My name is Kael Skyborn, friend of Clara Willer," he said. "I was here yesterday, and was expected today as well. You may check with her if you must."

Kael wasn't sure who was in charge, and he waited for one of the twelve to respond.

"Doesn't matter, expected or not," the soldier said. "No one enters."

"Under whose orders?" Kael demanded.

"Mine. Would you like to challenge me further, boy?"

Kael swallowed down his retort.

"No, sir," he said. "Have a fine day."

He turned and left, glancing over his shoulder once he was about fifty feet away. Beyond the line of soldiers, he saw nothing out of the ordinary about the mansion. No windows were broken, and the personal guard of the Willers still patrolled the grounds. So why the sudden change?

Kael cut left once he reached the main road, a smile growing on his face. The Speaker could put a thousand soldiers circling the entire holy mansion, and it still wouldn't prevent him from seeing Clara now that he knew the secret entrance. Only one man might cause problems, but a single old guard was a lot better than a thousand.

Locating the home was easy enough. Getting inside was another matter. Kael checked the front door, found it locked. He scrunched his face, thinking. The windows were shuttered, and Kael didn't need to check to know they were also barred. The house was meant to be small, unremarkable, and difficult to enter. Taking in a deep breath, Kael gambled and knocked on the door.

"Galvin?" he asked. When he received no answer, he banged much harder, raising his voice as he asked, "Galvin, are you home?"

Metal rattled within, and then the door swung open. Galvin stood blocking the way, a frown on his face and his sword held firmly in his left hand.

"You trying to wake the whole neighborhood?" the guard asked.

"Only until you opened the door," Kael said. He'd hoped the possible attention of a noisy visitor would force the guard to open the door, and he'd guessed correctly. "Is it all right if I, uh, come inside?"

Galvin looked ready to spit.

"Is Clara with you?"

"I was actually hoping to visit with her."

Something about the gray of Galvin's mustache made his frown all the meaner.

"I'm not here to help with clandestine trysts. I'll look aside for Clara's sake, but you don't mean much to me. I suggest you not coming here again."

The guard stepped aside, and Kael entered the house.

"I really am sorry," he said as he headed to the fireplace. "Next time, I'll make sure Clara's waiting here for me. Will that be better?"

Galvin snorted but did not answer. Good enough for Kael. Steeling himself for the crawl ahead, he dropped to his knees and entered the fireplace, and the tunnel within.

Traveling in the darkness alone should have been worse, but Kael had already made the trip once, and that familiarity helped keep him calm as he pressed ahead. Far more nerve-racking was his debate as to how he'd reach Clara before being spotted. If any guards discovered him before he found Clara he'd be in a tight spot. Perhaps they'd believe his lie that he'd been allowed inside. Perhaps they'd also believe he could sprout wings from his back and fly. It had roughly the same odds.

A thin line of gray marked a crease where the hidden door met the wall. It wasn't much, but compared to the pitch black of the tunnel, it was something. Kael approached, feeling the tunnel widening around him, and then with a satisfied grunt he stood to his full height and stretched his back. He was in the tiny room between the door and the tunnel, and now there, he realized he'd given no thought as how to get inside.

I'm not going back to Galvin to admit I couldn't figure out how to open the damn door, Kael swore as he steadily brushed his fingers along the wall, searching for a button or lever. To his relief he found it immediately, a groove along the edge that his hand easily slid into. The wall started to move, and Kael hesitated. There was no way for him to check the other side before exiting. What if someone saw him? He put his ear to the wall, listening for the sounds of voices or footsteps. He heard nothing, but with the wall dampening any potential noises, that was no guarantee.

Deciding to hell with it, he opened the hidden passage all the way, stepped out, and then slid it shut. So far, so lucky. No one there. If he made straight for Clara's room, he should be fine. So long as *she* was fine, of course. Thankfully the mansion felt too quiet for any sort of disaster to have unfolded. Nothing in the hallway looked smashed or disturbed. The increase in soldiers barricading the front must be a precautionary measure.

Just keep quiet and calm, Kael told himself as he walked the carpet. *You were here yesterday. The servants and soldiers inside might not even give you a second thought.*

Kael hurried down the hall, ears on alert for guards or soldiers. Every door he passed was closed, all but one, which Kael slid to a stop beside. Voices from within. He leaned closer, frowning. He recognized both speakers. One was the older brother, Lance, but the other...it was familiar, painfully so, yet he could not place a name to it. Whatever conversation they were having was heated, and Kael slipped closer to the door, ear pressed against it.

"...riots will stop in time," Lance said. "But you cannot expect results overnight."

"You act as if you or I have time to wait," said the other voice. Again Kael felt he should know who it was. That pleasant, yet authoritative tone. He'd heard it once before, just once, but where?

Kael no longer could help himself. Leaning closer, he peered around the half-open door and into the room. It looked to be a library of sorts, the walls covered with shelves filled with leather-bound tomes, their titles etched along the spines in gold and silver. Standing on one side of the room was Lance, looking flustered and angry. On the other side...

On the other side stood Marius Prakt, Speaker for the Angels.

"The people of New Galen must acclimate themselves to the Weshern way of life," Lance said. "Once they do, all this will settle down."

"Last night's riot was the worst of the lot," Marius said, and he shook his head as he crossed his arms. "It seems the people of New Galen would rather burn down homes than acclimate themselves. Such actions make me wonder if the measures you're taking are failing to improve the situation."

Lance blustered, clearly upset at the accusation.

"I've done everything I can to make the people of New Galen happy."

"Including armbands labeling them as outsiders, quarantining them inside their town?"

Lance let out a huff.

"They wear those of their own accord," he said, something Kael knew for certain was a lie. "As do they refuse to venture beyond New Galen's streets. The refugees are frightened of *assimilation*, Speaker, of becoming one of us. They hold on to the notion of being a separate nation, and so long as they do, they'll be angry, isolated, and eager for violence. Men of Galen think with their hearts instead of their heads. Do not blame me for the flaws they were born with."

Marius started to answer, but before Kael could hear it a hand grabbed his shoulder and spun him about. He caught a glimpse of gold armor and red robes, and then a mailed fist slamming his face. Pain exploded throughout his body, his vision a black sheet dotted with red light. His legs went weak, and he collapsed through the door and into the room with Lance and the Speaker.

Kael thought he might pass out, his consciousness swimming around and about like a drunk fish, but he fought through. Eyes watering, he watched as Marius leaned over him, analyzing him like a newly discovered puzzle.

"I recognize this young man," he said.

"Kael Skyborn," Lance said. "He's a friend of Clara's."

The Speaker's face was a mask, but it cracked ever so slightly at the mention of his name.

"Skyborn?" he whispered, rising. "How interesting. Take him alive."

A shadow fell over him as the soldier knelt, mailed fist striking once more, this time to the temple. Kael experienced a single moment of clarity, a realization of just how fucked he was, before the pain hit and he passed out for good.

CHAPTER

9

It was a long walk to the Aquila Forest from Lowville, but thankfully Bree found a merchant traveling northward from the docks, and she hitched a ride in the back of his wagon. Even better, he didn't seem to have any idea who she was. Left alone to her thoughts, she lay on her back, surrounded by rucksacks, and stared at the blue sky streaked with thin white scars of clouds. The calm was a welcome respite from the pressure that had robbed her of sleep the night before. It had been bad enough with Argus wishing for her to be the face of the resistance. Now to have Johan request the same, for her to be the igniting spark for the movement he'd built over the past few years…

Bree sighed. It was enough to make her wish she could hop off the wagon, run to the docks, and vanish to one of the other islands, just a nameless woman in the crowd. The cowardly impulse didn't last long, but it was fun daydreaming of a peaceful life in a new land. A land where Center's soldiers didn't patrol the streets, and her knights didn't occupy the skies. Though if Johan was right, Weshern wouldn't be the last to experience such subjugation.

"We're almost to Warwick," the merchant called over his shoulder from the front of the wagon. "I'll be stopping for a few hours before I continue on to Middleton, if you're still needing the lift."

"Warwick is close enough," Bree said. "And thank you."

The merchant, an older man with long white hair, waved her off.

"Think nothing of it," he said.

Warwick's proximity to the Aquila Forest granted it a lucrative, but tightly controlled, lumber trade, and from the moment she stepped foot inside Bree was immediately assaulted with traders in slender stalls offering her utensils, dishes, and even dolls and toys made of finely carved and stained oak. She kept her head down, ignoring them, no matter how rude or polite they were.

The lumber camps were a hectic bustle, dozens of shirt-less men hacking and sawing, using a variety of instruments to accomplish what appeared to be the same basic goal: turn-ing larger pieces of wood into smaller pieces. Bree skirted the limits of the camps, moving farther south so she could enter the woods unseen. The grass was soft beneath her feet, and she welcomed the return to solitude. Eye to the forest at all times, she searched for one of the signs the resistance had hidden that marked paths leading to the camp. It took a few minutes, but she found one, three small, connected circles cut into the bark, then slashed through the center. A broken chain.

Bree passed the marker, entering the dense oak forest. She quickly found a trail worn into the brush and followed it. Twice she lost the path, the first time finding it again due to another unbroken chain carved into a tree. The second time she crossed a thin stream and saw no sign of where to go. Picking a direction, she began walking. After only a moment she heard a voice cry out from up high.

"Halt," a man said, perched on a tree branch. He held a bow, arrow half-cocked and aimed at her chest. Bree raised her hands above her head.

"I'm one of Argus's Seraphs," she said.

"Your name?" the scout asked.

"Breanna Skyborn."

The arrow immediately relaxed.

"The Phoenix?" he asked. "Bloody hell, forgive me. I didn't recognize you."

He hopped down from the branch and offered her a gap-toothed grin.

"You're forgiven," she said. "I was trying to find the camp. It's a little harder on foot than when flying in."

The scout chuckled.

"Fair enough. Follow me, my lady, and I'll show you the way."

The scout led her to Camp Aquila, which despite her short absence, already looked to have grown considerably. Dozens more tents filled the area. She saw logs cut and dragged into loose circles for seating around dormant campfires. The beginnings of several little buildings lay in piles, slabs of wood cut and prepared to build.

"Where's Argus?" Bree asked the scout.

"At his tent. Do you know where it is?"

"I do."

The man bowed, then let her be. Bree passed through the camp to find the former commander sitting on a stump, sword before him, cloth in hand, and a cup of vinegar at his feet.

"Welcome back," Argus said. The cloth slid up and down the blade, slow and steady. "Are you ready to be our Phoenix?"

"Not quite," Bree said.

Argus paused, and he pulled the rag away to dip it in the vinegar.

"A shame," he said. "So why did you return?"

"Johan Lumens visited my home last night."

Argus paused.

"Is that so?" he said, careful to keep his voice even. "What did that self-proclaimed revolutionary say?"

"He believes our resistance is only the beginning, and he's pledged to help in any way he can. He... he also left a chest full of elements at my aunt's house."

Argus dropped the rag, and a hungry look entered his eye.

"At what price?" he asked.

"Freely given," she said. "I glanced over them before I left. There's at least thirty prisms of each element, other than light, which I guess to have an extra twenty more."

Bree could see the numbers twisting in Argus's head, re-adjusting what he thought he had available to him.

"I'll send men to collect them right away," he said, hurrying to his feet. "This changes things, Bree. If you'll excuse me, I need to talk with Rebecca."

Bree watched him go, trying not to be upset by how easily he dismissed her. Deciding some exercise might cheer her up, she crossed the camp toward the training field, hoping that Brad would already be there.

It wasn't Brad that she found at the clearing for training, but instead a far less pleasant face.

"You came back," Saul said as he slowly tilted his body to the right, arm reaching for the ground. The stretches were designed to both strengthen the muscles needed to perform their aerial maneuvers with the harnesses, as well as relieve any tension and tightness developed from such use.

"Why wouldn't I?" Bree asked.

Saul stood, then stretched in the other direction.

"Plenty of reasons," he said. "Cowardice. Hopelessness. Realizing this whole charade is doomed from the start. Things like that."

"Is that what you think this is?" she asked. "A doomed charade?"

Saul paused his stretching, and he wiped away the sweat that had collected beneath the bangs of his dirty-blond hair.

"You asked for reasons," he said. "Not if I believed any of them. Though you'd still be hard-pressed to find someone who thinks we have a real chance of success."

"Argus thinks we do."

"Good for him." He resumed stretching, this time bending down to reach for his toes. Saul grunted from pain occasionally as he talked. "Tell me, Bree, if you thought all this was hopeless, would you still keep fighting?"

Bree crossed her arms and frowned. It wasn't a question she needed to think on for long. She'd felt the sentiment from the very beginning, no different from when she donned Dean's wings and chased after his murderer.

"Yes," she said. "I would. Even if we don't succeed, it's still right to try."

"Consider me of equal opinion." She must have given him a look, for he immediately turned defensive. "What? Does that surprise you?"

She shrugged.

"After the Archon banished your parents, it does a little."

Saul stood to his full height, pulling back his shoulders in rapid circular motions.

"I told your brother, and I'll tell you," he said. "My parents raised me to be loyal to Weshern. Nothing Isaac or Avila did will ever change that. Now are you here to train with me, or just insult my honor?"

Bree felt guilty for her assumption, and truth be told, she'd neglected most of her stretches and exercises since leaving the academy.

"I've got a few hours to kill," she said. "Let's train."

As she began loosening up, Saul walked over to a nearby tree. Leaning against it was a crude rack containing more than a dozen wood training swords. He grabbed four, and he tossed two at Bree's feet.

"Swords?" she asked, raising an eyebrow.

"Elements are a rarity now," he said. "I have a feeling we'll need our swords far more than ever, and I never had the chance to train with them like you did. If you're willing to teach me..."

Bree picked up the swords, feeling awkward as she twirled them in her hands. She'd never trained anyone at swordplay before, always instead the student. She wasn't sure how to go about it, particularly since they didn't have near enough time to be patient.

"Let's start with a spar," she said. "I'll try to critique as we go."

"Fair enough," Saul said, readying his swords. Already she could tell his stance was wrong.

"Spread your feet wider," she said. "And pull your right foot back a little."

Saul did as he was told. Bree twirled her swords again, then nodded to begin. She started slow, at least what she thought was slow. Her wooden weapons danced in, both from the same side. Saul blocked the first, the other coming in too high. The wood smacked against his shoulder with a loud crack. Saul stepped back, and he swore.

"Every time you miss, it's going to hurt," Bree warned. "We can do stances if it becomes too much."

"You nearly broke my jaw with a broom handle," Saul said. "I think I can handle a few smacks to the arm."

Bree froze, but to her surprise, Saul just laughed.

"Don't think I've forgiven you for that," he said. "Consider me biding my time until the moment is right."

"And when might that be?"

Saul shrugged.

"If I knew, I'd tell you. Now are we going to spar or what?"

He settled back into his stance, and Bree was pleased to see his feet in the proper position without her having to tell him twice.

"Spar," she said. "But I'm warning you, I'm going to enjoy every single hit I score."

"Fair enough," Saul said. "Just know when I hit you, I won't be holding anything back."

Bree grinned at him.

"I might be worried if I thought you'd hit me even once."

Saul launched into an offensive, likely hoping to surprise her, but he was clumsy and straightforward compared to the grace Dean used to exhibit. Snippets of their training together flooded Bree's mind, and her easy smile vanished. She nearly missed her block, but as their swords connected, she intensified her focus, hoping to use the spar to block out the painful memories. She shoved Saul's blades outward, then rapped his chest with a hard thud before dancing away. Saul grimaced. Bree had no doubt left a bruise. He returned to his stance, no hesitation, no complaining.

"Again," said Saul.

They sparred for more than an hour. True to Bree's word, Saul never hit her once.

*   *   *

The Rea Brook flowed through the Aquila Forest, thin and rapid. Bree lay submerged up to the neck, enjoying the cold. She'd worked up a sweat sparring with Saul, and though he'd never scored a hit, he'd still improved immensely over time, forcing her to give effort toward the end. Saul had taken well enough to sparring that she had no doubt he'd have become one of the better fighters in their class if he'd had the chance.

For the most part Bree was alone, though occasionally a man or woman came by to fill a bucket from upstream. Bree had begun ignoring them, her eyes closed as she relaxed. Another approached, but this time did not go upstream, nor did they enter the water.

"I hope you didn't wear yourself out," Argus said.

Bree snapped her eyes open to see the commander standing above her. She fought an instinct to cover herself. Her pants and jacket lay in the grass beside the creek, and she wore only her thin underclothes.

"I'll be fine," she said. "Saul's the one who'll be sporting bruises for the next week."

Argus nodded. No amusement, barely even a recognition of Saul's name. Not good.

"I've received word," he said. "The elements are on their way, divvied up among more than a dozen runners I trust to avoid Center's watchful eye." He gestured to her clothes near the creek bank. "Get dressed. We've set a plan in motion, and Rebecca thinks it's time we fill you in. We'll be waiting for you in the command tent."

He left. Bree dunked her head underneath the water, came up gasping, and then rose to her feet. She had no way to towel off, so she rang out her hair, flung on her clothes, and walked dripping back to the camp. Men and women hurried about, showing more urgency than she'd ever seen before. Something was definitely up. Bree stepped into the commander's tent, where Rebecca, Argus, and a stranger waited around a table with a map of Weshern unfurled across it. The stranger was a middle-aged heavyset man with a long black beard and a smoothly shaven head. He wore a shining set of spotless chain mail underneath his black tabard, the blue sword of Weshern sewn onto the front with intricate detail.

"Bree, I'd like you to meet Varl Cutter," Rebecca said, gesturing to the enormous man. "He held the position of military general prior to Center's occupation."

"And as far as I'm concerned, it's a position I still hold," Varl said. He bowed to Bree. "It's a pleasure to meet you, Miss Skyborn. I've heard plenty about you."

Bree nodded politely. She'd heard of Varl only a few times in passing at the academy. For the most part, the Seraphim and the military guard did not interact. The military guard did the grunt work, patrolling the streets, ensuring the peace, and protecting the Archon. The Seraphim, on the other hand, took to the skies, deciding the fates of nations with their battles.

"I would not believe most of it," Bree said. "People tend to exaggerate when they tell stories."

"That they do," Varl said. "Though my men's stories tend to make me sound louder, dumber, and meaner. Consider yourself lucky to be pushed toward the better end of things instead of the worse."

Bree smiled, deciding she already liked the former general.

"Johan's gift allows us to be far more aggressive than we originally planned," Rebecca said, and she gestured to the map. "We can now safely arm every Seraph at our disposal, which means it is time to look to aiding Varl in doing the same for his military guard. While Marius has increased the overall military presence in Weshern, he has tried to do it incrementally to avoid further alarming the populace. I believe we can punish him for his caution."

She pointed to the northeastern portion of the map of Weshern, where a crude fort was drawn.

"When Marius ordered the academy shut down, he also disbanded the vast majority of the military guard," she said. "Fort Luster was forcibly evacuated. So far as we know, its contents have not been moved."

"Which means all our armor and weaponry are still there," Varl said. "I've got hundreds of soldiers eager to join your cause, but we've got nothing but our bare hands to do it with, unlike you Seraphs with your wings and elements. If we can liberate Fort Luster, we can haul out enough gear to outfit ourselves a fully equipped army. Once we do that, we can start hitting Center all over the island."

"It's a lot easier to hide a sword and a chain mail shirt than it is a pair of wings," Argus said. "We can position men in every single city and target smaller groups of soldiers. Every casualty will add up over time, greatly increasing the cost of occupying our island as well as making it far harder to stamp out any resistance."

"However, to ensure we have the time to unload the gear, we need to shift patrolling knights away from the fort," Rebecca said. "With the increase of elements, we can afford to use such a feint. I've picked out three cities, all many miles away from Fort Luster. We'll distribute half our Seraphim among these cities, with the goal of ambushing patrolling knights and eliminating them while they're vastly outnumbered. Afterward, our Seraphim will flee to the far corners of Weshern, guiding their pursuers away from the true goal. The other half of our

Seraphim will take part in the attack on Fort Luster, weakening it for Varl's men."

Bree frowned as she stared at the map, analyzing their planned attack.

"Aren't you afraid of escalation?" she asked. "We've already killed several of their knights. If we assault Fort Luster…"

"We'll be attacking a fort that belongs to us, one Center has no right to disarm," Argus interrupted. "And if Edwin and Lance had spines, it'd still be ours. Those cowards handed it over without a fight, but their appeasement only weakens our resistance instead of getting us closer to an actual solution."

"So where do I come in?" Bree asked, gesturing to the map.

"You'll be flying at my side," Argus said. "I'll be reorganizing our Seraphim into squadrons, and you'll be part of Wolf Squad."

"No more Phoenix Squad?" Bree asked.

"There's no Phoenix Squad until there's a Phoenix."

Bree nodded. Fair enough.

"I've over a hundred men making their way to Fort Luster," Varl said. "I'll be joining them just before your attack. Give us weapons, and I promise you, we'll pile up enough dead to make even you Seraphs jealous."

"A boast I pray you make true soon enough," Rebecca said. "We'll attack an hour before nightfall, in case the troops are prepared for a nighttime assault like our last. Each of you has much to do, so I suggest you get to it."

She bowed quickly, then marched off. Varl gave a quick two-finger salute to Bree and Argus.

"It's a long walk to Fort Luster, so I best get started," he said. "See you on the battlefield."

When he was gone, Argus gestured for Bree to follow.

"Olivia told me of your hesitancy about combat with ground

forces," he said. "While we have the time, I'd like to give you a crash course on proper tactics. Afterward, we'll run some drills with the new squadrons, and get everyone acclimated with one another."

"Very well."

He turned to her, and he lowered his voice after a glance at the many people hurrying about.

"We won't need your fire when we assault the fort," he said. "But afterward, when knights come flying in to their aid..."

"I'm aware of the danger we face," Bree said. "The decision is still mine to make."

"For our sake, I pray you decide soon," Argus said. "We need every Seraph we can get, but we need the Phoenix even more."

CHAPTER

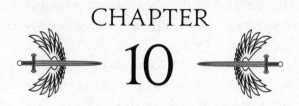

10

Bree flew at Argus's right side, the tips of their wings nearly touching. The rest of Wolf Squad trailed either side of them in a tight V formation. The ground flashed by in a great green blur, far too close for comfort. Bree knew they had to stay low to avoid being spotted, but sometimes she swore she could reach down and touch the tall grass swaying with the air of their passing.

Argus reached out his right hand, and he made four quick symbols with his fingers.

Attack speed on mark.

Bree relayed the message. The two Seraphs on the tail end of the formation flared out wide, flying closer to the other two squads trailing on either side so they could relay the message yet again. Bree kept her finger tight on the throttle, waiting for Argus to give the signal. The plan was to approach Fort Luster at full speed just prior to spotting distance.

I want us to hit them like a thunderclap, Argus had told the lot as they gathered in the Aquila Forest. *The only warning they get will be the flash of our elements.*

Bree lifted slightly as they passed over a particularly tall hill. The temporary rise allowed Bree to see a town far to their right. Porth, she believed. That was where General Varl was gathering a large portion of his soldiers. Assuming the attack went as planned, and they ransacked Fort Luster, the gear was to be taken back to the town, and from there, disseminated throughout the island to those still loyal to Weshern.

If the distant town was Porth, then Fort Luster was a little over a mile away. Close enough. Bree didn't even need to see Argus's right arm shoot out, fist clenched. She swung her own fist, then punched the throttle. The other two squads had no need of the signal. Wolf Squad's sudden burst of speed was obvious enough. Three squads, thirty Seraphim. Another thirty were broken into squads of ten and then sent out on distraction duty. Given how most knight patrols still flew solo, or in groups of two or three at most, Argus felt confident their ten could bring them down without casualties. Bree prayed he was correct. They couldn't afford the loss of a single Seraph. An entire squadron would be disastrous.

Wind blasting through her hair, Bree followed Argus over the landscape, which shifted from tall grasslands to shorter pastures full of dull orange and brown bovines. Argus tilted right, leading them toward a distant road, then straightened out, following it. Bree's pulse increased as the fort came into view far ahead. It was smaller than she'd expected, little more than a wood mole on the face of the land. Throttle pushed to maximum, Bree took care to manage every twitch of her muscles, eyes focused on her destination at all times. At such speeds, it would only take a momentary twist of an arm or leg to go veering off wildly, and with how close they flew to the ground, such a detour could be fatal.

Bree relayed another signal from Argus, this to arm their elements. Wolf Squad had two Seraphim with stone affinity, and they would be the opening barrage, knocking down the front gates along with portions of the surrounding wall. The rest of the elements would follow, raining death through the newly created openings.

"Don't expect this to be as easy as our ambush on the wagons," Argus had warned them all before taking flight. "Fort Luster was designed to repel an aerial attack. Surprise is our greatest advantage. If we don't hit them hard, and immediately, we'll be left with two options: a time-consuming barrage from beyond arrow range, or a costly melee engagement. Neither one is acceptable. When we fly that first pass, by God, make it count."

Bree's chest tightened with frustration. What would she be doing during that all-important first pass? Nothing. Not unless she wanted to burn through her single fire elemental prism in one clumsy ranged attack. That would deny her the option of wielding her burning swords, and given how the angelic knights were the true threat, she wouldn't dare leave herself so vulnerable.

If only you could control it, she thought as they raced toward the fort. Of course, there was another option. She could ignite the flame about her blades and go blasting through the troops, without a care as to who might witness and survive. This left her just as nervous as facing Center's knights without any fire element, and she pushed both ideas aside for the moment. Fort Luster was almost within reach, and she couldn't spare the distraction. The two stone wielders of Wolf Squad unleashed their barrage of pale gray boulders twice the size of Bree. The boulders soared to either side of her, gently turning as they flew. Bree kept one eye on Argus, the other on the stone, as the rest of Wolf Squad began their assault.

Fort Luster's outer wall was tall and circular, built of thick wood logs nailed together, the tops carved into points. Behind the sharpened points there appeared to be a thin rampart for soldiers to stand upon, and her glance saw only two atop it when the boulders smashed through the wood as if it were glass. The front gate shattered, the wall collapsing in on itself as supports broke and logs twisted and ripped down the center. Bree spotted dozens more soldiers wearing the red tunic of Center fleeing like ants behind the ruined wall, and then the rest of the elements hit. Balls of flame struck the ground, exploding outward in fiery rings. Lances of ice pierced armor as if it weren't there; those that missed and hit ground shattered into thin, deadly shards that flew in all directions. Last came the lightning. They were moving far too fast for any accuracy, so thick bolts of it slammed into the center of groups, killing those they hit and dazing others nearby.

Bree had but a moment to take it all in before a second barrage flew from the three squads. A ten-foot gap separated the outer wall from a second interior wall, this one half the height, twice as thick, and protecting a stone barracks. The boulders had far more difficulty with this wall. Wood splintered on contact, and even from up high Bree heard the loud crack of boulders hitting their targets, but they only managed to knock over a single portion of the wall, and only then because two other Seraphim focused their fire upon it as well. Ice and fire followed, first slamming into the wall, then raining down upon the barracks itself as the three squads flew overhead, doing little damage to the squat structure.

Another pass, Argus signaled. He waited two seconds for

Bree to relay the order, then their leader lessened his throttle, twisted his shoulders, and arced left. The rest followed, looping back around. Coming in from the other direction, Bree better saw the soldiers scrambling about. They raced up stairs on all sides of the outer wall, others climbing ladders leading toward the top of the interior wall. Nearly every soldier carried a bow, their quivers bristling with arrows. Bree thought Argus would lift higher, out of reach of the arrows, but instead he punched his throttle back to maximum and dove low.

Argus had insisted they hit hard and fast, and he showed every intention of maintaining that strategy. Bree clenched her jaw and focused on following him as arrows launched into the air, a great upward rain. Arrows from the soldiers on the ramparts, arrows from the men atop the barracks, even arrows from thin slits carved into the stone of the barracks' walls. There were so many firing in all directions, Bree saw no way to dodge, only race through, trusting their speed.

Ice focused upon the archers atop the barracks, easy targets to the thin lances. Those with stone blasted the soldiers atop the ramparts of the two walls. Fire wielders bathed the barracks in long waves that burned across the sides, hitting window after window, letting their flames flow into the interior. Amid it all tore bolts of lightning, taking down exposed soldiers attempting to climb to more advantageous spots. It was incredible the concentration involved, to aim at such speeds while fighting off any instinct to dodge the many arrows, but their foes showed no less resolve. Despite the destruction crashing down upon them, the soldiers released arrow after arrow, flooding the air with deadly bolts. Several passed within mere feet of Bree, at least two ricocheting off her silver wings. Others were not so lucky. One member of Wolf Squad took an arrow to the throat. He twisted sideways as his body went limp, spiraling wildly toward the ground. Bree counted herself lucky she couldn't see the moment of impact.

The second pass ended, and Argus looped the three squads around. Bree glanced left and right, counted at least three Seraphim dead, and several more wounded from arrows still stuck in their flesh. Argus's right hand twisted, three quick shapes.

Break rank.

Fort Luster was a broken, burning mess, but soldiers still rushed about, most heading toward the stone barracks. Protected within, they'd force the Weshern Seraphim into close quarters. Argus saw this, and he was giving the Seraphim free rein on attack. He led the way, flying both higher and slower, better able to aim. Bree followed him a moment, then decided against it. If she were to brave the arrows, at least she might accomplish something at the same time. Bree fell back, letting all others gain distance before resuming. Her wrists pushed down against the loops atop the hilts of her swords, connecting them to the safety cords before drawing the weapons free. She watched their next barrage pummel Fort Luster, dozens of soldiers dying in the blink of an eye, and then she punched her throttle.

She flew straight for the crumbled front gate, the grass a blur mere feet below. Archers stood upon the devastated ramparts on either side, firing arrows before ducking down to prepare another shot. Bree slowed, needing greater control lest she end up a splatter of flesh and metal on the interior wall. She shot through the broken gate, two arrows crossing the air above her, and then arched her back and slowed even more. Bree hovered for a brief moment, and once she'd straightened out she gave her wings a slight burst, charging two archers preparing their bows.

Her first swing opened up a gash across one archer's arm

and chest. The second swing shoved aside the other's bow so his arrow shot wild. Momentum carrying her forward, Bree punched both swords into his chest, lifting him up and over the spikes of the wall as she poured power into her wings. The corpse slid off her blades as she looped to the right. She focused on an archer whose back was to her, but a blast of lightning ripped through his body before she could get to him. Another two dashed through the gap between the walls in a panicked run for the barracks. Bree dove, trusting her fellow Seraphim not to kill her with friendly fire.

Just before impact, she shut off her wings and flipped herself feetfirst. Her heels slammed into an archer's back, and despite the pain to her knees, Bree maintained presence of mind to kick off toward the other. She thrust her sword, puncturing his rib cage and into lung. Blood soaked his tabard as she yanked it out, turned. The first had scrambled to his knees, bow in hand, arrow nocked. Fighting panic, Bree kicked left while flashing the throttle to her wings, just enough to give her some speed. The archer's arrow missed her waist by less than an inch. Bree's feet had barely touched ground before she leapt again, flashing her wings to give herself another boost. She landed heel first on the archer's abdomen, swords slashing before he might fire. His bow blocked one hit, but the other sliced across his throat, ending any resistance.

An arrow pinged off her wing, and Bree leapt into the air without daring to look for the shooter. A second arrow knifed the air beneath her as her wings thrummed to life, ripping her skyward. She turned, tracing the trajectory of the two shots to find her would-be killer, but an explosion of fire overwhelmed the wall where he'd have been. A Seraph flew past her, too fast for her to catch his face, but she heard his voice shout above the din.

"You owe me!"

Bree rose higher, wishing to survey the battle while out of bowshot. Turned out there wasn't much of a battle left. Any soldiers outside the barracks were dead or dying. Inside the barracks, though, was another matter. Bree watched as Argus had four of his men line up and flood the interior with flame. Others flew about the fort, scanning for potential survivors. Turning south, she spotted a trail of men and women approaching from Porth. General Varl's soldiers, coming to claim the gear they'd liberated. Though they were distant, she could tell they were jogging. Time was far from on their side. Bree unhooked the latches connected to her sword hilts, sheathed the blades, and then dropped down into the interior of the fort.

Everywhere was broken wood and spilled blood. Portions of the outer wall still burned, a faint, lazy fire steadily blackening the sides. The smell was the worst, of blood and meat and ripped-open bowels. Bree held a hand over her mouth and nose, focusing on keeping her breathing steady.

This is just the beginning, she told herself. *It's going to get a lot worse before it gets better, so don't you lose it now.*

Easy to tell herself, hard to do. She saw the burn marks marring the stone sides, the melting ice shards, the great boulders that lay in piles of splinters. The entire fort, designed for battle, now in ruins, and at the hands of thirty Seraphim. Meanwhile, Center had hundreds of knights at their disposal. What could they do to a town or village? How great would such devastation be? And what could anyone do to stop it?

Seeing the unleashed power of the elements, Bree both understood the dire need to defeat Center and the utter hopelessness of the task.

"Are you all right?" Argus asked, startling her. He'd come up beside her, and lost in her own private fears, she'd not noticed or heard.

"No," she said. "But I will be. We don't have much choice in the matter, do we?"

Argus glanced about the fort, understanding the reason for her unease.

"I've fought more aerial battles than most alive," he said. "But it's different on the ground. The damage feels more permanent, more real. We wield tremendous power, you and I, but it's an inescapable fact that so do our enemies. We can only hope to be better, and protect those we love from a similar fate."

"And if we're not?" she asked. "If we're not better?"

"We will be," Argus said, and he squeezed her shoulder. "As you put it, we don't have much choice in the matter, do we?"

Together they walked to the clearing before the barracks' entrance, where the rest of the Seraphim gathered. The door into the barracks was thick wood, presumably locked and barred from the inside. The door itself was incredibly narrow, and Bree had a feeling the interior was equally small. Argus was right; the building had been designed against attacking Seraphim. No pair of wings would fit through that opening, and even if they could, maneuvering the tight walls would be impossible.

"There's at least six inside," Olivia said upon their arrival. "We'll need to take them out. That, or wait for Varl's men to come and do the dirty work."

"There's no time to wait," Argus said. "We'll do this now. Olivia, Chernor, you two with me. The rest of you, take positions on the walls and keep an eye out for knights while Varl's men make their way here."

The other Seraphim scattered to take positions, but Bree remained behind.

"Let me help you," she said as the three Seraphs removed their wings so they might fit through the entrance. "I'm good with my swords, you know that."

"Your skill is in the air," Argus said. "We'll be in cramped quarters. You've no experience there."

"I can still help you."

"You'll help us more alive. At least, you will once you unleash your fire."

Bree gestured to the roof of the barracks.

"Can we not break through the ceiling or the walls?" she asked.

"Stone's too thick," Olivia said, setting her wings beside Argus's. "It'd take time and elemental prisms we don't have to spare. Best to do this quick."

Argus said something to Chernor, patted him on the shoulder. Chernor Windborn was one of the biggest Seraphim she'd ever seen, making even Loramere look small by comparison. He had the same build as Brad, and Bree wondered if Instructor Dohn had given Chernor similar harassment because of it. His black hair was twice as long as Olivia's, tied back in a ponytail with a pale blue cloth.

"Should have expected you to make me do the dirty work," Chernor said, grinning. His face was a mess of beard, bangs, and sideburns, and Bree couldn't imagine how he flew without it driving him insane. The man wore no sword belt, instead hefting a long maul he'd carried on his back.

"I'll be right there with you," Argus said.

"You'll be right there *behind* me, watching me kill everyone. Try not to pretend it's such a difficult task."

"Not everyone," Olivia said, drawing her swords and standing beside Chernor. Her head only came up to his shoulder. "I'll take down my fair share."

Argus's smile lasted only a moment, then he was all serious again.

"You have a job to do," he said to Bree. "Go. Keep watch with the others. We'll handle this just fine."

"Understood," Bree said, telling herself not to feel upset. She backed away as Argus put two fingers to his mouth and whistled. She glanced up and saw another Seraph waiting patiently above. One of the Wolf Squad stone throwers. The man nodded, aimed his gauntlet, and fired. A single stone shot at the door, smashing it to pieces. Chernor charged in immediately, Olivia on his heels. Argus drew his swords, saluted to Bree, and then dashed after.

The trio vanished into the dark corridor, and she wished she could follow after. Disobeying Argus would only get her reprimanded. Sighing, she lifted up into the air, just high enough to settle onto the roof of the barracks. From there she stared south, to the line of ants traveling from Porth. Time crawled along, and thankfully the skies remained clear of any sign of the knights and their golden armor. Bree tried not to be upset at being ordered to stay behind. Her experience in tight, shoulder-to-shoulder combat was nonexistent.

Varl's men were just arriving through the broken entrance of the inner wall when the three exited the barracks. Bree held back a gasp as she floated to the ground. Blood covered Olivia's neck, dripping from a cut on her chin. Chernor limped on his left leg, a thoroughly soaked bandage wrapped about it near the ankle. Argus had not a scratch on him.

Varl bellowed in greeting upon seeing Argus, and he clasped hands with the commander as he gestured to the surrounding wreckage.

"You made a hell of a mess," he said. "I expect you'll help me rebuild once we've taken back Weshern."

"Only if your men help me rebuild the academy first."

"Consider it a deal."

"How much time do we have?" someone asked Argus as the men poured into the barracks.

"Until we're noticed," was his answer.

"You heard him," Varl shouted. "That could be minutes, could be hours, so haul ass."

He hurried inside to supervise the retrieval of the military gear. Bree gently toggled power to her wings, rising up to the top of the inner wall and setting foot upon one of the few pieces of rampart still intact. From there she scanned the horizon, and she wasn't the only one. Several other Seraphs took position along parts of wall, so that eyes watched all directions. There was no telling when a knight might finally notice what had happened at the fort. If they were lucky, none would, not until they were all long gone.

Bree had a feeling they wouldn't be so lucky.

The first of many exited the barracks, swords and shields in their arms. They piled the weaponry onto carts, and when those were full, they began stuffing them into bags. Bree watched them occasionally, though not for long. She'd never forgive herself if a knight approached from her direction and she were too preoccupied to spot it.

She needn't have worried. Calls of warning came from the north, and she turned to see a single distant knight of Center flying toward him.

"Get down!" Argus shouted to the others. "See if you can get him in close enough to ambush!"

Bree hopped to the ground to avoid being seen, but she knew it was futile. The knight had already turned away, presumably to get reinforcements. The damage to the fort had been catastrophic. It wouldn't take too much imagination to figure out what had happened. Several other Seraphs dropped, pressing against the walls or ducking behind the barracks before Argus called out for them to cease.

"We're on a timer now," he shouted. "Knights are on their

way. Those of you on the ground, we'll buy you the time you need, so don't waste it."

Argus whistled, calling the rest of his Seraphim in. Bree hovered to his side. The commander stood in the center of the gap between the two walls, and he spun to address them all.

"Reform up," he said. "It will take too much time to summon a whole host of knights, so we're looking at facing one or two nearby patrols. That should still give us a numbers advantage, so let's make sure we use it. Stay grounded and hidden behind the inner wall until I give the signal. When I do, unleash hell. Show those bastards from Center how Weshern Seraphim fly."

"Unchained!" Bree shouted, and others joined up the call.

"We fly unchained!"

Argus grinned, a hungry wolf deserving of his squad's moniker.

"Damn right we do."

CHAPTER

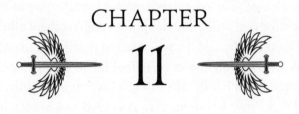

11

Kael had no way to know how long he was out. When he awoke, he was in a small, mostly empty room. He lay atop a bed, the frame of stained wood, the sheets bare white. Beside him was a similar bed. Beyond that he saw two shelves nailed to the wall above him, both currently empty, and a large trunk at the foot of the bed. Kael doubted there'd be anything of use inside it either.

A servant's room, Kael guessed by the minimal decorations and diminutive size. There were probably many like it scattered throughout the holy mansion. Kael attempted to sit up and was immediately rewarded for his effort by a sudden, sweeping sense of vertigo.

"Holy hell," he said as he collapsed onto his back and shut his eyes. It helped his vertigo, but also made him aware of a throbbing in his head that was growing angrier by the second. It was even worse than the ache on his face. At least both hits had missed his nose. Another good blow to it after the humiliating beatdown he received two nights ago and his face might never recover. Assuming there was even a point worrying about that right now. Still, if anyone wanted him dead, they had ample time and opportunity to do it. That he was alive at all had to be a good sign.

Well, not good, Kael decided. Hopeful, maybe. It might also mean he had a future of constant torture and depravation awaiting him, but that was a fate he tried very, very hard to ignore in his mind as he forced his eyes back open. Swinging his feet off the bed, he more stumbled than walked to the door, his movements like a controlled fall. Thudding against the thick wood of the door, he tried the handle, found it refused to budge.

Locked from the outside. Of course it was locked from the outside. Did he really think the Speaker and his soldiers would be so stupid? Staggering back to the bed, Kael collapsed onto his back, closed his eyes, and let his mind drift. No sense panicking, and with no windows and a single locked door, no point stressing out trying to escape. Besides, there was likely a guard posted on the other side, assuming the Speaker was the slightest bit worried about him escaping. Best he rest, and recover, for whatever might lay ahead.

Time passed. Kael drifted in and out of sleep. His headache lessened, and for that he was grateful. The long wait steadily wore at him, the fear of the unknown like a poison slowly dripping into his veins. When the headache subsided enough he could think clearly, and he was able to stand without vertigo, Kael paced the five steps from one side of the room to the other. Remain calm, he told himself. Remain calm...

A voice spoke on the other side of the door, coupled with a sudden turning of the handle. Kael retreated to the bed, fighting off a spike of panic. Had they finally come to kill him? Transfer him to a proper prison? Or merely investigate the reason for his being in the mansion?

The door swung all the way open. Kael had expected a knight, perhaps one of Clara's brothers, but instead in walked Marius Prakt himself. The Speaker for the Angels wore no armor, and he carried no weapon. Instead he wore his long red robes, adorned by a single black sash tied about his waist. No soldier accompanied him as he shut the door and stood, arms crossed, blocking the way. Face a perfect, emotionless mask, he stared at Kael, saying nothing. Analyzing him, Kael believed. Reading him like one would a book. Refusing to be the first to talk, Kael sat on the bed and tried to look equally emotionless. Here he was, the leader of the theocracy of Center. The question was, what did he want with Kael?

"I'd like us to have a talk, you and I," Marius said. "Do you think we can do that?"

Kael gestured to the empty room.

"I'm your prisoner," he said. "What choice do I have?"

Marius slowly shook his head, disappointed.

"You have more choice than you know," he said, arms still crossed. "You could scream and holler like a wild animal. You could shove your fingers into your ears, close your eyes, and sing the verses to 'Crystal Waters' at the top of your lungs. Or you could sit quietly and listen to what I have to say. Many choices, Kael. Just because a choice is foolish doesn't mean the choice ceases to exist."

Kael accepted the reproof, mildly confused. Was that why the Speaker had come? To lecture him?

"I'm right here," Kael said. "So if you want to talk, go ahead and talk."

"I want *us* to talk," Marius said. "That means I speak, and you listen, and then when you speak, I also will listen. Communication, my child. Open, honest communication. That is what I desire. Now remind yourself that I could have had you executed in your sleep hours ago, and show me the decency and respect I deserve."

Kael shifted farther away from the Speaker, sitting at the head of the bed. Marius's presence...it was so strong. The man exuded authority, but it wasn't overwhelming like Johan's. Instead Marius seemed pleasant, almost welcoming. Even when he berated Kael, he never outwardly appeared upset, nor did his tone shift all that much.

"All right, then," Kael said. "Let's talk. So what are we to talk about?"

Arms no longer crossed, Marius slowly paced before the door. Kael found it strangely amusing seeing the Speaker for the Angels, the most powerful man alive, walking those same five steps Kael had walked hours before.

"I want us to talk about Weshern," Marius said. "I want to talk about your people, and what you yourself believe. Right now, it seems everything has twisted and turned upside down, and I can no longer make sense of what I see and hear. Riots? Killings? Rebellion? Have your people gone mad?"

There was no telling what Marius knew, and what he was hunting for, so Kael chose his words carefully. Right now, he was merely the brother of the Phoenix, and friends with Clara. Marius should be ignorant of him and his sister's role with the growing rebellion. If he did suspect it, he lacked proof, which might be enough to escape the situation alive.

"You're right," Kael said. "We are mad. We're mad at the injustice you've performed against us, manipulating our people, stripping away our land and giving it to foreigners."

The words didn't represent his own heart, but it was a

common grievance of his fellows, and Kael was curious how the Speaker might respond to the accusation.

"Injustice?" Marius scoffed. "Yes, tell me more about your injustice. More than fifty thousand dead, their entire people and way of life destroyed in an instant, yet my handing them a single town on Weshern soil is a grievance worthy of riots and vandalism? Do you all forget that it is *Weshern* who's responsible for Galen's collapse in the first place?"

Kael failed to keep the indignation out of his voice.

"We're not responsible," he said. "And no one believes you when you claim we are."

Marius's calm veneer finally slipped. Kael had expected anger, derision. What he did not expect was complete and utter exasperation.

"Johan's lies," he said. "They're spreading, aren't they? Let me take a guess, Kael. You think *we* sent Galen crumbling to the ground, don't you? The absurdity of it all. That'd be like slaughtering your eldest son just to ensure your other four children obey."

His every word was far more believable than Kael anticipated. It made him uncomfortable, and he tried to cling to the rest of the evidence as he understood it.

"But what about overthrowing the Willers?" he said. "What about your presence here, the disbandment of our Seraphim, and the stationing of troops and knights?"

"An island died!" Marius said. His voice rose only the tiniest bit, but it was enough to fill Kael with an impulse to kneel. Every syllable was overwhelmed with earnestness. Every word felt like a request for Kael to understand, and believe.

"How stubborn and blind must your people be?" Marius continued. Kael had a feeling the Speaker's words were no longer just for him. "An entire island, one of six our entire race has left to survive upon, has vanished beneath the Endless Ocean. Yet you people want to argue over a little stretch of land? Your former Seraphim want to rebel, and for what? Promises of freedom you never lost, and the release of a royal family I would release on my own once matters settled? A royal family whom I never even took from Weshern, instead leaving them imprisoned in their own home as a matter of good faith?"

Kael tried to stay strong against Marius's arguments. He tried to tell himself Weshern was in the right, and Center the aggressive, lying invader.

It wasn't working.

"How petty you must be," Marius continued. "How small your world truly is. You think this is about power? About conquest? With but a word I dismantled your Seraphim and scattered your army, and you face only a fraction of my total might. If I wanted to rule Weshern, I'd have conquered Weshern, *not sent Galen crashing down.*"

Kael swallowed down a sudden knot in his throat.

"Then why are your soldiers here?" he asked.

"You have to understand, we are not the enemy," Marius said. "My theotechs are not the enemy. What everyone seems to have forgotten, what everyone refuses to acknowledge, is that what happened to Galen could happen *here*, and I have every reason to believe Weshern will be the next target."

Kael frowned.

"The next target?" he asked. "Whose next target?"

The Speaker shook his head.

"I've already said enough, and anything more would be beyond your understanding. You must believe me, I want to keep the people of this island safe, and not just this island, but all remaining five. Humanity must survive. Five centuries ago we escaped complete annihilation. Trust me when I say all I do,

I do to ensure we last centuries more. This fledgling resistance only puts everyone's lives at risk. We aren't leaving, Kael. We're going to stay until I know the threat is passed, and punish every guilty soul I must to ensure this tragedy is never repeated."

Kael fought to keep his face passive. Whatever zeal he held against Center felt irrational now, impotent against the Speaker's claims.

"So you're trying to keep us safe," he said. "So you're not responsible for Galen's fall. Then tell me who is. You've already let it slip that more is going on than just us fighting a battle against Galen without asking for permission."

Marius stared at him with those sapphire eyes, not flinching, not hesitating for a moment.

"I cannot tell you," he said.

Of course not. Kael shook his head, disappointed.

"Then how did Galen fall? We've always been told the Beam cannot be broken."

Silence was the only answer Marius offered.

"What about the elements?" Kael said. "Another secret you keep from us. Why won't you tell us how they're made?"

"The people are better off in their ignorance," Marius said. "Secrets become secrets for a reason, Kael, and it is not always because of power."

Kael pushed off the bed and onto his feet. He strode right up to Marius, determined to look the man in the eye. The Speaker would have no excuses for refusing to answer this final question. The other things he could claim the world was better for not knowing, or that the scope went beyond Kael's understanding, but not this.

"Your theotechs tried to have me and my sister captured after her first battle against Galen," he said. "I want to know why."

Marius stared at him, silence again the answer.

"You know," Kael said, meeting that gaze. "You know, and you won't answer. You tell me to trust you, then refuse to give a single answer to any of my questions. That's not how you garner trust, Speaker. It's how you hide."

"Kael," Marius said softly, "I am giving you one last chance. There is an entire world beyond your knowledge, and for the sake of your island, you must believe me. Will you accept reason, or will you cling to the comforting conspiracies of the rabble?"

Kael tried to decide what he believed. Much of what Johan had insisted didn't sound so certain when rebuffed by the Speaker, yet Marius was still clearly hiding so much. If he'd wanted to keep Weshern safe, why not work with the Willers instead of deposing them? And no amount of insistence would ever convince Kael that the many secrets Marius kept were better off as secrets than as open knowledge.

"You've come here to claim power over us," Kael said, wishing he believed as firmly as his words made it sound. "Nothing you've told me has convinced me otherwise."

Marius sighed.

"A shame," he said. "Such a shame. I'd hoped to avoid this unpleasantness. If you'd just listened, and stopped being so stubborn, you might have saved your sister's life."

"What are you talking about?" Kael asked, putting on a brave face despite his heart hammering in his chest. He took a step back, scanning the room for anything he might use as a weapon. The closest was the blankets of the bed, which would be good only for entangling the man, or maybe strangling him at best.

"I sent your sister a request for an audience," Marius continued. He didn't move to follow Kael's retreat to the other side of the room, instead remaining at the door. "I'd hoped she might be here with you to listen, but after tonight's display I find that doubtful. She's not coming, and you won't convince her, either. So be it. If she dies during the raid, we'll endure. We have you, after all."

Kael's heart was at full race now. What raid? And when did Bree reveal her presence? Had it happened while he was trapped in his room?

"You're bluffing," he said, wishing he actually believed that.

The left side of Marius's face twitched slightly, like an echo of a smile.

"A traitor in your midst gave us the location of your camp," he said. "My specters are already on their way to Aquila Forest. Your scouts have their eyes on the sky, I'm sure, but what about from within? What about from the ground, and the trees themselves?" Marius banged twice on the door. "Your rebellion dies tonight, Kael. Perhaps afterward we might have a semblance of peace, and a chance to keep your stubborn island from joining Galen beneath the ocean waters. Assuming your people can quit bickering with those of New Galen, of course."

The door opened, and two theotechs stepped inside. Despite wearing no wings, they both had golden gauntlets on their right hands, connected to gold cylinders attached to their backs.

"Take him to the Crystal Cathedral," Marius ordered. "Do not harm him. He's a gift for Er'el Jaina."

The three blocked the doorway, but under no circumstances was Kael going with them without a fight. He grabbed one of the blankets and flung it, hoping to screen his attack. He barreled straight for their center, thinking to slip through while catching them off guard. One reached for him, and Kael dipped below his grasp, but the other theotech swept his leg. As he dropped, the theotech jammed his open gauntlet against his chest. Lightning sparked from the palm. Kael tried to scream as pain ignited throughout his entire body, but his jaw locked shut. He couldn't even breathe.

The pain subsided, the lightning ceased. Marius leaned over him, frowning as Kael gasped in air.

"You'd rather suffer needlessly instead of bowing to your superiors," he said. "Just like the rest of Weshern."

When the two theotechs grabbed him by each arm, Kael's body went limp, his muscles unable to resist as they dragged him away.

CHAPTER

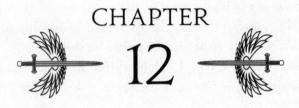

12

The former members of Weshern's military guard snaked an uneven trail south toward Porth, the largest of the groups escorting a covered wagon. Bree watched from her perch atop the inner wall, nerves steadily fraying. It'd been more than twenty minutes since they'd last seen the angelic knight scouting the fort, and the waiting was killing even the most patient of Seraphs.

"It shouldn't take this long to find a few patrols to help with an attack," said a woman beside Bree. A small group had gathered around her on the rampart, joining her in staring north, where they expected the knight to return from.

"Maybe they know they have the time," another offered.

"Or they're bringing a whole army," said the first woman.

"Let them," Chernor called from beneath. He leaned against the interior wall, wing harness beside him, leg freshly bandaged. "Even injured and flying like a lame duck, I promise

I'll score at least one kill, and Bree and Argus are both good for two each. That's nearly half a squad already, and we haven't accounted for the ones you all might luck into killing."

"Or the rest of Wolf Squad," Bree said, nodding south, to where the remaining eight gathered atop the outer wall, surveying the military's trek to Porth. "I'd say they're good for a few."

Those around her were smiling easier, their nervousness retreating ever so slightly.

"So is it true?" the man beside her asked Bree. "Will the Phoenix join us?"

She knew what he was asking, and she wished she had a better answer.

"I don't know," she said. "I guess we'll find out when the time comes."

Hardly the answer they were hoping for, and the smiles vanished as easily as they'd come. The guilt of it stung Bree like a wasp.

The first hint of the crawling darkness was peeking over the western horizon when they spotted the approaching force of knights. A knot caught in Bree's throat. Nine angelic knights of Center, flying in formation, their wings shimmering a soft golden glow. They'd lost three Seraphs during the assault on the fort, meaning they'd fight at a three-to-one ratio. Despite the bravado she'd shown, she feared it wouldn't be enough. They wouldn't be catching these knights by surprise. It'd be a head-to-head battle, and even if they won, she feared they'd suffer catastrophic casualties.

"Form up!" Argus yelled. "Form up, now!"

Bree flew to join Wolf Squad near the front as the other two squads gathered between the walls. Argus spun, eyes dancing, counting, a plan forming in his mind.

"Our soldiers are almost safely hidden in Porth with the supplies," their commander shouted. "But many are still on the road, and we need to buy them time. Center has sent her knights after us, and we're going to hit them head-on. Don't try to conserve your element, and don't hesitate or doubt your aim. Unleash hell on that first pass, because if we don't thin their numbers, we may not get a second. Am I understood?"

Scattered affirmatives greeted his question.

"Good," he said. "Now get in the air. We need those knights coming after us instead of our men on the road."

Wings hummed as the Seraphs took to the sky. Bree flicked the toggle, but stopped when Argus called her name.

"Chernor, Bree, with me," he said. Bree walked over, and she had a feeling she knew what the man wanted.

"What you need?" Chernor asked, burly arms crossed over his chest.

"I need you to lead Wolf Squad," Argus said. "Keep our Seraphim above the fort, and charge only when the knights are within elemental range."

"And where will you be while I'm doing this?"

"That's my own business—now fly."

Chernor thudded a fist against his breast, then kissed it.

"Always wanted to be in charge," he said, grinning. "Might as well lead when we're flying against the toughest sons of bitches in the skies."

He punched his throttle and shot into the air, silver wings glimmering brightly. Bree watched him leave, not wanting to meet Argus's hard gaze.

"So where do you wish me to go?" she asked.

"Nowhere," Argus said. "I want you here with me."

Bree's temper flared as she turned to face him.

"What, so I'm nice and safe in case we lose the battle?" she asked. "God forbid something happen to your precious mascot."

"Watch your tongue, Seraph," Argus snapped. Bree retreated,

her face and neck flushing. Her commander grabbed the front of her jacket and yanked her back, free hand pointing to the distant gold shimmers that were the angelic knights.

"Nine," he said. "I'd hoped they'd come in haste with only four or five, but there's *nine*. We have no hope of winning a prolonged battle. We must end this quickly, and that's where you and I come in."

"You and I," Bree said. Her tone had softened, and she felt embarrassed for her outburst. "As in you and the Phoenix."

Argus let out a long breath as he clenched his jaw and fought to cool down.

"The three squads up there will appear to be the entirety of our forces, and when they unleash their elements, they'll convince the knights of our desperation. Center is arrogant, and I'm betting our lives that they still underestimate us. When they circle around after the first pass, you and I can hit them from below, fast and hard. We don't need to kill many, just two or three to ensure our numbers advantage remains strong."

So not safe and hidden, but quite the opposite. Bree saw the wisdom in the plan, but there was the obvious need of her burning weapons.

"You said you'd never force me," she said. "You said the decision to bare my fire would always be mine."

"And it still is. I'll attack alone if I must. Come with me, or remain here, your choice." Argus stepped closer, spoke softly. "Bring your fire. Stop hiding, and show the world what you can do."

Bree drew her swords and clutched them tightly in her fists. Her left thumb tapped against the throttle, itching for speed. Eyes skyward, she watched the Seraphs and knights begin their volleys. Weshern's was by far the greater, all four elements flashing outward, illuminating the encroaching dark with fire and lightning. The knights' offensive lasted only a heartbeat before they flung up defensive walls of stone and veered out of formation to dodge. The fierceness of the attack had to have caught them off guard, and Bree pumped a fist upon seeing first one, then two knights plummet to the ground.

With reaction speeds bordering on superhuman, the knights flung their gauntlets to the side and blasted lightning and ice at the passing Weshern Seraphim. Three Seraphs died in an instant, and several others veered off injured. Argus twisted a knob on his right gauntlet, arming the ice element within. Bree thought he might offer one last argument, but that wasn't Argus's way.

"Decide," he said simply, then burst into the air with a sudden flash of silver. Bree flicked the throttle, felt power flood through the silver wings. In the end, her decision was no decision at all.

She ran, throttle easing forward until she leapt into the air and punched it to its fullest. Her arms stretched out to either side, swords pointed out and away like a second pair of wings. Momentum had carried both forces farther apart, but now they curled back around for another exchange. The knights' backs were to her and Argus, and they were not yet up to full speed. Wings screaming, air billowing across her body, Bree knifed upward on an intercept course, trailing just behind Argus.

Her commander lifted his right gauntlet, and blue light flared from the focal point in his palm as he shot shards of ice at the nearest knight. The shards were small and sharp, barely perceptible in the growing darkness. Most broke against the golden armor, but two found the soft flesh of the knight's abdomen and neck. His body went limp, and his final death flails sent him careening leftward. The now-falling knight had been at the rear, with no one to see his death, and Argus drained power from his wings to keep back and shoot at another.

Bree made no such hesitation. Foe in her sights, she released the power of her prism, then clanged her swords together. Fire bathed over them, and that flash of light was the only warning her target received. She flew past, sword slicing through his body and severing his arm. It would have been his head had he not dodged at the last moment. Bree twirled in the air, attacks from her fellow Seraphim screaming past either side, and then dropped to follow another knight who'd flown alongside the first. The woman's golden wings thrummed as Bree chased, the two streaking toward the ground like meteors.

The knight twisted about to face her, wings shutting off as she brought her gauntlet to bear. Bree weaved left, then rolled right, avoiding two thick blasts of lightning. Their light burned red in her vision. Bree punched her throttle to its absolute maximum, closing the distance between them. The knight rotated back and reactivated her wings, but she couldn't accelerate in time. Bree crashed down on her, burning blades hacking through her wings and harness like butter. The ground now frighteningly close, and getting closer, Bree kicked off, screaming in pain as she shifted her trajectory upward, the buckles of her harness digging into her skin as she arched her back. The knight, with her own wings damaged, could not follow. She slammed into the ground, then rolled, limbs snapping wildly as her body twisted like a rag doll. Teeth clenched, Bree fought against the pain as she missed the tall grass by mere feet before rising into the air.

The sky was full of silver wings, the remaining four knights now terribly outnumbered and surrounded on all sides. Bree flew into the center of the chaotic battle, swords leaving thin trails of flame. Lightning exploded on either side of her, and she saw a plume of fire rising from beneath, but she raced through. The crawling darkness covered half the sky, and against such a backdrop the knights' golden wings shone like beacons as she chased. Her chosen target was a knight weaving side to side, the two Weshern Seraphs on his heels alternating blasts of stone and plumes of fire. They always missed, but never by much, leaving the knight with no chance to retaliate.

Bree flew in from the knight's left side, the streaks of her swords easily visible to her fellows giving chase. They ceased their attacks, allowing Bree to close without danger. Wings thrumming a constant chorus in her ears, Bree shifted her angle once, then again, cutting the distance between them to next to nothing. Her prey spotted her from the corner of his eye, and he jolted into a hard right. The two original chasers appeared to have predicted such a reaction, and a combination of stone and lightning blasted into the knight's path, striking him down.

Arcing away, Bree scanned for the nearest foe, saw but one left. Darkness nearly covered the world, but even in the dim light she recognized the black line on Argus's wings as he chased after the fleeing knight. Bree forcing her wings to their maximum, relishing the feeling of speed. No matter how fast she went, it never felt like enough, and she pushed harder against the throttle. Fire dripped behind her as she flew, her blades hungry in her hands. Her vision narrowed down to that lone knight and Argus, weaving together in a deadly dance. Argus fired lance after lance of ice, a careful stream that never seemed to hit.

Bree grinned when she realized what Argus was doing. If allowed to fly straight, the knight could outpace them all with his superior wings. Argus was carefully, expertly guiding the knight's path, shifting it back toward her so he couldn't flee. Coming in from the side, Bree would have one brief opportunity of attack before shooting past. Vowing not to waste it, she judged the distance, tweaked her aim, and closed the gap. Too busy focusing on Argus behind him, he never saw her coming.

Bree shut off her wings just before impact. Shoulders and waist twisting, she spun in a circle, wrists together, twin blades forming a wall of fire at her command. She sliced straight through the knight as he passed, fire bursting with power the moment before the steel made contact. Her blades never felt a single moment of resistance.

Powering her wings back on, Bree watched the two separate pieces of the knight fall to the field, and she smiled bitterly.

The vultures spent centuries coming for our dead, she thought. *Will they know what to do when retrieving their own?*

Bree banished the fire about her blades. The battle was won, the Weshern soldiers safely arriving in Porth, carrying weapons and armor on their way to various safe houses established throughout the island. Adrenaline pounding through her, she surveyed the area, saw her fellow Seraphim joining into squadrons for a retreat back to the Aquila Forest. Bree did not go with them. Instead she flew straight up into the air, swords still in hand. Thankfully none of the other Seraphim tried to follow her. She didn't want to explain, and in a few moments, she wouldn't need to.

Higher and higher she climbed, thumb rammed down on the throttle. The island receded beneath her, nothing but a black blur as the darkness complete crawled across the sky. When it was at its darkest, the moment just before the midnight fire lit the west, she ceased her ascent, rotated her body, and ignited her blades. Flame burst to life about them, and she punched the throttle to her wings. Swords held wide to either side, she burned a trail across the blackened sky.

Silver wings shimmering, she streaked over the island of Weshern, wind gusting across her body as she left the rest of the Seraphim behind. Her fire burned and burned, unmistakable in the night. There might not be stars, but there would be twin red lines, the mark of the Phoenix, and all who saw would know. This was her promise to them. This was her open rebellion. Once word of the attack on Fort Luster spread, a single name would be assigned blame. Argus insisted she could give the people hope, and she prayed it was true as she twirled, twisting the burning lines together. Let the people believe her unafraid. Let them see her dance.

Far off in all directions golden wings took flight, their glow easy to see in the darkness. Knights spotting her during their patrols of distant towns. Despite it, Bree grinned. It would take several minutes for the nearest to reach her, and that was only if she remained still…something she had no intention of doing. She shifted her aim eastward, a path leading between two separate far-off knights. Behind her, the midnight fire continued its crawl across the sky. Bree kept her throttle punched to its maximum, and she veered north, then south, ensuring the few she saw rising from ahead would still need time to catch up.

Despite the danger, despite knowing that at least nine angelic knights raced after her, Bree felt free for the first time since meeting with Argus at Glensbee. No more hiding. No more debating the proper course of action. No more denying fire from her swords. She was Weshern's Phoenix, and she would fight for them, and if she must, she would die for them.

Bree glanced up, saw the midnight fire nearly overhead, and curled her back so she rose steeply. It would be tricky timing, but she trusted herself to pull it off. Higher and higher she climbed into the clouds, into the sky beyond. Weshern grew more and more distant, and the chasing knights had to shift their aim ever higher. They'd be watching her, chasing the trail of her swords and the silver shimmer of her wings, both easy to spot when outlined against the darkness.

But the darkness was at an end.

Bree veered so she flew through the heart of a gigantic stretch of clouds, then shut off her wings and banished the flame from her swords. The midnight fire crossed high above her, bathing the world in red. Wings and swords dormant, she'd be nothing but a speck amid the rippling, uneven fire. Eyes closed, she fell, felt the wind blow her hair, felt it push against her arms and legs. The knights would be searching for her, scattering, thinking her fire blocked by the burning sky or the silver of her wings hidden by the clouds. Let them look. Bree had done her part. Weshern knew, as did Center. The Phoenix was now an enemy of the Speaker and all who served him.

Twisting her upper body so that she faced the approaching ground, Bree angled her head downward into a dive. She acted as if her wings were already awake, and she spread her arms, pretending to be a bird descending upon its prey. Weshern approached, vague clusters becoming towns, purple veins becoming rivers and lakes. Bree waited as long as she could, then thrummed her wings back on. She kept the power low, trying just to slow herself as she shifted to fly parallel to the ground instead of straight at it. The change hurt her back, but the power of the wings could not be refused. She skimmed along the ground, so close she could sometimes reach down to brush the grass with her fingers. A glance over her shoulder showed none following, the knights still searching the skies high above. Gradually Bree upped the throttle, and like a shot she raced toward Lowville.

Bree flung her feet before her as she neared her home, changing the angle of the wings so they pushed against her momentum instead of with it. Slowing to a hover, she reduced the throttle, descending gently before the door to Aunt Bethy's house. The door was already open before her feet touched ground, Bethy rushing out to embrace her.

"I saw," she said, clutching Bree tightly. "I saw, you wonderful girl, I saw, and I cannot be more proud."

She was crying. At first Bree thought it was just out of relief, but then her aunt pulled back, blinking away tears, and apologized.

"I'm sorry, Bree," she said, pulling a scrap of paper from within a pocket of her blouse. "A soldier brought me this."

Frowning, Bree took it, angling the paper so the red light of the midnight fire shone upon its letters.

Breanna Skyborn,

Your brother is in my possession. If you care for his safety, come speak with me at the holy mansion. If you do, I swear neither of you will come to harm.

It was signed by the Speaker himself.

"When did you get this?" Bree asked, crumpling the paper in her fist.

"A few hours ago," she said. "I'm sorry, Bree, I didn't know what to do. I didn't know where you were, or how to find you."

Hours ago, thought Bree. Which meant before the attack on the garrison. Before she'd revealed her rebellion to all of Weshern. The Speaker's offer for Kael's safety might no longer be valid. Worse, he might have viewed her showcase as an open refusal of his invitation.

"Bree?"

She looked up. Her aunt was staring at her expectantly. Waiting for a decision.

"It's not safe here any longer," Bree said, her mind made up. "Do you know of a place to hide?"

"If you can get me to Selby, I can hide with the Briars," she said.

Aunt Bethy had married once, when Kael and Bree were toddlers, but her husband had died in an accident in the fields. She'd never remarried, but remained close with his family, the Briars, visiting them on occasion. It was a distant enough relationship that people from Center might not think to search there immediately, and even if they did, it would be difficult to find her given how many places she could hide among the fields.

"That'll work," Bree said. "I can drop you off on the way."

"Way where?" Bethy asked. "To the mansion?"

"No," Bree said. "To Argus. If the Speaker wants a visit, I'll give him one, but I'm not going alone."

CHAPTER
13

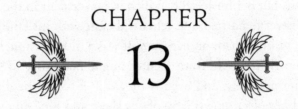

The glow of Bree's light element was fading when she and her aunt landed on the soft grass surrounding the small town of Selby.

"Thank God," Aunt Bethy said as she released her grip about Bree's neck. "I thought my arms would give out before we arrived."

"I'd have caught you before you hit ground," Bree said.

"I'm sure you would have, but it's not an experience I'd enjoy either way."

Bree could hardly argue with that. They'd fled their home on foot, the skies too full of knights to risk flight just yet. After an hour passed, and they'd left Lowville far behind, Bree decided it safe enough to take to the air. Aunt Bethy hung beneath her, her arms around Bree's neck, Bree's arms looped underneath her aunt's shoulders. They'd flown low and steady, skimming a few dozen feet above the ground while a nerve-racked Bree kept her head on a swivel, searching for incoming patrols from all directions. The fact that they'd made it without being spotted felt like a minor miracle.

"You'll need to lie low until Center's removed from Weshern soil," Bree said. "I'm sorry it has to be this way. I should have warned you first so you could prepare."

"Enough, Bree," her aunt said. "You just jammed your finger in the Speaker's eye, and you want to apologize? Worry about yourself, and let me handle my own. The weight on your shoulders is far greater than mine, and far more important."

Before Bree could argue, Bethy grabbed her wrist, forced her close.

"You did the right thing," her aunt said, as if Bree were ten years old once more. "And I'd never make you apologize for doing the right thing."

Bree stared into a face aged by countless hours in the sun and the demands of raising children not her own. Shadows danced across those worry lines, lit by the rippling midnight fire.

"You're right," she said. "But I also put Kael's life in greater danger. If something happens to him, nothing will wash away that guilt. Nothing. Which means we have to hurry. Kael's not going to spend another hour in the Speaker's grasp, not while I'm still breathing."

"Then fly on," Bethy said. "And don't you worry about me. It's not that far a walk to the Briar farm. On land that wide, there's plenty of places for me to hide should Center's soldiers come looking."

Bree flung her arms around her aunt, and she clenched her eyes tightly shut.

"Thank you," she said. "Stay safe, all right?"

"I will, I promise," Aunt Bethy said, holding her close and kissing the top of her head. "Now go. You've a war to fight."

Bree sniffled once but kept herself under control. Stepping back, she waved, thumbed her wings to life, and flew.

So far from Fort Luster, Bree felt safe enough to go full throttle so long as she kept low to the ground. Warwick was fairly close, and she envied the peaceful look of the town as she raced overhead toward the Aquila Forest. Bree spun about to ensure no knights lurked in the distance, then settled down beside the tree line and hurried within.

The mood was jovial when Bree entered the camp. She heard several cheer when they saw her, but it wasn't her name they shouted, but that of the Phoenix. Dozens of Seraphim rushed about, removing wing harnesses, checking gear, and sharing stories. Bree headed toward the leader's tent, not bothering to remove her own wings.

"Hey, did you think you'd get away so easily?"

She turned to find Brad barreling down on her, arms wrapping about her in a bear hug. Despite the weight of her wings, he still managed to lift her two inches off the ground.

"Good to see you, too," she said when he set her back down.

"People started landing, and you weren't with them," Brad said. "Been worried sick about you, especially when your little fire trail in the sky vanished."

"Well, I'm clearly fine," she said, trying to smile. She didn't want Brad to know about Kael, not until she had a plan. It would only worry him without reason. "Sorry to run on you, but I need to speak with Argus."

"Course you do," Brad said, and he gave her a goofy grin. "We kicked their asses tonight, didn't we?"

Worries for her brother aside, she couldn't disagree with that statement.

"That we did," she said, touching his beefy left arm and

giving it a squeeze. "And soon you'll be out there with us, kicking ass in person."

He laughed, and she hurried away, dashing into the command tent. Argus and Rebecca stood in the light of a single candle, poring over numbers the former over-secretary had updated. The commander had removed his wings as well as his black jacket, which hung over the top of a nearby chair.

"Bree!" Argus said when she entered the tent. He smiled wide in the candlelight. "I saw your display, as did half the island. I'm glad you made it back safely."

"We need to talk," Bree said. "It's about Kael."

"I'm sure your brother is safe," Rebecca said, eyes still on her parchment. "He's a resourceful lad, and he'll understand what your signal in the sky meant. He'll find somewhere safe to—"

"No," Bree said, pulling the paper from Rebecca's hand so she'd look up. "A soldier delivered my aunt a letter just before we attacked. The Speaker's captured Kael, and he's holding him prisoner at the holy mansion."

Both froze as if the blood in their veins had turned to ice.

"What does he want?" Argus asked.

"Supposedly for me to speak with him at the mansion. Beyond that, it didn't say."

The two leaders of the resistance glanced to one another, messages passing between them without either needing to speak a word.

"And were you planning to go?" Argus asked carefully.

"Not to speak," Bree said, steeling herself for the expected resistance. "I want to attack."

Blank stares from the both of them.

"Attack?" Rebecca asked. "When? Now?"

"Why not now?" Bree asked. She gestured out the tent.

"Our forces are gathered here, and because of Johan, we have the elements we need. We know where Marius is, right there in the mansion, vulnerable to attack."

"Nothing about him will be vulnerable," Argus said, anger pushing through his calm shell. "He'll be surrounded by the most skilled knights in all of Center, protected inside a mansion designed to withstand an attack by enemy Seraphim. If we're to have any chance, we'd need to surprise him, a task made impossible by the fact we've stirred up every single damn knight in Weshern with our attack on Fort Luster, not to mention that he's *expecting* you. This isn't a plan, Bree. It's a suicide, and I refuse to allow it to happen."

Bree clenched her fists at her sides, telling herself to remain calm.

"You misunderstand me," Bree said. "I *am* going. Whether I go alone, or with an army, is up to you."

"If you do this, you die," Argus said, slamming his fist on the table.

Bree flinched at the noise.

"An opinion I share," she said. "But I'm not staying here while Marius does who-knows-what to my brother. I won't leave Kael's fate in the Speaker's hands. I'm going to take it, and put it in my own."

Argus sighed through clenched teeth, and he glanced to Rebecca. The smaller woman tucked a strand of brown hair away from her face, lips stretched thin across her teeth.

"If Marius died there'd be enormous turmoil in Center while the Erelim picked a new Speaker," she said. "Between the threat of our rebellion and Johan's growing movement, it might cause the new Speaker to sue for peace."

"Might," Argus said, and he gestured to the stack of notes. "Or we fail, and dozens of our Seraphim die in a futile attempt to kill the Speaker and rescue a single captured Seraph. We're still building up our forces and supplies. Why risk it all in a hopeless gamble?"

"Then I go on my own," Bree said, heart pounding in her chest. "Is that a loss you're willing to accept?"

Argus turned to Bree, staring at her as if she were a brand-new person, one he failed to recognize. Outside, a few men shouted, something Bree couldn't make out.

"You overestimate your importance," he said. "You're a symbol, and a powerful fighter, but neither is greater than the lives of all those who'd die tonight. Kael is your brother, but to me, he's one single Seraph. We're not attacking. If you want to rush off and commit suicide, then so be it, but don't try to pass the blame onto me."

Bree felt her resolve breaking.

"I just want to rescue my brother," she said. "Is that so wrong?"

"And I want to keep you, Kael, and all my other Seraphim alive," Argus said. "We don't always get what we want, Bree. Sometimes we have to make do with the least terrible of fates. But..." He looked away momentarily. "I don't want you to think your sacrifices are unacknowledged. We will do all we can to confirm Kael's location and then rescue him the moment it appears feasible."

Bree was surprised by how close she was to tears. More shouts outside, but she ignored them.

"I understand," she said. "I'll stay and await your command."

Argus started to reach toward her, for an embrace or pat on her shoulder, she didn't know, but he pulled back and instead thudded a fist against his breast.

"You were beautiful tonight," he said. "It was a privilege to fly at your side."

And then a shard of ice pierced a hole through their tent and struck Argus across the temple.

Blood splattered as Argus's head snapped to the side. His eyes rolled, a strange mutter escaping his lips as he dropped limp to the dirt with a muted thud. Bree screamed, her entire body freezing in place. Rebecca dropped to Argus's side, amber eyes scanning his wound in the dim light. Bree forced herself to act, but before she'd taken a single step a blade pushed through the hole created by the ice lance and cut downward, ripping open a new entrance.

What stepped through made no sense to Bree. It was a man wrapped head to toe in black cloth, with only a single gap left for his eyes. In his left hand he held a short blade, one side smooth and sharp, the other viciously serrated. His right hand bore a silver Seraph's gauntlet, only he wore no wings. Instead the wires at the base of the gauntlet connected with a small metal cylinder strapped between his shoulder blades. The man spotted Bree and lifted his gauntlet. Blue light shimmered from the focal point, and Bree twisted to one side while drawing her swords. A shard of ice launched from the man's gauntlet, striking the metal of her wings. The ice shattered, leaving a deep dent that might interfere with the wing's proper functioning. At the moment, Bree couldn't care. All that mattered was closing the distance so her swords could do their work.

Bree launched herself forward while rotating, right blade lashing out for her foe's neck, left following up with a chop at his shoulder. The wingless man flung his gauntlet in the way of the first, Bree's sword clanging off the thick steel, hardly leaving a dent. With the other hand he pushed up with his sword, stepped closer while ducking underneath, and then thrust for Bree's chest. Poorly positioned, Bree retreated, using both blades to ward off a series of slashes. When she reached the edge of the tent, she braced for another barrage, but instead he stopped, gauntlet rising.

Rebecca lunged from the ground, shoving his elbow upward and saving Bree's life. The ice lance shot high, ripping another hole in the top of the tent. The man pulled free of her grasp, then swung his arm back, elbow leading. It crashed against her nose, blasting blood down across her lips and neck. She crumpled, but Bree rushed in before he could finish her off, taking the offensive with a series of thrusts and cuts she knew would have made Dean proud. Despite her skill, her foe danced around her, and not once did she draw blood. He was faster than her, more fluid, but she had one advantage. By blocking her swords with his gauntlet, it showed he didn't know who she was, and what she could do.

Bree parried a swipe, flung herself to one side to avoid another shot of ice, and then swung her right blade for his neck. As she'd hoped, he used his gauntlet to block while simultaneously setting his sword up for a killing thrust…only this time Bree activated the fire of her prism just prior to contact. The flame burst to life, hot and vicious. Compared to it, the metal of the gauntlet meant nothing. Her sword tore through steel, flesh, and then bone, severing the hand and gauntlet from the man's arm before continuing on. Quick as the fire appeared, Bree banished it right before her sword sliced open his jugular.

The last thing she wanted was her fire to seal the wound.

Her foe collapsed to his knees, then crumpled face-first into the dirt, blood gushing from his neck.

"What was that?" Bree asked, pointing a bloody blade at the black-garbed man.

"A specter," Rebecca said, returning to Argus's side. She pressed his jacket against the wound on his head, attempting to stanch the bleeding. "Wingless assassins from Center. You need to get out of here, Bree, now!"

"But what about him?"

Rebecca glanced up, blood still trickling from her nose. Outside, screams of fear and pain sang a grim chorus.

"The least terrible of fates," she echoed. "If specters are here, so are Center's knights. The camp is lost. Flee, Breanna. Flee to fight another day."

She wanted to argue, but she knew once Rebecca made up her mind, no force in the world would change it. Stone in her throat, she saluted with her sword.

"It was an honor fighting for you," Bree said, and before guilt could stop her, she pushed open the tent flap and stepped outside.

The entire camp was in chaos. Fires burned throughout, both trees and tents. Scorch marks covered the ground from blasts of lightning. Specters weaved through the camp, gauntlets unleashing endless streams of elements as they danced from prey to prey. Some Seraphim battled, others fled, weaving through the trunks as they flew higher. Those without wings could only run from the specters. Most died, shards of ice shattering their spines and bolts of lightning exploding their hearts in their chests. High above, wings thrummed. Stones crashed through the branches, crushing tent and bone alike as they slammed down. Balls of flame followed, exploding into rolling plumes upon hitting ground.

Bree couldn't take it all in, could barely fathom what she was seeing. So many bodies. So many dead. Releasing her fire, she bathed her twin blades. She'd promised to flee, but too many were helpless. She had to buy them time. Spotting the nearest specter, she poured life into her wings and flew. The specter's back was to her, and she died instantly, Bree's swords ramming through her back and out her chest. Pushing the body forward, Bree tilted upward, ripping her weapons free in an explosion of gore. Another specter spotted her, and he raised a gauntlet, tracking her flight. Bree curled right, and his shot of lightning thundered into the trunk of a tree instead.

Looping down, she killed her wings, and let her momentum carry her closer. She flung herself feet-forward, heels slamming the specter's back when he turned to run. He dropped, and Bree scissor-cut her burning blades across his neck, ending him.

"Bree!"

Hearing her name, she turned, saw Brad running toward her. He held a sword in his left hand. Blood covered his face and chest, and she wondered if it was his or not.

"What are you doing?" she screamed at him. "Get out of here!"

"I will!" he shouted back. "Once you have."

Bree heard another wave coming from up high, and she sheathed her swords and burst ahead, grabbing Brad by the shoulders as her wings carried both of them forward. The ground shook as a barrage of stone fell like an unreal hail, one boulder sinking a foot into the dirt where Brad had previously stood. Bree saw a Seraph and specter locked in battle simultaneously crushed by a boulder, saw another die as his head caved in from the force of an icicle's fall. Another pass of flame, this one setting alight every overhead branch so that it appeared the midnight fire had come in the daytime hour.

"We're almost out!" Bree shouted into Brad's ear. Her arms strained to carry Brad, and it felt as if her wings dragged sluggishly with every turn. Brad started to respond, but was given no chance. A blur of blue passed over Bree's head, then a great weight slammed against her wings. She twisted, cried out. Brad slipped from her arms, hit the ground rolling. Bree shut off her wings, needing control more than speed. Her wings clipped a tree, jammed her the other way, and then she was on the ground rolling. The bending and screeching of metal filled her ears, coupled with a tremendous ache in her back.

Screaming out her pain, Bree staggered to her feet, her entire lower back burning with pain. A glance over her shoulder showed her wings a broken mess.

"Brad?" she called out, retracing her path. "Brad!"

"Here," Brad said, leaning against a tree. She rushed to him as he smiled at her groggily. Blood trickled down his neck from a gaping wound across the top of his head. "That hurt," he said.

"I know," Bree said. "I know, but we have to run, all right? We have to run."

No one else was fighting. The world was fire and smoke, and those she could see through the haze were fleeing in all directions. Bree grabbed Brad's hand. He held it but showed no desire to move.

"Run," Bree said, pulling on his wrist. "We have to run, damn it!"

He didn't budge an inch. Another hand grabbed Brad's, and Bree turned to see Saul beside her. He lacked his wings, but he did wield a sword in his free hand.

"It's not a suggestion, you gigantic oaf," he said, yanking Brad off the bark. "We're moving."

Brad's legs moved, his balance uneven, but it was enough. Together the three fled deeper into the forest, Bree and Saul each supporting a shoulder.

"We have to find somewhere to hide until it's safe," Saul said.

"There's nowhere," Bree said, glancing at Brad. Her worry grew. His eyes were never focused quite right, and it seemed an awful lot of blood covered his neck. "They're burning down the whole forest."

"Then we go until we're out of the—"

Lightning ripped through the three of them from behind. The force sent Bree crashing into another tree, Brad to the ground. She heard the metal of her wings bending amid the ringing of her ears. Bree pushed off it, fell to her knees, and grabbed Brad by the shoulders.

"Get up," she said, voice hoarse and barely audible through the ringing in her ears. "Brad, get up."

He didn't move. His eyes were wide, his mouth open, but he wasn't moving.

"Brad," Bree said, and she clutched the cloth of his shirt, bunched it in her fists. "Brad, please, get up now, damn it, get up!"

He wasn't moving. He wasn't breathing. Bree looked up, saw through tears and smoke a specter chasing after a fleeing Saul. Looked down, saw a dead man. Not her friend. Not the joking, always ready to smile Brad. Just a dead man, heart ruptured by lightning, eyes locked open in the shock of death. Bree felt paralyzed, her mind melding into horror and anguish. She wouldn't escape. None of them would.

"I'm sorry, Kael," she whispered. There'd be no rescuing him, not anymore.

Something hard struck the back of her head, and she lurched, stomach performing loops. Hands grabbed her, rolled her onto her broken wings. A foot pressed down on each of her wrists as two specters pinned her in place. Bree cried out at the pain. Approaching through the smoke was a pale-skinned blond woman wearing the red robes of the theotechs. A smile was on her face.

"Hello, Breanna," she said, kneeling down before her. Her blue eyes sparkled with excitement. "I'm so very, very happy to meet you."

She looked to the specters.

"Bring her to the cathedral. Save the rest for execution."

"As you wish, Er'el Jaina."

Swords cut across the buckles of her harness, separating her from her wings. Bree struggled to raise her swords, failed. A thick cloth covered her eyes, and she screamed in protest until another solid blow to the temple knocked her out cold.

CHAPTER

14

When Kael couldn't walk, which was often, they dragged him across the hard stone road. Three knights had joined the trio of theotechs, two holding the length of rope they'd tied around his wrists. Kael's shirt was torn, his back bleeding from a multitude of cuts and scratches. Simply walking took his breath away, the aftereffects of the lightning from the theotech's gauntlet leaving his legs rubbery and weak. Not that he didn't try. The pain in his legs was better than the dragging.

They were passing through the heart of Byrntown on their way to the Crystal Cathedral when his legs gave out again. His knees hit cobbles, and he cried out at the pain. One yanked on the rope, attempting to jostle him back to his feet, but it only sent him lurching forward. Hands held up, he couldn't brace himself before his face hit the street. His forehead smacked stone, and his vision swam with color.

"Careful with the boy," one of the theotechs snapped. "Er'el Jaina wants him unharmed."

"We're long past chance of that," said the knight who'd yanked the rope. "He'll be breathing. That's good enough."

Kael curled into a ball, fighting to regain his composure. The world was spinning around him, the reds and yellows dancing across his sight. If he didn't stand soon, they'd start dragging again. His back was already on fire; he couldn't bear another mile or two of that. Breathe in, breathe out, nice and steady, but his attempt to rise was thoroughly ignored by his legs. He expected a yank on his rope, but it didn't come. Instead, the first theotech stepped closer to the knight and raised his voice.

"Good enough?" he asked. "Are you privy to the Er'el's plans? Do you know what she wishes to do with the boy? Or why he's important? Hostage, torture, experimentation, any of these for certain?"

The red of his robes floated before Kael's face. The knight backed down, and he cleared his throat before answering.

"No, I don't."

"Then listen when I speak instead of correcting me. The boy is to be delivered unharmed. A few scrapes shouldn't matter, but cracking his head open on the cobblestones damn well might."

Kael grabbed the hem of the theotech's robe and peered up at the man. It took all his concentration, but he forced out the words.

"Not...a boy," he said. "You prick."

The theotech, an ugly man with a milky left eye, grinned as he knelt beside him.

"Still some fight left in you even after all that?" he said. "I'm almost impressed." He lifted his gauntlet, opening his fingers wide enough to reveal the focal point, which sparked with faint yellow light. His other hand grabbed Kael's chin, preventing him from looking away.

"I can flood you with pain without causing any permanent harm," he said. "Insult me again, and I will drain my prism dry. It will take hours, Kael. I'll enjoy every minute of it. Will you?"

Kael bit his tongue, knowing any response he gave might put him in an even worse situation. Not that it could get much worse. Whatever this Jaina wanted with him, he highly doubted it was going to be pleasant. At least he might save himself a few jolts from the theotech's gauntlet. He'd had more than his fill back at the holy mansion.

"A wise decision," the theotech said. He smirked as he glanced at the nearby knight. "Get the boy up."

Kael grinded his teeth together as both knights pulled on the rope, lifting him to his feet.

"Keep him walking," another of the theotechs said. "Brace his shoulders if you must."

Kael's feet moved sluggishly below him as they approached Byrntown's center square. He still couldn't consistently maintain his balance, which forced both knights to grab a forearm and guide him along. The cobbles reflected the rippling light of the midnight fire, and Kael watched it with a growing detachment. His part in the rebellion against Center was done. Whatever he might have hoped to achieve with his life, it was over. Only the end awaited. Only the amount of pain he'd suffer mattered.

"Hold up," one of the knights said, stopping them in the center of the square.

"Why must we—"

"I said hold up!"

The milky-eyed theotech fell silent. Kael stood still, and he forced his eyes up from the cobbles. What was going on? What bothered the knight so? All he saw around him were squat rectangular homes, plus the burning sky above. Yet all three knights had drawn their swords, and light shimmered across the surface of their golden wings.

"We're being followed," the first knight said. "If we're to have Kael arrive safely, we need to fly, and now."

"Nonsense," said Milky-eye. "Who could possibly be a threat to three knights of—"

A blast of lightning ripped through the center of their group, connecting with one knight directly in the chest. The others spun about and readied their weapons. Kael spotted a man in brown robes lying flat atop the roof of a nearby home, gauntlet held out before him, aiming for a second shot. Milky-eye responded with one of his own, striking the man in the forehead. His smoking corpse went limp, arm still hanging over the edge of the rooftop.

Kael didn't have the strength to run, but he'd resist any way he could. The other two knights tugged on his rope, but Kael dropped to the ground, refusing to move.

"Get the hell up!" one shouted, kicking him in the ribs. It hurt, but Kael could endure some pain if it meant buying time for the ambushers. Shouts sounded from both up and down the road. More lightning flashed from one theotech's gauntlet, as did thin lances of ice from the other's. Kael watched two more men ascend the rooftops as shards of stone crashed frighteningly close by. The three theotechs scattered as they dodged, the two with gauntlets returning volleys as best they could. Craning his neck to see over his shoulder, he spotted another man in brown racing closer, a long blade in hand. He rushed the theotech who, lacking a gauntlet, instead wielded a long dagger.

"Back to us!" one knight yelled, flinging a ball of flame at the ambusher. It clipped the ambusher's arm, eliciting a howl of pain. Legs still kicking, he collided with the theotech. The theotech's dagger sank deep into the chest of the man, who fell atop him. Blood poured across his red robes, the corpse pinning him to the ground. The ambushers wasted no opportunity. Kael winced as a barrage of stones smashed both bodies into a puddle of blood and gore. The knight holding his rope flicked his wrist, bathing the entire rooftop with flame, but the ambushers were already gone, sliding down the other side of the building.

Kael watched three brown-robed men with long spears seal off the road. The milky-eyed theotech struck down one with lightning from his gauntlet, but the other two successfully flung their spears. One pierced him in the chest, the other his belly. He crumpled to his knees and then slumped forward, the spear shafts propping him up in place.

A man and a woman, both wielding swords, rushed the last surviving theotech from another corner of the intersection. Her back was to them, but she heard their approach and turned, ice erupting from her gauntlet. The shards were thin, rapid, cutting deep into their flesh. One stumbled and fell, a pool of blood beneath her, while the other closed the distance and swung his sword at the wires connecting the theotech's gauntlet to the pack on her back, successfully disarming her of her ice. His free hand struck the theotech across the face, sending her to the ground.

"Damn it," said one of the two knights holding Kael's rope. His wings flickered as he gave himself a burst of speed, bounding dozens of feet with a single leap. A thin jet of flame preceded his landing, boring into the ambusher's chest with enough force to deny him the killing blow. The injured theotech rolled, and the knight landed in her place, sword already swinging. It sliced cleanly through his abdomen. The body crumpled, and the knight turned to see if the theotech was all right.

The moment his back was turned, a familiar figure burst from around the corner of the nearby home, hood off to reveal the spiderweb of scars across his bald head. Johan wielded a blade in one hand, a gold gauntlet in the other, and he rushed the knight with furious speed. The theotech saw, screamed, and the knight spun with finely honed reflexes, barely blocking Johan's overhead chop in time. The knight's wings flared bright, and with his greater weight and armor, he tried to bowl over the smaller man. Johan twirled, deftly avoiding the charge, and in mid-twist he lashed out with his sword. The blade jammed into the knight's side, piercing up to the hilt through the gap in armor just underneath his armpit.

Johan released his sword as the knight's momentum sent his body crashing to the cobblestone. The fingers of his gauntlet spread wide, the focal point flaring red as it centered on the injured theotech. A gout of fire bathed across her, charring every inch of her body. Her dying screams were awful, but thankfully did not last long.

"Shit," the final knight said, and his wings flared a brilliant gold as he went shooting into the air. Kael screamed as the rope yanked him about, tightened, and began lifting him off the ground. Johan spun, another ball of flame shooting from his gauntlet. The ball slammed into the rope halfway up, searing it in half. Kael dropped to the street, landing painfully.

Johan retrieved his sword from the knight's corpse, then strode over to where Kael lay on his back. Three quick cuts and the ropes were off.

"Mr. Skyborn," he said, sheathing the sword and offering his hand. "It's a pleasure to meet you again, and under far better circumstances."

Kael had to choke down a laugh as he accepted the hand and rose to his feet.

"Better circumstances?" he asked, rubbing his painful back.

"Indeed, better," Johan said. "Your Seraphim defeated Center's soldiers occupying Fort Luster, and your sister burned a scar of fire across the crawling darkness. Two victories against Center, each in their own way, and I am glad to see them both."

"Forgive me if I'm not up for celebrating," Kael said. The remaining disciples gathered around him, at least nine in number. They each wore identical brown robes, and a few bore silver wingless gauntlets. "So where to now?"

"Now we get you to safety before that knight alerts others," Johan said, and he nodded to one of the men nearby. "Ready the wagon. The rest of you, return to your hiding places."

The nine crossed their arms over their chests in salute, then scattered. Johan followed the one tasked with the wagon, and when Kael stumbled after, Johan reached out and grabbed his arm.

"Lean on me if you must," he said. "We do not have time to tarry. The knights of Center are hornets, and your Seraphim struck one of their hives. They'll be swarming the sky for hours, and it's best we go far from here while they do."

Kael accepted his help, and they hobbled down the street. Several houses down waited a covered wagon, a lone donkey bridled at the front. The disciple sat at the front, and he'd shed his brown robe for less incriminating plainclothes. Johan led Kael around to the back, and together they climbed inside.

"We have a long journey, and the going will be slow," Johan said as Kael made himself comfortable. One corner of the wagon had a blanket, and he slumped into it and wrapped it about his shoulders. The wagon shook, the wheels rattling atop the cobbles as the donkey began to pull. Hidden from the skies, Kael finally allowed himself to relax. His muscles were painfully tired, much of his body bruised or sore, and no matter what position he put himself in, the cuts on his back were a constant bother.

"Are your injuries severe?" Johan asked, sensing his discomfort.

"I'll live," Kael said. Shivering, he closed his eyes and leaned his head against one of the sideboards. "How'd you know? That I needed help, I mean."

"We've had eyes on you for a while now, Kael, and have ever since Weshern's occupation. Your sister was a potential face of the growing rebellion, which meant you'd soon be a target for retaliation." He heard Johan chuckle. "Though I must admit, I did not expect you to be taken while inside the holy mansion."

Kael tried not to let it bother him, and he knew he was being sensitive. Of course they were watching him because of his sister. Without her, he was just another Seraph.

"I have friends in high places," Kael said, deciding not to mention Clara by name, nor his relationship with her. He was still unsure of how Johan might view her and the rest of the royal family. Kael had a feeling it was poorly.

"So I've noticed. Hopefully such friendships will prove useful during this blossoming war."

Kael's turn to chuckle.

"You're hardly the first to think so."

He heard a creak of wood, and he opened an eyelid to see Johan leaning closer, a frown on his face.

"You sound bitter," he said. "Do not diminish yourself because of your sister. If the theotechs want you dead, then I want you alive, no matter who you are. You're a skilled ally, and your Seraphim training makes you invaluable to this resistance."

"So you'd have staged this same ambush if my last name weren't Skyborn?"

"I cannot decide, are you merely proud, or slow in the mind?" Johan said, a fire burning in his blue eyes. "Like it or not, you are connected to your sister. If you were tortured, or held for ransom, it might compromise her will to fight. That I cannot allow. You are not without worth, nor is your worth defined solely by your own life. I will not lie to you to soothe your bruised feelings."

Kael closed his eyes, and he told himself over and over to stop being stupid. The mention of his sister jostled memories out of him, his conversation with the Speaker, and he fought to keep calm.

"Before they sent me away, I spoke with Marius," Kael said. "There's a traitor in the Weshern rebel camp, and Center's army is already preparing an invasion. You need to send them warning."

Johan's face darkened.

"I see," he said. "I'll send a runner to the Aquila Forest immediately."

"You know of the camp?"

"My eyes are everywhere, remember?" he said. "Don't worry. Nearly every word leaving Marius's lips is a lie, and no doubt this was a lie meant to break you as well."

"Let's hope so," Kael said, not so convinced. He shifted some more, trying to get comfortable while Johan called over one of his disciples and relayed an order for them to make their way to Camp Aquila. The disciple nodded, ducked his head back out from underneath the heavy tarp. The wagon hit a deep hole in the road, and Kael winced. The movement scraped his back across the wood, and he felt blood trickling down his spine. He sat up, bunching the blanket tighter for him to lean against.

"So where are you taking me?" he asked, settling back down. The exhaustion, the pain, and the stress of the night were all threatening to steal his consciousness away, and he fought to keep his eyes open.

"To my main base of operations on Weshern," Johan said.

"And where is that?"

"I'd hate to spoil the surprise. That, and if we're attacked before we arrive, I'd rather you not know."

"Glad you trust me so well."

Johan pulled his hood back over his head, hiding his many scars.

"It is not a matter of trust," he said, "but experience."

Kael decided the only appropriate reaction was to laugh. Closing his eyes, he abandoned his fight for consciousness and let the steady rattle of the wagon's wheels rock him away. Time passed as he drifted in and out, soft conversations between Johan and his disciples an indecipherable mumble to his ears.

Kael didn't know how long he actually slept before Johan tapped him on the leg, waking him.

"We're almost there," the man said.

Kael rubbed at his eyes as he sat up.

"And where is there?" he asked.

The robed man gestured to the closed flap.

"See for yourself."

Kael carefully climbed to the back of the wagon and pulled open the rough white canvas. What he saw was a town like any other, except for one key difference. Pieces of red cloth floated from nearly every home and street sign.

"We're in New Galen," Kael said.

"Indeed we are," Johan said, and there was no containing

his smug amusement. "Center's eyes are elsewhere, hunting for Weshern rebellion. But here? This is a new land for everyone, full of orphans and widows and wealthy living among the poor. No one will think twice at seeing an unrecognizable face. Its founding was chaos, and during the relocation of Galen citizens, it was child's play to bring my own people in."

Kael had to admit it was brilliant. Even if some of the theotechs had a suspicion Johan was hiding within the town, sending a search party risked igniting riots in an already riled and angry populace.

"What happens next?" he asked as he closed the flap and sat back down.

"We keep pushing," Johan said. "Sparks are landing everywhere, and it is up to us to ensure they become wildfire. The resistance is isolated here in Weshern, but I have eyes and ears in all other islands. Marius's invasion of your home has frightened everyone. My words of warning reach ears that were once closed to my wisdom. Protests gather at the royal cathedrals of Elern, Candren, and Sothren. People demanding answers, wanting to know what actually happened to bring Galen crashing to the ocean."

"No protests here?" Kael asked.

Johan smiled.

"What need of protests do I have when your people already outright rebel?" he asked.

The wagon halted, and Johan rose to his feet, head ducked to prevent hitting the covering.

"We're here," he said, pushing aside the flap and stepping out.

The building was larger than the others nearby, two stories tall and containing dozens of windows. One of the newer complexes meant to house multiple families, a rare sight on Weshern though he'd heard they were commonplace on Center. The roof was completely flat, and a man in brown robes stood atop it, acting as a sentry.

"How do you go about unnoticed?" Kael asked as he exited the wagon.

"I've purchased several of the nearby buildings to function as armories or storage," Johan explained. "And several other homes were given to us as gifts to house my members. It may surprise you, Kael, but even the people of Galen wish to see justice brought upon the true destroyer of their nation. Few believe the Speaker's lies when it comes to Weshern's guilt."

Inside the building was dark and crowded, the hallways uncomfortably narrow. Past two side doors they reached the stairs, and Johan led him up to the second floor.

"This will be your room for now," he said as he stopped before a door at the far end of the hall. "It's the best I can do given the circumstances. We have better rooms in distant houses, but I'd prefer to keep someone so important close by."

Inside was remarkably small, hardly enough room to fit the tiny bed. There was no place to store his personal belongings, so he removed his jacket, folded it, and put it in the corner beside the bed.

"It'll do," Kael said. "Thank you."

Johan bowed.

"I'll give you some privacy," he said. "I'm sure you could use the rest."

"Thank you," Kael said.

After his brief nap, Kael didn't expect much sleep, but lying down on something cushioned was far better than the rough wood of the wagon. Grunting at the soreness of his muscles, he lay down, closed his eyes, and let the tense minutes tick away.

Child?

Kael's eyes fluttered open. The room was dark, muddled,

lacking in detail. Sounds were muted, as if he were underwater. A face floated before him, beaming with light. Every feature was smooth, crystalline, perfect. There were no lips to open, no tongue to move, yet again he heard words.

Come to me, blessed child. We must speak.

Before he could answer, two loud knocks sounded from the door. Kael felt his body jerk upward in his bed. He wiped his forehead, felt cold sweat across it. His heart pounded in his chest. The face was gone, the room returned to normal.

A dream, Kael told himself, but he hardly believed it. Before he could dwell on it further, the door to his room opened, and Johan stepped inside without waiting for permission to enter. The robed man crossed his arms, and he used his shoulder to close the door behind him. His face was passive, but Kael didn't trust it one bit.

"Kael, I'm sorry to have to tell you this," he said. "The resistance camp inside Aquila Forest was attacked before my warning could arrive. Parts of the forest are currently aflame. It looks like the Speaker sent both ground and air forces to surround it, a skillfully coordinated attack."

Kael slumped down into his bed, head thudding against the thin wall. He forced his thoughts to push through the fog his slumber had created.

"Did any survive?" he asked. It was obvious who he truly asked about, and Johan answered accordingly.

"We've received no word of your sister, either dead, alive, or captured," he said. "Seraphim fled in all directions, and Aquila Forest is vast enough for people to hide within for days without being found." He put a hand on Kael's shoulder. "Once Marius pulls back his forces we'll send people in to search for survivors, as well as put out the call for those who escaped to join us here. Weshern's resistance will not die tonight, I promise. I won't let it."

Kael glanced up at the scarred man.

"You promise miracles," he said. "But then again, you always have, haven't you?"

Johan withdrew his hand.

"Rest for the night," he said. "Come the morning mist, we'll discover the true extent of the damage. Try not to worry. Your sister is a warrior, a true survivor. Wherever she is, she will endure."

The strange man left. Kael lay on his back, arm across his eyes, and prayed Johan was right.

CHAPTER

15

Bree awoke blindfolded, a burning liquid being poured down her throat. She coughed and gagged, but couldn't move otherwise. She lay bound on wood, that she was certain, her groggy mind distantly aware of a sense of motion as well. A wagon, perhaps. She didn't have much time to dwell on it, for the liquid she'd drank set her stomach to cramping and her head swimming.

"Just sleep," she heard Jaina say. "It's best for everyone that way."

Bree would have loved to deny her, but she had no choice. Her eyes closed behind the blindfold, and her consciousness blinked away.

When Bree emerged from the fog she was lying on her back atop a table. The ceiling above her was pale white, softly lit by a glowing light prism. Four leather straps bound her to the table, buckled painfully tight so that they dug into her skin. She heard a fire crackling near her head, its heat uncomfortable. Her clothes were different, a simple white linen shirt and pants that ended just below her knees. Someone had stripped and changed her while she slept, and the realization made her feel terribly violated.

"Where am I?" she asked. She craned her neck, trying to better see her surroundings. The walls were stone, the floors tile. Like everything else, they were a pale white. The room was thin and long, the walls to either side of her close while the space beyond her feet stretched out for a hundred yards. All of it was completely empty.

"Where am I!" she asked, this time screaming. Her voice echoed in the room, and still it went unanswered. She struggled against the leather straps. Her arms were bound at the elbows, but her hands were free, and she flailed them about, searching for a buckle or loop she could undo.

"She's finally awake," a familiar and now-hated voice spoke. Bree tensed as Jaina stepped around her table. Her hair was tied tightly behind her head with gold ribbons, her red robes immaculately clean. In her left hand she held an obsidian-handled knife.

"What the hell do you want with me?" Bree asked, but Jaina paid her no attention. A door opened behind her, she heard the shuffling of feet and the swish of robes. Several more theotechs joined the room, standing to either side of Bree. A man grabbed her left arm while Jaina grabbed her right by the wrist. Without warning or explanation, Jaina drew the knife's blade across Bree's palm and then put it away. Bree clenched her teeth against the pain, and she laid her head back down on the table.

More movement behind her, and a louder crackling of fire.

She heard a long, groaning creak, like the opening of a metal door or grate to a furnace. The heat blazed hotter so that sweat trickled down her neck and forehead.

"I've got it," a man said, and then Bree flinched at a sudden high-pitched shriek. Bree tilted her head back, but she only saw the top of what indeed appeared to be a furnace. The shriek ended as quickly as it started. Jaina reached out with her free hand, accepted something, and then placed it onto Bree's bleeding palm. It was a small red fire prism, and Bree cried out as both the prism and her blood burst into flame. Her skin blistered from the heat, yet when she tried to fling the prism away, Jaina grabbed her wrist with both hands and put all her weight on them, pinning her to the table. The fire lessened, much of her blood burning away to ash, until its flow from her cut palm ceased completely. The fire had seared the wound shut, ending the bleeding.

"The blood's reaction to the prism is within expectations," Jaina said. She removed the prism, handed it over. "Bring me an empty."

"Yes, Er'el," said one of the other theotechs.

She heard movement behind her, a shuffling of drawers. Jaina watched, then moved to join whatever was happening. The two discussed something, too softly for Bree to hear as more objects rattled about. There had to be a table or shelf of supplies near her head, Bree knew, but what was the purpose of the furnace? Why must she be so close, and the thing so damn hot? She couldn't dwell on it further, for Jaina reappeared, once more holding her obsidian dagger.

Bree screamed as Jaina reopened the cut on her palm, the pain far worse the second time around. She flailed her upper body, forcing a theotech to aid Jaina in holding her down. The Er'el put another prism in her palm, this one cracked and faded, the heart of it a smoky black. Bree winced, only this time she felt no pain. No flame. Instead, the prism shimmered, the black of the interior glowing like a dying ember suddenly exposed to wind. It swelled and swelled until it was a solid crimson, with only the cracks to show it was any different from the prisms Bree had accepted countless times during her training. The whole time a numbing sensation spread up Bree's arm, her strength draining away as if by leeches.

"Unbelievable," muttered one of the theotechs watching.

With the prism's return to color came the fire, flicking across her palm, but this time Jaina removed the prism with a pair of tongs before it could burn her flesh too badly.

"Subject's blood reinvigorates depleted prisms," Jaina said, speaking to someone over her shoulder. "Proceeding to gauntlet interaction tests."

"No!" Bree screamed, thrashing against her bonds. "No, enough, tell me where I am. Tell me what you want!"

Jaina grabbed Bree by the chin and held her still. She leaned in so close their noses nearly touched.

"Your blood may provide the way to a safer, better future," she said. "What I want is your cooperation."

Bree spat at her, missing her face and instead hitting the collar of her dress. Jaina didn't even flinch.

"Stand her up," she ordered her theotechs.

Bree heard a loud bolt releasing beneath her table, and then she was tilting. Still strapped down, they rotated the table ninety degrees forward. The bottom hit the floor with a thud. The straps holding her sagged, and she slid downward until her toes touched the cold tile. A theotech grabbed her right arm; another strapped a gold Seraphim gauntlet over her hand and wrist. While a normal gauntlet slid on smoothly and comfortably, this one hurt: a sharp needle halfway up her forearm jammed deep into her flesh as they tightened the buckles. Bree clenched her teeth together as it dug in deeper and deeper.

"Is the connection solid?" Jaina asked, examining the gauntlet.

"I don't know," Bree said. "Try it on for yourself and see."

Jaina continued examining the gauntlet, not bothering to look at her when she spoke.

"Urth, prepare a gag in case the subject refuses to be silent."

Bree glared but did not respond. Through the thick glass protector of the gauntlet she saw a red elemental prism softly pulsing. Filling the prism chamber halfway, and continuing to fill it, was her own blood. It swam over the prism, slowly hiding it from view. Before Bree could ponder the consequences, a theotech grabbed her gauntlet at the wrist and extended it forward. Jaina put on a gauntlet of her own, and she pressed it to Bree's neck.

"Activate it," she said.

"No."

The gauntlet tightened, and Jaina leaned closer, whispering into her ear.

"I can make you, Breanna. It will hurt, but you will release the fire within the prism. Cooperation will save you that pain."

Bree stared straight ahead, refusing to answer. Jaina tsked in her ear.

"Very well."

Jaina's gauntlet shifted, the focal point pressing against the base of Bree's neck. She heard a crackle, and then electricity flooded through her. Every muscle in her body tensed, and she'd have cried out if her tongue and lips cooperated. Her fingers widened, gauntlet still held firm by a theotech. Black flashed over her vision, and then she felt the tiniest of cracks within her mind. Fire burst out of her gauntlet, traveling in a great stream to the far side of the lengthy room. It splashed against the wall, charring a black smear across the stone.

Jaina ceased the lightning, but Bree could not cease the fire. It was wild as it always was, for Bree had no sword to center it on, nothing to narrow down its focus. It roared and roared until it ended, the prism drained. Bree slumped against the restraints, and she gasped in ragged breaths. It felt like she'd sprinted a lap around the academy without pausing for rest. Jaina leaned closer to Bree's gauntlet, observing the prism inside.

"Again," Jaina said.

"It's empty," Bree argued.

"I said *again*."

Another jolt of lightning coursed through her, igniting her nerves. Bree felt the connection between her and the prism reactivate, felt her jaw lock tight. Her entire body convulsed, and blood pooled in her mouth as her teeth clenched down on her tongue. Fire burst from her quivering gauntlet, another tremendous stream that shot across the room and splashed like liquid against the far wall. On and on went the stream, not quite as long as before, but each second felt like an eternity to Bree.

Finally the electricity stopped, and Bree hung there, lacking the strength to stand.

"Damn it," Jaina said as Bree stared at the blur that was the floor, blood dribbling down her lips and landing in vibrant spots upon the white tile. "Someone get me a cloth so she doesn't bite her tongue again."

One theotech lifted her head, another dabbed at the blood.

"Keep firing," Jaina said. "Or I will use the electricity again."

"It's... empty," Bree said, desperately wishing that were true.

"It was," Jaina said. "But not anymore."

The theotech shoved the cloth in her mouth, and Jaina sparked life into her gauntlet, letting the power race up and down Bree's spine. Tears trickling down her face, Bree watched a third stream of fire scorch the distant wall, then a fourth, then a fifth. Each one left her more drained than the last. By the sixth time, her consciousness flitted in and out, like a bird flying just shy of her reach. The white room spun, walls became ceiling, ceiling became floor. Jaina spoke with the theotechs, but Bree could no longer understand what they were saying. It took too much effort, and she had none left to give.

Another burst of fire. She barely noticed its heat, the flame pathetically small compared to the first few attempts. Despite this, it was the most horrible of the lot. She felt her mind breaking, felt her heart hammer in her chest as if it were about to explode. Worried voices chattered in her ears, speaking gibberish. The fire ceased. The straps around her body suddenly loosened, then were removed completely. Bree dropped to her knees, then landed in a limp sprawl upon the bloodstained tile. It should have hurt, but she was too numb to feel it.

I'm dreaming, Bree thought. Her head had turned to face the back of the room upon hitting the floor, and she stared at the furnace behind her bed. *I'm not here, only dreaming.*

Creatures stirred within the fire, black fingers slipping through the thin cracks of the grate. Red eyes peered out intently. Watching her.

She had to be dreaming, because if not, she'd lost her mind.

Eyes closed, she let the distant, worried voices lull her away as hands grabbed her arms and legs. *A dream,* her mind insisted. *Just a dream.*

The crackling sound of the furnace mocked her plea, mocked it with the shrill laughter of the creatures writhing within the smoldering fire.

CHAPTER

16

The waiting was the worst of it. Kael sat on his bed as the day crawled along, peering out the window at the sleepy street while wishing there was something he could do. There was too much risk someone in New Galen might recognize him, and according to Johan, signs bearing crude drawings of his face were already going up across Weshern, declaring him a fugitive with a substantial reward for his capture. In his tiny room he stayed, bored and frustrated, so that when his door opened, and a brown-robed disciple beckoned him to follow, Kael was torn between hope and fear. Hope that he might have something to do. Fear that the reason for the visit involved the fate of his sister.

"Is something wrong?" he asked, sliding off his bed.

The disciple, a smoothly shaven young man with enormous ears, shook his head.

"Johan desires your attention," he said. "Beyond that, I am not permitted to say."

Kael followed the man down the stairs, then to a door beneath the stairs leading deeper to a cellar dug into the earth. The disciple opened the door, beckoned Kael to enter. Kael did, and when the door slammed shut behind him he was swallowed in near darkness. Near, because at the bottom of the steps shone a hint of light through a doorway at the immediate right. A hand touching the cold stone to guide himself, Kael descended the stairs and entered the cellar.

Thin windows near the cellar's ceiling allowed in what little light they had. Shelves lined all four walls, each filled with thick glass jars containing sliced strawberries and apples. A single figure sat in a chair in the center of the cellar. Johan stood behind it, arms crossed, a blade held in his right hand. Kael squinted in the dim light. The person in the chair had their hands and feet bound. A woman, he realized when she looked up.

"Kael!" she cried, and his heart leapt.

"Clara?" he asked, and anger replaced his surprise as he turned his attention to Johan. "Why is she held prisoner?"

"She is held prisoner because I was waiting for you to confirm she is who she claims she is," Johan said. He lowered his knife, easily slicing through the rope. "Which I now have."

Free, Clara rushed across the cellar and flung her arms around Kael. He held her tight, and he whispered to her as she pressed her forehead against his neck.

"Did he hurt you?"

"I'm fine," she said. "Really, I am."

"She approached one of my disciples in Byrntown insisting she be brought to you," Johan said, a strange expression on his face. "A rash and dangerous act, but one I find admirable given the circumstances."

"It was so stupid of you to sneak into my home like that," she said, pulling gently from his arms. "My brothers told me of your escape, and they were all too happy to inform me of the bounty on your head."

"So you're saying I didn't make a good impression when we met at dinner?"

Clara forced down her laugh.

"No," she said. "You did not."

"Clara told me several interesting things before I summoned you here," Johan said, glancing at Clara. "Particularly about your sister."

What joy Kael had felt quickly froze in his chest. He stared at Clara's face, trying to glean information from her eyes and the twitch of her lip before she actually spoke the words.

"Kael...I overheard the Speaker talking to my brothers," she said. "They've captured your sister and are holding her prisoner."

Kael flinched as if he'd been punched, but he forced himself to remain calm.

"You're sure?" he asked.

"I'm sure," she said, nodding. "Marius was damn proud of it, too, as well as the attack on the resistance camp. 'The topper to a perfect day,' he called it."

Kael's hands balled into fists.

"Prisoner means she's still alive," he said, clinging to what hope he had. "Do you know where?"

"That's actually why I'm here," she said. "They're holding her in the Crystal Cathedral. There's still a chance we can save her if we act fast enough."

"And that there is the tricky part, isn't it?" Johan said. He twirled his knife in his fingers, watching the blade instead of them. "The remaining Weshern Seraphim are scattered and in hiding, and we've only begun finding and bringing them here safely. The Crystal Cathedral is the theotechs' primary stronghold on Weshern. Day or night, it is always guarded by angelic knights, plus additional ground forces."

"With surprise on our side we should still be able to overwhelm them," Kael insisted.

Johan waggled a finger at him.

"The moment we attack, they'll barricade the doors and hunker down to wait for reinforcements. Your sister is an important symbol for your rebellion, yes, but that importance doesn't mean we should carelessly throw away dozens of lives battling knights, especially when it likely accomplishes nothing."

"What if you don't need to defeat them?" Clara asked. "What if you just need to distract them long enough for someone to get inside?"

Johan leaned against one of the shelves, arms still crossed.

"I'm listening."

"Visitors to the cathedral are restricted, but I could get inside, especially if I pretend I'm there on some form of penance. My connection to Kael, perhaps. As the daughter of the Archon, I would naturally be accompanied by a house guard."

"I can be that guard," Kael said, filling in the rest of Clara's plan in his head. "Bring me inside. If I'm there when you attack, I can make my way inside before they lock everything down. All I'll need is for you to keep their focus outside instead of in."

Johan's blue eyes narrowed.

"A dangerous gamble," he said.

"But one that puts only me and Clara at risk," Kael said. "You just need to hit and run, stirring the knights and soldiers into battle."

"And once you find your sister, how will you escape?"

Kael bit his lower lip.

"I'll improvise."

He thought Johan would shoot him down, but instead the man laughed.

"A desperate plan," he said. "But better than none, and with far fewer risks. Bree is a valuable symbol, and even more so after the destruction of the camp in the Aquila Forest. We can't afford for the common folk to lose hope, and if her head were found atop a spike near the holy mansion the damage to morale would be irreparable." He pointed to Kael's face. "We'll need to make you unrecognizable. Cutting your hair will be a first step. The most trusted Weshern house guards also bear blue tattoos across their faces. We won't have time for a true tattoo, but I believe I can find paint to mimic it for a short period of time."

"Thank you," Kael said. "My sister and I owe you greatly."

Johan nodded, and he turned to Clara.

"I will need time to gather my disciples, as well as prepare Kael's disguise," he said. "We'll launch our attack first thing tomorrow. Can you return here come the morning mist, and bring Kael proper clothes to wear?"

Clara nodded.

"I can," she said. "And I thank you as well, Johan. If only my family had listened to you and your warnings, we might not be in the situation we're in now."

"There is no time to regret the past, nor wish for the present to be better," Johan said. "Return home, before your brothers suspect something is amiss."

Clara nodded, and she pulled Kael close so she could kiss his cheek.

"Stay safe," she said. "I'll see you tomorrow, all right?"

"You may not recognize me," Kael warned.

Clara smiled, kissed him again.

"Shave your head and tattoo your face, and I'll still know. But I'm not the one you need to fool, just the rest of the world."

*   *   *

Kael was in the armory beside the safe house when Johan found him. Red light of the midnight fire burned through the high windows, reflecting off the metal of dozens of swords, wings, and buckles.

"You should be resting," Johan said.

"My sister's held captive," Kael said, analyzing the sets of wings Johan had hanging from the wall. "Being tortured, interrogated, or who knows what else. Sleep isn't coming easy."

"Most important things don't," Johan said, joining his side. "But you should sleep nonetheless. Tomorrow is a great risk."

"One I'm willing to take."

"For all of us," Johan added, and he crossed his arms. "Not just you. Clara's involvement will likely be discovered given enough time. My disciples will directly engage knights of Center, and many will die no matter how great our surprise is. I have only a few trained to use Seraphim harnesses, and even fewer with combat experience. They are vital to my cause, and I am putting their lives in danger to aid in your plan."

"Then it's a good thing you've made it clear how important Bree is to everyone."

Kael moved to the next set of wings, searching for one that looked closer to his size. Most sets there were for larger men, full-grown Seraphim with many years on him.

"You won't find a set to your fitting here," Johan said. "I've already chosen yours and put it aside."

Kael paused, and he glanced at Johan from the corner of his eye. The man was watching him from underneath his hood, blue eyes smiling even if his mouth was not.

"All right," he said. "Where is it? I should make sure it fits."

Johan crossed the room to the opposite wall. A thick blanket hung over part of the wall, and Johan yanked it free with a flourish. Despite his predicament, a spark of excitement ran through Kael.

Hanging from the wall was a grand set of wings, larger than any available at the academy. There was no doubt in Kael's mind they'd once belonged to an actual angelic knight. The gold was scraped away, revealing the metal underneath. It wasn't quite silver, but it was close enough to Weshern's symbolic color. Kael stepped closer, touching the soft leather of the straps.

"Your task is so very close to hopeless," Johan said. "But such is the fate of our entire rebellion. If I'm to send you into the lion's den, I'm sending you with the greatest chance of success. This set was taken from a knight, one of very few that my disciples have managed to kill over the past few years. Tell me, what is your elemental affinity?"

Kael almost answered "ice" on instinct, but then shook his head.

"Light," he said. "I fight with ice, but it was my minor affinity when I took the tests."

He wasn't sure what reaction he'd expected from Johan, but laughter was not it.

"Excellent," he said, clapping his hands. "Most excellent. I've wondered when I might find someone to wield it, but you are the perfect man to try."

Kael was confused, but Johan didn't pause to explain. Instead he crossed the room to the near wall, removing another cloth to reveal a strangely shaped piece of metal. A shield, Kael realized, as he joined Johan's side. The outer parts were gold, the symbol of Center painted red in its heart. One side curled inward, design to neatly avoid the wings of a harness while carried.

"Why a shield?" Kael asked. He grabbed the top to lift it with one hand, found he couldn't even make it budge. "I can't fly with this. It weighs more than I do."

Johan grinned at him, stretching the little scars across his lips and cheeks. He used both hands to drag it away from the wall, then spun it in place to reveal the interior.

"Look here," he said. A leather strap was bolted to the metal, meant to loop around the forearm, and near it, a thick bar designed to be held. Above it was a square bulge of metal. A thick black cord connected the bulge to the handlebar. Johan pulled the lid off the metal, revealing an interior space remarkably similar to the prism slot for a gauntlet.

"Light element goes within," Johan explained. He pointed to a small switch on the handle. "It'll activate so long as you've turned it on. The shield will weigh significantly less, allowing you to fly and fight unhindered. You'll forfeit the use of a sword in that hand, but you'll be able to withstand attacks that would cripple most Seraphim."

"Swords have always been more my sister's thing," Kael said, running his fingers along the edge of the shield. It was so thick, so sturdy, he doubted anything but the most direct hit with a boulder would do much damage. "I think I can make do with a shield just fine."

Johan snapped the lid to the compartment shut.

"This shield is one of my most prized captures," he said. "The strain on the prism will be great, but with your light affinity, you should be able to wield this shield for hours." He leaned it against the wall and gestured to the front. "We'll strip the paint off before tomorrow. It wouldn't seem right to have you flying into battle bearing the symbol of Center on your shield."

"No, it wouldn't."

Johan tugged at his hood, pulling it tighter across his face, hiding the scars.

"I'll leave you be," he said.

Kael stared at the shield, and the wide circle of Center intersecting five much smaller circles.

"Johan," he said, turning before the man could leave the warehouse. "Thank you for trusting me. Even if it's for Bree, I still appreciate it."

Johan paused at the door.

"Kael, I have a suspicion that you're equally as special as your sister. You just need an opportunity to prove it." He softly chuckled. "Tomorrow, I suspect you will have that chance."

He left, and Kael knelt before the shield. He touched the half-orange, half-red circle of Galen, let his fingers linger. On a whim he pulled out the red cloth he kept in his pocket ever since that awful night. Kneeling down, he slid behind the shield as it leaned against the wall. Two quick loops and a knot tied the cloth to the shield's handle. No one would see it while he carried it. The reminder was for him only, of the damage done by Center. If Marius had sent Galen plummeting to the ground, there was so much for him to answer for. That done, he slid free, patted the shield once more.

"I'm coming, Bree," he whispered.

CHAPTER

17

Kael marched alongside Clara, feeling awkward in his new guise.

"You sure I shouldn't have worn the chain mail?" he asked. "All other personal bodyguards wear it."

"It'll hamper your flying, and leaving it in the cathedral will only link you to me," Clara said, keeping her voice even and pleasant. "And must I remind you that you've sworn a vow of silence, *Edward*?"

Edward was the name Clara would use for him should the guards outside the Crystal Cathedral question his accompanying her. A black tunic covered much of his body, bearing the blue sword of Weshern across the chest. He wore dark pants appropriate to both Seraphim and house soldiers, and hidden beneath his tunic was a plain gray shirt. A shield hung from his back, and he walked with a long spear in his right hand, the bottom striking the stone cobbles with a satisfying clack upon every step. His head was shaved, and the lack of weight coupled with air blowing across his scalp was distracting. Most irritating were the fake tattoos, a thick blue line of dots that started just above the ear, crossed over his eyes, and ended at the other ear. The paint itched terribly, but he couldn't dare scratch it. They'd had to layer it on thin as best they could to mimic the appearance of a tattoo.

Kael had hardly recognized himself by the end of it all, which was exactly the point. If one of the guards outside the Crystal Cathedral identified him, the game was over before it began.

"We're almost there," Clara said, keeping her gaze straight ahead. "When we're within the vicinity of the Cathedral, I won't address you or acknowledge your presence. Keep stiff and still. Pretend your face is a mask, and you've sworn to never leave my side. Focus on those two things, and we should be just fine." She blew out a breath. "I hope."

"Comforting," Kael muttered.

"Vow of silence, Edward. Don't make me remind you again."

The day was early, the morning air pleasantly crisp. They'd recently passed through a quaint farming town, the merchant sellers still setting up shop on the main roadway. Beyond that was a lengthy stretch of green pasture that surrounded the Crystal Cathedral on all sides. Elsewhere in Weshern, a road cutting through pasture would be plain dirt, but the carefully maintained cobbles continued beyond the town. On the seventh-day, thousands of people traveled to the Cathedral, hoping to be one of the lucky few allowed inside during Theotech Vyros's services. The rest had to sit outside and listen to another theotech's lecture. Kael had visited a few times, mostly after his parents' deaths when Aunt Bethy had been heavy in mourning. They'd sat in the grass atop a blanket, so far away Kael could barely make out the words the theotech spoke as he addressed the crowd.

There'd be no crowd this morning, not with the seventh five days away. They saw nary a soul on their walk to the cathedral, which was fine with Kael. The fewer around, the better. The last thing he wanted was innocent lives lost during Bree's rescue.

"Almost there," Kael said as they passed through the tall grass fields on either side of them. "Are you sure you're up for this?"

"It was my idea, remember?" Clara said. "And don't worry. Once the battle starts I'll flee back to the mansion, and it'll be easy to say my escort came back with me. So long as you do your part, I'll be fine."

She made it seem as if she were in no danger, but Kael knew that was far from the truth. Even if all went according to plan, and any who witnessed Kael's arrival with Clara died during the engagement, the timing of the attack coinciding with Clara's arrival would still draw suspicion. Clara insisted the risks were worth it, and Kael knew better than to try changing her mind. He looked to the tall grass fields as they walked, searching for signs of movement. Hidden deep within the grass crawled Johan's men, who had entered the fields during the midnight fire. Kael saw no unnatural wave of grass, no gap to signify the presence of a man, but he trusted them to be there, waiting for Johan's signal to attack.

Ahead, the Crystal Cathedral rose above the green in a splendid display of glass and steel. The front resembled a multi-layered triangle, nearly every bit of it colored glass. The chosen colors were blue and white of varying shades, smoothly integrating together so the many jagged, overlapping glass sheets seemed one singular piece. The sheets rose out of the ground, on thick steel poles expertly camouflaged by the paintings that decorated the lower portions of the building. They depicted theotechs administering crowds and performing miracles while above them Seraphim battled red-eyed demons made of fire and frost.

The only nonglass structures Kael could spot were the ancient wood doors painted white and the marble steps leading up to them. Four knights stood at attention, one for each corner of the pyramid-shaped structure, while two armored soldiers with spears and shields flanked the doors. Kael thrust his shoulders back, trying to make himself seem as tall as possible. He'd be young for a personal bodyguard, and while the tattoos and weapons helped, there was still the chance a soldier would sense something was amiss.

"Have you come to pray, Miss Willer?" asked one of the soldiers as Kael and Clara stopped at the foot of the steps.

"I have," Clara said. "I fear for the salvation of my parents, and the safety of my home."

One guard looked to the other.

"The family of the Archon is always welcome," he said, and he pushed the door inward. "Come seek the angels' guidance."

Kael kept his face passive lest his relief show. Could it truly be that easy? Clara nodded respectfully to the soldiers, then climbed the steps. Kael followed, trailing behind her and slightly to the side. His optimism plummeted the moment both soldiers crossed their spears before him.

"Just her," they said.

Keeping in character as best he knew how, he glared at them while waiting for Clara to speak.

"He is my personal bodyguard," she said upon hearing their proclamation. "Would you deny me my safety?"

"You are within blessed halls watched over by knights of Center herself," the first guard said. "There is no place safer, not on this island."

"Where I go, Edward goes," she said. "Or must I find Theotech Vyros and inform him of how you've disrespected me by
wasting my time?"

The mention of Vyros's involvement removed their stubbornness immediately.

"Very well," the guard said. "But he leaves his shield and
weapon here with us."

They'd anticipated such a request, and that was more than
fine with Kael. The long spear and heavy shield weren't the
weapons he planned on fighting with. Kael glanced to Clara,
waited for her accepting nod, and then handed his spear to the
nearest soldier, followed by the shield off his back. That done,
the guards parted, allowing Kael to follow Clara into the cathedral. Together they entered the main hall, where the cathedral
opened up immensely.

Kael gaped at the ceiling, unable to help himself. The many layers of glass ended at random intervals as the four sides approached
the focal point of the cathedral. The sunlight filtering through the
various colors blended them together into a seemingly singular
ceiling. Theotech tradition declared all sermons must be given in
open air, and it was above the raised dais where the four thick-
est and longest glass plates came to a halt, leaving a gap barely a
foot wide for sunlight to stream down in a thick beam. The floor
was marble painted green, the benches an earthy brown. Instead of
theotechs and crowds, trees and sprawling bushes full of blooming
flowers were painted across the interior walls. The many layers of
glass were expertly weaved together while leaving narrow passages
so that a gentle breeze blew throughout the building. The wind
was always chilly, fueling rumors that ice elements were embedded
deep within the glass. The overall effect was a feeling of being in
an open field with a clear blue sky, the sun shining directly down
upon the lecturing theotech as he spoke the wisdom of the angels.

Clara traveled down one of the rows splitting up the benches, chose one near the center, and took her seat. As he'd been instructed during their preparations, Kael sat in the row directly behind her, crossed his arms, and stared vacantly ahead.

"So far so good," Clara whispered while pretending to pray.

Kael didn't acknowledge her, only casually glanced about the cathedral. He saw several robed young men and women at the outer walls, carrying buckets and rags as they cleaned the glass. They wouldn't be any threat when battle came. Behind the dais stood a single knight guarding what appeared to be steps downward. From where he sat, Kael could barely see the top of a metal door. The rest of the complex was built underground, just as Johan had predicted. It was from there Kael expected reinforcements to emerge when Johan attacked. He'd need to be patient, and Johan's timing equally perfect. Telling himself it would all be fine, he fought against his growing nerves. Just sitting there, he felt so exposed, so vulnerable.

Kael heard Clara speak his name, and he brought his attention back to her. It hadn't been meant for him, though, as he realized she was praying for real. Asking for his safety, as well as Bree's rescue. Hearing her worried plea, hearing her fears expressed so personally, made Kael feel like an intruder. Worse, he could do nothing to comfort her, not even something as simple as touching her hand, without potentially exposing the charade.

Time dragged on. The door in the back opened, and an older theotech emerged. He spotted Clara and immediately made his way over the dais and then down the aisle toward her. The bushy white of his beard and eyebrows contrasted sharply with the extreme dark of his skin. He sat down on the bench directly ahead of Clara and turned to face her. Clara sensed his arrival and pulled up from her prayer.

"It's always a pleasure to see members of the ruling family

within our crystal halls," the theotech said. "Is there something heavy on your heart you'd like to speak with me about, Clara?"

"No thank you, Jorg," Clara said. "I need no advice or counsel. I only wish to express my fears over those I love."

Jorg coughed, wet and full of phlegm.

"As you wish," he said. "Know I am close, and always willing to lend an ear. The wisdom of the angels was meant for all, but it is most important for those of the Archon's blood to hear and understand. Your decisions shape the hearts of your people, and right now, I fear Weshern's faith is tenuous and brittle." The theotech chuckled. "Then again, it is the gardener who must accept responsibility for the state of his garden, and no one else."

"Who is the gardener, you, or my family?" Clara asked.

Jorg smiled at her as he rose from his seat.

"I meant my order, but I suppose your family's hands are in the soil as much as our own."

The old man was four steps down the aisle when Johan's army attacked. A boulder smashed through the ancient wood doors at the entrance, crushing the bones of the two guards along with it. Crackles of lightning flashed in the sky above, shining through the blue paint of the glass. The young cleaning the sides of the cathedral stood shocked and confused as to what was happening. Kael joined Clara's side as Jorg rushed to the door behind the dais. They ducked down below the bench; Kael removed his house guard tunic.

"Get out of here the second the fight shifts away from the cathedral," he told her, handing over his tunic. Should he be caught, he needed to reduce every possible link to Clara's involvement.

Clara grabbed the top of his shirt and yanked him close enough for a kiss.

"You come back to me, you understand?" she said, breath

coming out rapid between her lips. "You get your sister, and you get out."

Her iron stare made it seem like she believed she could will it to be with a mere order. Kael yanked off the glove of his right hand and brushed the side of her face with his palm.

"We're not dying here," he said. "Not today."

Jorg reached the back door, flung it open, and began shouting for reinforcements to come and aid the battle outside. Kael kept low, watching armored soldiers arrive from the far door, some bearing spears, others bows and arrows. They rushed the broken entrance, shouting orders as they exited. Three knights followed, emerging single file in their golden armor and glimmering wings. With professional calmness they marched to the exit. Kael kept his eyes low and his body crouched next to Clara's, praying the three didn't notice them hiding there. They didn't, not with the battle outside occupying their attention. Upon reaching the gaping hole that was once the front doors, the knights flooded light into their wings and took off.

With the knights outside, the sounds of battle heightened tenfold. Kael kept crouched, legs tensed for a sprint. It would be any moment, and he'd have to act quickly. Jorg had returned to the inner door, standing before it while talking to two soldiers positioned beside him. Everyone's attention was on the outside, but those three might be an issue if he weren't fast enough...

Even though they expected it, the shattering of the Crystal Cathedral's eastern ceiling was still an overwhelming spectacle. Two stones blasted through, smashing the blue glass into a thousand shards that fell like rain upon the tiles and benches of the cathedral's eastern portion. The roar of its fall was deafening. The stones struck the floor, cracking marble as they shattered into pieces. The pieces rolled, mist leaking off them as the stones already began the gradual process of fading away into smoke and dust. Kael looked to the newly opened gap and saw a man wearing the brown robes of Johan's disciples flying above. He held a huge bundle in his arms, silver wings sticking out from one side. The man dropped the pack unceremoniously through the gap, then took off, a blur of gold and red chasing after.

Kael sprinted the moment he spotted the pack. It fell at a strange speed, about half of what should have been normal. The two soldiers with Jorg stood dumbfounded at the damage to the ancient cathedral, their surprise giving Kael the time he needed to reach the pack as it softly thudded atop one of the benches. Kael tugged at the rope holding the pack together, removing the knot and yanking aside thin burlap to reveal his harness and wings. Tied to it was the enormous shield, newly painted so that the blue sword of Weshern hung over a black background, two white wings spreading from either side of the blade's base. Between the wings and shield was his sword belt, along with a single sword. The light elements of both shield and wings were activated, allowing the disciple to carry it in the first place, as well as fall without taking damage.

Skipping the wings, Kael thrust his right hand into the gauntlet, flicked the knob to arm the ice element inside, and then whirled on Jorg and the two soldiers. One was running toward him, the other standing confused beside the theotech. Kael sent a lance of ice straight through the neck of the far soldier, a second shot trailing a heartbeat behind to smash the theotech's ribs. Both dropped, dead or dying. The final guard lifted his shield to protect his body, but Kael lowered his aim and widened his palm far as it could go. His mind shaped the shot, turning the ice into a spray of frost that painted the tiles. With his shield and heavy armor, the charging soldier had no chance to keep afoot, slipping and falling painfully onto his back. He lay there, groaning, as Kael jammed his arms through the harness and hoisted the wings onto his back. Next came the sword belt, which he looped around his waist and then yanked the buckles tight. His left arm slid through the strap of the shield to grab its handle, and despite its size, it lifted as if it weighed less than a pound.

"Here we go," Kael whispered, breathing out a nervous sigh.

Kael flicked the throttle while jumping. He rose into the air and curled his body so that he rolled forward, then killed the throttle, going upside down. His momentum kept him sailing toward the inner door, and he thrust his gauntlet out as he soared over the prone soldier. The man pulled his shield up from the floor, but not fast enough. A thin shard of ice jammed through his eye, ending his movements. Kael curled more, somersaulting to a standing position and then punching power back into his wings just before his feet touched ground. It jarred his knees, but not as bad as it could have. Kael sprinted toward the open door upon landing, weaving around the bodies of the dead and then dashing down the steps into the hidden recesses of the theotechs' cathedral.

CHAPTER

18

The hallway was wide, and clearly designed for winged knights to pass through comfortably. The walls were clean, undecorated marble. The hall descended for at least a hundred feet without a turn. Doors lined either side, many of them thrust open. It should have been dark, down so deep away from the sun, but soft lights embedded into the ceiling shone across everything. Light elements, Kael realized as he passed them every few seconds. Smaller than normal, and set into slots carved out of the marble. Strange runes marked all four sides, and Kael could only guess as to their purpose.

Kael wiped the paint off his face as he walked. With his paint and tunic gone, and his remaining clothes nondescript, he'd hopefully appear as nothing more than one of Johan's attacking Seraphs. When Kael passed the first door, he glanced inside, his shield and gauntlet ready. A soldiers' barracks by the looks of it. Four beds pressed against opposite walls, the remaining space used for racks of armor and trunks of clothes, both of which were scattered about, reflecting the frantic nature of their defense against Johan's assault. Kael checked a door on the other side. Another empty barracks, also lit by a single light element shining from the ceiling like a ghostly stalactite.

Kael continued deeper into the complex, his footfalls echoing in the dreadful silence. He checked each door, ready to fire his ice element should he encounter resistance. One door revealed a far nicer room with a single bed instead of bunks. A knight's quarters, he assumed. The bed's stained oak frame and silken crimson sheets looked like they belonged to royalty rather than servants of Center. An empty stand stood in the corner, a holder for the knight's golden wings. Kael spotted two more such rooms on his way down the hall. All of them, thankfully, were empty.

As Kael approached a turn, he paused, swearing he heard footsteps. Standing there he heard nothing, no footsteps, no distant calls, but he didn't trust the quiet. Carefully he neared the corner, then stopped, waiting. It was faint, but Kael heard it, the distinct rattle of armor from around the corner, but how far? Holding his breath, Kael slowly crept closer, soft blue light wafting from the focal point of his gauntlet as his nerves stretched tight. One tiny step, followed by another, and then he stopped. Listened. Absolute silence. He didn't buy it.

Kael leapt around the corner, twisting his body so his shield covered all but his head and everything below the knees. A winged knight waited in ambush, sword in his left hand, gauntlet spread wide in his right. The sword smacked against the shield, not even scoring a dent, as a ball of flame burst from the gauntlet. It splashed across the shield, then dissipated with a puff of black smoke, its energy expelled on the thick steel. Kael's momentum carried him shoulder-first into the wall, and he cried out. The hit spoiled his aim, his thin spike of ice shooting past the knight's head and shattering against the ceiling.

Before he could fire a second the knight hopped backward to gain space, braced his hand, and released a torrent of flame. Kael lifted the shield knowing it was hopeless. The fire stretched near floor to ceiling, its center focused right at his chest. It was a rolling inferno that made a mockery of his shield's cover. Kael tensed, anticipating the fire's heat on his skin, but his shield flared with light the moment the attack hit. Kael felt a tug on his mind, a pull on the element akin to when he released the ice element from his gauntlet. The fire swirled against the shield, but it went no farther, the enormous burst crackling and breaking into plumes of black smoke that hung in the cramped corridor.

Kael's foe looked just as stunned as he was. Refusing to lose what advantage he had, Kael jumped toward the knight while flaring his wings, his shield leading the charge. Kael thumbed off the switch to the shield's light element just before impact. Immediately he felt the weight on his arm, pulling him forward and down with its momentum. It slammed into the knight, who'd braced against the impact. His strength meant nothing against that thick, heavy steel. The knight toppled, Kael landing atop him, the shield crunching armor and pinning his limbs. Kael reactivated his shield's element, rolled off him and onto his knees, and yanked his sword free of its scabbard. The knight started to move, but Kael lunged with his sword. The tip jammed into his throat, scraping across spine on its way to clack against the stone floor.

Kael knelt there on one knee, gasping for air, as he yanked the blade free.

"Holy shit." He looked to his shield, the blue paint of the

sword singed black in a few spots. It should have been burned away completely, just like the rest of him, but it wasn't. "Holy shit."

If Kael survived, he swore, he would find out if Johan knew the shield was capable of such things. Sure, the strange man had called it his most prized possession, but what he'd just witnessed went far beyond that. Heart pounding, he rose to his feet, shifted the shield on his left arm to a more comfortable position, and then resumed his search for his sister.

The hallway before him wasn't quite as long as the previous, and it contained far fewer side doors. Near the end of the hallway a second passage branched sharply to the left. Kael barely gave it thought, for his eyes were locked on a pair of majestic doors at the very end of the hall. The ceiling itself rose up to make room, the hall two times higher by the door than anywhere else. Multiple blue lines looped and curled throughout the white marble of the doors, forming circles and whirlpools before joining together in the center as a thick circle. Painted into that circle was a pair of white wings. Along the walls on either adjacent side of the doors, forming a perfectly straight line from floor to ceiling, were dozens of runes painted gold.

Kael found himself approaching the double doors without thinking, and he blinked and shook his head, surprised he was already halfway down the hall.

Keep it together, he told himself, figuring he was still recovering from the brief skirmish. He'd passed one door to his right, but before he could backtrack to check inside it, he heard the soft echo of conversation from up ahead. He froze, torn between hiding and attacking, and then the pair turned the corner from the left branch near the hall's end.

The first was a blond woman wearing tall black boots and tight red robes cinched at the waist with a silver buckle. Beside her, golden armor shimmering in the white light, was an angelic knight.

"...don't know what the disciples are after," the knight was saying before they realized Kael was there. The theotech froze, but the knight reacted without the slightest hesitation, lunging forward with a sudden burst of his wings. Kael lifted his shield, trusting it to keep him safe after the previous display. Stones the size of his head shot from the theotech's gauntlet, and Kael cried out as they struck his shield with bright flashes of light. The stones shattered at the contact, and again Kael felt the faint strain on his mind. The impact still jarred his arm, but nothing like the damage he should have endured.

The knight closed in, sword drawn in his left hand. Kael braced his legs and let him come. This time the knight's sword bounced off his shield, and in that moment, Kael pulled his shield back with one hand and pushed his other hand forward, fingers curled to narrow the focus of his gauntlet. Three lances of ice flew forth, sharp and thin, their aim for the knight's exposed head.

Victory wouldn't be so easy. The knight dropped to one knee, the lances breaking upon the wall, and his gauntlet dropped to the floor. Two more stones, except this time aimed at Kael's legs. They were small, each the size of his fist, but they flew with more than enough speed to cause harm. They passed beneath Kael's shield, both striking his left leg, one at the kneecap, the other his shin. Kael screamed in pain, and his leg buckled. Realizing how vulnerable he was, Kael acted out of desperation. Instead of retreating, he kicked off with his right leg while punching his wings to their full power. The moment he began moving he shut the power off to his shield. His scream intensified as the harness wrenched his back and his shield strained his left arm.

That pain of carrying his shield was nothing compared to what it did to the knight. They collided with a screech of metal, the heavy shield ramming the knight against the wall. His wings bent and broke, and the knight let out a cry as Kael pushed harder, crushing him. More sounds of twisting metal, and then with a sudden gasp the knight's body went rigid. Kael cut off his wings and staggered backward. The knight collapsed face-first to the ground and lay still. Blood pooled around him, flowing from where the metal of the wings had pushed through the harness and into his back to impale him.

Gasping in air, Kael looked to the hall, but the theotech in the red was long gone, having fled back the way she'd come. Kael could only guess whether or not she'd return with reinforcements. Still, there was no turning back, nor giving up. He had to find his sister. Weaving around the dead body, Kael limped to that first room, continuing his search for Bree.

The room stretched on seemingly forever to his left, needing at least eight light elemental prism shards to keep it lit. The walls were pale white and covered with scorch marks. An empty table rested in the center of the room. A small furnace burned in the corner opposite the door and was the only other object he saw. Kael frowned, for the furnace wasn't like any he'd seen before. There was no flue to release smoke. On the bottom, the four iron legs were connected to wheels, as if the furnace were meant to be portable. The grate at the front bore thick, heavy bars to keep it locked shut. The gaps in the grate were thin, but Kael could barely see through them to the smoldering fire inside.

And from within that fire he heard shrill, cackling laughter.

Kael stepped closer, dreadful curiosity overwhelming his sense of urgency. Eyes wide, he stared through the grate. All he saw were black embers shimmering with orange and red flame.

Nothing to explain the laughter. Two more steps, and then he knelt before the furnace, felt its heat upon his face. Watched. Waited.

Several embers rose up, collecting, reshaping into arms and legs. Burning hands grew claws, and beady black eyes opened from the heart of the suddenly roaring flame. A spiked tail whipped about the back of it, showering the enclosed chamber with sparks. It smiled, revealing a yellow serpent's tongue slithering between teeth made of liquid fire.

And then it laughed.

Kael fled the room, convinced he was lost in a nightmare.

What was that?

His mind didn't have an answer. He feared even pondering the question. Shock crept through his body, making his fingers tingle and his mouth dry.

What in God's name was that, Kael?

He didn't know. Didn't want to know. He more stumbled than ran back to the main hallway and then to the next door, the one closest to the giant double doors. His shoulder slammed against it, the handle refusing to turn like the others. Kael tugged on it, saw a bar the top of the door holding it shut. Kael pulled it free and flung open the door.

"Bree," Kael said, relief flooding through him. The room was a prison, albeit a nice one. There was barely room for the single bed, which Bree lay upon, the blankets pulled up to her neck. Kael had to twist so he would fit his wings through the door, and he could barely move without one tapping against the walls.

"You need to wake up," he said, brushing her side. She stirred, her eyes flitting open and shut. Kael's relief quickly drained away. She didn't recognize him, and didn't seem to understand the urgency of their situation. Praying she was fine, he took her by the wrist and tugged. As she sat up the blanket fell away, revealing a silver gauntlet strapped to her hand, though unconnected to any wings or harness. Kael was confused as to why they'd give her a gauntlet, even without a set of wings or armed with a prism. Frightening, too, was the dried blood he saw caked along the interior of the empty prism compartment.

"Come on, Bree," Kael said, fighting to keep his voice calm. His sister forced open her eyes again. She was looking at him, he could tell, but her eyes weren't properly focused. Drugged? Deprived of sleep? He didn't know. Kael could only hope she'd be fine enough to endure their escape.

Slowly, as if sleepwalking, she slid her legs off the bed. Kael pulled her to a stand, and though she wobbled, she managed to stay upright. With achingly slow progress Kael slid her out of her prison and into the hallway beyond. He glanced in both directions, wanting to ensure no one had crept up on him while he got his sister out. Just empty hallway toward the exit, and the blue-white doors on the other side.

Kael stared at the doors longer than he meant, feeling a terrible compulsion to race over and thrust them open. There was no reason to do so, not with Bree in his arms and a desperate need to escape, but he felt the need as strong as his desire to draw breath. As he stared, a deep sensation of familiarity came over him. Distant words, as if from a forgotten memory, echoed in his mind.

Come inside, child, and speak.

Electricity raced from his heart to his throat in a sudden jolt. He knew that voice, recognized those words. The voice haunting his dreams.

"Kael?" Bree murmured, snapping him out of his stare.

"Sorry," he said, shaking his head and trying to focus on the here and now. "Can you walk?"

No answer. Kael grabbed her left arm and forced it around his neck. Her grip tightened—whether instinctual or not, he didn't know, nor did he care. They had to get out of there.

He half-walked, half-carried Bree back down the halls, doing his best to keep Bree's weight on his good leg and limping with his left. When he passed the empty room with the furnace he refused to look inside. Inside was something his mind couldn't deal with right now. Back around the corner, to the stairs leading up and into the cathedral proper. The sight of natural light shining from the open door was a blessing to his eyes.

"Almost there," he told his sister. She grunted but said nothing.

The two emerged into the Crystal Cathedral. Daylight shone down on them through the broken ceiling shards. The sounds of battle were gone, though it was only a matter of time before more knights and theotechs arrived to assess the damage and begin repairs.

"We need to fly," Kael said, still unsure of his sister's awareness. "You'll have to hold on to me, all right?"

Bree's left arm was already around his neck and shoulder, and she turned to face him so she might loop her other arm around. Kael undid the two harness straps that crossed over his waist and chest, and he yanked on the buckles to stretch them out. Pulling his sister closer, he wrapped them both around her and cinched them tightly, buckling her against him. That done, he locked his arms around her waist, his shield forming a sort of sling as it covered her body. Kael eased the throttle higher, wanting to gently ascend and test the straps before going full speed.

Their feet lifted off the ground, and Kael was pleased by how secure his sister felt.

"We're going to be fine," he whispered into her ear. "Just hold on, and trust me."

Still no response, just a nod of her head that he might have imagined. Swallowing down his fear, Kael pushed the throttle halfway to maximum, and together they soared through the ceiling of the cathedral and into open sky. Kael slowed to a hover, twisting to look about. Maneuvering was difficult and awkward with his sister hanging on to him.

"Not good," Kael muttered. Johan's disciples had taken the fight away from the cathedral before fleeing, but not far enough. Two knights flew less than a quarter mile away, and they had both clearly spotted him. Turning east, Kael resumed flight, heading toward the distant edge of Weshern. Wind whipped across his body, and Bree's grip around his neck tightened. Teeth clenched, Kael increased speed until the throttle was all the way to its maximum. Kael's wings were faster than anything he'd flown before, but he was carrying extra weight. If either Bree or Kael moved in the wrong way, he might lose control and careen into the blur of hills below.

Find somewhere to hide, Kael told himself as a town rapidly approached. *Hide, just hide.*

He slowed upon reaching the town, and he dipped lower to the street. Bree immediately pulled her lips to his ear, and she finally spoke.

"No," she said. "Keep going."

Kael didn't even hesitate. He jammed the throttle back to full with his thumb and shifted his back to lift away from the gray blur beneath that was the town's buildings. A quick glance behind him showed the knights slowly closing in, their gold wings shimmering in the blue sky. The town vanished, replaced by farmland. Seeking only distance, only to flee, the twins raced over Weshern, Kael unsure of where they went, only knowing that they needed speed.

A ball of ice dropped fifteen feet to his right, whistling as it sliced through the air. Kael craned his neck, baffled. He'd thought the knights too far away to accurately attack, but apparently he was wrong. The two chasing knights lobbed shots of ice and stone as smooth, heavy orbs far into the sky, accurately predicting Kael's path despite the significant time it took the projectiles to both rise and fall. Another ball of ice fell, this one far too close for comfort. Kael veered left, and he nearly steered into a chunk of stone the size of his head.

Stay calm, Kael told himself. *Small weaves. Whatever you do, don't lose speed.*

Towns and streets passed beneath him in a blur. The edge of Weshern was closing in. Keep flying, his sister had told him, and so Kael would do just that. Perhaps, if he was lucky, the two knights wouldn't realize just how insane he was. Several more barrages landed to either side of them, some too far ahead, some far behind. Homes vanished beneath him, then a thin strip of green, and suddenly he was over open air. Far, far below, hidden by thin strips of white clouds, the Endless Ocean glimmered.

Kael shot east like a comet, never changing his direction. The same, however, could not be said for the knights. One veered north, the other south, both keeping close to the island.

They know I have to come back, Kael realized. So long as they never lost sight of him, they could always get him when he attempted to return to the island. Which left Kael with one direction: straight out, in hopes of losing them completely. Wings thrumming, he let the island of Weshern recede behind him. Nothing but blue stretched out before him but he refused to let the sight unnerve him. He had to fly. He had to keep steady.

Kael shifted his arms for a moment so he could see the glow

246 Brief moment of clarity

of his light element. Just below half. He could fly more than a hundred miles on that, but he had to be careful and save enough to get back home.

By now the two knights had realized his plan and resumed chase, but he'd already added more than a mile to the distance between them. Kael checked on them occasionally as they soared east. It was strange how peaceful he felt, flying with his sister in his arms, while also knowing that he likely flew to his death. There'd be no outmaneuvering the knights, no eventually outracing them. Hiding would be near to impossible, especially with the sky as clear as it was. Just a desperate turn back to Weshern and a suicide rush in hopes the knights somehow missed their mark.

Another glance at his light element. Barely a quarter of the bright glow it started with.

"We have to turn around," he told Bree, lips pressed to her ear.

"No," she responded.

"We can't make it to land if we don't."

Bree shook her head. She still looked drowsy, and her speech was slurred, but there was no changing her mind.

"Do you trust me, Kael?" she asked.

Kael glanced over his shoulder at the two knights. They'd fallen farther behind, showing no hurry. They knew the limits of a light element. They knew he'd need to turn about soon.

"Yes," he said. "I do."

A brief moment of clarity hardened in Bree's eyes.

"Then fly."

And so he did. No turning back. No retreat. Over the Endless Ocean they flew, the miles passing by amid thin tufts of clouds and over a sheen of blue stretching from horizon to horizon. Weshern was but a brown and green speck in the distance, easily blotted out by a passing cloud, the beam holding it aloft all but invisible. The knights hung back even farther, and Kael sensed they were afraid to chase. No one went this far out from the islands. There never was reason to.

After what Kael guessed to be another fifteen minutes, the two knights turned about and returned to Weshern. Kael checked his prism, saw it painfully faint. He kept on flying until his shield felt heavy on his arms and his speed decreased to a lazy drift as the thrum of his wings lessened. Kael angled them lower, and settling to hover above the water, he released the power of his ice element. Round and round he spun, layering it atop the ocean, freezing it wide enough for him and his sister.

"Here we are," Kael said as he removed the buckles and lay Bree atop his shield on his little island of ice. Bree curled her knees to her chest, and she closed her eyes as she shivered.

"Thank you," she said.

Her voice was so soft, so tired. Kael brushed strands of hair from her face and smiled down at his sister.

"You'd have done the same," he said, and he crossed his legs, turned off his wings, and let the ocean carry their refuge away.

CHAPTER

19

Bree drifted in and out of sleep with the gentle rocking of the water, and despite the cold, she felt like she could relax for the first time in days. Kael hovered over her, always quiet. Occasionally she'd hear him activate his gauntlet, adding more ice to their island to keep it from fading away. Mostly he stayed near her, shifting his weight often in an attempt to keep any part of his body from becoming too cold.

By the time Bree felt like herself, the sun had begun its descent. Bree opened her eyes, and she smiled when her brother noticed.

"I like your new look."

Kael's shaved head made him look older, and she'd barely recognized him when he first entered her prison.

"Thanks," he said. "We needed the disguise."

Groaning against the pain of her stiff limbs, Bree slid up to a sitting position. Her head pounded, but that she could ignore. She pulled the shield out from under her and handed it to Kael.

"Nice shield," she said. "Your wings aren't exactly Weshern issue, either. Where'd you get them?"

"Johan."

"I have a feeling that answers my next question. Last I knew, you were being held prisoner at the holy mansion. Did he rescue you?"

Kael nodded. "They were taking me to the Crystal Cathedral, to join you in that cell, I'd wager. Johan and his disciples ambushed them on the street and took me to his hideout in New Galen. Clara overheard Marius telling her brothers about your capture, so she found us and told us where you were. We set up the rescue immediately after."

"Remind me to thank Clara as well, then," Bree said. "Thank God your rescue attempt went better than mine. I was trying to convince Argus to launch an attack on the holy mansion when Center's troops ambushed our camp." What little good mood she'd felt quickly drained away with that memory. Bree glanced to the ice, preferring to watch it instead of Kael's reaction. "Have you heard anything about that? About who might have survived, I mean?"

"No," Kael said.

Damn it.

"It was awful," she said. "While running...me, Brad, and Saul, we were trying to get out when a bolt of lightning hit Brad in the chest. He's...he's gone, Kael."

A long period of silence.

"Are you sure?" Kael asked.

Bree swallowed down her sorrow, fighting against the haunting image of Brad's face locked still, eyes wide, jaw unhinged.

"Yes," she said. "I'm sure."

More silence. Bree dared look up. Kael sat at the edge of their ice island, fist pressed against his lips. His entire upper body was shaking.

"He shouldn't have been there," Kael said with a sniffle.

"Kael, don't…"

"He wanted to leave the academy," her brother continued. "He wanted to leave, and I convinced him not to. I told him he was going to stay. He was going to make his parents proud."

Kael's tears were infectious, and Bree clenched her jaw as she wrapped her arm around his shoulder and held him close. She let him grieve, let her own tears fall. Brad wasn't the only one. Others had died, many she didn't even know. But Brad was the one who made it real. Brad had been the only one impervious to all the ugliness around them.

The ocean rocked their island, and together they rode the waves.

"A shame he never got to fight," Kael said, long minutes later. He'd splashed water across his face, cleaned his tears, and collected himself well enough to speak. "We had a goal, you know? He'd score a kill in battle, and then we'd rub it in Instructor Dohn's face. We'd show him just how well fat could fly." He shook his head. "This sucks. This fucking sucks."

Bree hugged him tightly.

"I know," she whispered.

They fell silent again. High above, the sun continued its crawl toward the western horizon.

"The theotechs tried to capture both of us," Kael said. "They got you, and they almost had me. What do they want with us, Bree? What were they planning to do to us inside the cathedral?" He glanced at her, worry painted all over his face. "If you're able to talk about it, of course."

Bree waved off his concern. Instead, she lifted her right arm to show him the gauntlet still attached.

"They wanted me to unleash fire from this modified gauntlet," she said. "It's... Something is special about my blood, Kael, and I have a feeling I'm not the only one."

Kael frowned.

"I don't understand."

"It'll be easier to show you," she said. "Remove the light element from your gauntlet."

Her brother didn't follow, but he did as instructed, popping the prism out from his gauntlet. It was gray and cracked, thin veins of black running throughout. Bree took it from him, then gestured to his sword.

"Cut your palm," she said. "Just like when we had our affinity tests."

Kael's uncertainty grew. Carefully he pressed the tip of his sword against his palm, then cut. Blood pooled in his hand. Before Kael could ask why, Bree pressed the light prism into his hand and closed his fingers about it. A question was on his lips, but it died as his entire body stiffened. His eyes widened, his jaw falling open. A soft light grew in the center of the prism, shining brighter and brighter until it spilled through his fingers. The cracks and veins steadily vanished.

Bree pulled the prism from Kael's grasp, and immediately he relaxed.

"You felt that, didn't you?" she asked. "Like it's draining something out of you, making you weak?"

"I feel like I just ran a mile," Kael said, and he stared at the prism with a mixture of elation and horror. "This is it, isn't it? This is why the theotechs always treated us like we were special."

"Seems like it." Bree twirled the prism in her fingers as she stared at it, letting her mind slip to the past. "There's a needle jammed into my arm, along with a tube allowing my blood to drain into the compartment holding the prism. When I fired, I drained it in a single shot like always, but moments later I could fire again, the prism once more glowing with light. And they made me keep going, Kael. Over and over again. I think it was six times, maybe seven, before I passed out."

Bree's mind flashed to the eyes in the furnace just before unconsciousness took her away. What she'd seen, it couldn't have been real. She'd been so exhausted, it had to have been her delusional mind imagining things. Dismissing the faint memory, she handed the light element back to Kael. He slid it into the compartment of his gauntlet, flashed his harness off and on. It was as if he still didn't trust it to be true, that his blood could replenish the prism.

"I wonder if Mom and Dad were like this," he said, staring at the cut on his hand. "Like us, I mean. Their blood. When Center took all those people during the ghost plague, maybe they were looking for people like them."

Bree thought of the clinical coldness in Jaina's voice as they strapped her to the table and forced her to release fire from her gauntlet.

"Or making people like them," she said. "What if our parents were the only ones to survive whatever it is the theotechs did?"

"We're just guessing now," Kael said. "Sure, it's possible. But why let them go if they succeeded? This changes everything we know about the elemental prisms."

"No," Bree said, shaking her head. "We don't know that for sure. We don't know *how* they're made. We don't know what this means, not entirely. Center's still keeping secrets from us, and we'll have to keep prying them out into the open."

Kael nudged her side.

"Well aren't you a killjoy. Here I was hoping we'd made progress."

His cheer didn't last. A change had come over her brother, and he slumped his shoulders as he rested his head in his palm, staring into nothing. Bree watched, waiting. Years together had taught her that if she kept silent Kael would reveal whatever he was thinking on his own, without need of prodding.

"Bree, when you were in there, did…did you see what was in the furnace?"

Bree hesitated. She'd been so exhausted, she didn't believe it to be true. But what did it matter if she told Kael? The worst he would do was laugh at her, and given her circumstances at the time, she doubted he'd do even that.

"I thought I saw something in it watching me," she admitted. "It was right at the end of their experiments. I'm sure I just imagined it." She looked to her troubled brother, horror licking at the edges of her consciousness. "Unless I didn't. What did you see, Kael? Why even ask?"

He tapped the ice with his fingers, looked away.

"I saw it, too," he said. "Something inside, watching me. A creature, small, humanlike, yet not. It was…it was made of fire, Bree. Coal and fire. And when it saw me watching it, it drew its claws, flicked its tongue at me, and…laughed."

Kael rubbed at his eyes.

"Tell me I'm crazy," he said.

"I wish I could," she whispered. "That's the same as what I saw. I never thought it could be true. How could it? What could that thing possibly even be?"

"The stories of the Ascension," Kael said, glancing up at her. "Of angels warring against demons. What if they're all true?

What if that...thing...was one of the demons we fled to the skies from?"

"Then why haven't we ever seen them before?" Bree asked. "All that's left of the world is the Endless Ocean."

"Is it?" Kael asked. "How do we know?"

It was a simple enough question. Bree started to retort with the obvious, how everyone knew in all directions there was only ocean, but then paused. She didn't know. The theotechs always insisted that was the case, but since when did she trust them to speak the truth?

"We don't," Bree said. "Maybe no one's flown far enough. Maybe in some faraway place, there's land. We're in the dark, as we always are. It's a position I'm pretty damn sick of."

Kael chuckled.

"Amen to that," he said. He looked to the west, to the far distant brown speck that was their island home. "So what do we do? With my light element charged, I can easily get us to Weshern. They might still be looking for us, though. The knights may not know what our blood does, but the theotechs likely do."

"Then we wait until dark," Bree said. "We'll fly low along the water. With the midnight fire's reflection rippling on the water, I doubt anyone will see us coming."

"Good enough for me," Kael said. He armed his gauntlet, added another chunk of ice to their little island, then slid over to it. "Now if you don't mind, I'm going to close my eyes for a bit. You weren't kidding about how it feels to refill an element. Wake me when the rolling darkness comes. That, or our little ice island needs another layer."

Bree pulled her legs to her chest and wrapped her arms about them for warmth.

"Will do," she said softly, and watched the sun fall.

*   *   *

Bree shook Kael awake from his slumber as the darkness complete rose from the east, and she pointed with a hand as she stared at the sky.

"What?" Kael asked, sucking in a deep breath as he looked about in confusion.

"The crawling darkness," she said. "It's . . . wrong."

Kael frowned, and he blinked rapidly as he gazed at the sky, searching for whatever it was she meant. After a moment, he saw it, too. It had begun when the inky darkness reached overhead. Normally it rolled along as a solid line, but as it neared, it was curling inward as well as moving at a far more rapid pace. It felt frighteningly close, like a wave crashing down directly atop them.

"What does it mean?" Bree asked, the last light of the sun fading behind the horizon, bathing them both in absolute darkness. She felt Kael's hand touch her own, and she held it, her mind transported back years ago, when they caught a glimpse of a single star prior to the battle that claimed their parents' lives.

"I don't know," Kael said. "I'm not sure I want to know."

The midnight fire erupted, and Kael and Bree watched its progress across the sky in silence. Bree noticed even the rippling fire looked wrong from their perspective on the water. In the vast emptiness of the ocean, she could clearly see the dividing line between fire and shadow, and it wasn't perfectly even as it approached. Instead it curled to the far north and south She pointed that out to Kael.

"Strange," he said. "Maybe it looks different because we're far from Weshern, or we're watching from so low?"

Bree didn't believe it was that simple. With much of the sky consumed, the crawling fire swarmed downward, again like a sharp wave to bury the eastern sky.

"It looks so *close*," she said. "Like we could reach out and touch it."

Kael watched the fire seal off the eastern horizon, the two of them bathed in red. His eyes narrowed.

"Grab hold of my neck," he said.

"Why?"

"Because I think you're right," he said, rising to his feet. "I think we *can* reach out and touch it."

Bree swallowed down her apprehension, wrapped her arms around her brother, and held on as he flooded silver light into his wings. Kael curled his right arm around her waist and gently raised the throttle. They flew into the air, leaving their little island of ice behind. The wind whipped through her hair, and though they flew at a gentler pace, it was still enough to flood her ears with the sound of wind.

"I see land!" Kael shouted.

Bree's eyes widened. It couldn't be. Land, amid the ocean? But how? Their speed lessened as they descended. Twisting to see, she scanned the distance for this supposed land. She saw only fire, a pure wall of it blocking star and sky, but she searched too far. Kael slowed their descent even more, and glancing down, she saw it, a strange island of bare earth less than a few feet wide. Its length, though, seemed to stretch for at least a mile toward the north and south. Water lapped the western edge. Blocking the other, a massive wall of flame.

The two landed. The ground sank beneath Bree's feet, wet and muddy. Side by side they stared at the rippling fire before them. The dirt rose toward it, as if pulled out of the water, but then halted upon contact. Despite their proximity, the raging fire made not a sound and cast no heat.

"What is this?" Bree asked. Her insides trembled. It was too much. First the burning creature within the furnace, and now this. The implications were beyond her understanding. Kael looked equally shaken. Despite standing on somewhat solid ground, he refused to shut off his wings, and their soft hum was the only sound of the night.

"It's the midnight fire," Kael said. "It's here. Right here. We're at its very edge."

"But that can't be," Bree said. "It's supposed to swallow up the heavens. No one can reach it. No one could ever fly to touch it."

Kael took a step closer to the fire.

"Then it's another lie," he said. "So strange. There's no sound. No heat. Almost as if..."

The flame rippled before them, strangely distorted. Bree tensed, her breath catching in her throat as Kael pushed his fingers toward the fire.

And stopped as he touched a shimmering wall. It was translucent like glass, shining a faint white at his contact. Kael's mouth dropped open as he slid his fingers across it. The rippling effect increased, spreading out as if he were disturbing the surface of a pond. Bree neared, and she dared to touch it with her own fingers. Just as Kael said, she felt no heat. Though she'd expected something cold and smooth, like stone, instead her fingers tingled with the faintest hint of electricity.

"How far does it go?" Bree wondered aloud.

"I don't know," Kael said. "We're not that far from Weshern, maybe a few hundred miles."

Bree looked up and down the wall. Now so close, it was much easier to see its gentle curve, a dome stretching high into the sky holding back the flame, and a thin cropping of dirt where it sank deep into the earth.

"It's like we're in a giant cage," she said.

"Or a shelter," Kael said, pushing harder against the barrier. "See how we're protected? Outside this...dome rages a tremendous fire. Yet inside here, somehow, we're kept safe from..."

The image shimmered, far worse than ever before. The silence broke with a rumble, tremendous and terrifying. Both Kael and Bree fled from the wall, Bree sinking up to her ankles in water. White light sparked like spiderwebs across the image before them, and the protective dome thinned. The fire behind the barrier thickened, brighter, louder. And in the heart of the rippling formed eyes and teeth. Several implike creatures clung to the other side, fire dripping off their bodies like water. Their claws dug into the translucent barrier, the spiderwebs of light focused where they touched. The creatures grinned, and seeing those obsidian eyes, there was no denying it was the same being as what Bree had witnessed laughing at her from within the furnace.

"Kael," Bree said, reaching for her brother.

"It's all right," Kael said, eyes locked on the creature. "It's all right. Just listen. It's already fading."

Sure enough, the rumble of the fire was but a murmur, and diminishing still. The spiderwebs of light softened, the fire rippled, and the creatures faded away, hidden behind the resurging flames. And then all was silent once more but for the hum of Kael's wings and the pounding of Bree's heart in her ears.

"They lied," Kael said softly, eyes locked on the fire. "They lied like they always lied. Every story says the Endless Ocean washed away the demons during the Ascension. But they're not gone. They're outside waiting, while we're stuck in here, behind this..." He gestured to the massive fire. "This barrier. What other lies have we been told? What's out there, Bree? How much of the world remains while we're locked inside our dome?"

"I don't know," Bree said. "I'm not sure we'll ever know."

Kael stared at the towering inferno, as if wishing his eyes could pierce through to the other side.

"The flickering," he said. "The change in the midnight fire that no one can explain. What if it's this barrier breaking after all these centuries?"

Bree put a hand on her brother's shoulder.

"If it is, then there's nothing we can do," she said. "It's time we go home."

"You're right. It is," he said, and he started unfastening the chest straps of his harness. "Buckle in, sis. It's a long flight back to New Galen."

CHAPTER

20

The entire flight made Bree uncomfortable, not that she told her brother so. It wasn't distrust in his abilities, nor how the wind blasted through her hair and face since she lacked the protective loop that Kael wore around his neck connected to the harness. It wasn't the endless waves of the ocean below, cold and dark and eager to swallow her whole. No, what set her nerves constantly on edge was how she lacked any control over their flight. Wearing a set of wings always felt freeing to her, but now she flew with a decided lack of freedom. She was little more than a package Kael carried to safety. It was maddening, to say the least. Every twitch and shift was magnified, and no adjustments of her own body would offset them.

"Getting closer," Kael shouted, not that there was any need. At the very start of their flight they'd followed the white Beam beneath Weshern, easily viewable through gaps in the red-tinted waters of the swirling Fount. They'd followed that beacon home, the darkened shape of Weshern steadily growing larger.

"Just stay low and we'll be fine," Bree shouted back. "If we're spotted, drop me and flee."

"Never happening."

Given how she hung beneath him, it was easy enough to elbow his ribs. He jerked on reflex, sending them sliding dozens of feet to the side.

"What? I can swim."

Kael laughed and shook his head, nerves already gone. Bree turned her attention to their flight path. Before leaving the fiery barrier, they'd discussed their plan. In case people had been left at the island's edge on watch, they'd stick as close to the waters as possible, letting its waves, combined with the reflection of the rippling fire above, disguise their travel. Once at Weshern, they'd pass beneath the island, weaving around the Fount and then up the southeastern side, where hopefully no guards would be stationed. Plus once there they'd only be a quick flight away from New Galen, and the relative safety of Johan's hideout.

The minutes crawled along. Crossing from one side of Weshern to the other was almost an hourlong flight, and going underneath made it no faster than above. They saw no sign of Center's knights, which was a welcome relief. Much as she'd joked about it, Bree really had no desire to take a midnight swim.

Once they were near the southwest corner of the island, Kael angled their flight upward. They'd be passing near Lowville, coming up over the edge and directly into New Galen. The rocky ground grew closer. Bree held her breath. They passed over the lip, suddenly flying over homes and green grass.

No knights. No patrols. Bree breathed out in relief as Kael's wings gently hummed.

They kept dangerously low to the ground, and they traveled slow enough that Kael had to keep their bodies positioned halfway upright. Any higher and they risked being spotted from afar by a patrolling knight. Bree glanced about the quiet streets. New Galen looked like any other Weshern town, the houses having belonged to people forced to relocate to make way for the new inhabitants. With so little time having passed, few had had the chance to redecorate or remodel. If not for the many thin red flags and cloths flying from various posts, Bree wouldn't have known they were in New Galen at all.

Kael stopped before the tall hideout and shut off his wings. Bree quickly unbuckled herself and stepped free, groaning as she stretched her arms.

"I hope we never, ever have to do that again," she said, wincing as her back popped multiple times.

"Me neither," Kael said. "You're not the lightest person to carry, you know."

"The straps did most of the work."

"I still did the rest."

Bree approached the door, but hesitated just before opening it. Was there a secret knock required, or maybe a password to alert guards that she and Kael were friendly? Before she could ask Kael, the door flung open. It wasn't a guard or a lowly disciple. Instead, it was the last person Bree expected.

"Kael?" asked Saul, a look of shock on his face. "Bree? You're both alive!"

Bree had no clue how to react, so she stood there dumbly. It wasn't like she'd been close to Saul, but to see any familiar face, let alone someone she'd thought long dead, filled her with happiness. She moved to hug him, thought it inappropriate, and then was given no choice in the matter as Saul flung his arms around her.

"I thought you were dead," he said, quickly letting her go. He seemed embarrassed by his reaction.

"I thought you were, too," she said.

"Looks like dying is something we're all bad at," Kael said, stepping past Bree to shake Saul's hand. "So how'd you get here?"

"Johan's been taking in Seraphim refugees wherever he can find them," Saul explained. "I'm on watch for anyone I recognize. Speaking of which, we need to get you inside before unfriendly eyes see you." He pointed to Kael's wings and shield. "There's no room for those in here. Next door's our armory. Stash them in there, and I'll make sure someone polishes them up."

"All right," Kael said. He approached the nearby building while Saul ushered Bree into the hideout. Inside was dark and poorly lit. A long hallway past many doors led to a set of stairs to the upper floors. Bree stood opposite Saul, her arms crossed. For reasons she couldn't identify, she felt suddenly nervous.

"So how'd you escape?" she asked, breaking the silence.

"Pure luck, really," Saul said. "I ran as fast as I could into the forest, with no real direction in mind. Center's troops did their best to search, but the woods are too big. Once things calmed down, I figured out which way was south and began making my way out. I didn't get far before one of Johan's disciples spotted me in Warwick and guided me here."

"Were you alone?"

Saul shook his head.

"Alone? No, there's others here. Not enough, though. Not near enough."

Their mood sobered, and Bree crossed her arms and looked to the floor.

"Well, I'll tell Johan you're here," Saul said, turning to leave.

"Saul," she said, stopping him. "I'm... I'm glad you're alive."

It sounded like such a stupid thing to say upon hearing it exit her lips, but thankfully Saul accepted it for the sentiment it represented.

"You too, Bree," he said. "Maybe when things calm down we can get another training session in with our swords. I have a lot of bruises to repay, after all."

Despite her exhaustion and stress, Bree flashed a smile.

"Sure," she said.

Saul vanished down the hall. Bree heard the door open behind her and turned. Kael stepped inside, now without his harness.

"Where's Saul?" he asked.

Before she could answer his eyes widened, and Bree turned about to find Johan approaching, his scarred face covered ear to ear with a grin.

"Never in my wildest dreams did I think to see either of you again," he said. "Please, be welcome in my home. Forgive me for being in a hurry, but follow me. We have much to discuss."

They passed the stairs, then entered a room Bree guessed to be Johan's. At least it seemed that way, though it lacked any signs of life. Even the solitary bed looked mostly unused. Johan shut the door behind them, then rubbed his hands, barely able to contain his excitement.

"We've steadily gathered surviving Seraphim from the attack on the Aquila Forest and hidden them in safe havens within New Galen," he said. "Plus many that had been hesitant to join Argus's resistance have come searching for us, pushed into action after hearing of the deaths of so many. Not the reaction Marius was hoping for, I'm certain. I've also been in contact with a man you might know, Varl Cutter. We've begun coordinating movements and supplies between my men and his ground forces stationed throughout the island. As of this moment, both Weshern's resistance, and my own movement, have unified in our fight against the Speaker's tyranny."

Bree wondered what such a cooperation meant. Johan's disciples sought far more disruptive changes than Argus and Rebecca's original list of demands. Working with them felt like another escalation in a conflict rapidly approaching complete and total warfare. But did they have any other choice? Without Johan's help, their resistance might have already disbanded.

"What of Clara?" Kael asked. "Did she make it out of the cathedral all right?"

"She's safely back at her family's mansion," Johan said. "I'm sure she'll be suspected, but I believe without further proof no move will be made against her." Johan stared right at Kael. "Though I'd caution against further contact with the Archon's daughter from now on. The eyes of Center will certainly be watching her more closely."

Kael was clearly unhappy but accepted Johan's wisdom. Bree leaned against the wall in the corner, resting her head against it as she closed her eyes and asked a question whose answer she feared.

"Do you have a list of the dead?"

"Nothing complete, but as survivors arrive we're writing down the names of those whose deaths they witnessed. I can bring the list to you, if you'd like. I'll also have Corm, one of my disciples, come speak with you later so you might add your own names to the list."

Bree nodded, wishing she could hide the hurt creeping into her neck and chest. There was only one name she could add to that list. Though she couldn't guess as to what happened to Rebecca Waller or Argus Summers, both of whom had been alive when she fled, she did know for certain Brad's fate.

"We need to retaliate," Kael said as he sat down on the bed. "We can't let Center have such a huge victory and then go unpunished."

"That's actually why I'm thrilled you arrived when you did," Johan said. "Marius has prepared a public execution for several people they captured during the attack at the Aquila Forest."

"Who?" Bree asked, feeling every muscle in her body tighten.

"We're mostly relying on rumors," Johan said, turning toward her. "But one name we do know for certain, because Marius made sure everyone heard: Argus Summers."

Bree was glad to hear Argus had survived his injuries, but her relief was temporary.

"We have to free them," she said. "If Argus dies, we'll lose what little support our resistance has left."

"Of course we're to free them," Johan said. "At every turn we must challenge Center's control. The eyes of Weshern will be on this execution. We've already given Marius a black eye with our attack on the Crystal Cathedral. Bloody his nose with a second humiliation, and even the common folk might believe we stand a chance at victory." Johan gestured to them both. "If you're able, I'd like you to join tomorrow's attempt."

"You couldn't make me stay if you tried," Kael said. "Bree?"

"He's killed enough of my friends," she said. "I won't let him kill even more."

"Excellent," Johan said, clapping his hands. "If the people witness the Phoenix battling against Center's troops, the ramifications will be enormous. Assuming you don't die in battle, of course."

"I'll do my best," Bree said, and she smiled bitterly.

CHAPTER 21

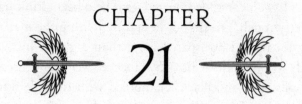

Sleep was stubborn in coming, helped little by Bree's snoring on the bed above him, which he'd forfeited to her given all the trials she'd endured. Kael lay on the floor, a thick pile of blankets beneath him, but no rearrangement made them comfortable enough for him to slip into dreams. The sounds of laughter flitted in and out, coupled with visions of burning skin and obsidian eyes. Amid it all, the strange door beneath the Crystal Cathedral kept reappearing in Kael's mind, as if calling out to him. Sighing, he wrapped one of the thinner blankets around his shoulders, exited the room, and climbed the stairs. Being cooped up in Johan's little headquarters for any amount of time did not agree with him. Fresh air sounded wonderful. The stairs ended at a short ladder leading to the roof, the top blocked by a thick wood hatch. Kael pushed it aside and climbed up. He'd expected to be alone, but to his surprise Johan stood at the rooftop's northern edge, gazing up at the midnight fire. His hood was down, revealing his bald, scarred head.

"Difficult time sleeping?" Johan asked as Kael closed the hatch. His voice sounded slurred, as if he'd been drinking.

"Pretty much," Kael said, hesitantly joining the man's side. So far Johan had not spared more than a glance his way, so intently did he stare at the sky. His eyes were unfocused, too, the pupils wide and black. Combined with the pale skin and scars, it only made Kael's unease worse. He kept silent, and he refused to watch the midnight fire. Now that he knew what it was, or at least what was partially responsible, it gave him shivers to think on it. How many of those creatures might be crawling above them, clinging to the mysterious protective dome? Did they peer down at him, laughing through the consuming shadow?

"Can you not sleep, either?" Kael asked, shaking himself free of such thoughts.

"I tend to avoid the daylight," Johan said, his slurring suddenly gone. "Too many eyes. I cannot risk being handed over to Center, not when we're so close to succeeding. The night has become my freedom." He gestured to the sky. "The ripples worsen. A sign of coming changes."

"I've never been one to put much faith into such readings," Kael said. Sometimes older men and women claimed they could divine the future from the way the midnight fire burned, and would point out patterns and symbols. Kael wondered how they'd react if they learned their divine portents were nothing more than laughing demons of flame.

"And you're probably wise to have done so," Johan said, and he smiled sideways. "You seem on edge, my young Skyborn. Are you nervous about tomorrow?"

Kael shrugged.

"I am," he said. "But that's not it."

"Then what bothers you? We're alone beneath the burning sky. Share, and I promise I will take your secret to my grave."

Kael breathed in deep and then slowly let it out. He needed to talk about what he'd seen with someone, anyone, and Johan had once been a member of the theotechs. Perhaps, just perhaps, he'd actually believe Kael's outrageous story.

"Johan... is it safe to say the theotechs have been lying to us?" he asked, deciding to ease into the subject. "About a lot of the things we believe?"

"Kael, I'd wager they've been lying to you since the day you were born. If you'd like to discuss the falsehoods of the theotechs, you must narrow down the subject."

Kael drummed his fingers against his leg as he stared out at the quiet, cramped homes of New Galen bathed in the red light of demon fire.

"The stories we've heard of the Ascension," Kael said. "About how mankind was besieged by demons, fireborn and iceborn and the like..."

"Evil creatures serving the shadow that swallowed the world, desiring nothing but destruction and ruin," Johan said. "I am well aware of the tale, and of the beautiful, flawless angels who grabbed the holy islands in their hands and lifted them to the sky as God washed away the foul creatures in a terrible flood." The man chuckled. "It paints quite a picture, doesn't it?"

"So you don't believe it?"

Johan raised an eyebrow as he glanced sidelong at him.

"Did I say that?" he asked.

Kael shook his head.

"No, sir."

Johan put a hand on Kael's shoulder and squeezed once.

"There is truth buried in those stories, now twisted and

changed over the years to fit the theotechs' agendas. Or perhaps I give the theotechs too little credit. Perhaps they tell the stories humanity is capable of hearing. The truth is a hard edge, and not all can endure its cut. Some need it blunted with fantasy and fable." Johan removed his hand. "But I have a feeling your troubles are not born of a few bedtime stories. Tell me what really bothers you, Kael Skyborn. I will hear it with open ears and an open mind."

"Are you so certain of that?" Kael asked. "I'm worried you'll think I'm insane."

Johan smiled.

"I earned my scars by challenging wisdom long accepted by my brethren. I will not condemn you for believing what others may deem strange or wrong. Now what troubles you so greatly that you're up here on a rooftop in the middle of the night?"

He didn't have to answer. Kael knew he could leave now, return to his room, and toss and turn the night away. But there was a chance Johan would believe him. That tiny chance someone might tell him he hadn't lost his mind.

"When I rescued Bree from the Crystal Cathedral, I...saw something," Kael said. "In a room where they'd been torturing my sister. It was a furnace on wheels with nothing connected. Just the furnace, all by itself. And inside..." Kael looked to the fire burning across the sky. Imagined it listening. Laughing.

"Inside was a living creature made of fire and coal," he finished.

He glanced at Johan, dying to see his reaction. Only there wasn't one. Johan stared at him, silent, his face a perfect mask, his eyes windows into nothing. Waiting for him to continue.

"Bree saw it, too," Kael said, convinced Johan didn't believe him. "It had eyes, a tail, and these thin, long claws. It wasn't some beast, either, Johan. It laughed at me. It looked right at me with these black eyes and laughed. And that wasn't the only time I saw it, either. When we fled the island, we flew miles and miles to the east. We reached a clear wall of some sort. I could touch it, and feel it, but we could see right through. And then the midnight fire came. It was spread by those creatures, Johan. We're in a cage, and that fire above us, I think it's swarming with them. Watching us. Mocking us." Kael shivered. "Waiting to get inside."

The excruciating silence dragged on. Kael wished he could read the strange man's mind. Was he thinking of a way to dismiss him without hurting his feelings? Perhaps debating a more rational explanation for what he witnessed? Kael looked away, pretending he'd said nothing as he tapped his hands against his sides and waited.

"There were... whispers," Johan said after clearing his throat. "Rumors of things we might one day witness for ourselves as we ascended the ranks of the theotechs. When I began asking my questions, I lost my chance of climbing higher up the chain, but those whispers still reached my ears. Fanciful stories, Kael, ones I easily dismissed as nothing more than the imaginations of the youthful members wishing for extravagant explanations for the source of the prisms and the power for the Founts. Fanciful stories that perhaps I should not have dismissed so easily as I did."

Kael shivered. He felt like he stood at the edge of a cave, and Johan was about to give him one final push into the light. Johan turned from the rooftop's edge and leaned closer, his voice dropping to a hushed whisper.

"Stories of captive demons in the deep pits of Heavenstone," Johan said. His blue eyes narrowed in the red dark. "Of knives cutting into their flesh, drawing out their blood to make the elements humankind needed to survive."

"Their blood?" Kael asked, thinking of how his blood

regenerated the power of a light element, and his sister, a flame element.

"Always their blood," Johan said, nodding. "But that couldn't be true, could it? The theotechs harboring demons while also preaching that God wiped them all away during the Ascension? Why, that would make them liars and deceivers. And if they know of the demons, then they'd know the true reason for the midnight fire, which they've always insisted they have no explanation for."

The bitterness and contempt dripping from Johan's words was so thick Kael felt he could reach out and touch its hovering presence. Despite the underlying horror such revelations meant, Kael couldn't help feeling excitement. He wasn't alone. He didn't have to hold on to such secrets and wonder at their meanings.

"So you'll tell the people?" Kael asked. "That's what you do, right? Unravel the theotechs' lies?"

Johan stood to his full height, and he shook his head as he smiled sadly.

"If I spread such stories, the people will believe as I once did," he said. "They'll hear nothing but fanciful tales told by a man doing all he can to smear and discredit the Speaker and his theotechs. We have no proof, Kael, and proof is what we need if we're to shake the faith of the public. The grander the lie, the harder the people will cling to it over acknowledging their own gullibility. Right now, there is only one greater lie in all of the five islands."

"And what is that?" Kael asked.

"That the theotechs care about the lives of their subjects."

Kael's nerves retightened, his anxiety reawakening.

"So we tell no one?" he asked. "We keep it to ourselves and let them get away with their lies?"

"Only for a little while," Johan said. "We'll need to find a way to capture one of these demons if we're to have any chance in persuading people to abandon the beliefs they've been taught since birth. Right now, we must remain focused on the task at hand: saving those the Speaker would execute tomorrow morning."

Kael felt a mixture of relief and disappointment. Part of him wanted to investigate the mystery of the demons. Part of him never wanted to see them again.

"You're right," he said, heading for the ladder down. "I'll leave you in peace."

"Peace is no preference to your company," Johan said, and he smiled. "Sleep well."

Kael reached the stairs, paused. Something still bothered him, nibbling away at the back of his mind. Before leaving, he turned around.

"Johan...there's something strange beneath the Crystal Cathedral. I can feel it. And I know it makes no sense, but it feels like I'm being called back there."

Johan's mouth twitched into a frown.

"Is that so?" the man asked. "Do you have any idea what calls you down there, or why?"

Kael shook his head.

"I don't. It's a feeling I have, along with blurry dreams I barely remember upon waking."

"Interesting. If you happen to learn more, please, let me know. Now go rest, Kael. A monumental task awaits you tomorrow, but you've succeeded at the impossible once, and I believe you and your sister capable of doing so again."

When Kael returned to his room, Bree was quiet, her snoring ceased. He slipped into his blankets, trying not to wake her, but it was an unnecessary kindness.

"Kael?" Bree asked from atop the bed.

"Yeah?" Kael responded as he moved pillows about in an attempt to get more comfortable.

"Are you all right? You were gone a long time."

"Just went to the roof for some fresh air," Kael said. "I'm fine, really. Johan was up there, too, and he wanted to talk, so we talked. I...I told him about the creatures we saw, and the wall they're behind." He sighed. "Do you think that was a good idea?"

He heard the bed squeak as she shifted.

"I don't know. I'll trust your judgment," she said. Kael suppressed a laugh. Trust *his* judgment? He hadn't the slightest clue what he was doing. "Kael, did you tell him about what our blood can do?"

He frowned.

"No."

"Why not?"

Kael rolled onto his side, facing away from the bed.

"I don't know," he said. "Never had reason to, I guess."

A long pause.

"Until we know what it means, or what we even are, can you keep this between only us?"

"Of course," Kael said. "Whatever you want."

Another long pause.

"Thank you, Kael."

"Don't mention it."

He closed his eyes in an attempt to sleep. It wasn't long before he heard his sister's breathing slow and the first inklings of snoring resume. Exhaustion clawed at his own eyes, but every time he felt sleep coming to take him away, the blue-white doors with gold runes and painted wings flashed into his vision, hovering over the darkness, calling him, demanding he return and enter within.

CHAPTER

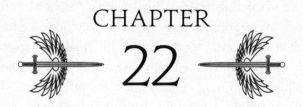

22

Marius entered New Galen in the early morning mist, flanked on the ground by four of his most trusted knights and several more hovering in the air above. Er'el Jaina Cenborn walked alongside him. None of the news she'd come to share was good.

"Breanna's blood was everything Er'el Tesdon hoped for when he began the program," she said, shaking her head sadly. "Her escape is most disappointing."

"Is there any way of replicating the results?" Marius said as they passed posts pounded into the ground, long red strips of cloth fluttering from nails at the tops.

"Not in the short term," Jaina said. She smoothed an errant strand of hair away from her pale face. "Perhaps not even in the long term. When we last tried, the casualties from the blood implantation were catastrophic. Liam and Cassandra's survival bordered on a miracle, and given our lack of explanation as to why, we might as well accept it as nonrepeatable."

Marius refused to let his frustration show. At all times in public he kept his head high, his shoulders back, and his lips in a smile. Exuding confidence was a vital aspect of maintaining the persona he'd so carefully crafted. People mustn't doubt his authority. They mustn't wonder at his capabilities of handling even the most difficult of situations. Despite trusting his knights completely, he lowered his voice and leaned even closer to Jaina as he spoke.

"Demon blood may be lethal, but the gift emerged in the second generation," he said. "What if the blood of the Skyborn twins is far more suitable for transfer than anything we used previously?"

Jaina tapped at her lips as she thought.

"Interesting," she said. "But we've used Liam's blood in transfusions before. We never discovered any latent gifts in the recipients."

"We've also never seen what Breanna Skyborn's blood accomplished, either," Marius said. "The idea is worth pursuing, at the least."

"It is," Jaina said. "But first we must capture one of them *alive.*"

The street broadened, the town center of New Galen nearing. Already Marius heard the murmur of the gathered crowd.

"Do you know who rescued Breanna from the Crystal Cathedral?" Marius asked.

"We've only guesses. It was a male, bald, likely a member of Johan's rebel ministry. He wore a stolen harness from one of our knights as well."

"A disguised male," Marius said. "One who flew far beyond the distance my knights felt comfortable traveling. Kael Skyborn's affinity was of light, and if his sister's blood can revive an emptied fire prism, it's not much of a stretch to assume her brother is capable of doing the same with a light prism."

There was no hiding the excitement blossoming in Jaina's blue eyes.

"If that's true, and Kael was the rescuer, then the two likely survived," she said. "Why didn't you post a watch for their return?"

"I did," Marius said. "But Weshern has hundreds of miles to its border. It's not unreasonable to assume they managed to slip onto the island without being spotted."

"Then we must find them and bring them in," she said. "Both of them. They're the key to Tesdon's dream. I only scratched the surface of what we might learn prior to Breanna's escape. With the two of them together, and with more time..."

"Patience," Marius said, and he gestured before them. "For now, we focus on the task at hand. Those who would spit on all the good we've done must pay the price."

The murmur was now a rumble. Hundreds of people, massed together in New Galen's market square. Many were Galen refugees, but Marius had ordered a significant amount of Weshern natives to be herded inside as well. All four roads leading into the square were blocked off by soldiers forming a solid wall of shields and spears. A dozen knights stood in a ring at the center, forming a perimeter around the enormous pit he'd had his soldiers dig over the last twenty-four hours. It was ten feet across and thirty feet deep, the very bottom lined with jagged stones. Four tall beams of wood, one at each corner, held aloft crossbeams that formed an X above the pit. Hanging above the pit by ropes tied to those crossbeams were the nine men and women waiting to die.

The bodies softly swayed in the gentle morning wind. Their hands were bound behind their backs, their ankles tied together, and their chests carefully wrapped. All three loops were then connected to a single major rope attached to the beam, the only thing that held them aloft. Their mouths were gagged, for there was no need for repentance or confession, only execution. Some were conscious, others not.

Marius recognized several, particularly those who'd been involved with the Weshern Seraphim academy. Rebecca Waller glared at him from where she hung, her eyes never leaving his. Marius smiled at her, pleased by the woman's fiery spirit. Capturing her had been the second-most important success of the raid on the Aquila Forest. She was the intelligence of the resistance, the hidden bones holding it all together. Near her was a former instructor, Randy Kime, if Marius remembered correctly. One of his hands was missing from an old injury, and it had required an even trickier set of knots to keep his arms pinned behind his back. Between them was a smaller woman with copper skin and dark hair. The academy's librarian, though Marius couldn't recall her name.

In the center of the X hung Marius's most prized capture, and the one death he knew would reverberate throughout all of Weshern: a fully gagged and blindfolded Argus Summers.

"A shame such a legend must die this way," Marius said, pausing before the pit. "Reports say Argus was surprised and taken down without a chance to fight back."

"And it's for the best," Jaina said, frowning at the hanging man. "How many more knights might we have lost if he'd been given that chance?"

"A great many," Marius admitted. "Argus deserved a better end to the legend he crafted, but that is his own failing. I did not force him to rebel. Misguided loyalty and pride did that, and neither will save him from the drop."

An elevated wood platform stood on one side of the pit, and Marius climbed its stairs, Jaina at his heels. Another dozen shield bearers lined the front of the platform, separating Marius from the rest of the crowd. Two men waited for him atop the platform, Lance and Edwin Willer, come at his request to grant legitimacy to the executions. Not that he needed it. This was about sending messages. The people would see Lance and Edwin beside him, calm, silent, and most important of all, obedient.

"I've never seen tensions this high before," Lance said, accepting Marius's offered hand and shaking it. "Half the crowd looks ready to kill the other half."

"And both halves wish to see *us* dead," Edwin added, shaking his hand as well. "I know you brought plenty of knights, Speaker, but I wish you'd brought even more."

Marius beamed his widest smile, his well-trained response for when he wished to frown in public. Lance was a hot-blooded fool drunk on his own importance. He'd do anything Marius asked so long as it allowed him to believe Weshern remained loosely under his control. Edwin was more troublesome, his tongue sharp, his eyes always laughing. Thankfully that one had shown no inclination to work with Argus's crumbling resistance.

"We are quite safe, I assure you," Marius said. "I have with me twenty of my best knights, each worth a dozen Seraphim from any minor island. We are safe from any threat."

"It's not rebel Seraphim or Johan's deluded disciples I'm worried about," Lance said. "It's the hundreds of people ready to tear each other limb from limb. No offense, your holiness, but I have a feeling they'd do the same to you if they got the chance."

"They're welcome to try," Jaina said, listening to the conversation even as her eyes never left the nine waiting to drop. "Spoiled children throwing tantrums, that's all they are. Beat them hard enough with a switch and they'll behave."

"Today's not about punishing the guilty," Marius said, taking in every fearful glare, every muttered sigh, to gauge the temperature of the crowd. "If I wanted that, those hanging there would have been dead days ago. I'm here to enlighten the misguided and warn the foolhardy."

Marius beckoned one of his knights closer, the armored man hovering close from a perch near the rooftop behind the platform. A dark beard covered much of his face, and that which wasn't covered was the color of coal. Hanging from his back, locked in place between his two wings, was an enormous chain flail. A patch on his shoulder identified him as a knight lieutenant, one of the most skilled of all his knights.

"What is your name, Knight Lieutenant?" Marius asked him.

"Beograd, your holiness," the man answered.

"Is the area secure?"

"It appears so, though with so many people in such a wide area, we can never be sure."

That was good enough for Marius. He knew this performance was inherently dangerous. All important things tended to contain some measure of risk.

"The angels will not take me until my time has come," Marius said. "But keep close, and keep your eyes open. I have no intention of giving the angels a reason to hurry."

Beograd saluted, then hovered back into the air, positioning himself between two other knights who watched the row of homes behind the platform. Marius ran the opening few sentences of his prepared speech over in his head. *Project,* he told himself. *Dominate. Their ears are yours, so captivate them with your charisma.*

All the while, he kept a calm smile on his face. No matter what doubt or concerns were inside his mind, he would never, ever let the public see anything other than complete confidence. Deciding the time was right, he stepped to the edge of the platform. The crowd immediately hushed, as eager to hear the words of the angels as Marius was to speak them.

"Citizens of Weshern," Marius began, spreading his arms wide as if he were to embrace them. "Survivors of Galen. I greet you as voice of the angels, servants of our mighty Lord. I wish the message I brought was one of joy, but that cannot be. Turmoil is the norm, and even on this island the risk of collapse remains. The Ascension was to save us from the trials of the old world, but the evils have followed. Under such a threat, we must have the strength of unity to endure. We must be one voice decrying the darkness. But instead…"

He spun to face the hanging nine.

"Instead we have liars and warmongers!" he shouted. "Instead we have those who would seek death over union, destruction over safety, and the bloodshed of war over the sanctity of peace!"

He thrust an accusatory finger their way.

"They have decried my authority. They have spread falsehoods and denied the very words of the divinity spoken to me by God's angels. For their pride, and their bloodlust, they risk the fall of Galen being repeated here in Weshern."

The very mention of Galen's fall sent a ripple through the crowd. Many bearing red armbands tilted their heads and raised a single fist. The pose was both a solemn remembrance of their fallen homeland and an undeniable demonstration of defiance. It was a sentiment Marius wanted to both tap into and end forever.

"These nine are not the reason I have come," he said. "These nine are not why I have dug this pit in New Galen's square. Daily I receive word of the conflict born in these streets. Galen's memory is not to be forgotten, nor her people dissolved into dust. But let all old grudges fall with the island. Let all bitterness and regret sink beneath the waters of the Endless Ocean. Galen and Weshern, you are one people, one race, one existence. The conflict between you ends now. I will not let it stand. I will not endure it, nor let it risk all the good I have sought to build during my time as your Speaker for the Angels."

Marius stepped closer to the edge of the platform. All eyes were upon him, and he let it add power to his voice as he gave his decree.

"The segregation must end," he said. "The killings and violence must stop. This pit is far too large for these nine, but by God, I will fill it if I must. Peace, my children. We shall have peace, no matter the cost."

"The Speaker is right!" shouted a man, his voice rumbling over the crowd like thunder. "There must be peace between the people of Weshern and Galen, for you are not enemies."

Marius scanned the crowd for the shouter, but he was not among them. From atop a distant rooftop he emerged. He wore a long brown robe and a hood covering half his pale face. Marius's heart leapt at the sight.

"Johan," he whispered. There he was, the phantom whose name spread fear and bloodshed throughout the remaining islands. The man who would bring every piece of order and stability crumbling down into chaos.

"The army of *Center* is your true enemy," Johan continued. "Their authority over you ends today. All islands must rise up and demand true freedom and prosperity. Chains of bone bind you, and only blood will set you free." Johan pointed a gloved hand right at Marius. "His blood."

"I want him alive," Marius ordered one of his knights, not the slightest bit afraid of the madman's threat. "Bring him to me. His execution will be the greatest achievement of my reign."

A deep thrum accompanied the knight's wings flaring to life. "With pleasure," the knight said.

As the knight rose into the air, Johan bent down, his hand sliding into the folds of his robe.

"We cannot afford cowardice. We cannot endure peace. Meager lists of demands will not result in justice." Johan's hand came out from the robe covered with gold, and this time Marius did feel afraid. "Only war."

Marius dove to the ground as ice shot from Johan's gauntlet. His knights flung into action, one leaping atop Marius, another forming an enormous pillar of stone on the platform, creating a barrier. Marius winced at the heavy weight, the golden armor far from gentle as it jabbed into his skin, but better it than the lances of ice that shattered against the protective wall. He heard screams, coupled with the roar of the crowd. A hand grabbed him, pulled him upward. One of his knights, pushing him against the wall of stone, Jaina propped beside him.

"Stay here until it's safe," the knight said, activating his own gauntlet.

Jaina bobbed her head, her outer appearance calm but for her wide eyes.

"Don't let them escape," Marius said.

The knight flew into the air as more gathered on either side of him, watching, gauntlets up and ready. Marius leaned out, glimpsing the battle that suddenly roared about him. Edwin Willer lay on his stomach atop the wooden platform, hands on his head. Lance, meanwhile, had fled into the crowd, frantically shoving his way toward one of the exits.

"Capture him!" Marius shouted to his knights, and he pointed over the barrier. Likely neither brother was involved in Johan's attack, but he'd have them questioned nonetheless.

One knight heard his command and lifted into the air, hovering low above the chaotic crowd as he chased.

"They'll suffer for such foolishness," Jaina said. She'd spun around and risen to her feet so she could peer over the stone wall. "Surprise means nothing without Seraphim to battle our own."

Marius joined her overlooking the battlefield. All across the rooftops he saw dozens of men and women, some wearing brown disciple robes, most not. A few bore wingless gauntlets, like those of his specters. The rest carried bows and arrows, and they flooded the air with their shots. The crowd on the ground swarmed like a stirred hornets' nest, pushing in all directions against Marius's soldiers who were attempting to keep order. Many in the crowd were armed with blades, and scattered pockets of battle filled the square. Maddeningly, his soldiers were dying as frequently as Johan's supporters, overwhelmed from all sides, with seemingly every man or woman a foe, regardless of whether they bore the distinctive brown robes.

At the very heart of the crowd gathered several women, and they lifted crossbows hidden underneath their dresses. Marius's eyes spread wide as he watched them fire at the knight he'd sent after Lance. Bolts thudded into the man's chest and shoulders, and his wings dipped low. With a horrific shriek of metal and crunching of flesh the knight crashed through the crowd. Limbs snapped. Bodies crumpled. Lance, fleeing directly beneath the knight, had only the slightest warning before the knight rolled over him. The sharp, broken edges of the wings tore into his body as he fell to the ground, hidden by the crowd. Marius had no delusions as to the man's survival.

"Damn it," Marius swore, and he pointed to the cowering Edwin. "Get him to safety, now!"

His knights heard and obeyed, one rushing over, grabbing the man from underneath the arms, and soaring into the sky.

Wherever the knight took him, Marius trusted it to be safer than the current battlefield.

"They're not retreating," Marius muttered, returning to the ebb and flow of the battle. He searched for Johan, furious he could spot neither the man nor his corpse. While the chaos on the ground worked against his soldiers, the rooftops were a different story. The angelic knights looped in circles, dodging arrows and occasional shooting lances of ice and lightning back at their attackers. One by one the rooftops collapsed under a barrage of elements. It was clear Johan's people would be overwhelmed in time, yet they did not retreat. But why? What else could they hope for? Marius was surrounded by knights. It would take an entire army to kill him, so what other objective could they have?

Marius turned to the nine traitors hanging from ropes over the pit, saw the answer.

"Cut their ropes!" Marius shouted to a knight beside him. "Carry out the executions this instant!"

The burly knight drew a sword and saluted.

"As you wish," he said.

He flew to the first of the nine, the former Weshern Academy's librarian, and hovered in the air before her. The woman's eyes widened, and she twisted and thrashed as the knight pulled his sword back to swing. He never got the chance to finish. A blast of lightning ripped through his chest. His body went rigid, his wings dark, and down into the pit he fell. Marius pressed his back tighter against his stone shelter as he searched for the interlopers.

Johan's Seraphs flew in pairs, six total, one just behind the other, knifing through the chaos. Starting on the outside, the leading Seraphs jerked to a halt before a hanging prisoner and swung their swords, cutting through the rope. The trailing

Seraphs barely even slowed, slamming into the newly freed prisoner and catching them in their arms. The pairs then shot away, the burdened three fleeing while the others looped back into the fray, elements flashing from their gauntlets.

"Weshern's Seraphim working with Johan?" Marius seethed. "Do they not understand the monster they ally themselves with?"

"Our knights are faster," Jaina said, leaning in close beside him to watch. "They won't outrun them to safety."

Two knights chased after the fleeing Seraphim who carried the prisoners, slowly closing the gap between them. Jaina was right; they couldn't outrun them.

But they weren't trying to.

The Phoenix blasted in from the street below, streaks of flame trailing behind her. Despite racing headlong toward a collision with the two knights, she showed no hesitation, no fear in the slightest. Her entire body twirled as she neared. One knight died instantly, arm and head sliced free of his body. His wings careened wildly to the ground, slamming into a distant home with an explosion of dust and stone. The other knight immediately veered to the side, attempting to flee, but Bree had the better angle. She curled up and around, and now above the knight, she punched downward, using gravity to give her even greater speed. Marius's knight sensed his vulnerability and twisted in air to face Bree. Lances of ice shot from his gauntlet. Bree dodged with perfect fluid grace, the lances passing so close Marius couldn't believe she escaped unharmed.

Bree and the knight collided with a flash of flame. Bree rose higher, hurtling toward New Galen's square. The knight fell to his death upon the hard stone streets, his wings cut from his back. Marius was stunned by the relief he felt. He knew it would be advantageous for them to capture Bree alive and deliver her into Jaina's hands for continued testing, but that didn't explain it, not quite. What then?

"Incredible," Jaina said, equally mesmerized. "Watch how she increases her fire just before contact. I doubt she even knows she's doing it, but that gives her swings tremendous cutting power. No wonder she uses tactics other Seraphim cannot attempt."

That was it, Marius realized. Bree was a pure pleasure to behold in combat. She never hesitated, never even showed the slightest moment of doubt. No, the Phoenix sliced through the air as if her entire body were a weapon carving the skies, twin trails of fire ensuring all eyes remained upon her. Unlike other Seraphim, she didn't avoid proximity or turn in wide loops while fighting for a better angle than her foe. She always attempted to intersect, her path direct, relying on her speed and maneuverability to protect her. Though she warred against him, Marius could not bring himself to cheer for such beauty to be snuffed out. The only thing that bothered him was that she was foolish enough to ally with Johan's movement.

Marius turned to the knights keeping him closely guarded. Recognizing one, he rushed out from protection to grab him by the shoulder.

"Forget me!" he shouted to Beograd. He pointed to the twin trails of fire knifing through the sky. "Bring her down, and bring her alive."

The knight looked as if he were to protest, then shut his mouth and bowed.

"I obey," he said, pulling the chain flail off his back. The handle was half the size of Marius, the chain links thick and black, the head a solid sphere of steel with winglike protrusions forming a crown of razor spikes. With a burst of light, his wings carried him into the air, his path directly intersecting Bree's.

So far, Bree appeared unaware of his approach as she raced toward the center of New Galen's square, right into the thick of battle. To Marius's confusion, she sheathed her right blade, and the fire vanished from the left. What was she trying to accomplish? Was she hoping to enter the battle unnoticed? His angelic knights had turned their attention to the ambushing Seraphim, wisely deciding them the greater threat than the scattered few archers still firing from the rooftops. Three Weshern Seraphs engaged from one direction, and Bree flew in from the other, with Marius's knights caught in the middle. Marius thought they would hold their own just fine, but then Bree unleashed her fire.

A tremendous plume of flame flew from her gauntlet. Marius's jaw slackened as it blasted two of his knights, consuming them completely. Even if a knight had attempted to drain his fire element so quickly, Marius doubted one could do so. There were limits to the power one could unleash, but Bree wasn't bound to those limits. The remaining knights scattered, dodging the blast as Bree twirled in place, unleashing the flame in all directions. It took only a moment, but the fire ceased, and the Weshern Seraphim raced through the smoke in chase, their own elements flashing from their gauntlets.

"She must be ours again," Jaina said beside him, eyes locked on Bree. "We witness the future of our evolution."

"That may not be an option," Marius said as Beograd closed the distance between him and Bree, who redrew her right sword and bathed both blades in flame. The idea was chilling. The Phoenix suddenly able to harness the power of her gauntlet along with the fire of her blades? Only the most skillful of foes could hope to stand against her. No matter how much Marius hoped otherwise, Beograd would be hard-pressed to capture her alive.

Bree noticed Beograd's approach mere moments before he swung his enormous chain flail. Marius clenched his jaw, angry to see the knight attack so recklessly after being commanded to capture her alive, but as Bree twisted to dodge, he realized Beograd wasn't aiming for her but instead her wings. The flanged head passed close, but it failed to puncture the silver metal. Beograd extended his gauntlet as he flew past her, narrow bursts of flame slicing through her path, guiding her upward. Bree looked more than happy to give chase instead of fleeing, following after the knight with a shimmer of silver about her wings. Higher and higher they climbed, bringing their battle to the skies.

The two whirled about each other in a dance, and oh what a dance it was. Marius watched, enraptured by the sight. Bree was smaller, faster, able to twist and shift her body into curves and arcs Beograd could never hope to achieve. But where she had speed, he had experience, and it seemed the knight knew every move she made before she began it. Bree would chase after him, knifing in at various angles, and Beograd would redirect his path the tiniest bit. Never much, but a rotation here, a momentary drop in speed there, Bree's swords always left cleaving air. Anytime she overshot, his flail would lash out, the long pole and even longer chain giving him reach her swords had no hope of competing with. Sometimes all it took was a perfectly placed swing by Beograd to convinced Bree to pull off completely lest she be crushed by its flanged head.

The two circled and circled, while below them the conflict winded down. Another wave of rescuers came swooping in for those hanging in wait of execution. Marius seethed as he saw Argus Summers cut free of his ropes, pulled into the arms of a Seraph, and then whisked off into the distance. The battle was nearing its end, with Bree and Beograd dueling high above and the rest of the knights either scattered, aiding the ground skirmish, or chasing after fleeing Seraphim. Only two prisoners remained hanging from hopes. Marius's insides boiled. Such a paltry example left to make, but he would make it nonetheless.

Several knights remained at his side, guarding against any potential ambushers, and he shouted to one.

"Forget protecting me. Kill the prisoners, now!"

A knight raised his gauntlet, electricity sparkling across the focal point of his gauntlet.

"As you wish," he said.

He turned to the remaining two. One was a member of Argus's vaunted Wolf Squad, and a single blast of lightning ripped through his chest. His body convulsed momentarily, swinging side to side, then hung still. The other was the one-handed instructor from the academy. The man had his head tilted back, watching Bree battle Beograd. Bizarre as it was, he was smiling.

The lightning bolt struck him directly in the forehead, ending that smile forever.

Two prisoners of nine, Marius thought, shaking his head. *Johan already has his victory.*

But perhaps the day would not end as a complete waste. Marius turned back to the aerial battle. Beograd was clearly frustrated with being on the defensive. He was also holding back, that much was clear, unable to unleash his fire for fear of outright killing Bree. When he swung his flail, its aim had to be for the wings instead of the body, for such a heavy weapon would crush her bones like twigs. Bree, meanwhile, flew like a wild creature, using more and more aggressive attempts to close the distance between them. She'd been clipped by the flanged edges of the mace twice, once on her leg, once on her arm. Despite the bleeding and pain, it never slowed her down.

Bree broke for a brief moment of separation, then dove right back after Beograd in a head-on attack. Beograd swung his flail, attempting to force her to pull back, but this time she continued on, flipping upside down while swinging one arm wide. Her sword struck the flail's chain, bursting with fire so bright it was nearly blinding. The head of the flail flew free, smashing through the roof of a home. Suddenly weaponless, Beograd lifted his gauntlet, and instead of fleeing, he unleashed the fire of his prism.

The problem was, Bree did the same.

Fire connected with fire, but Bree's billowed forth with far greater strength and volume. It washed over Beograd, melting his armor and blackening his skin. The light around his wings faded, and he dropped limp to the stone of the square. His wings twisted and cracked upon landing, and Marius winced against the shriek of metal.

With Beograd defeated, Bree looped in the air, surveying the battlefield, then turned to the execution pit. Even from so far below, Marius heard her scream, a keening most appropriate to her Phoenix name. Despite the knights all about, despite the retreat of the remaining Seraphim, she dived straight for Marius, who pressed against his stone barrier, the only protection he had. The knights guarding him and Jaina scrambled, lifting into the air while unleashing bursts of lightning and stone. Bree danced through them. Panic trickled up Marius's spine. The girl looked possessed. No element would stop her.

His knights flung up one last barrage, then positioned themselves in the way of her target... except her target wasn't Marius. Bree's body arced, and she curled underneath the double beams of wood above the well. Her left sword lashed out, slicing through the rope holding the dead instructor and dropping him down into the dark pit. She never slowed. Body still curled, she rose higher, shooting over the rooftops, fire trailing into smoke behind her as she dismissed the flame of her blades. A few chased, but Marius ordered them back. They wouldn't catch her, and thinned out, they were a prime target for another ambush.

The diminished crowd was largely subdued, with most having fled down the various openings in the square. Knights still circled above, searching for potential ambushers or disciples of Johan in hiding. Marius walked to Beograd's charred corpse, torn between anger and awe. The fire on Bree's weapons was incredible, and she wielded it with a control he doubted she fully understood. Calm and constant when in movement, yet growing into a burning fury just prior to an attack. Combined with her natural grace in the air, it was no surprise she'd already become a fabled hero for Weshern.

But if her fiery swords could be mimicked by his superior skilled knights...

"The rescued prisoners are already in hiding," Jaina said, returning to Marius's side. "Soldiers are sweeping nearby buildings but it's a slow and likely fruitless process."

"This was an ill day," Marius said, staring at Beograd's corpse. "And an overwhelming victory for our foes."

"We each suffered casualties," Jaina said. "And we can afford to lose far more than they."

Marius gestured to the crushed body of Lance Willer.

"We were humiliated before the eyes of the populace, and we'll be blamed for his death. The damage will range far and wide. Today should have ended any resistance, but it will endure. We must plan a retaliation, Jaina. Something terrible and swift to stomp this out before—"

He stopped as a knight raced in from the east and slammed to his knees mere feet away.

"Forgiveness, Speaker," he said, head bowed in respect. "But we are under attack and need immediate reinforcements."

Marius's eyes narrowed, and he knew the answer to the question before he ever asked it.

"Where?"

"The holy mansion," the knight said. "The Weshern military have stormed the grounds, and they've come with disciples of Johan as well as traitorous Weshern Seraphim."

The fire in Marius's breast burned brighter. This wasn't just a few Seraphim aiding Johan Lumens. This was a coordinated attack by all of Weshern's former military. If the rescued Archon and his wife also felt they owed Johan their loyalty, today's bold attacks would be the beginning of the war Johan had been craving for years.

Two fingers to his lips, he whistled, summoning the rest of his circling knights.

"Send all we have to the holy mansion," he ordered. "Every pair of wings, get it airborne. The Archon must not escape, do you hear me? The Archon must not escape!"

CHAPTER

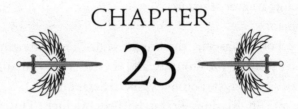

23

The gathered ground forces of Weshern's military marched toward the gates of the holy mansion, and Kael flew high above them as one of the six Seraphim sent as escort. Chernor Windborn was their squad leader, and he kept low and slow as they closed the final distance.

"Looks like they've locked the gates on our welcome party," Chernor bellowed over the wind. "Would one of you care to knock?"

"I got it!" shouted another of the five, an older Seraph with bronze skin named Aven. The black stripes of Argus's Wolf Squad were still painted on his silver wings. He casually aimed his gauntlet and lobbed four large stones through the air. Golden-armored soldiers fled from the gate as the stones smashed down, making a mangled mess of the iron and stone supports. The way now free, the ground troops rushed through the outer gate toward the mansion's entrance, Varl Cutter leading the wave of spears and shields.

With the Weshern forces numbering in the hundreds, Center's forces couldn't hope to compete in open warfare. Instead they retreated through the thin doors. Another stone knocked those doors down, clearing a path. Spears slammed against shields as the two forces collided. Even within the cramped space there was little the vastly outnumbered soldiers of Center could do to withstand the tide.

Chernor took them through a loop above the mansion, then slowed to a hover. The rest of the Seraphs gathered around him to hear his commands.

"Reinforcements are bound to show up soon," he said. "Kael and I will rescue the royal family. You four, set up ambush points around the premises. The moment any knights show up, hit them fast and hard before they can retreat."

"What if they come in too great a number?" Saul asked. At first Kael thought him merely being pessimistic, but to his surprise Saul looked earnest in his question.

"Then you fight, you die, and you fall from the sky like Seraphim," Chernor said. "Buy us the time we need. No matter what, we're getting our Archon and his family out of there."

"We've got this," Aven said. "Get in there and give them hell, Chernor."

The six saluted one another, and Aven took charge, directing the remaining Seraphs to hidden alcoves of the building and deep shadows beneath the carefully cut trees. Chernor watched them leave, then smacked Kael across the chest.

"Let's go," he said.

Chernor and Kael dove for the broken entryway doors. The

sound of distant combat met their ears as they landed, soldiers stepping back to give them space.

"Remember, we find Clara first," Chernor said as he pulled his enormous maul off his back. "Isaac and Avila should be relatively safe inside their cells during the combat."

"Or they'll be killed immediately," Kael said, readying the shield Johan had given him.

A brief flash of worry crossed over the big man's face.

"Yet another reason to ensure Clara's safety," he said. "With the two brothers licking Center's boots, Clara might be the only heir worth saving. Now lead on."

Chernor had chosen Kael to accompany him inside because of his time in the mansion. Taking point, Kael passed through the entryway, walking single file for his wings to fit, and then into the taller, wider hallways. Bodies lay about, many bearing the circle of Center on their tunics. Among them were the Willer house guards, and Kael swallowed down his unease at the sight. There'd been no way to send Clara warning prior to the attack, and Kael could only pray she'd safely endured the chaos.

The deeper into the mansion they traveled, the louder the sounds of combat grew. Kael flexed his right hand, feeling the connection to the ice element within the gauntlet, letting it calm his mind despite the many signs of violence. Paintings were ripped down, vases broken, and blood spilled across the carpet. Center's soldiers had immediately turned on the house guards the moment the Weshern military was spotted. If Clara had been unaware and vulnerable...

They turned a corner, stumbling upon three of Center's soldiers standing shoulder to shoulder with their shields linked. Five of Varl's men engaged them, trading thrusts with their spears as they searched for weaknesses. Beside them was the door to Clara's room. Fighting off panic, Kael raised his gauntlet and aimed through the chaos. The shields were thick and tall, and combined with the relative lowness of the ceilings, there was no way for Kael and Chernor to safely fly over them and engage from behind.

"Patience, lad," Chernor said, lowering Kael's gauntlet with a beefy hand. "Wait for an opening."

The ground troops battled, the Weshern soldiers growing more aggressive with each passing moment. Time was not on their side, and every single person inside the mansion knew it. The aggression left the Weshern men vulnerable, and their greater numbers weren't enough to overtake their highly trained foes. One soldier pulled his shield back to thrust, only to find a spear in his chest. Center's other two soldiers jammed their spears in a coordinated assault, bypassing another shield to clip a Weshern soldier across the neck. His jugular opened, the doomed man fought weakly on before collapsing. With two down, the Weshern line broke.

"Now," Chernor ordered, and he readied his maul. Center's soldiers rushed forward, trying to press their newfound advantage. Kael met their advance with lances of ice aimed below their tall shields, cracking knees and breaking shins. Chernor leapt into the heart of the fight, giant maul lifted high above his head. His target raised a shield in protection, screamed as the heavy head rammed down upon it, wrenching the soldier's arm violently and snapping bones. Another thrust for Chernor's chest, but Varl's men recovered and rushed back into the fray. Their shields crowded to either side of the Seraph, protecting him. Chernor shifted the maul to his left hand, extended his right, and blasted a bolt of lightning straight through the forehead of another of Center's soldiers. The man died with his spear raised up to thrust.

Suddenly outnumbered four to one, the final soldier went

fully defensive, retreating step after step with his shield before him. Kael flung a single shot of ice at the man's feet, tripping him up. The moment he slipped, spears punctured his body, ending him.

"Link up with another squad," Chernor told the soldiers as they regrouped. "We need numbers on our sides at all times."

"Understood, sir," one said, saluting before leading the rest back down the hallway. Kael paid them no attention. He tried the door to Clara's room, found it locked. He kicked at it a few times, growing more frantic when the lock refused to give.

"Clara?" he shouted at the door. No answer.

"Did you forget who's with you?" Chernor asked, pulling Kael aside. "If you need a door opened, all you need to do is knock."

He swung his maul, blasting the wood open with ease. Kael rushed in, searching for Clara. Instead he found five servants huddled together on Clara's bed.

"Where's Clara?" he asked.

"We don't know," the oldest of the servants answered. "We locked ourselves in here when the soldiers started killing each other."

Kael fought down a curse.

"The way out is safe," Chernor told them. "Stay the night with family or friends. You don't want to be here when the rest of Center's army arrives."

The servants hurried out, and Kael kicked a wall in the now-empty room.

"Stay calm," Chernor said. "There's a dozen other places she could be safely hiding."

"Or she could be lying dead in a hallway somewhere," Kael said. He felt his subdued worry breaking free in his chest, every possible nightmare scenario crawling through his mind.

Chernor put a hand on his shoulder.

"You can't think like that," he said. "Now come on. You said you know where the dungeon is, right?"

Kael nodded, gaze locked on the bed, caught in flashes of memories of him and Clara together.

"Not for sure," he said. "But I have a strong guess."

"It's the best we have to work with. Stay with me, Seraph. You still have responsibilities."

Kael breathed in deep, then blew out all his weaknesses.

"I know," he said. "Follow me."

Kael led Chernor down the corridor, his destination the elaborate dining hall. Earlier in the day, they had hoped Clara could lead them to the dungeon entrance once they'd found her. Without her, Kael's best guess was that the cells were located somewhere beyond the door from which Vyros had entered the grand dining hall. They passed more corpses on the way, and Kael checked every one. It was selfish, he knew, but each face that wasn't Clara's filled him with a sliver of relief.

The dining room door was ajar, and Chernor peered inside before backing away.

"A single knight's in there," he said, keeping his voice low. "I'll rush in, and if I can't kill him immediately, I'll position his back to you. Once he's distracted, take him out from the doorway with your ice."

Kael nodded in affirmative, blue mist softly floating from his palm as he made the softest of mental connections with his prism. Chernor hefted his maul with both hands, breathed in deeply, and then charged through the doors of the dining hall. Kael counted to three, then peered around the corner to watch.

The angelic knight stood in the center of the dining hall. In his left hand he held a sword, its blade covered with the blood of three dead Weshern house guards lying at his feet. His other held a ball of flame that swirled steadily above his palm. The control was incredible, a feat Kael had never seen, never even known was possible. Chernor flew above him, darting about the high ceiling, anticipating an eventual attack. The knight tracked Chernor's movements, waiting for the slightest mistake. His entire body looked ready to burst into motion, and Kael bit his lip as he debated attacking or waiting for a moment when the knight's back was to him completely.

Chernor's wings darkened, the Seraph suddenly descending for an attack, and then the ball of flame burst upward. At first it held together, but halfway to Chernor it exploded outward like blooming petals of a flower. Chernor shifted to one side, saw it wouldn't be enough. The ball, which had started out as the size of a man's head, looked wide enough to cover half the ceiling. Chernor tucked his arms and rolled, wings flaring to life to aid his speed as he dropped beneath the inferno. Fire charred the painted ceiling, the angelic figures now blackened splotches. The knight's wings shimmered gold, and he crashed into Chernor before the Seraph could safely land. His sword clashed with the maul's thick shaft. The men spun around one another, their weapons seeking flesh.

Kael watched them duel, thin wisps of blue frost gathered around the focal point of his gauntlet.

Should have taken the shot earlier, he berated himself. Now the two were incredibly close. Getting a clean shot would be difficult, if not impossible. The knight attempted a retreat, and Chernor chased, falling back only when a wide circle of flame flashed from the knight's gauntlet. Chernor momentarily halted, ducking the fire, and the knight pounced at the opportunity, sword leading. Chernor twisted and kicked as their bodies rammed together, momentum carrying them to the floor. Together the men crashed atop the long dining table, wood shattering beneath their combined weight.

The humming of wings increased in volume as the knight leapt back into the air. Chernor shot a blast of lightning at the knight hovering above him, missed. Fire bellowed down, a tremendous blast dwarfed only by what Bree could unleash. Chernor rolled across the debris, trying to stand, but Kael knew he wouldn't recover quickly enough.

"Get down!" Kael screamed as he stepped through the door and into the dining hall. Ice poured from his gauntlet. Chernor dove, and the stream crossed above him, forming a protective wall. The fire hit it. The ice melted, but it withstood long enough for the knight's blast to end.

The knight glared Kael's way. In response, Kael lifted his shield, braced his legs, and grinned.

"Am I interrupting?" he asked.

The knight lobbed a ball of flame straight for the doorway, then leapt into the air to avoid two shots of lightning from Chernor's gauntlet. Kael ducked low and closed his eyes, establishing a mental connection, not with the ice prism in his gauntlet but instead with the light element hidden in the mechanisms of the shield. It flared brightly, and when the ball of flame struck he felt the impact but not the heat. His feet skidded a step back on the carpet, then held. When he lowered his shield, only black smoke remained of the attack.

The walls shook as the Chernor and the knight collided with one side of the dining hall, battling while Kael defended. Charging closer, Kael scanned for an opening as ice formed in the palm of his gauntlet. Chernor's maul weaved through the air, twice missing, both times puncturing holes in the ceiling. A single hit would prove lethal, but the knight was too fast, too quick. The knight kicked off the ceiling, dipped underneath a streak of lightning, and then curled straight back up, sword lashing. Blood sprayed the air as Chernor rolled to one side, the sword slicing across his chest. He struck the wall with his shoulder, twisted, and then dropped.

Kael screamed, barely aware he was doing so. He soared into the air, gauntlet up, scattered shards of ice racing toward the knight. The knight circled, wings humming, ice shattering against the ceiling all around him. One icicle he even cut with his sword, deflecting it before it could find flesh. Distance closed between them, Kael flung his feet before him, reversing the angle of his wings to retreat. Bree was the sword fighter of the two; his only hope was to catch the knight with a shard of ice before being cut down like Chernor.

Kael's escape wouldn't be so easy. The momentary halt to his movement made him an easy target, and a burst of flame roared toward him, hungry and bright. Kael punched the throttle to his wings, painfully jerking himself out of the way. More ice lances flew from his gauntlet, bigger, sharper. The knight weaved through them as he chased, and running out of room, Kael rolled and tried to dash away to the other side of the dining hall.

Fire exploded before him, and panicking, Kael turned, far too hard for how fast he flew in such confined surroundings. He crossed the room, and despite shutting off his wings, there was little he could do prior to striking the opposite wall other than shift his shield to take the brunt of the damage.

The impact rattled Kael's skull, and he fought to keep control. He more glided to the ground, left wing scraping along the wall. His shield landed beneath him, trapped by his own body. Still on his stomach, he tried to rise, but then the knight slammed on top of him. One heel hit his neck, the other pinned his right gauntlet to the ground to prevent any attempt at defense. The knight said nothing, only raised his gauntlet to unleash his flame.

A single lance of ice whistled through the air, puncturing through one side of the knight's neck and out the other. The knight stiffened, mouth open in shock, blood pouring down and staining the ice purple. He dropped dead, and Kael turned to see Clara rushing into the room. She wore a silver pair of wings, but instead of black her Seraphim jacket and pants were white and hemmed with gold. They looked ceremonial, but there was nothing ceremonial about the ice shard that had slain their foe.

"Where have you been?" Kael asked her as she helped him up.

"Fighting my way here from the armory," she said. "And you?"

"Looking for you and your parents," Chernor said, wincing in pain as he staggered to his feet. His left arm pressed against the deep cut in his chest. "At least, we were. I won't be much help now."

Kael hurried over to him only to be pushed away.

"I'll be fine," he said. "I'll have to fly and maneuver like a newborn child, but I'll be fine."

"Most of the angelic knights and soldiers were at the public execution," Clara said as she frowned at the blood. "Me and Kael can handle whoever's left to guard my parents."

"You sure about that?" Chernor asked.

Clara glanced toward him, and Kael nodded.

"Not in the slightest," he said, grinning at the bigger man. "But we're going to do it anyway, because we're the only ones left who can. Get out of here, Chernor. That's an order."

Chernor choked out a laugh.

"You don't order me around, you little whelp."

"While you're wounded and unable to hit me with that maul of yours, I sure as hell will."

Chernor waved his hand in surrender.

"Stay safe, both of you," he said, taking a step toward the door. He winced, his arm clutching his chest tighter, but he held in any cry of pain. "But if outside's calm, I'm sending more Seraphim inside to replace me."

Kael watched him leave, praying Chernor wasn't downplaying how badly he'd been injured.

"The entrance to the dungeon's this way," Clara said when he was gone, and she pointed to the opposite door, the same one Vyros and her two older brothers had come from that first time he'd visited.

"Great," Kael said, but instead of following her, he grabbed her wrist, pulled her close, and kissed her lips. She tensed for a moment, then relaxed as his arms wrapped about her.

"I'm so glad you're safe," he whispered when he finally pulled back.

"Me, too," she said. Her hand brushed his forehead, and he winced. "That bruise is going to be amazing in a few hours. Are you sure you're all right?"

Kael nodded. "Like I said, there's no choice in the matter. Now lead on. We've your parents to rescue."

Clara hurried through the door, into a dark corridor lit by long oval windows on the ceiling. At the far end of the corridor was a heavy metal door, halfway open. Stairs led deeper underground, the oval windows now tunnels through the dirt to allow in light. The walls were stone instead of wood, and Kael was thankful they were still wide; otherwise they'd have felt terribly claustrophobic.

A familiar face blocked the way deeper into the dungeon at the bottom of the steps. Vyros wore no wings, but he bore a thin gold cylinder on his back, attached to which was a heavy gauntlet. Fire swirled around the gauntlet's focal prism, ready to be released. Both Kael and Clara shot lances of ice, but instead of finding purchase, they melted in a sudden flash of heat and light. Kael could barely see what it was, only knew that it came from the theotech's gauntlet.

"You flail like children with your elements," Vyros said. "You know nothing of true mastery."

He spun his arm. Fire lashed out like a whip, bathing all four walls before rolling toward them. Kael had never seen fire move in such a way, never even known it was possible. He and Clara dove through the center of the wave, the only safe spot from the fire on all four sides. Vyros's arm continued looping, and the fire tightened, cascading down as it closed in on them. Fighting off panic, Kael lowered his gauntlet and released a spray of ice straight down, forming a curved wall. He dropped behind, Clara following, as the hallway flooded with fire behind them.

"You Seraphim," Vyros said, calmly approaching. "You fling your elements like arrows from a bow. Such limitations. Such lack of imagination."

As if to show them, his next blast roared out in the visage of a dragon, teeth widening to bite. Clara shot a chunk of ice straight into its mouth, and as the fire scattered, Kael followed up with lances of his own. Vyros's gauntlet was a blur as he intercepted each shot, bright flashes of yellow light scarring Kael's vision. The lances lost their shape, splattering across Vyros's robes as harmless water.

"After all our hopes, and all the potential your blood has shown in our reports, you'll still die here, accomplishing nothing," Vyros said. "How disappointing."

He stretched out his hand, his fingers spread as wide as possible. Fire burst from it, enormous, widening out so that no space in the hall was safe. It looked similar to what Bree could do, only more steady, more controlled. Kael braced himself for the flame, baffled by the attack and unsure if his shield would be of any aid, but then Clara acted first, charging straight at the widening spray. She dipped at the last moment, sliding underneath the inferno, and then slammed her gauntlet to the floor. Blue light flashed. Ice spread wall to wall, and she flung her arm back as it grew from the focal point of her gauntlet into a rapidly growing barrier. The ice sealed Vyros off completely, but it wouldn't stop him for long.

"Kael, run!" Clara screamed, but Kael had a different idea. Swallowing down his fear, he dashed straight toward the ice barrier. Orange light blossomed from its center, heat from the theotech rapidly thinning the wall. Kael leapt off his feet and slammed the throttle to his wings while readying his shield. He smashed straight through the weakened wall, shards exploding in all directions. Vyros's fire bathed his shield, but it flared white, absorbing the fire, denying its power. Kael crossed the distance, not slowing in the slightest.

The two men collided, Kael's shield ramming the theotech's upper body. A spear of flame shot above Kael's head, charring a black mark onto the pale wall. Vyros fell to his back while Kael continued on, wrenching his body a half circle so he towered over and behind the theotech. His wings killed his momentum, and in that momentary pause hovering over Vyros's body, Kael braced his gauntlet with his free hand and let loose his ice. An icicle the size of Kael's arm exploded downward, puncturing Vyros's heart, the tip shattering against the stone floor as it pierced his body.

Kael dropped to his knees, staring at the theotech as he gasped in ragged breaths.

"Still disappointed?" he asked, frost falling from his gauntlet. Ice sheathed Vyros's face, locking away his final death cry.

A single iron key dangled from the dead theotech's sash, and Kael tugged it free, stood, and twirled it in his fingers.

"Give you two guesses what cell this opens," he said.

"I only need one," Clara said, yanking it from his grasp and hurrying ahead.

Windows in the ceiling gave the pair their only light as they continued downward. At the far end was a heavy iron door, and Clara yanked it open. Light flooded into the darkened space, and as it did, Kael grabbed Clara by the arm and pulled her back. A single knight guarded the cramped passageway, and he raised his gauntlet to fire. Kael braced his shield, flinching as a blast of lightning struck its center. More light flashed about the metal of the shield, shimmering a rainbow of colors as it rapidly dissipated. The knight prepared another shot, looking equally baffled and unnerved by the shield's ability to protect against lightning when it should have conducted the electricity straight into Kael's heart.

Clara never gave him a chance. Though she couldn't fly over Kael's head with the ceiling so low, she could still lift up above his shoulders. Twin lances of ice shot from her palm, one puncturing the knight's unarmored abdomen, the other opening a gash in his forehead. He dropped, gasping for air as he bled out.

"Did you know your shield could do that?" Clara asked as she settled back to her feet.

"Not for lightning," Kael said. "Glad I guessed right."

Clara looked torn between amusement and horror. If circumstances weren't so dire, Kael would have laughed.

The two hurried deeper into the dungeon, Clara staying as close as she could despite their wings.

"Who gave you that shield?" she asked.

"Johan. He said it belonged to one of Center's knights."

"I've never seen a knight wielding anything like that. Are you sure Johan told you the truth?"

Kael shook his head.

"Of course not," he said. "But given the situation, there's not much choice but to trust him."

They left the few windows behind as they entered the dungeon. Their only light came from the focal points of their gauntlets, which they both kept shimmering the faintest blue. They passed one empty cell after another.

"Mom?" Clara shouted, adding her voice to the quiet that had been broken only with the sound of their footfalls. "Dad? Where are you?"

The voice was deep and startling in the quiet, but it put a tremendous smile on Clara's face.

"Here."

She dashed ahead, stopping before one of the cells and jamming in the key to the lock. Kael kept his gauntlet high, giving her light to see with. The lock clicked, the door swung open, and Clara sprang inside, wrapping her arms around the tired, pale, dirty royal family of Weshern. They were both dressed in plain white robes that covered them from neck to ankle. Isaac's blond beard, which had once been neatly trimmed close to his mouth and chin, was now ragged, a faint shadow of it growing all across his face. Avila's long hair was pulled back behind her head, wet and matted as portions of it clung to her neck.

"Clara!" Isaac exclaimed as he hugged her in return as best he could due to her wings.

Avila pulled their daughter free of him so she could embrace her fully, kissing Clara's forehead as she held her tight.

"You foolish, reckless, wonderful girl," Avila whispered as tears trickled down her cheeks. "I never thought I'd see you again."

Kael kept his gaze to the stone floor, feeling like an awkward interloper to such intimacy. Isaac would have none of it. He exited the cell and offered Kael his hand.

"I suspect you deserve equal blame for this idea?" he said.

Kael shook his hand, and he fought for words. Cell or no cell, bare robes or not, this was Weshern's Archon, and Kael tried his best not to be intimidated.

"Johan's, actually," he said. "I just do what they tell me to."

Isaac's face twitched at the mention of the name.

"So we have thrown our lot in with him and his disciples. I suppose I shouldn't be surprised. Desperation results in a lot of strange bedfellows."

Clara kissed her mother's cheek, hugged her again, and then finally pulled away.

"We're getting you out of here," she said, sniffling as she pushed her emotions down to resume a more dignified demeanor. "Follow us."

They left the dungeon, returning to the mansion and then hurrying through the halls. The few soldiers they passed raised their spears and shouted in excitement, with several taking up escort as the royal family exited the mansion. Kael squinted as they stepped out into the bright sunlight, a welcome change from the horrible darkness of the dungeon. Smoke rose from the mansion behind them, many of its windows broken. Dead bodies littered the grounds. Chernor waited beside the entrance, bandages wrapped about his chest. Nearby, Saul and Aven stood over the corpse of an angelic knight.

"Two knights on patrol," Chernor explained, leaning on his weapon. Blood dripped from his bandages. "Never stood a chance." The big man bowed his head low. "Great to see you two alive and well."

"I'm merely glad for daylight," Isaac said. "Where is General Cutter?"

"Most of the soldiers have already begun scattering to nearby safe houses," Chernor said. "They don't have the benefit of wings to carry them out of here before Center's forces show up royally pissed. As for Varl himself, he's near the front gate, preparing you an escort."

Avila pulled on Isaac's arm, keeping him moving.

"Come," she said. "Our soldiers and Seraphim died to free us. If we don't escape, their deaths will have been in vain."

The others hurried down the stairs to the main gate but Kael hesitated at the top with Chernor.

"Will you be all right?" he asked.

"I'll be fine, I promise," Chernor said. "Now go with the royal family. Keep them safe, you hear?"

Kael nodded, smiled at the big man, and then hurried to the main gate. A dozen soldiers waited, spears in their hands and shields on their backs. General Cutter stood among them, red-faced as he shouted out orders. Kael thought his head looked ready to pop off.

"There you are," Varl said when he realized Isaac and Avila were with him. "About bloody time the Seraphim got you out of there. I've an escort ready to move, the finest men available to me."

Isaac glanced over the soldiers, then shook his head.

"We'll never cross Weshern unnoticed with so many," he said.

Varl scratched at his long black beard, and the redness of his face only worsened.

"If you're spotted, I'd rather you have a fighting chance than no chance at all," he said.

"Give me an escort of Seraphim instead," Isaac said. "I need speed and stealth now, Varl, not spears."

Varl turned his head away to hide the rolling of his eyes.

"Where's Chernor?" he said, then cried louder toward the shattered doors of the holy mansion. "Chernor! Get your ass over—"

He stopped. A Seraph sped in from the west. Kael saw him too, and a surge of unease shot through his veins. The lone Seraph surely came from the battle in New Galen, where the Speaker had meant to hold his public executions. The Seraph easily located them at the gates of the holy mansion and dove to the ground.

"I've come from the executions," he said, dropping to one knee before Isaac. "Dozens of angelic knights are on their way. We need to get you to safety immediately."

"Is Bree all right?" Kael asked, unable to contain himself. The Seraph glanced his way, nodded.

"She battled as I left, but I saw her trails of fire in the distance long after. I believe she is well."

"What of our sons?" Avila asked. "Are they safe? If Marius knows we've escaped, they may suffer in our stead."

The Seraph frowned, and he hesitated a moment before carefully addressing the both of them.

"Archon, milady, Edwin was arrested and taken away by knights, but Lance...perished during the battle. I'm sorry."

Isaac's hands balled into fists and Avila looked as if stabbed. Kael looked to Clara and took her hand as he saw the first of a few tears trickle down her face. She squeezed his fingers to show him her appreciation, then went to her father's side.

"Now's not the time for mourning," Clara said. "If knights are on the way we won't be safe for much longer."

"I know," Isaac said, shaking his head. His voice trembled, but only a moment. "We'll have to stay grounded until we're in the clear, keep low, and find homes to hide in as we travel."

"It's a long way to New Galen by foot," Varl said.

"Which is why we'll have an escort," Isaac said, and he nodded to Chernor, who had finally limped the distance to join them. "Seraphim to protect us."

"I won't do you much good myself," Chernor said. "But the rest here should still be at your side."

He made a quick signal above his head, bringing in the remaining three Seraphim. Aven landed beside the Archon, his silver wings sparkling. Another Seraph landed beside him, a man Kael had met only that morning named Sig. Last was Saul, who walked instead of flew, and kept farther back from the others with his arms crossed.

"These five will keep you safe," Chernor said. "Even from knights, I'd wager."

Archon Isaac turned in place, and even in his worn clothing he commanded their attention and respect.

"My life, and the lives of those I love, are in your hands," he told them. He hesitated only the briefest moment on seeing Saul. "Honor that, and do not let me down." The Archon then turned to General Cutter. "It's time to scatter. Send soldiers out in all directions, and get them hidden."

Varl dipped his head.

"Yes, my lord," he said. Immediately he rushed away, bellowing orders.

Chernor said something to the messenger Seraph, then turned back to the Archon.

"Allen here will help me get to safety," he said, bowing low. "Safe travels, all of you."

"Fly well," Isaac said. "And fly unchained."

Chernor soared into the air, the messenger Seraph escorting him and aiding him in keeping balanced. Isaac took his wife by the hand, then led them down the road.

"We'll need to stay off the streets until nightfall," he said. "We've several safe houses nearby, and one has a hidden cellar large enough to hold us all."

Kael looked west, saw the distant gold dots. Knights, coming in search of the Archon. They were many, so many...

"We don't have much time," he said, turning back around.

"Then it's best we run," Isaac said. "I have no intention of returning to that cage."

CHAPTER

24

Bree was on her way to the rooftop when she found Devi Winters hunched in a chair, candle burning on a table beside her. A stack of papers lay on her lap. Ink stained her fingers.

"Shouldn't you be asleep?" Bree asked her.

"Can't," she said, sounding so very tired. "I'm chronicling the dead."

"How many?" Bree asked.

Devi rubbed her forehead and closed her eyes.

"Too many. Always too many."

Bree let the sober comment hang in the air as she climbed the stairs. After that she ascended the ladder and flung open the hatch, stepping out onto the rooftop of Johan's New Galen hideout. Arms crossed, she walked to the edge and watched the fire burn across the black sky. The ferocity of its rippling disturbed Bree greatly. It reminded her of when Kael put his hand upon the dome to the far east, revealing the laughing, biting things lurking on the other side.

"It seems you and your brother share many things in common," Johan said, startling her. "A penchant for staring to the sky when in thought is one of them."

"Solitude hasn't been easy to find," Bree said, glancing over her shoulder to see the man exiting the hatch. "Not since entering the academy."

Johan joined her side and pulled back his hood, revealing his many scars. Whereas the rippling flame made Bree nervous, the strange man smiled up at the midnight fire as if comforted by the sight.

"How are your injuries?" he asked.

"They hurt, but they'll heal," Bree said, downplaying how much they actually bothered her. During her battle against the knight lieutenant he'd nicked her twice with the sharp, flanged edges of his mace, once on the right arm, another on her left leg. Luckily for her, neither had been deep, though they'd bled plenty before she could finally have them stitched. They pulsed with pain, and when they weren't hurting, they were itching. Thick cloth was wrapped around each, both stained with dried blood.

"I'm glad they weren't worse," Johan said. "And you are lucky indeed to escape with such minor wounds. No, not lucky. That belittles your accomplishments." He closed his eyes and breathed in deep. "You were incredible out there today. A true beauty. It's rare for any Seraph to match a knight in battle, and you took down several, including a knight lieutenant. I cannot adequately express my pride in your accomplishments."

The praise left Bree feeling more awkward than flattered. If she'd not taken so long battling the skilled knight lieutenant she might have saved Instructor Kime instead of cutting him free to fall into his grave.

"Thank you," she said.

He opened his eyes and glanced sidelong at her.

"I also saw you unleash fire from your gauntlet between exchanges with your swords. Perhaps rumors were wrong, but I was under the impression you were unable to wield flame in the conventional sense."

Beyond awkward now. Bree crossed her arms and kept her eyes on the burning sky, debating an answer. Prior to the battle, she'd spent time in the warehouse where Johan stored his various weapons and harnesses, examining the gauntlet Jaina had strapped upon her hand. She'd learned how the needle and tubing worked, and despite the pain, forced it back into her skin. At no point had she told anyone what she was doing, or why.

"I'm...learning," she said. "Not much, but I believe I can release a blast or two in battle without exhausting myself completely."

She didn't like lying to the man, but she preferred it over discussing her blood and the potential experiments performed upon her and Kael's parents. Until she knew more of what was going on, she wished to keep such information to herself.

"Good," Johan said, and she found it hard to tell if he believed her or not. "Very good, Bree. Our cause is furthered the more dangerous you become."

Silence fell over them as together they stared down the empty road lit by the harsh glow of the midnight fire. Bree thought of what she could say to fill the void, for Johan showed no desire to leave, and she didn't want him prying further into her sudden ability to control her fire.

"Any word from my brother?" she asked.

"My runners say he's with the royal family," Johan said. "With knights swarming the island, caution is of the utmost importance, and they've a long way to travel from the holy mansion. They'll arrive before morning, I'm sure, and if not, who on Weshern would deny their royal family a place to hide?"

"Who indeed?" Bree said.

"Once they're here, Weshern will finally be on the proper path toward freedom," Johan continued. "And a far better path than the one those two sons of theirs were leading us on. Cowards, the both of them."

"They did what they thought was best for Weshern, in their own way," Bree said, feeling compelled to defend them. She'd never met either Lance or Edwin, only knew them by name, but she'd not pretend they'd been in an easy situation after the Archon and his wife were imprisoned.

"Their best was to kneel before Marius and kiss his feet," Johan said. "They aren't worthy heirs to the Willer name. The older brothers begged, yet the younger daughter donned her wings and fought for her parents' freedom. Marius would have done the Archon a favor by killing Edwin along with Lance, clearing the line of succession for someone infinitely more deserving."

Such callous dismissal of the royal family's recent loss put Bree on edge. Did Johan care about anything other than his crusade against Marius and Center? She doubted it. For all his talk of pride and amazement at her abilities, he'd sacrifice her in a heartbeat if it brought the theotechs crumbling down.

"We're just playthings for you, aren't we?" she said, surprised by her own boldness. "Pieces for a game you've been playing with Center for years. Things are not so clear as you claim."

"Things are painfully clear," Johan said. "It's just that far too many want to keep their eyes squeezed shut. I am not one to avoid the truth just because it hurts, Bree. I remember the name of every disciple who dies fighting for my cause. I bear their sins upon my shoulders, and I use them to fuel my anger. My guilt, my sorrow, my failures; they must all be swallowed down so I might succeed. What does my suffering matter when compared to the fate of our world? Who I *am*, does that even matter?" He shook his head. "I am scars and a name, Breanna. Like you, I am a symbol. Ever since taking on that responsibility, I have lost my right to act on my own selfish desires. All I do now is for a greater future. In many ways, I have ceased to exist. In time, you will, too, replaced by the entity that is the Phoenix."

It was a sobering thought. Bree started to respond, then stopped. The sky...something was wrong with the sky. The fire burned brighter than it ever had before, and it twisted and coiled with unprecedented speed.

"Playthings," Johan said, chuckling. "You'd accuse me of using you as playthings. Such a hard heart you believe me to possess. Do you think I dream of war every time I close my eyes? Do you think hatred is the only thing left in my blackened soul?"

Bree frowned, already regretting her earlier outburst.

"I'm sorry," she said. "It's just...the way you speak of Center and the theotechs, it's hard to imagine you as anything else."

Johan looked to the rippling fire, but his eyes must have gazed inward instead of outward, for he didn't seem to see the chaotic swirling.

"You may not believe it, but I once considered myself a friend of *all* humankind," he said. "Regardless of birth, royalty, or nation, all were under my care. The best for them, that's what I wanted. A peaceful world, for everyone. And unlike my fellows, I did not consider this task hopeless, or one that must be compromised with half measures and watered-down justice. I did not seek war. I did not desire bloodshed. But I dared ask the questions no one else would ask. I dared confront the truths no one else wanted to acknowledge. And for that, I was betrayed."

His hands clenched into fists, and he looked ready to strike an invisible being before him in the air.

"Marius overplayed his hand," he said. "He revealed the desperate lengths he'll go to maintain power. He'd hang Weshern's heroes, even a legend like Argus, all while claiming it's to protect Weshern? Only the willfully blind will still buy the lie. I've ensured that word of the hangings and the enormous pit dug in promise of more dead spreads to all the other islands. Everything I've sought to accomplish is reaching fruition. Rebellion is coming. Destruction of the old and ill is at hand, and it won't be confined to this island alone."

He lifted his hands before him, staring at his open palms.

"The day of my betrayal, the day my brethren rejected me and I suffered these scars, I learned something," he said softly. "Something I myself, in all my wisdom, had still refused to see."

"What is that?" Bree asked, feeling her chest tighten as enormous ripples shook the heavens, like water disturbed by a heavy stone.

A tired smile spread across Johan's face.

"So long as those who desire power and control live, we will never have our peaceful world."

The sky cracked. It was first a single long line snaking through the fire, shimmering gold like a heavenly vein. Then a second, a third, a spiderweb of gold growing brighter and brighter, outshining the deep red of the midnight fire. It was accompanied by no sound, no reverberations. Bree turned, saw the dome covering their islands flare into existence, no longer veins but a single solid sheen of gold.

And then the gold broke, vanished, and the waiting demons above began their descent.

This isn't happening, Bree's mind begged. *This isn't happening, it isn't, it isn't what I think it means...*

Johan and Bree watched the rain of fire fall from the sky. Thousands upon thousands of thin meteors approached the surface of their world, little dots against an impenetrable blanket of smoke. Bree's body locked up, her every muscle tense, her veins pounding with horror throughout her every limb. They were so many, a hellish field of stars unmatched by any picture or painting. The closer they fell, the easier they were to distinguish, and Bree watched several nearing her perch on the rooftop. Balls of flame struck homes, the street, distant towns and fields, all of Weshern, all of every island, bathing them in infernal rain.

One struck the rooftop with a strange, soft thud, fire extinguishing as it rolled. The sight flooded Bree with terror. It was one of the imps from her time of torture beneath the Crystal Cathedral, only now it wasn't hidden behind a steel grate or a shimmering dome. Its body was black as coal, with veins of fire rippling through it. Its eyes were obsidian rings, their center sparkling with faint white ghost-light. A spiked tail wrapped around its left hind leg, which bent backward, like that of a goat or horse. A yellow serpent tongue hung from its open mouth, and though it bore no teeth, in their place were globs of liquid flame that dripped down the sides of its chin. The drool landed on the rooftop with a sizzling *plop.*

The creature turned toward Bree, and it eyed her with terrifying intelligence.

"Human," it snarled with a voice like scraping glass. The sound of speech coming from its mouth was enough to finally snap Bree from her paralyzed state. She dashed for the hatch,

but the thing cut her off, easily outmatching her speed. A thin trail of fire marked its movement, burning into the ancient wood of the roof. It laughed at her, high-pitched, mocking, as it raised both hands. The coal-like part of its fingers extended, sharpening into long claws that scraped and twitched like the legs of a spider.

Bree didn't know what to do. She didn't know how to react. It leapt, and she braced her arms before her as she fell back. The creature's mouth opened midair, obsidian eyes sparkling, clawed fingers reaching.

It halted mere feet before her, a knife stabbed through its body. Johan lowered the knife, guiding the thing to the rooftop, then rammed it deeper into the wood, pinning the demon's dying carcass. Bree watched as it thrashed, a strange blood seeping out from the wound. Liquid fire flowed from the creature, then coalesced, hardening into a substance like glass. The demon stiffened, limbs curling inward like an insect as it finally died.

"Are you harmed?" Johan asked as he yanked the knife free.

"No, I—" She shook her head, trying to clear it. "I'm fine."

The robed man used the rooftop to scrape the dying liquid fire from his knife as he stared at the dead creature.

"Your brother told me of the creatures you two witnessed beyond a wall far from Weshern," he said. "Creatures just like this one, am I correct?"

Bree nodded, still fighting through the shock.

"What are they?" she asked.

"Fireborn," Johan said, rising. His gaze never left the thing. "Creatures from the age prior to the Ascension. We witness history before us, Bree. We witness undeniable proof of what the theotechs have hidden for centuries."

"The fireborn," Bree said, eyes widening as she looked to the distant homes and fields. Already she saw great blazes spreading, heard the distant screams of fear and panic. "What do they want?"

"To do what they were always meant to do," he said. "Ready your wings and swords, Breanna. Tonight, Weshern burns."

CHAPTER

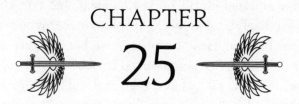

25

The midnight fire's...changing," Clara said as Kael stared at the rippling sky. The farther they'd traveled from the holy mansion the easier it had been to remain on the road, for there were too many paths for the knights to cover them all. Now they walked between homes in Elan Village toward New Galen, a wary eye locked on the sky above. Kael had been searching for knights, but instead he watched as the midnight fire shimmered and shook in a way that reminded him of when he placed his hand upon the dome encasing the islands.

"I'm not sure what's going on," Kael said. "I have an idea, but I hope I'm wrong."

He'd not had a chance to tell Clara about discovering the edge of the dome, or the fireborn lurking on the other side, but it appeared he wouldn't have to. The rippling widened, violently increased, and then the first of seemingly a thousand cracks of gold broke across the protective dome that filled their sky. Wordlessly their band watched the gold spread, thickened, the protective dome now clearly visible in all directions.

And then it silently shattered into nothing. The crawling darkness appeared for the briefest moment, and then the rain of fire fell. Kael stared in shock, unable to make his body move. His mind blanked. He knew what it was, but he didn't want to believe it. The implications were too terrible.

"Kael..." Clara said, grabbing his arm and freezing in place.

A thousand meteors, a fiery, living swarm. How could he explain it? What could he say that wouldn't sound like nonsense? The dome that had protected them for centuries, the dome they'd not even known existed, had somehow broken. The fireborn that had leered down from above now fell, glowing balls of flame slamming across Weshern, a torrential explosion of light and fire in the night. The number of creatures that fell was staggering. Kael guessed six landed in Elan Village alone. Already blazes flared in the distance. To think of how many must cover all of Weshern, setting fire to fields, buildings...

"What's going on?" Isaac asked, equally stunned by the sight.

"Is the world ending?" Sig asked.

Kael swallowed down a stone in his throat.

"Close enough," he said. "They're fireborn."

The others looked at him like he was insane.

"The demons were slain," Isaac argued. "The Endless Ocean drowned them all during the Ascension."

"Clearly not," Aven said, the skilled man drawing a sword in his left hand and pointing with his gauntlet. "Because otherwise what the hell is that?"

The coal-black body of a demon climbed the wall of a nearby home, claws sinking into the stone with ease. When it reached the roof it rolled about, cackling as the thatched material burst aflame.

"Fireborn from the sky," Isaac said. His voice was soft, stunned. "Dear God in heaven, what did we do to deserve this?"

The fireborn pulled up from its roll, gaze locked straight on the Archon. A smile spread across its face, grin filled with glimmering yellow teeth of liquid fire slobbering down its chin. It leapt off the roof in a shot, legs a blur as it charged across the street.

"Kill it!" Sig shouted, an entirely unnecessary order as all five had already lifted their gauntlets. None were prepared for its incredible speed. Kael's first shot misjudged terribly, as did the others. The fireborn dashed left and right, avoiding the elemental attacks, its destination never wavering. Panicking, Kael drew a sword and turned, lunging toward the Archon while Clara's silver wings filled his peripheral vision. The fireborn knifed between two Seraphs, then leapt into the air. It howled with pleasure, Isaac almost within its grasp, but finally Kael correctly judged its path. He swung his sword, cutting the creature in half. Its two pieces flew on, burning blood splashing the air. It would have washed over the Archon but Clara was already there, shoving him out of the way.

With the fireborn dead, the five Seraphs gathered over the body. They stared at the two halves of the creature and the smear of blood between. Smoke wafted up from the blood as it began to crystallize on contact with the air. The arms and legs twitched, flexing through some sort of power Kael could not understand.

"What does it mean?" Avila asked, returning to her husband's side as he stood.

"It means we've been lied to for centuries," the Archon said. "We all knew something was strange with the midnight fire, but we didn't know what it meant." He gestured to the dead creature. "The theotechs knew. They had to have known. Those bastards in Center knew this might happen yet they left us abandoned and unprepared."

"We'll pay them back in time, but it isn't now," Aven said. He pointed to Isaac and Avila. "We're getting you two airborne this second."

"Sounds like a fine idea to me," Saul said. "But where do we take them? Fires burn all across Weshern."

"We go to New Galen," Aven said. "Once surrounded with soldiers we can keep the royal family safe."

"It'd take us at least twenty minutes to fly there," Clara said. "If we're spotted by knights while on the way..."

Saul gestured around him as his temper flared.

"You really think knights will be searching for the Archon in the middle of all this?" he asked her. "You're more naïve than I thought."

"Quit bickering," Aven snapped, glaring at Saul. "You're Seraphim, not little children, so act like it. If we are to survive tonight, it'll be as a cohesive unit." He turned to Isaac. "We'll fly low and slow, but we'll still fly. I'll carry you, and Sig will carry Avila. Is that acceptable?"

Isaac glanced to his wife, then nodded.

"It is," he said.

The two older Seraphs started undoing the front buckles of the harness to wrap around their passengers. Kael turned about, scanning the sides of the streets. Homes were dark, everyone asleep. How long until the fire awoke them? How many would die across Weshern, suffocating in smoke, or worse, their bodies torn apart by the vicious fireborn?

"Are we to just leave them here?" Kael asked. He pointed to a fire not two streets down. "Can't we warn them somehow?"

"Our responsibility is to our Archon," Saul said, thumbing the switch to his wings. A soft white glow shimmered across the steel. "Until then, they'll have to fend for their own."

Not the answer Kael desired, but neither was it one he could argue with. The entire purpose of the dual-pronged attack at both the execution and the mansion had been to rescue the royal family. To succeed in escaping the mansion, only to die in this otherworldly chaos, would merely add to the tragedy, particularly when Weshern was going to need its leaders more than ever come morning.

"Let's go," Aven said, buckles tightened around Isaac and arms holding him securely in place. His wings flared, and Kael punched his throttle to follow.

Aven and Sig flew in the center, each holding his precious cargo before him. The other three formed a protective flank, Kael on the left, Clara the right, and Saul hovering a few dozen feet back. Homes passed below them, and Kael did his best to ignore the steadily spreading destruction. Already alarms had begun to sound from the town's bell tower, as they would all throughout Weshern. The people would fight the flames, fight the fireborn, but how many would die, overwhelmed by the shock and ferocity…

Stop it, Kael said, shaking his head to banish the thoughts. He couldn't dwell on the loss. He couldn't try to count the dead. His mind would break long before. They had to survive. They had to endure. Eyes back up, he scanned ahead, then slowly peered east, the flank he was assigned to guard. A glimmer of golden light in the distance shot panic into his chest.

"Knights!" he shouted.

Aven glanced his way, saw the telltale golden glow, and let out a curse.

"Get down!" the Seraph ordered.

The five dove lower, skimming along the rooftops. Kael waited for an order to land, but it never came, Aven instead powering his wings to increase his speed. Kael watched the approaching knights as he flew faster to keep pace. There were three of them flying high in the sky. So far it didn't seem like the knights had changed their path, yet surely they'd seen the Seraphim. The silver glow of their wings would be easily visible despite such distance. Perhaps they weren't looking down?

Kael frowned. Or perhaps they didn't care. The world was in turmoil, and given Center's far greater size, the number of fire-born that landed there had to be massive. Kael glanced to his right, saw Aven watching the trio of knights. It seemed he had the same thought, and he shook his head in disgust.

So much for keeping Weshern safe, Kael thought, bitterly reminded of the Speaker's promise.

Directly ahead shone the glow of another fire. Aven tilted his wings, guiding the group upward. Before they had climbed far, a spear of flame shot out from the wreckage, soaring into the air. Kael was too shocked to react, and could only watch in horror as one of the fireborn slammed against Aven's body. Claws swiped, fire bursting across the Archon's clothes. Aven twisted ninety degrees, angling him into a downward spiral toward ground.

Powering up his gauntlet, Kael dove after the two. If he could catch them in time, he might...

Their angle became steeper, and with a horrific screech of metal Aven and Isaac crashed into the hard stone street of an alley. The first wing to hit snapped in half, the other bent as their bodies rolled. Telling himself not to panic, Kael closed the distance, gauntlet leading. A burning ember had tumbled free of Aven and Isaac upon landing, an evil thing of fire that lay dazed in the street. It didn't take long to recover, and seeing the bodies, it hopped to its feet and sprinted. Patience kept Kael's shots in check for a second, giving him a chance to judge the creature's speed and path. Heart in his throat, he launched a lance of ice straight down.

The fireborn never even hesitated. The lance pierced the shrieking fireborn mere feet away from where Isaac lay. The momentum of the lance slammed the creature to the street, the ice shattering from impact against the stone while ripping the creature in half. Kael breathed a sigh of relief, then landed to survey the damage.

Aven's body rested against a wall, his neck at an odd angle, his face locked in a terrible death scream. The Archon lay on his back beside him, hands clawing into the dirt as he choked down cries of pain. While Aven had taken the brunt of the damage from the creature's claws, swaths of burns still marked Isaac's left arm and chest. That he was breathing at all seemed a miracle.

The others landed around him, Avila tearing at the buckles of Sig's harness to free herself.

"Isaac?" Avila said, kneeling beside her husband's body. The Archon hissed as his back arched in pain. Flesh curled and peeled off his burns.

"Get...get her to safety," he said.

"I'm not leaving you, so worry about yourself." She examined his wounds further. "Where does it hurt?"

Despite his horrid condition, Isaac coughed out a pained laugh.

"Everywhere," he answered.

Sig stepped over to Aven's body, and he wiped his eyes before shutting off the dead man's wings. That done, he gathered the other Seraphs to him.

"We can't move Isaac like this," he said. "The burns are bad enough, and God knows how many bones he's broken. Carrying him may outright kill him, so that means we're staying put."

"It's not safe here," Clara said.

"It's not safe anywhere," Saul countered. "At least we've got walls on either side of us. I say we set up guard and wait for rescue. The rest of our Seraphim are bound to come looking for us."

They all looked to Sig, the only experienced Seraph left among them. He ran a hand through his sandy brown hair, turned away for the slightest moment. When he looked back, his posture straightened, his words hardening as he assumed leadership.

"Clara and I will guard the entrances," he said. "Saul, Kael, you two search the nearby buildings for fireborn. The safer the surrounding areas, the safer the royal family."

Kael thudded a fist against his breast in salute, wishing he could feel as confident as Sig sounded. The older man walked to Isaac's side and knelt down to speak with him and his wife and quietly explain their current plan. Before assuming her post, Clara wrapped her arms around Kael's neck and pulled him close.

"Stay safe," she said. "I've lost enough today. Don't you dare let me lose you, too."

Kael forced a smile to his face.

"Wasn't planning on it," he said.

She smiled back, but it was fleeting. Too much worry. Too much danger. When Clara stepped away, Saul nodded toward him, arms crossed over his chest.

"Let's go," he said.

Kael walked alongside as they exited the alley.

"How do we find them?" he asked.

"Seems simple enough," Saul said, and he gestured to the many distant blazes. "Look for the fires."

"I guess that'll work," Kael said, toggling life into his wings. "So circle above and slowly spread outward as we clear?"

"That's the plan."

Together they lifted off. Kael shifted his shield back and forth to stretch the muscles of his left arm. Though the light element within greatly reduced its weight, it was still a burden that steadily wore on him as the night continued. Keeping his sword sheathed, he flexed his open palm, the firing prism faintly glowing blue as the ice element within readied for battle.

The nearest homes appeared quiet and dark from above. The two Seraphs hovered a moment over the alleyway, Kael sending a worried glance Clara's way. He doubted she could see his face, but his silver wings were easily visible, and she offered him a small wave. Breathing in deep, Kael took lead as they circled above the alleyway, gradually spreading outward to the surrounding homes. Kael spotted plenty of distant fires, including a particularly fierce one to the north, but he kept their path consistent. Chasing after every blaze they saw would only have them flying lost throughout the town, likely missing the fireborn as they raced about.

Kael caught movement from the side, turned to see Saul signaling with his hand.

Possible enemy.

He pointed to a home with flickering yellow light leaking through the closed shutters of its front window. Kael flew closer, choosing to remain in the air while Saul landed in the center of the street. With the height advantage he could guard Saul against an ambush from the rooftops. Saul drew a sword in his left hand, his right pulled back, ready to unleash his ice at a moment's notice. Carefully he crept to the window, angling himself to the side to make room for his wings. Kael readied his own gauntlet, eyes dancing back and forth from the rooftop and the window. Saul tucked the fingers of his right hand into the blinds, braced, and then yanked them open.

Three fireborn burst from the home, cackling wildly. Saul screamed as he retreated, his wings flaring with light. Not attempting to fight, Kael realized, only fleeing into the air so they couldn't overwhelm him. Kael dove downward, gauntlet open for a shot. One fireborn latched on to Saul's right leg as he climbed, obsidian claws sinking into flesh. The other two leapt but missed, tumbling back down to the street. Four thin, sharp shards flashed from Kael's palm as he closed the distance. The fireborn split in opposite directions, the ice shards shattering upon the stone. Kael pulled up and spun back to Saul.

"I'm fine," Saul said, his sword jamming into the open mouth of the fireborn. It hissed, its blood dripping down on Saul's leg, charring his clothes. A hard shove, and the body gave way, plummeting to the ground.

"Your leg," Kael said, hovering still. Saul's pant leg was torn where the creature had ripped into him, much of the exposed flesh a frightening red from burns.

"I said I'm fine," Saul said. "I'm flying, not walking; now don't let them escape!"

Kael chased the one north, Saul soaring south into the air. The fireborn weaved back and forth in front of Kael, occasionally glancing over its shoulder and laughing at him. He shot two more thin shards. It wouldn't take much to kill the small creature, and he wanted to conserve his element as much as possible. He had a feeling he'd need it over the course of the long night. The shots missed, but they forced the fireborn to dodge, slowing it down long enough for Kael to close the distance.

"No you don't," Kael said as it suddenly veered left and

dashed for the door of a home. In a maneuver that would make Bree proud, he cranked the throttle of his wings while twisting his body in a diving twirl. Killing his wings as quickly as he'd powered them, he came to a hard landing on one knee between the door and the fireborn. The creature lunged, but Kael's shield was ready. Light flared across the metal as the fireborn made contact with its claws. It immediately recoiled, pale smoke rising from its hands as it let loose an unnerving shriek. Its claws, Kael realized. The shield had melted the demon's claws, leaving nothing but smoking red nubs. The pain left it stunned, and Kael gave it no chance to recover. A shard of ice punched through its forehead, snapping it to the street, where it lay still, its shriek finally ending.

Kael walked closer to it, a shiver traveling up his spine despite his best attempts to remain calm.

"How did you break through?" he asked the corpse. "Why now, after all these years?"

A scream from farther up the street stole Kael's attention. A couple sprinted down the center, the man wielding a sickle, the woman carrying a baby so young it was swaddled and hidden against her breast. Two fireborn imps chased after them, laughing as if playing a joyful game. Kael sprinted toward the family while powering up his wings.

"Get inside!" he shouted.

The father stumbled in the road and then collapsed, a fireborn leaping atop his back and sinking glowing fangs into his spine. The man howled with pain, thrashing on the ground in a futile attempt to shake the creature off. The mother stopped, screaming in horror at the sight. Kael barely heard it over the roar of distant fires and the cries of the dying father. The second fireborn neared, eyes on the mother. Kael aimed with his gauntlet, desperately begging that his aim would be true.

His lance of ice caught the demon in mid-leap, ripping through its chest and sending it flying into the nearby home. It lay there, still cackling, as its blood fell and hardened at its feet. Kael pushed the throttle higher as the other fireborn tore into the father with renewed ferocity. Clothing and flesh burned away, the claws digging deeper. Kael flew overhead, shield swinging low. He clipped the thing across the collar, throwing it off the man's corpse. Twisting as hard as his waist and shoulders allowed, Kael tracked it with his gauntlet, then shot. His ice lance ripped through its throat as it reared up to howl in anger at being interrupted.

Killing his wings, Kael landed beside the mother, who rushed toward him.

"You have to help us!" she shouted. "You have to—"

"There's nothing we can do for him," he said, putting his hands on her shoulders and meeting her gaze. Tears filled her eyes, but she seemed to be hearing him through her shock. "Go inside and stay until morning, do you understand? It's not safe here."

"We tried," the woman said. Her brown hair was matted on the left side of her head. Blood, Kael realized. He wondered how long she'd had the wound. "We tried to hide but they burned us out. They burned us out, and then they followed us, laughing. They killed my husband, they killed my . . . my . . ."

Her legs gave out and she collapsed to her knees. Kael felt horror rising in his chest, and he looked down to the wrapped bundle in the woman's arms. The very quiet, very still bundle.

"I'm sorry," he said. His words were empty, meaningless. She saw his sorrow, glanced at her child, her eyes bloodshot pools of denial as she realized what he'd seen.

"He's fine," she said. "He's sleeping because of the pain, you hear me? He's only sleeping."

The woman dashed to the nearest home, beating and kicking on its door.

"Let me in!" she shouted. "Let me and my boy in!"

The door cracked open, someone inside said something, and then it swung wide just enough for her to enter. When it slammed shut, Kael felt his body trembling. Whether it was shock, rage, or sorrow he couldn't even begin to guess. His nerves were fried. He wanted nothing more than for the night to end, yet it felt like daylight was still a lifetime away. With numb fingers he powered up his wings. He had to check on Saul, make sure he'd caught the other fireborn. Almost lazily he flew into the air, looking for the telltale silver glow. Sure enough, he found it, but not where he'd expected. Kael landed beside Saul, who leaned with his wings pressed against the front wall of a home, all his weight supported by his good left leg.

"I got it," Saul said. His eyes were closed, his hands clenched into fists at his sides. Sure enough, a fireborn lay in two pieces at his feet, crimson blood hardened in a puddle between.

"Saul...," Kael said, eyeing his wounded leg. Blood had begun seeping through the fabric, the exposed skin starting to peel.

"I'm fine."

"That's a lie and you know it."

Saul opened his eyes and glared.

"I...am...fine," he said, limping away from the wall. His wings lifted him up off the ground. "Right now there's a hell of a lot of people in worse shape than I am, so let's keep going."

Kael grabbed the arm of his jacket to prevent him from leaving.

"You're going to get yourself killed," he said, locking gazes with Saul. "At least go back to protect the Archon. Clara or Sig can come with me instead."

Saul pulled his arm back, but Kael refused to let go. The two stood there a moment, Saul's feet hovering inches above ground, neither relenting to the other.

"All right," Saul said. "Let's go back. We should check on them anyway."

If that was the excuse Saul needed, Kael was fine with that. They rose into the air, then returned to the alley where the royal family was hidden. Despite having no reason to fear otherwise, Kael was relieved to see Clara and Sig standing guard unharmed, one at each entrance. They landed beside Clara, who winced upon seeing Saul.

"What happened?" she asked.

"What do you think happened?" Saul said, his left leg gingerly accepting weight. His balance wavered, and Clara reached out to grab his shoulder to steady him.

"I need someone else with me," Kael said.

"I'll go," Clara said. She cast Saul a look. "Rest here. Sig's more than capable of keeping my parents safe."

Saul pulled back from her grasp and braced against the wall.

"I'm not resting," he said. "I'm taking your post. No one here has the right to rest while our people are dying." Despite his obvious pain, Saul stood up as straight as he could and saluted to Clara. "I will protect the royal family," he said. "Go help Kael patrol."

Kael couldn't decide if Saul's stubbornness was impressive or annoying. Turning back to the street, his thumb dropped to the toggle to power his wings, then stopped. Kael tensed, torn between shock and disbelief. A single fireborn crouched on the opposite side of the street, its tail curled around its legs. No attack. No setting homes ablaze. Just calmly watching them. Kael lifted his gauntlet as he locked eyes with the creature. A grin spread across its face, sick and dripping with flame. That look of pleasure, of intelligence, was far more frightening than its sharpened claws.

"Don't let it escape!" Kael shouted, flinging a single lance of ice. It had barely left his palm when the fireborn dashed into the street and beyond their sight. Two quick strides and then a leap took Kael into the air, his wings flaring silver as he gained speed. Clara followed, her own wings humming. Kael curled north in chase, racing high above the street.

"There!" Clara shouted. A trio of shards flew from her gauntlet, guiding Kael's vision. The creature fled at a blistering pace, not even bothering to weave as it ran. Clara's attacks landed just short, alerting the fireborn to their presence. It glanced over its shoulder once, hissed, and then slammed itself against the door of a nearby home. The wood charred and crumpled, offering little resistance to the fiery demon. Kael signaled to Clara, the two splitting to guard opposite ends of the two-story building. Kael kept his gauntlet ready, debating whether to enter the house in search. The fireborn knew the Archon's location. If it somehow understood who he was, or his importance, it could find and bring others. No matter what, they couldn't let it escape.

"Damn it," Kael muttered as smoke began wafting out from a window on the second floor, followed by a frightened scream. Trusting Clara to catch the fireborn if it fled, Kael dropped down to the smoking window and smashed it open with his shield. Two children huddled atop a bed. Fire burned in little patches across the floor. Lying facedown before the stairs was the body of a man, his clothes aflame. The fireborn stood atop the dead man's back, ripping into his flesh with its claws. Upon hearing the shutter break, it looked up from its work. Again that grin, that understanding. Kael let loose another lance of ice, this time anticipating the creature's dodge. The fireborn fled down the stairs, exactly as Kael hoped. His lance ripped through its arm, severing it from its body. The thing howled bloody murder as it vanished.

"Bottom floor!" Kael shouted to Clara, who hovered directly over the rooftop in an attempt to cover all avenues of retreat. She spun, searching, and then he saw her jerk to one side and zoom away.

The children were crying, but Kael couldn't do anything for them, couldn't even spare the briefest moment to comfort them. The fireborn was off, Clara in pursuit, her silver wings a beacon amid the smoky black sky. Kael kicked off the building, rotated, and then pushed his wings to their maximum. Rooftops vanished in a blur beneath him, the great fire to the north rapidly approaching. Except buildings weren't burning as he'd expected. None appeared aflame. Instead a great yellow glow washed over them.

Clara slowed, and Kael flew up to her side.

"I lost it," Clara said, her eyes still sweeping back and forth below.

Kael pointed to the ominous glow.

"Seems like the obvious place to check," he said.

Clara agreed. Together they dropped closer to the ground, flying just over the rooftops and into the cul-de-sac.

Kael and Clara both froze at the horrific sight. After the host of nightmares they'd already witnessed, this was too much to even understand. Kael lessened the power to his harness, his feet gently touching down on the rooftop. At first he thought a hole from Hell had somehow opened in the ground of Weshern. Fire bubbled in a grand circle, filling the street from side to side. More than a dozen fireborn flitted around it, rushing down streets or lunging unaffected into the pool. Those that fled from the hole went empty-handed, while those returning moved slower, burdened...

They were dragging dead fireborn, Kael realized. Some carried whole bodies, others what limbs they could find. With relentless haste they tossed them into the pile, which simmered and boiled with an unearthly red glow. Worse were the bodies of humans that joined the pit. The body parts of adults were tossed in piece by piece, full bodies too big to be carried by the diminutive creatures. Children, though, they could manage, and Kael watched two demons drag a boy's body into the pit's center, flesh peeling away as it sank into the magma.

"What do we do?" Clara asked softly over the faint hum of their wings.

"I don't know," Kael said. "There's so many of them."

"What are they trying to create?"

"Your guess is as good as—"

He stopped. Not far to their left he saw another child being dragged toward the molten pile. She looked no more than two years old, her arm terribly burned from where the demon clutched her.

She was still alive.

"This whole night can go to Hell," Kael said as he drew his sword and tore through the air. The many fireborn turned his way, a multitude of obsidian eyes glaring at him as they bared their molten fangs and hissed like feral cats. Kael stayed above and out of reach, the child his only goal. The magma pool passed beneath him, the heat uncomfortable to his skin despite the distance. Pieces floated within, thick chunks of black stone amid the orange and red. Claws, legs, and even faces of dead fireborn floated atop it, a macabre graveyard for the otherworldly beings.

Kael landed before the creature, which snarled and refused to release the child. When Kael lashed out with his sword, the fireborn ducked beneath the swipe, but its refusal to let go kept it pinned in place. Kael looped the sword around, and as it ducked again, he pushed his shield closer. Its light flared, blinding the yelping fireborn. The next sword thrust pierced it between the eyes, killing it instantly. The body collapsed, black tongue lolling out of its mouth. Still it kept its grip tight on the crying girl's arm. Kael cut it off at the wrist, and as its blood pooled out on the stone, the severed hand hardened, cracked, and then released.

"It's all right," Kael said as he scooped the girl into his arms. "I've got you."

Two fireborn dashed closer, weaving around Clara's protective blasts of ice. Kael jumped into the air while punching his throttle. The fireborn leapt. Kael's wings thrummed. Their claws missed by inches as Kael flew down the street, Clara keeping back to defend his retreat. The girl sobbed in Kael's grasp, tears trickling down her dirty face from big blue eyes as she squirmed and held her burned arm.

"We're safe," Kael lied as he dropped lower now that the fireborn circle was so far away. "We're safe, I promise."

Guilt and frustration tightened his chest. He didn't know where her parents were, assuming they were still alive, or where her home might be. He felt as helpless as when Galen collapsed, his actions pitiful and meaningless against the overwhelming carnage unfolding. But at least this girl would live. That meant something, he told himself as he banged on the door of the first home he came upon. Kael heard movement from within, but no one came to answer.

"I'm a Seraph of Weshern!" he shouted. "In the name of the Archon, open this door!"

A lock rattled, and then the door cracked open, revealing a haggard man's face. Huddled behind him was the rest of his family.

"Take her," Kael ordered, handing the girl over to the father. The man did so without argument, too stunned and frightened to speak a word. Kael gave one last look to the child, prayed she'd be safe, and then flew back toward the molten pit.

Clara circled overhead, keeping far out of reach of the frantic fireborn. She rained ice upon them, her gauntlet a relentless cannon. Some dodged, others scrambled faster, carrying what body parts they could. As Kael neared he spotted a familiar one-armed fireborn rushing ahead of him. It weaved side to side, its pace uneven. Kael did his best to judge, then flung a small thin lance. It shattered upon the road, barely missing the creature.

The fireborn glanced over its shoulder, saw him, and laughed.

More ice, shot after shot as Kael chased, the fireborn bolting for the molten pool. Kael saw others abandoning their own tasks and rushing straight in, melting into the liquid fire. Such suicide made no sense to Kael, but he knew that whatever the reason, it wasn't good. Diving lower, he launched one last barrage at the fleeing fireborn. The demon sensed the attack coming and tucked into a roll. Kael's attacks missed the diminutive target, which launched itself into the center of the molten pool with a victorious screech. With a burst of flame, it sank down deep and then vanished.

Kael flung his feet forward and rotated the angle of his wings so they pushed back against his momentum, effectively hovering him in place as he lashed the ground with ice. The rest of the fireborn were charging the pit, and his gut said to stop them at all costs. He attempted to form a wall encircling the glowing red pool, but it melted from the heat faster than he could build it. Clara flew beside him, and without a word between them they tried again, redoubling their efforts into a single stream that layered the molten ground. Steam rose in great plumes, but it seemed nothing could deter the fire. The ground shook, the flames roaring hotter and hotter.

And then the molten pool began to rise.

The remaining few fireborn dove into the lava, their bodies melding into it, becoming yet another part of the growing monstrosity. Chunks steadily hardened, turning black as the pool gained form. Taller and taller it grew, thirteen feet high, a horrific facsimile of the smaller fireborn. Its legs were thick and stocky, its chest bulky and covered with hardened stone. Jagged pieces jutted out from its knees and elbows. Veins rippled over the surface of its body, glowing red as molten fire pulsed through them. It bore no tail, nor did it have lengthy claws. Instead a ring of jagged horns protruded from its forehead like a demonic crown.

The fireborn giant reared back its head, stretched its shoulders, and let forth a cry that shook the walls of the nearby buildings. Beneath it, where there'd been a gigantic pool of flame and melted stone, was now nothing but blackened char.

"This is bad," Kael said. "This is very bad."

"Higher, now!" Clara shouted. Sound advice, Kael agreed, and together they shot into the air. The giant took a lumbering step, the weight of its impact audible even from up high.

"I don't know if we can bring it down," Kael said as he hovered beside Clara.

"I don't know, either," Clara said. "But we're sure as hell going to try."

She reached into her pocket, pulling out two spare ice elemental prisms.

"Here," she said, handing over one of them. She popped out her old element and replaced it with the new. Kael did the same, not wanting to run out in the middle of fighting the fireborn giant. Clara looked to see if he was ready. He nodded.

"Give it all you've got," she said, leading the way. Her arm stretched out as she aimed with her gauntlet. The giant had its back to them as it rammed straight into a nearby building, knocking it to the ground as if it were made of cards. Clara spread her fingers wide, releasing an enormous torrent of ice from the focal point in her palm. It slammed into the back of the fireborn like a club, not meant to pierce or cut but instead crush and overwhelm. Steam hissed as the ice melted against its form. The force of the impact knocked the creature to one knee, and it turned about, hatred glinting in its obsidian eyes.

Kael struck it in the face with two boulders of ice, rocking the thing backward. The boulders broke into pieces, but they did their damage. A thin stream of orange liquid dribbled from the fireborn's mouth and down its chin. They gave it no reprieve, Kael rising higher while firing three large lances. Clara kept low, blasting at its knees with another beam of ice. The fireborn shrugged off both attacks, its stony skin seemingly impenetrable. Its hands dug into the street, scooping up slabs of dirt and stone. Biting back a swear, Kael turned and flew away, weaving as the fireborn hurled the collection at him through the air. After a glance over his shoulder he weaved again, dodging a thrown chunk of a nearby home. A heavy stone struck his thigh as he turned, and he clenched his jaw to hold in a pained scream.

Once he was safely away, Kael turned about for another assault. Clara continued throwing ice at the fireborn's legs, undeterred by its apparent lack of damage. As if to mock her, the giant dug its hands into the street and ripped the stone and earth upward, forming a barrier to protect its lower body. Forced to clear it, Clara rose into the air, joining Kael as they flew in for a barrage. Lances and boulders shot from their palms, battering the beast, but it kept its back to them as it crashed through the center of a home, its very touch setting the wood aflame. Kael led them closer, trying to focus on the same spot on the fireborn's back. Their attacks might have seemed to be causing little damage, but the ice dulled the creature's fire as their attacks slowly chipped away at the thick rock that made up the monster's body. Perhaps if they could weaken it enough, or break through its armor to the blood flowing underneath...

Their path took them close, too close. The fireborn giant whirled around, one of its mammoth arms outstretched. Its palm opened, and like a demonic version of a Seraph it released a torrent of flame that mocked even Bree's tremendous blasts. Kael and Clara split to either side, muscles protesting as he forced the turn. The flames licked his heels as he banked, avoiding two more tremendous sprays. Then it turned its attention to Clara, thinner, faster lances ripping from its palm and shooting through the air. Kael curled about, his heart in his throat as he watched Clara dance and weave in retreat. The shots appeared on target, but she narrowly avoided each one, twisting and dodging no differently than if an enemy Seraph were in chase.

The attacks stopped, the fireborn giant again putting its back to them and hurrying away. Kael joined Clara, looping over the rooftops to fly to her side.

"You all right?" he asked as she slowed to a hover.

"Yeah," she said, chest heaving as she sucked in air. "Where's it going?"

Kael returned his attention to the fireborn. It was marching with purpose, but where? He lifted higher, tracking the direction the creature walked. Seeing its path, he felt the pieces clicking into place in his head. The one-armed fireborn. It had seen the royal family. Somehow it understood who they were, and its intelligence was now part of the giant. There seemed no stopping it as it blasted through homes, crumbling planks and stone all around it as it lumbered for the alleyway where the Archon lay wounded within.

"It's headed for your parents!" Kael exclaimed.

She turned his way, then looked to the creature. She saw its path and made the same connection. Fear etched into her face, she flared her wings with light.

"We have to warn them!"

They pushed their wings to their limits. Speed was all that mattered as they flew over the fireborn in a desperate bid to beat it to the royal family. Kael veered slightly, just in case the fireborn flung another blast of flame, but it did not, so focused it was on its destination. Not much of a surprise, Kael decided. So far he and Clara were but pests to the thing, posing no real threat.

The alleyway approaching, Kael slowed as they dipped lower. Sig stood at the nearby entrance, then dashed after them as the two soared over his head to land in the alleyway.

"We have to get them out of here!" Kael shouted.

"Why? And how?" asked Sig.

"It doesn't matter," Clara said, kneeling down beside Isaac. "We have to . . ."

A red glow washed over them, and she tensed, knowing what it was.

"Holy shit," Sig said, jaw falling slack at the sight of the fireborn giant halted at the edge of the alleyway, flames licking off its body in swirls. A horribly familiar grin was on the creature's enormous face.

Kael lifted his shield, positioning himself before the royal family. Pure light washed over its surface. Despite the shield's amazing properties, the protection felt meager in the presence of such a beast.

"No running," Kael said. "We have to take it down together."

The fireborn's mouth opened, and from deep within its belly rumbled a spine-chilling laugh.

"Try," the creature said as it stepped into the alleyway, its voice like stones cracking together. The buildings on either side crumbled to make room for its enormous frame. "Nowhere left to run. We are here now, humans. We reach you at last."

The other Seraphs powered up their wings as the giant took another step. Light swirled across their palms as their focal points filled with power. Kael readied his own, imagining the ice as a sharpened spear, an enormous ballista to pierce through the creature. Before he could let it loose, the fireborn flung its arm. A massive chunk of stone ripped free of its form, swirling with flame. The boulder flew straight for Kael, mocking his shield with its size. The other Seraphs unleashed their elements upon the fireborn, bathing it with ice and lightning from above, but they could do nothing against the boulder.

Kael couldn't move, couldn't dodge. The royal family was behind him. Shield raised, gauntlet arm extended, he let loose a defiant scream. His element unleashed from his widened palm, Kael demanding every bit of its power. His vision filled with ice and fire, an explosion of steam, and then he braced for the fatal collision.

CHAPTER
26

All around Johan's hideout was insanity. Seraphs dashed in and out of the warehouse, grabbing wings, swords, and their respective elemental prisms. Bree already wore her pair, having been one of the first to alert the others of the fireborn's attack alongside Johan. Rebecca Waller stood in the heart of the chaos, a small table before her as she created an impromptu command post in the center of the street. A map of Weshern was unfurled across her table, pinned at the corners by two lamps to give her light. Dozens of marks and symbols were scrawled over it, names of Seraphs attached to towns and hastily circled districts.

"Where's Argus?" Bree asked as she and Johan pushed their way to her side.

Rebecca didn't even look up from her map.

"Argus is too hurt to leave his bed," she said. "So that leaves only me."

She pointed to a trio of towns, one after the other in a tight bunch on the map.

"Scour those three," she told two Seraphs beside her. "When you're done, don't return here. Head northwest, and skip Gainesville as you clear out the fireborn on the way toward the island's edge. Varl's stationed twelve men there, and we'll have to trust them to protect the village instead."

The Seraphs saluted in unison, then tore into the air. With them gone, Rebecca finally turned her attention their way. As the flicker of candlelight washed over her features, Bree winced. Rebecca's nose had been broken during her capture at the Aquila Forest, and it was still swollen and red, with a crook near the center that didn't quite belong. It certainly looked painful, and when Rebecca spoke, her voice had a slight muffle to it.

"I hope you're here to share some good news," she said. "There's been precious little of it tonight."

"I've spoken with my disciples," Johan told her. "They're spreading out in all directions to the nearby towns to aid in killing the fireborn."

"That'll help," Rebecca said, not a hint of enthusiasm reaching her words. "I'll ensure further patrols skip over the locations that your disciples can reach on foot."

Johan bowed low to the woman.

"As always, at your service," he said. "Now if you don't mind, I have work to do."

The man left, leaving Bree standing awkwardly before the little table.

"As for you," Rebecca said, looking to her map. "If you don't mind flying solo, I think there's a spot near your home of Lowville we could..."

"I do mind," Bree said. "I need to find Kael."

The woman looked up, her face iron.

"Tens of thousands of helpless lives in danger," she said. "And you'd abandon them all to go looking for one of the few people actually capable of defending themselves?"

Bree's face flushed with heat. Before she could respond, another Seraph joined them, still in the process of strapping on her wings.

"What's my patrol path?" Olivia West asked.

"I haven't decided," Rebecca said. "I was planning to send Bree to the southwest, starting with Lowville, but she wants to look for her brother."

"Not just my brother," Bree said. "He's with the royal family. They're out there somewhere, in danger of both knights and fireborn."

Rebecca hardly looked convinced.

"By diverting resources toward a search, we're dooming others to die," she said. "The Archon already has an escort. I don't see how we can afford to take such a risk."

"Yet we risked dozens to save the Archon earlier today," Bree argued. "How is this any different?"

Olivia crossed her arms and lowered her voice as she leaned closer to Rebecca.

"The people are going to be frightened by what happened tonight," Olivia said. "We'll need Isaac to keep them calm and help pick up the pieces. With Center breathing down our necks, the last thing we need is a power vacuum."

Rebecca glared at Bree.

"It's a poor excuse," she said. "But I'll allow it. Take Olivia with you. If you both fly a direct path toward the holy mansion, chances are good you'll pass one of the towns they're in. Even if you don't spot them it will still give them a chance to signal you as you fly over."

Rebecca stood, and she braced herself with the edges of the table as she sternly addressed them both.

"Waste no time in searching," she said. "Just fly with your eyes wide, and trust that either they see your wings, or you see theirs. If you reach the mansion without finding them, put an end to your search. Our island needs every Seraph on defense. We can't spare you for longer than that."

Bree quickly nodded in acceptance.

"Thank you," she said. "Thank you so much."

Rebecca waved a dismissive hand. Not daring to wait lest the leader change her mind, Bree powered on her wings and looked to Olivia.

"Let's go," the woman said, her own wings thrumming. Together they soared into the air, Olivia taking point. The older Seraph adjusted their angle twice as they flew, taking them along the main road leading from New Galen to the holy mansion. Bree saw Seraphs glimmering all around her, each with their own part of Weshern to defend. Knowing the size of the island, and how few Seraphs they had left, made the task feel borderline hopeless, even with the military guard helping.

The people will defend themselves, Bree told herself to ward off such dire thoughts. *Knives, swords, shovels, anything they can. The fireborn aren't invincible. They'll die tonight, every last one of them.*

Easier to believe than to do, though, and the scattered fires across the horizon were a strong reminder of that.

After a few miles, Olivia swung closer and grabbed Bree's arm to stabilize their flight together. With her free hand, she pointed to her left.

"Knights!" she shouted. Bree followed her finger, saw a distant flicker of gold wings piercing the smoky night.

"Where are they going?" Bree asked.

Olivia hesitated a moment before answering.

"They're not helping the people," she said. "I'd guess they're on the way to the Crystal Cathedral."

The thought put a fire in Bree's gut. The knights, who'd sworn to protect Weshern against any and all threats, would flee to their fortress at a time when the people needed them most? Bree couldn't decide which stung worse, the cowardice or the betrayal. Never before had Center's true allegiance been so clearly displayed.

Towns vanished beneath her, each and every one bearing signs of fire. Worst was a field not far from New Galen, dozens of acres consumed with billowing flame. A steady stream of people flooded out of the town to combat it, but Bree couldn't imagine what they could do against such a blaze. Rebecca's words calling her selfish echoed in her ears as she witnessed the destruction. Though her desire to find her brother had not wavered, she found she agreed with Rebecca.

The longer they flew the more Bree felt guilty for her request. Every fire they passed felt like one more opportunity to help, lost forever. Over Elan Village, while Bree was pondering abandoning their search, she saw a sign of hope.

"There," she said, pointing. Two sets of wings glowed silver in the night. It had to be the group with the Archon. No other Seraphs had yet come so far from New Galen. The pair dipped down into an alleyway, and with an excited burst of speed Bree led the way straight for it. The alleyway neared, and instead of feeling relief, Bree's heart flooded with fear. A nightmare of a monster lumbered through the street, fire and obsidian given life, a crown of horns protruding from its forehead like a sick joke. For the briefest moment Bree felt her mind blank, refusing to believe what she saw. What in all her training taught her how to battle such a creature? What could mere swords of steel do against something so gigantic?

Kael stood guarding the Archon, who lay injured on the ground behind him. His shield lifted, light blazing off it in defiance of the fireborn's flame.

Don't think, Bree's mind ordered as her fear formed a noose about her throat. *Just go. Go, damn it, go!*

Her thumb cranked her throttle, flaring her wings as she blasted toward the giant. It swung its arm, and a boulder ripped from its body, flinging to the alley like a comet. Clara, Saul, and Sig took to the air, their elements blasting the fireborn, but Kael stood his ground, a torrent of ice flowing from his palm into the center of the flaming boulder. It slowed the attack, but not nearly enough.

Despite knowing it madness, Bree aimed her gauntlet for the boulder. She had to do something, no matter how desperate. The boulder passed below her, so close she felt its heat on her skin. Her gauntlet jerked backward, wrenching her shoulder as the fire blasted downward, striking the boulder. The push wasn't much, but she didn't need much, especially with Kael's ice already slowing it down. Instead of landing atop of Kael, the boulder fell lower, striking the ground with an explosion of stone. The ball of liquid fire rolled forward, slamming into Kael with the last of its momentum. Bree screamed, certain she was about to see him crushed, but his shield flared with light so brilliant Bree had to squint and turn away.

When her vision returned, she looked for his corpse. Instead she saw Kael standing before the royal family, bathed in steam, his shield shimmering white. A cracked and broken pile of debris was all that remained of the fireborn's attack.

"Let's go!" Bree shouted to him as she looped above, relieved beyond measure.

Kael saw her, and a grin spread from ear to ear on his face as he took to the air.

Olivia had joined the other three in swarming the fireborn giant, her lightning coupling with Sig's. The electric strikes swirled off the demon's obsidian form, seemingly doing little beyond angering it. Saul's ice fared better, battering the giant again and again with thick chunks, the melting frost dimming the glow of flame in the creature's crisscrossing veins. Bree closed in, wondering what good her flame might be against such a beast. The smaller fireborn were vulnerable to her naked blades, but this thing? Their situation dire enough to try anyway, she tilted sideways and slashed while passing over the giant's shoulder. The fire on her swords flared, but despite their power she felt resistance reverberate through her hands. The steel cut a shallow groove into the obsidian, the inner parts oozing a deep red down its shoulder and arm.

"Little bees!" the fireborn roared, the sound of it terrifying Bree to her core. It blocked a lance of ice from Kael, staggered a step when twin blasts of lightning hit its back from Olivia and Sig. "Do you think your stings will harm me?"

Kael shot a boulder of ice in response. The giant caught it in both hands and immediately flung it back. Bree circled about for another charge, eyes wide as her brother dodged the retaliatory strike. The ice shattered behind Kael as he retreated farther down the street, safely out of range. Sig dove in from behind the giant, attempting to cover Kael's retreat with a blast of lightning from point-blank range, but the giant's reflexes were far faster than he expected. An enormous hand shot into the air, snagging Sig by the leg. Bree felt her heart lurch as the Seraph unleashed a desperate stream from his gauntlet into the giant's hand. It only made its grip tighter, crunching armor and bone. Sig screamed, but not for long. The giant slammed him to the ground, smashing his body and wings upon the stone. Its foot lifted, dripping with molten rock.

"You monster!" Saul screamed, and he charged while releasing a massive stream of ice from his palm. The ice caked across the monster's upraised foot, slowing but not stopping it as it smashed down on Sig's immobilized form, burning him to ash and twisted metal. Saul shifted his aim to the giant's face as Kael battered the back of the thing's knees from the other side. The fireborn endured, pointing its fingers at the approaching Saul. Thin stones erupted from the tips, each the size of an egg. They numbered in the dozens, a massive spray Saul had no hope to avoid. The stones battered his body, dropping him blind to the ground. He knelt there on his knees, gasping for air as he tried to regain his bearings. The giant gave him no time, widening its palm like an enormous Seraph about to shoot.

"Saul!" Bree screamed.

He attempted to leap back into the air but his injured leg buckled. His wings lifted him, but his takeoff was uneven, and he shot more sideways than straight up. A flash of flame bathed Saul's chest, and he collapsed before the entrance of the alleyway.

The giant laughed as it took a step closer to Saul's limp form, thick, sharp chunks of obsidian rattling across its form. Something about the way the creature moved sparked a thought in Bree's mind. It stepped heavily, almost clumsily, like a beast wrapped in an enormous set of armor. And if those chunks of obsidian were in fact armor, then she just needed to find its weak spots...or create one. Bree circled around, zeroing in on the giant's chest while trying to put her worry for Saul out of her mind. Best to go for an easy target, she decided, a spot the others could consistently hit. A blast of Olivia's lightning hit the giant's shoulder, spinning its attention toward her as it snarled. Bree came in from its blind side, rotating so she was close to its body. Fire bathed her swords as she slashed across its chest, both blades showering sparks across the street. Her speed carried her away before it could retaliate, an impotent cry of anger sounding behind her. Twisting about, she flew backward while dropping her throttle to survey the battle. Twin gashes of red glowed like angry veins where she'd struck the creature.

"Focus on the same spot!" Bree shouted to the others. "Weaken it enough and I'll break you an opening!"

Kael and Clara halted their retreat and hovered in place. As one they braced their arms and shot streams of ice at the giant's chest. It howled as the ice blasted into it, the ice initially shattering on first contact, then sticking as it slowly encased the fireborn's molten armor. The giant lifted an arm as a shield, snarling at the two Seraphs. With its other hand it reached down, grabbed an enormous chunk of road, and flung it back at them. They scattered in opposite directions, narrowly avoiding the explosion of stone as the chunk collided with the ground and broke into pieces.

Lightning struck the fireborn's chest, quick, rapid bursts ripping into the small space between Bree's twin sword marks with surgical precision. The giant turned its attention to Olivia hovering above him, but when it grabbed a chunk of the street to throw, Bree had returned, her swords slicing across its fingers. The chunk dropped and hit the ground with a loud thud, followed by another angry roar. Bree zoomed away as a torrent of fire nipped at her heels. She circled higher, watching as Clara and Kael alternated boulders of ice. The giant blocked several with its arms, its feet sinking into the street as it fought to maintain balance. Anytime it dropped its defenses to attack, the ice would slam into its chest with a blistering crack.

The giant suddenly ran down the street toward them, bellowing as it rushed Kael and Clara. The two split, streaking away as the giant belched fire from its throat like a legendary dragon of old. Lightning struck the demon's face again and again, Olivia taunting it as if it were a plaything. At no point could it assault her in return, for the moment it tried, ice blasted its chest. It was weak and angry, its enormous arms flailing wildly at them as if they were the swarm of bees it had mockingly named them. Mindless rage bellowed out of its throat, a horrifying primal cry that Bree refused to dwell on as she vaulted over the fireborn's head. Her wings off, she passed upside down, swords swatting at its eyes. She didn't expect to hurt it, just keep it distracted. Completing the turn, she landed on her knees facing the fireborn, which howled in anger. Another burst of ice shot over her head, four lances with blunted ends like battering rams. They weren't trying to pierce the armor, just weaken it. The elements cracked and scattered into mist, but the impact sent the fireborn giant staggering back a step. It flung another boulder, its aim frantic and poor. A nearby house collapsed from the attack, its wood bursting into flame. Kael and Clara refused to relent, another barrage of ice flying over Bree's head. The first few shots hit its shoulders and legs, knocking it off balance, and then the second wave battered its already weakened chest. It howled, and from overhead Olivia sent a stream of lightning down its throat.

The giant staggered on unsteady feet. Bree saw her opening and didn't hesitate. Leaping forward, she ignited her wings and thrust with both swords. She crashed straight into the fireborn, her weapons sinking to the hilts in its cracked chest. So close to the creature she'd expected fire and pain, but either her affinity protected her more than she'd anticipated or the creature's flame was too dimmed by their overwhelming attacks.

Screaming to give herself strength, Bree put a foot on the giant's chest and kicked off. Her swords tore free, and the dark stone tore with it. Pebbles showered the street as a bright orange liquid dripped from the opened wound, flickering with flame from contact with the air. Bree rose higher, swords to either side as she screamed victoriously.

"Take it down!"

The two ice Seraphs were now below her, and they lifted their arms and flared their gauntlets. Two enormous lances shot from their palms, and this time their points were long and sharp. The giant defended Clara's with a swipe of its forearm, but Kael's struck the heart of the weeping wound and sank deep inside. The giant's body convulsed, chest jerking backward. It collapsed on weakening knees, thick hands sinking into the street to support its weight.

Olivia dropped from the sky, sword in her left hand, lightning swirling around the palm of her right. She pressed her hand directly against the wound, showing no fear for the creature's fire. Her teeth clenched, her body tensed, and then lightning poured out of her in a tremendous explosion, every bit of her element's power releasing in a blinding display. The giant screamed a sound like thunder. Its arms fell limp, the fireborn sinking down on its haunches. The shimmering red veins across its body dulled, the obsidian stone that made up much of its form now weak, cracking and crumbling. Pulling back her hand, Olivia slashed the thing across the throat, then kicked. Its head tumbled free, the horns of its crown breaking as it rolled to a stop farther down the street.

Bree lessened her throttle, gently drifting back to ground. Her swords were caked with the giant's blood, and no amount of shaking seemed to clean them off. When she touched down, she beat both blades together. The brittle blood cracked and broke, pieces showering the ground at her feet. Bree stared at them, a sudden revelation striking her. The pieces of dried blood, they looked familiar, so familiar...

She knelt down and grabbed one of the pieces, rolling it in her palm. It was smaller, and weirdly shaped compared to what she was used to, but there was no doubt it was an elemental prism.

Demon blood, she thought, chilled to the bone. *The theotechs harvest demon blood for our wings.*

"Did we get it?" Saul asked, stirring Bree from her thoughts. He lay nearby, propped up by his wings. His hand pressed against his injured leg, his face locked in a permanent grimace as he stared up to the sky. Burns covered much of his chest. Bree smiled at him, trying to remain hopeful despite his wounds.

"Yeah, we got it."

"Good." He closed his eyes, shifted in an attempt to get more comfortable. "Good."

A hand touched her shoulder, and she turned to embrace Kael, her brother looking tired and drained.

"Great timing, sis," he said.

"I do what I can."

Clara was with him, and she flung her arms around Bree's neck next.

"Thank you," she said. "I thought I'd lost Kael for sure."

Bree hugged her back.

"So did I," she said. "Thank God I'm more stubborn than smart."

Olivia landed with them, her outfit blackened in places, her beautiful face blistering from the heat of the fireborn giant.

"Well done," she told them. "Fine Seraphs, each and every one of you."

Praise from Olivia was rare, and despite all the awfulness and insanity of the night, Bree felt proud to receive it.

"What do we do about them?" Kael asked, nodding toward the royal family. Olivia glanced farther into the alley, frowned.

"Wait here," she said as she and Clara approached the royal family. For a moment she knelt down and discussed something quietly with Avila, then nodded. Conversation over, she returned to the three, with Clara remaining behind with her parents.

"I'll send for others back at New Galen," she said. "We'll have a Seraph carry Avila, and a stretcher for Saul and the Archon. Until I return, keep an eye out for more fireborn."

"I'm pretty sure we're in the clear," Kael said. "It'll be nice to catch our breath."

"It's not over yet." The older Seraph flicked her throttle, powering up her wings. "With Isaac and Avila safe, we'll need to turn our attention to the rest of the island."

Bree pointed a sword at the smoking corpse of the fireborn, its form slowly disintegrating into rubble.

"We took down a giant," she said. "After that, the rest of the fireborn don't stand a chance."

Olivia smiled despite her own exhaustion.

"Amen," she said. "They can run and burn all they want, but this time, we're the ones hunting."

CHAPTER

27

The light of day was a most welcome thing to Kael's tired eyes. The morning glow made it feel like the nightmare was almost at an end. Only almost, though. As Kael stood atop a roof, he gazed in all directions. The smoke drifting skyward was so thick it made a mockery of the morning mist. At his feet lay a dying fireborn, his sword still embedded in its chest. Blood bubbled out of it, slowly crystallizing as it made contact with the air. The color faded from its skin as its body ceased to move. Kael yanked his sword free, smacked it against his shield to shake off the dried pieces of blood still sticking to the steel.

"I think that's the last of them in this town," Bree said as she landed beside him. Dark circles ringed her eyes, and faint burn marks blackened much of her uniform. She'd handled the northern parts of the village while Kael scoured the south. Once the Archon had been retrieved, they'd spent the rest of the night hunting.

"Want to keep looking?" Kael asked. He pointed east, to a distant town with a particularly heavy haze of smoke above it. "Welton might still have a few lurking within."

"Can't," she said. "Olivia sent word. Isaac's ordering all Seraphim to join him and Johan back at New Galen."

Kael shrugged.

"Well, hate to disappoint the Archon," he said. "Hopefully he'll give us a royal decree to sleep for the next twenty-four hours."

Bree laughed despite her exhaustion.

"I fear it'll be the opposite," she said. "Forty-eight hours without a rest, but let's hope you're right instead. Since it's on the way, let's swing by Selby first. I want to make sure Aunt Bethy's all right."

Kael eased his wings back to life.

"Sounds like a plan," he said. "Lead on, sis."

Together they flew southwest, Kael scanning the ground for signs of any remaining fireborn. He saw none, but he did see plenty of the damage they'd caused. Homes throughout every city burned or burning, with civilians scrambling to contain the damage. Worse were the crops forming charred rings around the towns. Sprawling fields of wheat and corn, consumed in a single night. Kael feared the starvation that might follow. If the damage was equally vicious throughout the entire island, then the death toll from the attack might rise long after the last fireborn were hunted down and slain.

Kael had not been to Selby in years, having visited the Briar family only once at their farm. He remembered being taken aback at the sheer chaos of the place. Three families, totaling more than fifteen people, lived in the two-story wood home, which on the bottom floor looked more like a barn, given the mess left by the many animals the Briars kept inside during the harsher winter months. Kael and Bree had been forced to share a "bed" in the corner of the kitchen. The bed had been made up of a collection of pillows and a single blanket not long enough to keep Kael's feet from poking out the bottom. A blanket that smelled like goats, too. Not exactly his fondest of memories.

"There!" Bree shouted, pointing to the distance. They flew over a huge field, and in the middle was the home Kael remembered. Not far from the house was an impressive barn, built entirely of wood and layered with thick black shingles across the roof. To Kael's relief, neither was aflame. Less comforting was the thin cloud of smoke coming from the heart of one of their fields, but from what he could tell, it appeared to be dying.

Together they landed before the home, shutting off their wings. A mop-haired young boy Kael didn't recognize stood before the door, jaw agape and eyes wide.

"Bethy!" he shouted, suddenly springing to life and dashing through the door. "Bethy, your nephew and niece are here!"

In less than a second Aunt Bethy came rushing out. Her face and clothes were smeared with ash, her eyes bloodshot, but she was alive and unharmed.

"Praise God you're safe," she said, flinging her arms around Kael's neck. "I feared the worst when the fire fell from the sky." He hugged back, too tired to be embarrassed. Bree was next, and she smiled briefly as she embraced their aunt.

"We don't have much time," she said. "We just wanted to make sure you were fine."

"Of course, of course," Bethy said, stepping away. "Look at you two in your wings, so mature. I'm sure Weshern owes you a great debt for all you've done tonight."

"We did save the life of the Archon," Kael said, unable to help himself. When she looked his way, disbelief in her eyes, Kael grinned wide. "We did, I swear."

Aunt Bethy smiled as she shook her head.

"You two are little miracles," she said. "I wish your parents could see you now. They'd be so proud."

"How was your night here?" Bree asked. "We saw the fires as we flew over."

"Ashton was awake when it all began," Bethy said. "Out in the field with the neighbor's girl, though he's shy to admit it. Their little tryst is why we were able to save what we did. He woke up the whole house, and when the fires started we were able to dig a ditch to keep it contained."

"Did you encounter one of the fireborn?"

Bethy's face twitched, and she hesitated. Members of the other families were filtering out of the home, all looking equally as tired and disheveled as their aunt. A deeply tanned man, Jared Briar, if Kael's memory was correct, put his hand around Bethy's shoulder.

"We did," he said. "Found it in the field, cackling as it set the corn ablaze. We were lucky enough to have come carrying shovels, so we weren't defenseless. Burned my boy pretty badly, but we managed to take the damn thing down."

"How is the rest of Weshern?" asked a woman beside Jared. Her hands were calloused, her hair tied back in a bun. "Is it as bad as here?"

"Worse," Kael said. "But we've slaughtered the fireborn. We'll be safe now, I'm sure of it."

Bree glanced his way, not sharing his optimism. Still, the people were tired and frightened. What harm was there in offering them a sliver of hope?

"If the Archon's safe, then he'll lead us through," Aunt Bethy said. "Now go on, you two. I'm sure there's plenty left for you to do."

Bree and Kael gave her another hug, then powered up their wings.

"Stay safe," Kael called to his aunt, then shot into the air, Bree following. Kael's relief at seeing his aunt safe lasted only as long as it took to reach the nearest town and see the smoldering devastation. He did his best to put it out of his tired mind. A long day lay ahead of them. Worrying about something out of his hands wouldn't help anyone. Silently they flew to New Galen, to meet up with the rest of the Seraphim. Hopefully there they'd hear what the Archon had in mind, and how they'd respond to last night's tragedy.

When they landed at Johan's headquarters it was swarming with both Seraphim and soldiers. Dozens sported burns on their flesh and uniforms, the marks thin, like the claws of the fireborn.

"Where should we go?" Bree asked as she glanced about. The hum of conversation was heavy and tired, and no one appeared to be taking charge.

"I don't know," Kael said. "Let's find Clara."

Kael led the way, weaving through the group and into the large building. Inside was equally crowded, and occupied mostly with injured. Kael winced at the sight of burnt and peeling flesh. The pain looked unbearable, and based on the cries of many as they pushed through, sounded unbearable, too.

"These poor people," Bree whispered as they checked inside the rooms they passed, searching for the Archon.

"Better us than the innocent," Kael said, wishing his trembling insides were as steeled as his words.

At the last room in the hall, Kael found the Archon and his family. Isaac lay on the bed, thick bandages wrapped around his bare chest and left arm. Avila sat beside him on a little stool, holding his uninjured hand. Even after escaping prison and fleeing the fireborn, an air of regal dignity hovered over her. Clara stood in the corner, wings beside her on the floor.

"Are we interrupting?" Kael asked, but Clara immediately waved off the concern.

"Welcome back," she said, wrapping her arms around his waist and giving him a tired kiss on the cheek. "I'm glad you didn't get hurt after I was gone."

"Me, too," Kael said. He kissed her back, then reluctantly pulled apart.

"The Skyborn twins?" Isaac asked in a heavily drugged voice. He leaned up in his bed and opened his eyes. They poorly focused on Kael. "Th...thank you, both of you."

"Not now," Avila said, gently pushing him back onto the bed. He crumpled with minor resistance.

"Thank you," Isaac continued after grunting in pain. "My wife and I...we're in your debt."

"It's nothing," Bree said, sounding incredibly awkward.

"It's not," Avila said, and she smiled at both of them. "Please, accept our gratitude. If not for your aid, we'd never have survived the night."

A knock on the door stole their attention. Rebecca Waller stood in the middle of the entrance, brown eyes darting about the room.

"Forgive me, but we must discuss our responses to last night's chaos," she said. "Johan is waiting. Would you come with me, Avila?"

The Archon's wife shook her head.

"I won't make decisions for Weshern without Isaac."

"I was under the impression he is unwell."

"I am," Isaac muttered. "But you'll have it in here anyway."

Rebecca bowed.

"As you wish," she said, and then left.

"Should we leave, too?" Kael whispered to Clara.

"No," she whispered back. "I want you here. Leave only if my father makes you."

Kael doubted that would happen anytime soon. His eyes were closed, and it seemed he drifted in and out of sleep. As bad as it looked, Kael knew it could have been much worse. That he'd survived his fall at all was incredible.

Bree started removing her wings, and Kael did likewise. The room was already cramped, and their harnesses made it worse. Kael groaned as he stretched his muscles. A tiny part of him envied the Archon. At least he got to sleep. If Rebecca and Johan were discussing responses, Kael had a feeling rest was still many hours away. When both their wings were carefully stacked atop Clara's, they slumped against the wall. Kael closed his eyes, enjoying what rest he could. Clara sat next to him, arm around his waist and head on his shoulder.

"You're making me too comfortable," Kael said. "I'll be out in minutes."

"Sleep if you must," Clara said. "I'll wake you when Johan arrives."

Kael cracked a half smile. It surely wouldn't take that long for Johan and Rebecca to return. He doubted he could fall asleep that quickly, even if it felt so good cuddled up against her, his arm wrapped over her shoulder, her head leaning against him...

Her elbow jarred him awake, and he sucked in air as feeling returned to his limbs.

"The Archon needs his rest," he heard Johan say. "You should act in his stead until he's capable of resuming his duties, Avila."

"I'm here, and I'm alive," Isaac said as he pushed his blanket off him and struggled to sit up. Avila grabbed his side, helping him slide his back up against the headboard. His upper body shook, but he remained upright. "For now, that's good enough. So talk."

The two stood side by side in front of the door. Johan appeared spry and energetic as ever, while Rebecca looked like her mind was in a thousand places. She carried a board with several pieces of paper upon it, and that familiarity seemed to calm her hands from the fidgeting mess they'd been recently. If either was upset by Kael and Bree's presence, they didn't show it. Rebecca glanced at Johan, who gestured for her to start.

"From what we can tell, nearly all of the fireborn have been destroyed," she said. "The damage they've done, though, is catastrophic. Preliminary estimates put the loss of this year's harvest at two-thirds. We're still counting livestock, but I'd estimate at least a quarter of our total supply killed. We'll need to begin rationing immediately."

"The animals," Isaac said, breathing heavily with every word. "Focus on the dead animals. Get them butchered as soon as possible, before the meat spoils."

"I'll spread the order," Rebecca said, marking something on her paper. "After that..."

"After that is the matter of retaliation," Johan interrupted. "And we must decide on it quickly, while Center still burns."

"Retaliation?" Avila asked. "Have you seen the state Weshern is in? How are we to retaliate? And how do we know more fireborn won't fall from the sky tomorrow night?"

Johan addressed his comments directly to Isaac.

"Center is far larger than Weshern," he said. "Countless more fireborn landed upon her soil than ours. Take the devastation you've seen here and then magnify it tenfold. I doubt they've even killed the last of the fireborn like we have. They've lost more crops, more lives, and have more mouths to feed. We need to strike now, while they're still recovering from the chaos. And as for further fireborn attacks," he glanced at Avila, "the fireborn are incapable of flight. The protective dome about us broke while the fireborn swarmed atop it, hence their fall upon our islands. If there are more, and they wish to attack again, they'll have to cross ocean waters, and even then, they have no way of ascending the Beam."

Isaac kept silent a moment, wincing against his pain as he thought.

"If we were to retaliate, what is it you suggest?" he asked.

Johan stepped closer to the Archon, his every action growing more animated.

"We drive them off Weshern, now and forever," he said. "It won't be difficult, will it Rebecca?"

The smaller woman seemed to understand Johan's plan, and she looked thoroughly displeased with it.

"All reports indicate that the forces of Center who didn't flee the island gathered at the Crystal Cathedral," she said.

"The Crystal Cathedral," Johan echoed. "The last theotech stronghold on your soil. If we're to have any semblance of true freedom we need to wrest control away from pawns of Center. It is there that they control the Beam that keeps your island afloat. It is there they purify your water and control the Fount. Such control cannot remain in their hands."

"You speak of things only they understand," Avila said. "Nobody else knows how to control those forces. Taking over may put Weshern at greater risk."

"Then have the theotechs there swear allegiance," Johan said. "My disciples can ensure their loyalty. The power they hold is too great. If you're to be free, that freedom must be ripped from their hands."

"And what is your opinion on this?" Isaac asked Rebecca.

Rebecca shifted uncomfortably, eyes on her notepad.

"I think our men and women are exhausted and would

like to check on their families," she said. "If Center is as weak as Johan says, then now is the time we should sue for peace. Demand they withdraw all claims of wrongdoing by our island and apologize for Isaac's and Avila's imprisonment. Our people are in turmoil, and they're asking questions about the fireborn and the meaning behind their fall. Center surely suffers even greater, and if they dont give answers, they'll suffer further riots and chaos. The threat of war is greater now than it ever has been before. I say we use that to end this conflict and begin rebuilding our homes."

Isaac sighed, and he shifted so that he could rest his elbows on his knees. His gaze stared into nowhere as he thought.

"I cannot ignore the fate Marius almost sentenced us to," he said. "He disbanded our Seraphim and military guard, stripping us of our wings and elements. When the fireborn fell, Center's knights *abandoned* us. Marius tried to deny us our ability to defend ourselves and then left us to burn and die."

"Left you to burn and die to an enemy I assure you they knew existed," Johan added. His voice was a solemn whisper. "An enemy that torched the skies overhead every night, praying for the day they might fall upon our cities."

Isaac looked up, fury burning hot in his eyes.

"If Center is weak, then now is not the time for peace. Now is when we repay them for their centuries of lies. Marius's knights hid in the Crystal Cathedral while all around them innocent lives burned. Gather our forces. We'll show them the punishment they deserve for such cowardice."

"And what of Edwin?" Avila asked. "We still don't know where he's being held. If we attack, Marius may execute him as punishment."

Isaac winced, and he refused to look her way.

"No matter what we do, Edwin may suffer," he said. "We must act on what is best for Weshern."

Hardly what Avila wanted to hear, but she did not argue further.

"Your risks are great," Johan said, bowing low in respect. "You have my gratitude for your bravery. I shall spread the order to my disciples. We'll assault in tandem with your own military. Our foes won't stand a chance."

He left. Rebecca started to follow, then hesitated.

"There will be no going back after this," she said. "Center won't view this as the attack of a few angry disbanded Seraphim. This is war. If we fail, all of Weshern will face Marius's wrath. Are you sure it's not wiser to sue for peace?"

It was a sentiment Kael found himself agreeing with, but it seemed Isaac did not.

"Do not fear the coming change," he said as his wife pulled a blanket over him. "We're so close. So very close . . ."

Rebecca bowed low even though Isaac couldn't see it.

"As you wish, my Archon," she said. "I will send a flyer to General Cutter with orders that he bring his troops to the cathedral."

The woman left, and with Isaac already drifting off, Kael felt like an interloper amid the family.

"We should go join the other Seraphim and prepare," he said, pushing to his feet. Clara stood beside him, and she wrapped her arms around his shoulders for another embrace. "Do you want to come with us?"

"I want to stay here, with my parents," Clara said. "For what little time we have left."

He kissed her lips, quick, keenly aware of her mother's watchful eyes.

"We'll find you before liftoff," he said. "Keep an eye on our wings until then, all right?"

Clara smiled in acknowledgment, then knelt beside her father's bed. Kael stared at her a moment longer, part of him wishing to remain, but then Bree nudged his side.

"Let's go," she said.

Bree opened the door, and they exited together. Once in the hallway they heard the growing commotion from outside the building. Bree glanced at him, curious, but Kael could only shrug.

"I guess Johan's already spread the word," he said.

Bree didn't look satisfied. Her leading, they crossed the hall and stepped outside. The crowd was mostly soldiers and Seraphim, but Johan's disciples were also scattered throughout, easily detectable in their plain brown robes. Johan stood on a makeshift platform made up of four crates stacked beside one another. He kept his hood pulled low over his face against the rising sunlight, hiding his many scars.

"You all have now seen the reason for our struggle," Johan said, his voice thundering through the crowd. "You have now seen the lies Center has woven over your eyes. Let the hope of peace die and a fire of vengeance kindle anew. We have suffered, all of us, suffered deeply for their arrogance and pride, and today we shall let them know the truth of our rage."

"Isaac should be giving this speech," Bree said, shaking her head with disgust. "Or at least Argus. He's not one of us, Kael. He's as foreign as Marius, yet here we are, cheering as he gives orders to our troops..."

Johan continued, his figure seeming to grow larger, his voice louder, as his excitement heightened.

"Soldiers of the Archon," he cried. "Seraphim of Weshern, hear me! Long have I preached against the lies of Center. Some of you listened, while others responded with scorn. This morning, as we stand among the destruction that rained down upon us from the midnight skies, I trust only open eyes and ears greet me now. The fireborn have fallen, my brothers and sisters. The skies burned and bled while we too burned and bled, and why? Because Center kept yet another secret from us!"

Johan spun as he spoke, ensuring all saw the fire in his eyes.

"The theotechs knew of the demons' existence, yet we were never warned. They left us unprepared for the disaster that befell our islands. The demons were swept away by the Endless Ocean, they claimed. Our burned crops say otherwise. Our lands were kept safe by the hands of the theotechs, they insisted. Our beloved dead say otherwise."

He jammed a finger toward the crowd.

"What else do they hide from us?" he asked. "What other secrets do they keep that we will one day suffer for? This cannot stand. This cannot endure! On Elern, my disciples rise up. On Sothren, my followers sharpen their blades. On Candren, my believers are ready to take the lives of those who would oppress and enslave. Here on Weshern, where your people have suffered more than any other due to the Speaker's thirst for power, will you remain peaceful? Will you lie down and wait for Center to return with chains and collars for the disobedient animals they think you are?"

Cheers of adamant denial met his question.

"Your Archon has given the order," Johan said. "And I am proud to accept it alongside you. People of Weshern, rise up against Center, starting with their lone and final stronghold. The cowards lurk within the Crystal Cathedral. Let them not remain. Those who prepare our water and keep our islands afloat must swear their allegiance to the people they serve, and not those who would rule from beyond. Do you hear me, Seraphim? Are your blades sharp? Are your wings ready? Freedom awaits you. Have you the strength to take it?"

He hopped down from his little platform amid cheers. Kael shook his head, tired and upset.

"We go to war," he whispered to his sister. "And we go with Johan leading the way."

Bree patted his arm, and she smiled in a vain attempt to calm his fears.

"I'll get our wings."

CHAPTER

28

The Weshern Seraphim flew to Castnor, the town nearest to the Crystal Cathedral. Battle was close at hand, but it would not begin until both Johan's and General Cutter's ground troops arrived. Rebecca Waller had insisted they attack with all their forces combined, something Bree had found unnecessary, and she stated as much during their flight over.

"Why wait?" she'd asked Olivia West, who'd helped take over Argus's duties since his injury. "We can destroy the soldiers from the air without fear for casualties."

"And if they hide inside the cathedral?" Olivia asked. "Or worse, retreat into tunnels and bunkers built underneath it? We send everything, Bree. This battle may decide Weshern's freedom. There's no point going in at half strength."

Bree accepted the point. With the size and weight of their wings they weren't the greatest combatants in enclosed spaces. Best to let those with shields, spears, and armor fight the more confined battles. And if their armies did meet in open ground, whoever had the greater aerial power would arise the victor. Given how at least forty Weshern Seraphs flew with them to Castnor, Bree couldn't imagine how that wouldn't be them.

The Seraphim gathered in the town center, mingling about the wide empty square. Bree arrived alongside Kael and Clara, and together the trio landed near the center. Voices washed over them, dozens talking with one another, sharing their outrage, their thirst for vengeance. The quieter ones discussed tactics, or admitted their concerns for the coming fight.

"This way," Clara said, tapping Bree's shoulder to gain her attention. They worked their way toward the corner of the square, Bree following in the other two's wake. She glanced at her comrades, seeing their determination amid their exhaustion, and tried to draw strength from it. They'd all suffered and lost family and friends last night. No matter how badly exhaustion weighed on her shoulders, she would push through, no differently than anyone else.

As they walked, Bree spotted one Seraphim markedly smaller than the others, her blonde hair almost as white as her skin. Bree paused, glancing over a second time at the tiny woman with wings bigger than her entire body.

"Amanda?" Bree asked as she recognized her former roommate. "Amanda, how've you been?"

She hugged the tiny girl, who shyly hugged back. Clara and Kael quickly joined her in greeting their friend.

"Not as well as you," Amanda said. "My name's not known from here to Sothren."

"Sometimes that's a good thing," Kael said, and she smiled as he hugged her as well. "It's good to see you, even if it's, well..." He gestured to the gathering soldiers and Seraphim. "Here."

Clara was last, and the least enthusiastic with her embrace.

Bree remembered Clara's concerns about Amanda's hesitancy to kill in battle. Perhaps she still shared them, but given all the losses they'd suffered, any trained Seraph was better than none.

"I didn't expect a class reunion," Amanda said, smiling as she pulled back from Clara. "Is anyone else from ours here?"

Bree exchanged a look with Kael, and she fought down a wave of fresh hurt. Who should she mention first, Brad's death, or Saul's injury?

"No," Kael said. "For now, it's just us four."

Amanda didn't inquire further, which allowed Bree an inward sigh of relief. So close to another fight, the last thing she wanted was to dwell on all they'd lost. The four walked through the crowd, pushing their way to a corner of the town center so they had some measure of privacy.

"So what brought you out here to join us?" Kael asked as he leaned against the door of a closed pawnshop.

"The same that brought many others here," Amanda said, gesturing to the gathered Seraphim. "Last night's destruction. It can't be ignored."

"That's one way to put it," Clara said, and she glared east, as if she could see the distant Crystal Cathedral and the theotechs lurking within.

Bree watched Amanda as the woman nodded, her eyes fluttering to avoid eye contact. Something troubled her greatly, that much was easy to see.

"Are you all right?" Bree asked, touching Amanda on the shoulder. The contact startled her, but it also forced her former roommate to meet her gaze. Her eyes were heavily bloodshot. From tears, Bree wondered, or lack of sleep?

"Yeah," Amanda said, and she crossed her hands behind her as she leaned against the pawnshop wall. "It's just, last night, when the fire fell from the sky, I..." She paused. "We didn't know what was going on. Most of us had nothing to fight back with. We fled and hid until Seraphim arrived to cleanse our village." Her lower lip began to quiver, but her voice held strong. "Those creatures killed so many, and they laughed as they did it. Laughed, just laughing as they burned my mother until she..." Amanda took in a deep breath. "I was scared what would happen to my family if I joined everyone in fighting against Center," she said after recovering. "But now it doesn't matter. We never should have been so unprepared for what happened. Marius and his theotechs need to pay for what they cost us."

She looked to them all.

"I'm sorry," she said. "I should have joined sooner, I really should have, but I was a coward."

Bree wrapped her in another embrace.

"You're not a coward," she said. "You never were, not then, not now."

Amanda didn't look like she believed it, but she was relieved by the words nonetheless. She wiped at her face, then smiled.

"Such mighty warriors are we," she said.

"The most terrifying in all the land," Bree said, and she laughed.

Their laughter grew stilted as Olivia emerged from the crowd of Seraphim to join them. When she spoke, Bree noticed she addressed only her, ignoring the other three.

"Our numbers are too devastated to use our old squads," she said. "And there's not enough time to officially form new ones. Do you have preference for whom you'll fly with?"

Bree gestured to her three friends.

"I'd like to stay with them," she said. "We've all trained together. The four of us should be a solid squad."

Olivia hardly looked convinced, but she acquiesced.

"Very well," she said. "Will you fly with them, or far ahead, like you did with Phoenix Squad?"

Bree imagined holding herself back to keep the others with her, or worse, Amanda attempting to keep up with her complicated maneuvers and constant high speeds.

"I know my role," she told the dark-haired woman. "The Phoenix leads the way into battle, does she not?"

"Until her death, she does," Olivia said, and she quickly saluted before moving on to the next cluster of Seraphim. Amanda watched her leave, biting on her lower lip.

"I'm not sure how well I can do this," she said when Olivia was outside earshot. "I was never able to keep up with you during drills…"

"You don't need to keep up with me," Bree said, and she glanced at Kael. "Just my brother. Follow his signals, and you'll be fine."

"You don't know that."

Kael chuckled as he nudged Amanda's side.

"Come on, now," he said. "Give me some credit. Stick with me, and we'll make it out unscathed. I don't hold a candle compared to Bree, but I've survived several battles myself."

"Maybe it's just all luck," Clara said, poking him.

"Then may it not run out for many years to come," he said, grinning.

Olivia flew into the air above the town center, and she cupped her hands to her mouth as she shouted.

"Cutter's forces are massed east of town and ready to march. We're their escort, so form up and follow me!"

The first inkling of nerves jittered inside Bree's chest, and she exhaled them slowly as she looked to her friends.

"I won't let anything happen to you," she said. "Any of you. I promise."

"Stick with promises you can keep," Clara said, her wings humming to life. Together the four lifted off, joining a parade flying east. Sure enough, several hundred soldiers stood armed and ready just outside town, formed up in ranks along the road. Olivia led the way, positioning the Seraphim hovering above in escort. Bree settled into a hover as distant shouts echoed below them, the combined forces slowly stirring into a march.

The first dozen lines of soldiers were Weshern's military, but more than one hundred people crowded near the back wore the distinctive brown robes of Johan's disciples. Most carried spears and swords, though she spotted a few wearing the single gauntlet and backpack setup that Center's specters had used when assaulting Camp Aquila. Having elemental users sprinkled throughout the ranks would certainly provide a huge advantage in battle, yet for some reason the sight of so many disciples gathered together made her nervous. At least Johan marched with them in the heart of the formation. He was no coward or hypocrite, chanting for revolution and then hiding when it came time to bleed and die for it.

When the soldiers marched, a motion from Olivia set the Seraphim into a forward drift. At agonizingly slow speeds they made their way to the Crystal Cathedral, which shone like a jewel in a sea of green grass. Bree watched for signs of defense, and sure enough, hundreds of soldiers poured out the doors and down the front steps, outnumbering the Weshern counterparts. Knights hovered above the building, slowly circling. Bree counted fifteen, though something was off with half of them. They lacked armor, she realized, and wore red instead of white. Theotechs, then. She'd never heard of them flying into battle before, but then again, there'd likely never been reason to before today. The minor islands rebelled, and demons rained down from the sky. It seemed it was a time of firsts.

Despite their approach, Center's aerial forces kept calm, maintaining their steady circling. No fear of the coming battle, nor Weshern's superior numbers. Bree hoped the same could be said for their own Seraphim. She glanced behind her, to the other three in her squad. Clara looked focused as ever, but Amanda appeared a mess of nerves. Bree hovered closer to Kael, grabbing a hold of his shoulder to keep themselves steady.

"Keep to the back," she said. "Hit the ground forces instead, and leave the knights to me."

Bree wished she could read her brother's expression as he stared at her for an uncomfortably long time.

"Fine," he said. "We will."

"Thank you," she said, smiling with relief.

He nodded but said nothing. Bree drifted away, settling into a comfortable lead ahead of the other three. The minutes passed, the ground forces closing in toward one another. Bree maintained her calm, eyes always on the knights and theotechs, watching for the moment they broke off.

And then they did, like bees fleeing a hive. All fifteen swooped out, soaring over their soldiers. Bree cast one last look to Kael, who gestured toward their foes.

"Fly on!" he shouted. "Go do what you do best!"

Bree drew her swords. She knew what that was. A mental connection clicked into place, simple and easy, and then fire erupted over her twin blades. She steadily increased the throttle until her wings were screaming, and like a comet she blasted through their ranks to emerge at the forefront. Bree held her swords out to either side, ensuring their waiting enemy saw them well.

When the Phoenix comes crashing in, I want them afraid, Commander Argus had told her once. Bree let the memories of the past few weeks flash before her eyes, of Galen's destruction, of the demons raining down from the sky, of Brad's collapse, his heart burst by a bolt of lightning. She channeled that sorrow and fear into rage, let it peel back her eyes as she punched her throttle to its absolute maximum. She saw every knight, every theotech, with crystalline clarity. They would fear her. They would see her and know their deaths approached. She refused to allow it be any other way.

The first barrage released, stone and ice lobbing into the air. Bree whirled her body, darting upward and then plunging low. Lightning flashed past her. Stone flew through the air around her. None would touch her. None would stop her assault. It didn't matter if she scored a kill on her initial charge, only that all eyes were upon her, distracting them, breaking up formations and granting openings for her fellow Seraphim to seize. The knights' fire flooded her vision, and she arced again. The straps of her harness pulled against her body, a comforting pressure as wind blasted past her.

Bree spun while flailing out her arms, almost decapitating a knight racing overhead. Her spin continued, a corkscrew of fire trailing behind her. She dove and pierced through the heart of Center's knights, her ears overwhelmed by the sound of humming wings, breaking stone, and booming thunder. One knight unleashed a blast of lightning sideways as he flew past, just barely missing as Bree pulled up and cranked back on her throttle. Multiple lances of ice punctured the man's body, his concentration stolen for that brief moment as he watched Bree. The knights and theotechs scattered under pressure from the overwhelming number of Weshern Seraphim.

Bree searched for a target, found one in a theotech flying backward while aiming toward her. Bree weaved side to side, spheres of stone as big as her head flying past. He couldn't track her, his shots always a half-second behind, but it was enough to force Bree to dodge instead of soaring straight at him. She rose higher, hoping to dive down on him from above, but while he might not be equal to the knights in aim and flight, his mastery over his element was incredible. As she rose, the theotech flung his arm, his gauntlet firing. A web of stone formed above him, pale and thin and sprawling dozens of feet in all directions.

Bree clenched her jaw and forced herself to stay calm in the face of such a bizarre attack. She rose higher, outracing the climb of the stone. As the web slowed, she spun about, diving down with arms forward as if into a lake, her grip on her swords flipped so the blades angled out and away from her body. The stone web cracked at the apex of its climb, pieces already weakening due to its thin form. Trusting her swords, she picked the largest gap and shot straight through. Her swords flared with fire, cutting clean through two lengths of the web so that when her wings connected the stone shattered. Bree saw the briefest moment of panic on the theotech's face before she cut him down, neck to hip.

Bree pulled up on her wings, leveling out as she raced away from the stone pieces falling like rain. She glanced to the ground once, saw their armies colliding with one another. As she'd hoped, the knights were too busy focusing on the aerial battle to aid below, whereas the Weshern Seraphim rained elements down upon Center's soldiers, crushing their numbers with stone and burning through their ranks with flame. Bree would gladly help, but first she would deal with the knights...

A lance of ice struck her wings, and she felt its vibrations travel all the way up her harness. Biting down a swear, she immediately twirled. A knight had fallen on her tail, and if she'd been traveling any slower he'd have torn through her side with the lance. So far it seemed her wings were undamaged, and she prayed it stayed that way. Another lance shot past her, missing by inches. Bree weaved side to side, wings pushed to her limits. She kept her movements erratic, raising or lowering the tiniest bit, and dragging on some dodges longer than others before veering back the other way. Several more lances pierced the air around her, each one far too close for comfort.

Can't shake her, Bree thought, glancing back over her shoulder. The knight matched her movements, right arm stretched out and tracking her. The prism in the knight's palm glowed blue, and another lance knifed through Bree's path. Bree pulled upward, screaming against the pain in her back. The sky and ground changed places as she performed a full loop, and on her downward dive she readied her swords to attack the knight... only the woman had mirrored the loop perfectly. Much thinner shards of ice, no bigger than knives, rained down on either side of Bree as she frantically dodged. Several broke against her wings, but luck was with her, and none pierced flesh.

Shit shit shit, Bree thought as her eyes danced left and right. The knight was back on her tail, her ice momentarily halted as she steadily closed the distance between them. Bree spotted two fellow Seraphim chasing after a fleeing theotech, and she altered her path to intersect. Trusting her comrades, she went racing past the theotech, driving the pursuing knight directly into the Seraphs' path. Sure enough, they saw and immediately switched targets.

Bree slowed the briefest moment while arcing her back, curling up and around to tail the fleeing theotech. Cramming the throttle, she burst after him. He never dodged, too busy firing ice at the other two Seraphs to realize she'd looped about so quickly. Her swords swung, the fire about them bursting to life the moment before impact. She sliced the theotech in half at the waist, both parts tumbling to the ground as the gold wings went lifeless. Meanwhile her original chaser frantically dove and twirled, avoiding the vicious barrage unleashed upon her.

Not so fast, Bree thought as she angled back into the chase. Getting to melee range against someone so skilled was unlikely, so she sheathed her right sword and banished the flame around the left. Bree followed just behind and above the other two Seraphs, watching the fleeing knight dodge, waiting for her to make a desperate maneuver...

The knight cut off her wings, swung her body, and then burst them back to life to make a sharp ninety-degree turn. The two Seraphs shot past, unable to turn in time, but Bree was ready with enough space to react. Her body rotated and, hand outstretched, she released a massive torrent of flame directly into the knight's path. The woman flew through it, emerged on the other side screaming. Her wings lost their shimmer, and the scream died as the woman passed out from the pain.

Bree collided with her hovering form. Her sword punched through the woman's breast, putting her out of her misery. A shove and they separated, the knight's body tumbling to the grass while Bree relaxed and flew away.

The release of flame sapped her breath, and she dipped lower, attempting to avoid any ongoing fight. The battle on the ground flashed beneath her as she flew. So far it seemed their forces were crushing Center's. Johan crashed through the middle of the conflict, fire exploding out from his gauntlet at a furious pace. None could withstand his assault, and it seemed the entire battle revolved around his presence. Just like her, she realized. Twin demons of war. There would be no defeat so long as they lived. The realization was equally terrifying and intoxicating.

It seemed that only two knights remained, and she chose the nearest and raced after. Two Seraphs weaved in chase, firing the occasional lance of ice or spray of flame. Neither seemed capable of corralling him, his dodges perfectly timed, the tiniest of shifts or twists in direction enough to avoid the attacks. Bree gauged his overall trajectory and then flew to cut it off. She only needed a moment, maybe twenty seconds at most. If the two Weshern Seraphim could keep him fleeing for that much longer...

The knight spun a full rotation, hand lashing out. His aim was incredible, and the two chasers had been on the offensive for so long they'd stopped weaving and dodging. A shot of lightning struck one through the chest, sending her flying off course. Bree prayed it wasn't lethal as she closed the distance, her fury seeming to give her wings that much more speed. The knight spotted her just before impact, and he fired a shot of lightning that passed over her shoulder, so close she felt the hairs of her neck stand on end. Bree twisted her upper body so she spun, hands lashing out so that both swords could slice through the knight's armor. One cut through his chest, and the other severed his leg at the knee.

Bree dropped her throttle to a hover as she turned, gasping for air. She watched the body fall to the grass, blood dripping, then a blowing horn stole away her concentration. She whipped about, searching for the source. They'd crushed their aerial foes, so what possible warning could they need? In answer, she saw Olivia flying away from the cathedral and to the north. Dotting the sky were ten red and gold forms racing toward the battle at incredible speed.

Reinforcements from Center. What had happened to their information? Marius wasn't supposed to have any knights to spare. They were all said to have fled to Center to lick their wounds and recover from the damage the fireborn had wrought.

Marius hates us more than we realized, Bree thought as she clanged her burning swords together. *That, or fears us...*

Bree angled her body parallel to the ground and punched her throttle, soaring past Olivia to face the coming challenge.

He should be afraid, she thought as the Weshern Seraphim followed her twin trails of fire. *And I'll show them all why.*

The knights unleashed their elements, fire and ice, lightning and stone. Bree danced through it all, fiery blades thirsting for blood. They would not be denied.

CHAPTER

29

Kael looped around the backside of the Cathedral, pulling himself around for a straight charge against the approaching knights of Center. Clara flew alongside him, so close she could reach out and touch him if she wished. Amanda Ruth trailed after, treating him like her squad leader. The three leveled out, joining the dozens of other Seraphim facing their enemy. Bree led the way, fire dripping from her blades, and Kael wished he could share her courage. Below them the ground battle waged, the Weshern soldiers now unaided by elemental attacks.

"It's starting," Clara shouted as the space between the forces rapidly shrank. Wind whipped across their bodies, and the first volley of stone arced into the air from opposing sides. Kael stared at the knights, ten of them, each one skilled in ways he could barely comprehend. Did it matter that the Seraphim outnumbered them more than four to one?

Kael felt a tug on his arm and he glanced Clara's way. She

flew beside him, waiting for an order. She was frightened yet determined, and he choked down his fear. No, he would not fly near the rear like he had in the previous confrontation, wishing he had his sister's bravery. He had his own bravery. Time to use it. Phoenix Squad might be disbanded, but Kael had once been a member, and he had two others he trusted to follow him. He knew where he belonged, even if Bree desired otherwise.

"Trust me!" he shouted to Clara, then used his right hand to convey with signals his next command to both Clara and Amanda.

Stay close, and follow.

Stones smashed into one another, pieces ricocheting, dust billowing in the air, and into that carnage they flew. Bree danced and weaved through the knights' formations, and a barrage of lightning and ice trailed after her. Knights dodged, retaliatory shots fired off with frightening accuracy given how little time they took to aim. Lightning thundered above Kael's head, and a lance of ice passed between him and Clara. An instinct to peel away filled him, to pick one of the knights lingering near the edges of the battle, but he denied it. He was Phoenix Squad. He had his orders.

Through the very center of it all they flew, wings shrieking, air exploding with fire and boulders. Refusing to be afraid of the chaos, refusing to lose sight of his sister's twin streaks of flame, he cranked his throttle to its maximum. The tiniest shift of his head and shoulders weaved him left of an ice lance knifing upward; a dip of his back dropped him below a wide, flat wall of stone meant to screen a retreat. He didn't look to see if Clara and Amanda followed. He couldn't afford the distraction.

Bree had yet to score a kill, but she'd scattered the knights, none willing to directly engage her. They wanted to kill the others, to slowly whittle down the numbers so they could assault her on more favorable terms. This clearly frustrated her, and she raced after them with reckless speed, refusing to be ignored. It should have left her vulnerable, but that was what Kael's trio was for. He caught sight of a knight disengaging from one duo of Seraphim to flank Bree several hundred yards directly ahead.

"Amanda!" Kael shouted. She wouldn't hear him, but she didn't need to. A blast of lightning ripped overhead, passing so close to the knight, Kael thought Amanda had scored a lethal hit. The retaliatory sphere of flame said otherwise. Kael lifted them over it as the ball of flame exploded in a wide ring, rippling through the air with a tremendous roar. The knight turned his attention from Bree to their trio, and Kael felt his nerves spike with adrenaline.

Screen, he signaled, and all three released a torrent of ice and lightning as they curled left, following Bree. The knight twisted and dodged, forced to break off his pursuit long enough for other Weshern Seraphim to spot him and take up chase. Kael continued leading his group after Bree. Amanda released occasional shots at knights in the distance, her lightning the most accurate of the elements. She was such a small thing, more wing than body, but Kael was proud of how well she remained with him in her very first battle. She was performing better than he'd done in his first fight against Galen's Seraphim, that's for sure.

Given their interference it was inevitable that they gained another knight's attention. Directly ahead, a knight looped in a circle, avoiding attacks by two Seraphs in chase. Kael dared not attack for fear of hitting his fellows, but the knight had no such reservations. His arm swung as he flew past, a lance of ice shooting with incredible accuracy directly into Kael's flight path. He didn't retreat or try to dodge. In the brief heartbeat of time he had to think, he lifted his shield and braced his arm.

The ice hit his shield, which flared with light. It shattered, Kael hardly feeling the impact beyond a tug on his mind as the light element within spent its power. He heard Clara shout nearby, frightened for his safety, but he glanced over his shoulder and grinned to show her he was fine.

"Let's go," he shouted to the two women on his tail as he curled his body and chased after his sister. They followed without hesitation, wings shimmering silver as they knifed through the air.

Bree raced after a knight, steadily closing the distance. Several hundred yards away a knight finished off a Seraph and then looped in chase. Kael judged the angles, and swore as he realized Bree likely had no clue the knight was there. He tried to follow, but two knights fleeing an entire squad of Seraphim flew between, flooding the space with an assault of ice and stone. Clara and Amanda twisted aside on instinct, avoiding the sudden barrage and going on the defensive. Kael refused to follow. Damn his safety. Protecting Bree was his mission. She was the one who could single-handedly turn the tide of war. He rolled through the air, the muscles of his lower back screaming as obstacles whisked by terrifyingly close. The sky and ground traded positions like dance partners, but he focused on his prey and let all other distractions fade. It didn't matter that he had no clue of his surroundings. It didn't matter that someone might pick him off. What mattered was that knight closing in on Bree, and how Kael could stop him.

Ice sprayed from his gauntlet. He didn't try to conserve it. He barely even aimed. Shot after shot of sharp-edged lances flew unending as his body twirled. Kael kept his eyes on the knight, his hand tracking just ahead of his path. His foe

appeared just as hell-bent on killing Bree as Kael was on bringing him down, and the knight shifted and weaved, never once
turning his attention away from the deadly Phoenix.

Come on, Kael thought as he pushed his wings harder, their
thrumming a scream in his ears, the world a spinning nonsense
of blue and cloud and fire trails. *Come on, come on, come on!*

He willed himself faster, begging speed out of his light
prism...and then he felt its presence no differently than the
ice prism. Something in his mind clicked, he felt a connection
made, and then the pressure on his body tightened as his wings
pulsed with blinding light. Kael blasted through the air, outflying his sister, outflying everyone as lightning and stone flashed
on either side of him, their paths greatly misjudged due to the
sudden, tremendous burst of speed.

Bree dove at her target, who'd finally given up fleeing to turn
and shoot one last desperate barrage. He missed, and her burning blades sliced through his armor like it were nothing. The
temporary slowing of her speed made her an easier target, but
Kael was far closer and had a far better angle on her chaser. He
fired a single long lance, and he cried out in excitement as it
blasted through the knight's neck, showering blood as his body
suddenly twisted and veered wildly.

Heart hammering in his chest, Kael had no chance to dwell
on his sudden increase in speed. The moment he tried rotating
around to follow his sister his muscles tightened up and he felt the
air fighting against him. He eased the throttle, but his momentum carried, and letting out a cry, he realized he was spiraling
out of control. The rotation had left him dizzy and disoriented,
and as Kael twisted the opposite way to counter his spinning, he
saw the Crystal Cathedral above him and closing fast.

Keep calm, he told himself as he shut off his wings, descending in free fall. A few seconds more of panic and he'd die a

splatter of gore on the cathedral floor. He had to relax. He had to regain control. Tucking his head to his chest and pulling up his legs, he rotated forward, until his feet were facing the ground, then extended. The remainder of the cathedral's glass ceiling was so close now, so close, and he wasn't stopping. No chance to be gentle. He jammed the throttle, screaming as the straps dug into his body.

He tucked his feet and lowered his shield beneath him so that his shield absorbed the bulk of the impact. The glass cracked beneath him, then shattered as he rolled sideways in the air. Kael found himself falling headfirst. Twisting his arms, Kael rotated just enough to reactivate his wings a mere heartbeat before his feet hit the ground.

It didn't kill him. Didn't even break any bones in his body. Despite the horrendous pain shooting through his muscles and the throbbing ache of his knees, Kael decided he couldn't hope for more than that. He groaned as he lay there on the cold floor, waiting for his heartbeat to return to normal. Shards of glass cut into his skin, and he grimaced at their sting. His vision swam, the aerial battle above weirdly muted to his ears.

"Get up," he muttered to himself. He pulled one knee beneath him, planting a foot, and then the vision hit. It struck his head like a blow, and he gasped in vain for air. All sight left him. The sound of the battle vanished completely. Instead he heard a roaring, saw a darkness gradually growing with light.

You return, a voice spoke in his mind. *Come, so we may speak.*

"Come where?" Kael asked. He didn't know with whom he spoke. He didn't even know where he was. The words slipped off his tongue, but he did not hear them. The voice in the darkness must have heard, for the shadows peeled away, revealing plain tile and dim white light. His eyes lifted, and there before him towered the doors that had haunted his dreams. The gold of its runes pulsed with light, the white marble so bright no light of day could match it. From the other side he felt an aura of calm, of peace. Kael reached out a hand for it, overwhelmed with a desire to enter through. The vision vanished, and his hand brushed the stained wood of a pew.

"Shit," Kael said as the real world returned with vicious suddenness. He knelt in one of the aisles between the pews. Two soldiers were rushing toward him from the hidden door of the cathedral, spears at ready. Kael pushed off one pew to get to his feet, whipped his gauntlet around to fire. Ice shot out, a trio of poorly aimed lances. Only one hit its mark, colliding with the soldier's breastplate. The armor held, but the impact sent him stumbling backward.

The other crossed the distance, spear thrusting. Kael pushed his shield in the way, winced at the sound of metal striking metal. As the spear pulled back for a second thrust, Kael flung his free hand forward, and as expected, his foe prepared his shield to block. Except Kael didn't fire thin lances; it was instead a wide spray. It coated the shield, thickening about the metal, adding to its weight. The soldier struggled to keep it raised, and realizing what was happening, he dropped the shield, clutched his spear with both hands, and desperately lunged.

Kael hopped backward, pushed the throttle so he lifted out of reach and into the air. Another spray of thin, sharp lances flew from Kael's gauntlet in a rapid flurry, puncturing the vulnerable flesh of the soldier's neck and abdomen. Kael turned on the second soldier, but only a single, stubby shot of ice flew from his gauntlet to break ineffectually against the knight's shield. Kael choked down a swear as he glanced at his ice prism through the protective window of his gauntlet. Instead of a soft blue glow, he saw a pale, cracked prism.

With his element drained, Kael had only one other recourse. He drew his sword and readied his shimmering shield. The soldier braced in the center aisle between the pews, peering over the top of his shield with his upraised spear pointed at Kael from the side. He seemed to be daring Kael to charge, a dare he willingly accepted. Kael dove, and just before impact he shut off the element to his shield. It slammed into the man with tremendous weight and force, but he stubbornly held on.

"For the Speaker!" the soldier cried, jamming his spear forward again and again. Kael pulled away and let his shield block two thrusts, sidestepped a third, then reclaimed the offensive. He hit the other man's shield, parried a thrust from the spear, and then pushed closer. His wings hummed, giving him strength. When his glowing shield struck his foe's, sparks flew between, and he heard the man scream. He swung again, was blocked, then pulled back for a thrust. When the soldier countered, Kael abandoned the swing to fling his shield in the way. It hit the shimmering surface, spear tip driving harder and harder. Kael felt a painful tug on his mind, and then the spear exploded into splinters.

Without hesitation, Kael used his wings to slam their bodies together, then sidestepped, his sword smacking his foe's shield out of the way. A single thrust ended the man, steel piercing through his eye and into the vitals behind. Kael stood over the corpse, and he gasped in air as he felt his adrenaline easing.

"I don't care where Johan got you," Kael said to his shield, and he shook his head as he sheathed his sword. "You're goddamn amazing."

Kael looked to the sky, peering through the broken ceiling of the cathedral. A guilty part of him knew he should rejoin the battle, but there was no shaking the feeling deep in his chest. He'd felt it when he rescued Bree, but he'd turned away out of their need for a hasty escape. Not this time. It had haunted his daydreams and troubled his sleep. This was his chance. One way or another, he was getting answers.

Kael opened the compartment of his gauntlet, tossed the blackened ice crystal to the floor, and then reclosed it. Adjusting the shield on his left arm, he descended the steps and entered into the hidden corridors beneath the Crystal Cathedral. As before, light elements softly glowed from insets in the ceiling. Kael saw no sign of guards. Likely all were battling Weshern's ground troops. The silence unnerved him, making his footsteps echo that much louder in the empty hall.

A lump grew in his throat, and Kael had to fight down his growing nervousness. It made no sense, none at all. Why such fear? Why such attraction in the first place to those stupid doors? What did he think would be behind them? Why did he feel so certain it was worth going inside while his friends and his sister warred in the skies against Marius's knights...

And then he turned the corner and saw it. The doors with the painted wings loomed at the far end of the hall. The gold runes didn't shimmer like in his vision, and he heard no voice, but the pull in his chest grew all the stronger. It took all of his willpower to keep from running as he crossed the distance. Yet with every step, he also felt his fear growing. It was terrifying, feeling so little control over his own actions. A rather important question echoed in his head. Did he even *want* to know what was on the other side of those doors?

Didn't matter. The door was before him, the cry to open it overwhelming his mind. Kael put his hands on either side, and he saw his fingers shake as they pressed against the cold gold runes. His fear made him angry, and he clenched his jaw as his weight leaned against the doors. *Stop it,* he told himself. *You're braver than this.*

Kael stared at the doors, envisioning a hundred things that might await him on the other side, some wonderful, some terrible. He sucked in a long, deep breath, then slowly let it out.

"Here goes nothing," he said, and he pushed open the doors and stepped inside.

CHAPTER

30

This is my purpose, thought Bree as she swirled through the air. Twin trails of fire marked her passage. *This is where I belong.*

Her muscles ached and exhaustion clawed at her eyes, but nothing would stop her. No attack would touch her. The skies were her home. She would defend her home. A solitary knight flew ahead of her, weaving side to side while circling above the dwindling ground forces. Lances of ice flew from his gauntlet, striking down Weshern soldiers. Bree's blood boiled at the sight, and she pushed her wings harder, closing the gap.

The knight spotted her approach, rotated in air, and aimed backward as he flew firing blindly. Bree danced around two lances, above one, below another. The knight never had a chance for a third. She pushed her wings to their limits, curling downward while using the pull of gravity to give her even greater speed. Her right blade lashed outward as she flew past, cleaving his firing arm at the shoulder. She saw the severed limb fall past her as she climbed, blood spraying into the air as the knight fell after it, overwhelmed with pain. Her mind blanked away the horror, refusing to let any of it sink in.

Do what you must, she told herself. Death and blood were inevitable in battle.

Bree rose higher, surveying the area as she sought a new opponent. The battle had gradually spread out, all pretense of formations and group tactics long gone. The knights had begun to ignore the ground battle altogether, instead spreading out far and wide. They were trying to fight the Weshern Seraphim in smaller engagements to take advantage of their greater skill. Given how badly they were outnumbered, it was the knights' only real chance. Bree spotted the nearest fight and increased her throttle. The longer the battle wore on, the more of her friends would die. She couldn't rest. She couldn't wait.

The thrum of her wings was so loud it sounded like a scream as she crashed through the nearest battle. Three Weshern Seraphim were dancing about a single knight, trying to fence him in as he expertly weaved and dodged. Bree attempted to cut him off, knowing her burning blades would immediately steal his attention. As expected, he saw her coming and banked hard upward. It was exactly as she'd hoped. The maneuver cost him speed, and Bree raced ahead as the other three Seraphim struck him down with a combination of fire and stone.

A Seraph and a knight battled one-on-one directly ahead of her. Bree recognized the black lines of Argus's Wolf Squad on the Seraphs' armor, which explained how the fight remained even. The two followed alongside one another, weaving in and out, testing each other for a break in concentration. Bree came up behind the knight, slowly closing in the distance. Both combatants flew just shy of their wings' maximum in case they needed a sudden burst of speed. Bree felt no such need, and she sheathed her right blade as she neared.

A shard of ice crossed the path of the Seraph, which he dodged. He retaliated with a stone of his own, and when the knight curled to the right, Bree was there, arm extended. A great explosion of flame filled the air, and the knight flew straight through, momentarily vanishing amid the red and black. When the knight reappeared, her trajectory was wild, her body hanging limp as the wings carried her in a death loop.

The Seraph twirled once to show his thanks, then arced right, chasing a knight fleeing two other Weshern Seraphim. Bree curled back around over the Crystal Cathedral, needing a moment to gather herself. Releasing her flame left her lightheaded and out of breath, and she didn't want to search for another fight while disoriented. Her speed eased, her path steadying. She just needed a few seconds to recover, that was all, but she never had the chance. From the shadow of the cathedral flew a hidden knight, his aim straight for her.

Oh shit...

A blast of lightning sent her rolling out of the way. The afterimage flashed in her eyes, and she twisted her body to fly higher, realizing only too late that the lightning wielder was already in chase. Another bolt hit her wings, and they sputtered, the deep thrumming sound becoming a high-pitched whine. Bree flicked the throttle, trying to force speed out of it as her body careened through the air at the mercy of her momentum.

Though it felt like an eternity, it took only a few seconds for the glow to return about her wings. She pushed the throttle while turning her body about, slowing her descent. The rapid approach of the ground ceased, her body began to climb, but then her pursuer raced past. A sword lashed out, slicing through the chord connecting Bree's left gauntlet to the wings. Immediately they died, and she dropped straight down. Bree flailed, feeling so helpless, so vulnerable.

She landed with a hard jolt near the bottom of the cathedral steps. She heard metal twist and groan from the landing, and she screamed as the interior of one wing jammed into her back. Through tears in her eyes she saw the knight circling above her like a bird of prey. Bree rolled, her wings dragging on the stone, one hanging limp and leaning against her side. Pain shot through her back and shoulders. She could barely get to her feet. Panicking, she ripped at the clasps of her harness. The wings were just deadweight now. She had to move. She had to find cover.

The harness dropped to the ground, followed by her gauntlets. Her sword belt remained, one weapon still sheathed. The other she spotted nearby on the ground, and she stumbled over to it. Irrational relief filled her once she had it in hand. She drew the other, then turned to flee up the stairs, only to find the way blocked. Nickolas Flynn landed before her, sword drawn in his left hand. Blood stained the lower half of his white tunic. Electricity sparkled from the focal prism in his right palm. Hatred flooded his brown eyes.

"You never listened," he said. "No matter how wise the advice, you just . . . never . . . listened."

Light swelled around the focal point, and Bree dove aside. Her shoulder hit the steps hard, and she cried out as she rolled down two more, the sharp edges jabbing into her skin. A blast of lightning sundered the spot where she'd been, blackening the stone and scattering loose tiny pebbles.

"I told you to stay away from Johan," he said. Another blast, this time faster than Bree was able to dodge. It ripped into her chest, the pain reminiscent of when she was strapped to the table at the mercy of Er'el Jaina. She flailed, muscles tightening,

fists about her sword hilts clenched so hard she feared her
fingers would break. The electricity flowed through her, she
screamed, and then all at once it ended.

Bree gasped as she rolled onto her knees, pushing with the
hilts to rise back to her feet.

"I told you to remain loyal to Center."

A straight blast through the chest should have killed her,
which meant either Nickolas was holding back, or his elemental
prism was too badly drained. Clarification came from another
short burst, this one a pale reflection of the first two shots. Bree
hopped aside as it blasted the steps. Nickolas shook his head as
he twirled his left sword while drawing another into his right
hand.

"Now look at what you've become," Nickolas said. "A
pathetic idol for a misguided nation soon to crumble."

Bree rose to her full height, biting down a grimace as her
bruised back twitched, and she lifted her swords.

"We're not afraid of you," she said. "None of us are."

Nickolas smirked.

"No matter how brave or frightened, if put your hand in fire,
you burn."

Bree dashed toward him, knowing surprise was her best
hope. Nickolas had both the size and height advantage while
above her on the steps. If she didn't equalize the situation
immediately, she might as well stretch out her neck and await
the beheading. She swung both blades for his nearer leg, hoping it would be too low for him to easily block.

He didn't need to. He jumped, wings flaring momentarily
to lift him overhead. She rotated, blades swirling above her,
but Nickolas spun before landing, weapons ready to meet her.
Steel clashed with steel, and skilled as she was, Bree could not
match his strength. He shoved her backward, and she struggled

to keep her footing as her heels struck the steps. His swords attacked, and she weaved back and forth, parrying as she climbed two more steps.

Nickolas kept up the attack, showing no real hurry. He thrust for her chest, and she smoothly swept it aside with her left only to find his other blade already slicing in for her abdomen. Her frantic parry pushed it just shy of her skin, but her balance was now precarious, and he took advantage of it immediately. Both his swords crashed down in a powerful overhead swing that she had no hope of blocking. Bree dove aside, landing hard on her shoulder. Nickolas's swords struck the stone steps, the loud clack sending shivers down her spine.

"What is it you hope for?" the knight lieutenant asked as he stalked closer, weapons twirling in his hands. High above, ice shattered against a boulder of stone, thin shards raining down on them like hail. "Fame, perhaps? Or did Argus promise you a position of power when his suicidal rebellion succeeded?"

He leapt toward her, his speed incredible. One moment he was walking toward her, and the next his swords were crashing down upon her, her finely honed reflexes the only thing keeping the steel from burying into her flesh. Bree screamed as she pushed against him, buying a momentary separation. A double-thrust forced him to defend, and as their weapons rattled against one another, Bree dashed up three more steps.

"I'm fighting for my home," she said as Nickolas stalked below her like a panther from the old world. "You'd never understand."

Nickolas swung at her ankle. Slowly, like an insult. She flicked it away as he shook his head.

"I serve the will of God and his angels," he said. "As if your home means anything in comparison."

He climbed a step, swung for her waist. Bree blocked,

countered with a swing toward his neck. His other blade easily blocked its path, and as their weapons collided, he shoved her away like an unworthy child. Bree retreated, nearing the very top of the cathedral's steps.

"Marius is a liar," she said. "You follow the will of a tyrant."

"You're a babe ranting against the rod in her father's hands," Nickolas said. "Your protests mean nothing."

Bree's hands tightened around her hilts, and she let her anger fuel her. Enough retreating. She descended in a blur, assaulting Nickolas with all she had, her momentum giving her strength in the opening exchange. Their weapons danced. Bree pushed herself to her limits, her vision narrowed, her entire existence just her and Nickolas. The movements of his blades, she predicted, every twitch of his body and shift of his feet, she saw and reacted accordingly. Bree kept the offensive, refusing to back down. Sweat poured down her neck, and her muscles screamed as she hammered her blades again and again on Nickolas's seemingly impenetrable defenses. Nothing she did surprised him. No feint worked, no swing fast enough to connect.

Despite all her skill and training, Bree was outmatched, and Nickolas knew it.

"Enough," he said, and it seemed his hands moved faster than her eyes could perceive. He attacked from both sides, guiding Bree's blades closer together, and then looped up and around, thrusting directly between them. Bree fell back, pulling her swords even tighter together to block. It was exactly what Nickolas wanted. His swords flung outward, separating her weapons and forcing her arms out of position. In came Nickolas's swords, and despite knowing it was futile, Bree tried to block anyway, her body braced in expectation of the lethal blow.

But the killing stroke never came. Instead he struck the sword in her left hand with all his might, sending the weapon

404 David Dalglish

clattering down the steps. His boot struck her chest, and she stumbled out of reach, her other sword flailing in a pathetic attempt at defense. Nickolas didn't press the attack and instead patiently closed the distance. He had no fear of her. No uncertainty in his movements.

"*Phoenix*," he spat. "What a joke. Consider yourself fortunate Marius wants you alive."

Bree closed her left hand about the sharpened edge of her sword. Only one last desperate play left to make. The idea had been squirming through her mind ever since she saw the blood of a dying fireborn harden into an elemental prism. Magic, Instructor Kime had called it. But it wasn't magic, not quite. They stole it from the fireborn, drained it from their bodies, bent it to their will. And if her own blood was capable of restoring that power...

Nickolas swung high. Bree ducked down a step, spinning, her own blade slicing into the flesh of her palm. Nickolas's swords passed above her, and they looped back around to block a strike that never came. Bree completed her spin, left arm lashing outward. Blood flew from her hand in a great spray, and as it filled the air, Bree made the mental connection now second nature to her, but this time the connection was not with a prism tucked carefully into her gauntlet. She had no need of a prism, no need of a gauntlet. The power of the fireborn already flowed within her veins.

Her blood ignited, exploding with flame. It splashed across Nickolas's face and neck, and he screamed as it seared his eyes and melted into his skin. Bree gave him no chance to recover, her sword thrusting for the opening beneath his breastplate. The blade sank up to the hilt. Warm blood poured across her hands as the knight lieutenant collapsed to his knees. His scream halted as his lungs struggled to pull in breath. His swords fell from limp hands, and his body collapsed onto her, held in her arms as if he were a long-lost friend. The smell of charred flesh filled her nostrils.

"Did you ever care for us?" she asked as she pulled her blade free. "Or was it all pretend?"

There would be no answer, not from the burning corpse crumpling at her feet halfway up the stairs of the cathedral. Bree stepped away, and she looked to the dwindling battle in the sky.

My blood is fire, she thought, exhaustion eating away at her shock and replacing it with dawning horror. *My blood is fire.*

The forces of Center flew in retreat, the ground forces crushed at last. Johan's disciples rushed up the steps while Seraphim circled above like carrion birds. They'd successfully taken the cathedral, and yet Bree could not bring herself to care. Too much pain. Too much death. Too much she feared to understand.

"My blood is fire," she whispered, and she stared at her bleeding palm. But not just fire. With every beat of her heart, she felt an awareness growing of the demon blood coursing through her veins. There was no hiding it, no pretending it meant anything else. She glared at Nickolas's corpse, tears building in her eyes.

"What am I?" she asked. "Am I even human?"

Johan ascended the steps, bloody dagger in one hand, shimmering gauntlet in the other. She watched him as if lost in a dream.

"The cathedral is ours!" he shouted, and the gathered forces cheered.

All but Bree, who sat on the steps, closed her eyes, and begged for the day to end.

CHAPTER

31

Kael had thought himself prepared for anything. He'd stood at the edge of their world and put a hand upon the dome separating them from the fireborn. He'd survived an assassination attempt, flown through battles filled with unleashed elements, and stood his ground against a giant demon that had mocked his very existence. The lies of Center no longer blinded him. His mind was open to the truths of the past. He should have been prepared.

He was not.

"My God," Kael whispered, mouth slack as he gazed upon the naked creature that stood before him.

More than sixty feet tall, she filled the cavernous room whose roof stretched a good ten feet above the creature's head. Her skin was smooth and white, without the slightest wrinkle or blemish, so that it more resembled porcelain than skin. Chains looped around the creature's wrists, neck, waist, and arms, bolted into the walls and ceiling of the spherical room to lock her in place. Piercing her luminous skin were a legion of tubes. Thick, giant tubes sank into her spine, while hundreds of smaller, thinner tubes pierced the exposed flesh of her arms and legs. Pearlescent blood pulsed through them, traveling up the tubes as they vanished into the pale gray walls surrounding her.

The creature stirred, leaning closer to him as she strained the chains binding her. Even that slight motion shook the walls and vibrated the floor beneath him. Her face was smooth, hairless, a marble mask with eyes that shone gold. A soft glow emanated from her, and he felt it on his skin like he would the light of the sun on a bright summer day. Her presence was calming, peaceful, and only it kept him from fleeing the room in fear. Though she had lips, they were sealed, without any actual opening. When she talked, the lips never moved, but her voice sounded clear in his head.

"You come at last," she said.

Kael's knees were weak, and he struggled for something, anything, to say.

"I have," he said. "Who are you?"

She tilted her head. The rattling of chains echoed on and on.

"You don't know?" she asked. It was hard for Kael to describe, but he felt a shift in that glow. Curiosity and worry tinged the calmness he felt radiating from her.

"No, I'm sorry, I don't," Kael said. "Are you...are you an angel?"

She straightened, her shoulders widening slightly. The mountain of tubes moved with it, groaning as they stretched and shifted.

"I am L'fae, lightborn of the heavens," she said. "And 'angel' is one of many names humanity has used for my kind. Now tell me your name, stranger, so we may be strangers no longer."

"Kael," he answered. "Kael Skyborn."

"Welcome, Kael," she said. "For many days I have called you. Your presence has shone in my mind, in ways no human has before."

"Calling me?" Kael asked.

"In dreams. In visions. Have you not seen them?"

The voices he'd heard from the L'fae's doors when he stood before him. The fleeting words when he'd crashed through the cathedral roof. The dream he'd had just before Jason Reigar's kidnapping attempt, of wings and a face piercing an endless battle. Not any face. L'fae's porcelain visage.

"I have," Kael said. "But always faint and fleeting. I never knew what it was."

"Only my fellow lightborn can hear such a call, yet you did, human," L'fae said. She tilted her head again, and Kael felt like a simple curiosity, a piece of string before an amused cat. "Our blood is within you. I do not understand. How do you survive with the blood of an eternal in your veins?"

"Eternal?" Kael asked, his head spinning. "I don't understand. I didn't even know lightborn existed until meeting you."

The bright glow about her body faded, and Kael felt it stronger this time, a mixture of sorrow and disappointment.

"You...don't know," she said. "What of the others of Weshern? Do they know of my suffering?"

Kael hated upsetting her so, but he felt a strong impulse to tell the truth while in the angel's presence.

"No," he said. "I don't think they do."

L'fae sank into the chains, her entire weight supported by them. The walls groaned as she, too, groaned.

"All our blood," she said, softer, a whisper in Kael's ears. "All our pain, our suffering, yet we mean nothing to you. You don't even know our names. Is this what the world has become over the centuries?"

"It's the theotechs' doing," Kael said, feeling his anger rising up to counter the angel's despair. "They've lied to us, hidden your existence from us. They're the ones that did this to you, aren't they? They trapped you in this prison."

L'fae slowly shook her head.

"This is no prison," she said.

"Then what is it?"

"The hope of your people," she said. "The continued existence of humanity. The only choice left to us come the Ascension."

The Ascension. Growing up, Kael had always believed the stories exaggerated, particularly the account of winged knights battling demons as the angels lifted the islands into the sky. Deep down, he'd assumed it a fanciful retelling of their flight from the Endless Ocean as its waters buried the world. Now he'd witnessed the demons, and he stood before a bound angel of heaven.

"Why would you submit to something like this?" Kael asked. "What happened during the Ascension? All we have are stories of that time, and I don't believe them anymore."

L'fae lowered herself as far as the constraints allowed her, and she stretched her right hand toward him, the rattle of the chains nearly deafening. Fingers the size of tree branches neared, and Kael straightened his spine and swore to be brave. The lightborn's forefinger stretched out, closer and closer. As the aura of her existence bathed over him, Kael felt his many cuts and bruises healing. It only frightened him more.

"I will tell no stories, Kael Skyborn," L'fae said. "I will *show* you."

Ever so gently, the lightborn's finger brushed Kael's forehead. Her touch was soft and surprisingly warm. An electric feeling pulsed through him. His vision swam with color. All sensations faded away, and suddenly he occupied a body not his own and saw from eyes not his.

Ocean waters stretched out before Kael, thousands of miles to the horizon. His eyes stayed still, unfocused, scanning the wide rocky shore. Trees stood behind him. They didn't need to be in his vision for him to know. He sensed them through the noise of the wind rustling their leaves, from the soft touch of life that flowed through their trunks.

A man joined Kael's side. He stared down at the man, such a small thing reaching no higher than Kael's ankle. His robes were a faint red tied at the waist with thin strips of brown cloth. A name came to him as he spoke words that were not his own.

"Is it as we feared, Barukh?" he asked.

The man tried to hide his reactions, but Kael felt them so clearly they might as well have been his own. Unease and fear gripped Barukh's chest, but bravery fought equally hard, and Kael was proud at the dark-haired man's strength.

"Worse!" Barukh said, shouting despite the effort being thoroughly unnecessary. Kael heard the beating of his heart, heard the blood pumping through his veins. "The Oceanic Wall collapsed last night."

The words meant nothing to Kael, but he felt sorrow at hearing them. Whatever the Oceanic Wall was, it had been important.

"We covered too great a space with the wall," Kael said. He realized his lips weren't moving at all when he spoke, but still the words emerged as audible sound. "Collapse was inevitable."

"Inevitable, but not so soon. We needed more time. Much of the greenlands is yet to evacuate, and boats from Eshern arrive daily."

Kael shook his head.

"Did Y'vah and Gh'aro escape the fall?"

Barukh's silence was answer enough. A weight settled on Kael's shoulders.

"I feared as much. L'adim continues to strip away all that was good in this world of yours."

"That bastard won't be satisfied until everything is crushed and burned," Barukh said.

Kael's eyes closed, and in the darkness he saw far-off shimmering orbs of light, somehow knew their distances. Names for each orb came to him immediately. The nearest was Ch'thon, and Kael sensed an immediate bond between them.

"You may be right," he said, "but we will not allow it to be this day. I sense the shadowborn's approach. We must prepare. We failed at war. We failed at fortification. Only one path remains if humanity is to escape extinction."

"You speak of cowardice," Barukh said. His disgust radiated off him in waves.

"I speak of survival," Kael said, a shudder of fear in his own heart. "And there is nothing cowardly in choosing the fate awaiting me and my brethren."

He turned from the ocean, eyes now falling upon the great forest before him. Kael offered his hand to Barukh, who climbed into his palm and sat. Kael stepped forward, but instead of smashing down the tall pines, he hovered over them, rising up as if the world were but an inconvenience he could ignore as he wished. The miles passed below him, and Kael relished the abundance of life. Squirrels raced up the sturdy trunks, birds nested in a thousand branches and hollowed spaces, wolves and coyotes slumbered as they waited for night-fall. A river ran through the woods, and Kael knew the presence of every little bug racing across its top, every little tadpole squirming through the mud of the slower branches and pools.

Below was life, and Kael cherished its feel, for he feared he might never bear witness to it again.

A city of stone sprawled across the countryside, stopping just shy of the forest's edge. Ch'thon stood in its center, towering over the buildings as he patiently waited for Kael's arrival. Kael landed opposite him, and he lowered his hand so Barukh might climb down. Barukh bowed to them both, then hurried away. The streets were crowded, with many men and women staring from the corners of their eyes as they walked. Neither Kael nor Ch'thon let his words be audible as they conversed.

"Are your preparations complete?" Ch'thon asked. The lightborn's physical representation was similar to L'fae's, despite a more masculine shape, but Kael could detect a thousand variations of white in their porcelain skin distinguishing them from one another. Ch'thon was most pleasing to look upon to Kael, his aura that of a dove recently bathed in spring waters, the feathers not quite yet dry.

"We will need years for them to be complete," Kael said. "You know that."

"Are they complete enough for the land to ascend?"

It was the question that mattered, and Kael felt the first inkling of fear in his breast when he answered.

"I believe so."

"Good," Ch'thon said, and he made a gesture with his shoulders and released a strange pulse of emotions that Kael interpreted as a form of a sigh. "Then it is time, L'fae. L'adim's army has already begun surging toward these lands. Prepare the people. Call forth what animals will listen and find them homes. There will be no second chances."

Kael put a hand on Ch'thon's shoulder, light sparkling between them.

"Do not fear these sacrifices," he said. "Embrace the opportunity to make amends for our failures."

"I do not see it the same as you," Ch'thon said. "I see a new failure to replace the old. What humanity asks of us, it may be our deaths."

"We will die even if we do not make this sacrifice," Kael argued.

"We are eternal-born," Ch'thon said, and though he spoke no audible words, his rage was so potent that hundreds of humans suddenly dropped to their knees in fright. "For millennia we never felt death's touch, yet here in this world, among these creatures, we suddenly feel its sting."

Kael's fear continued to grow deep in his chest.

"For millennia, L'adim was our brother and friend," he said. "The light is gone from him. He is shadow, and he bears death's kiss for even the eternal."

Ch'thon's body shuddered.

"All he represents is an affront to God," he said. "Why has he not been struck low for such blasphemies? Why let this destruction befall the world without intervening?"

"This world was put into our hands to nurture," Kael said. "It is still in our hands to save."

"Or it was never given to us to begin with," Ch'thon said.

Kael stood to his full height, and whatever fear he'd felt building vanished beneath waves of fury.

"Those are L'adim's words!" he shouted. "And I will not listen to them. We were brought to this realm to protect it, and so we shall. Send for the Seraphim. When the armies of the eternal-born rise against us, we shall fight until the end is upon us, and we are given no choice but to take to the skies."

More humans were cowering now. Kael looked to them, felt sympathy, and stabilized his burning emotions.

"Go to your lands," Kael told Ch'thon. "Despite all the unknown in this world, know that L'adim's hatred and slaughter is not righteous, nor just."

"And so we hide," Ch'thon said. "And so we are enslaved."

Kael stood with his head held high.

"And so we fight, and so we live."

Ch'thon took Kael's hand and brushed it with his fingers.

"You are everything to me, L'fae, and I love you dearly," he said. "But in this, you are wrong."

The lightborn rose into the air, flying away over the city, light trailing after like a cloud. Ch'thon flew to his own designated spot, where the machinery and tech was being installed by theotechs like Barukh and thousands of others. Kael felt immediate regret in his chest. In all likelihood, he would never see Ch'thon in person again. What terrible final words to exchange with one another.

"Damn you, L'adim," Kael muttered. He flew several miles north, to a sprawling field of grass beyond the city. A quarter mile of it was already excavated, dug into and laden with stone and steel in preparation for the ascension. In the very center waited dozens of tubes, and Kael winced at their sight as his feet set down.

"Welcome, L'fae!" shouted one of the older theotechs. "Come to oversee our work?"

"Not oversee," Kael said. "I come to help."

Time loosened around him. Days slipped, faster than a breath, until the sun had spun twice in the sky as he tore enormous chunks of soil up from the earth with his fingers and repositioned massive slabs of stone. Men and women scurried like ants around him, building, shaping their salvation, and L'fae's cage.

Come the third dawn, time hardened. Golden-winged soldiers gathered about L'fae, armor sparkling in the sunlight. Kael could sense every one of them, not just their innate presence of life, but also the lightborn blood pulsing in their left gauntlets, powering their wings. Theotechs walked among them, praying and blessing the elite soldiers for the coming battle.

"The shadow comes," Kael declared after scanning the east. "Take to the air, and hold nothing back. The fate of your race is now in your hands."

The Seraphim saluted L'fae, hundreds assigned to protect this specific stretch of land. With a great hum they flew skyward to join the distant legion of soldiers forming a perimeter a dozen miles long. They were the combined might of humanity, the final army to fight in what L'fae prayed would be the final battle. The lines of conflict were nearly fifteen miles away, but the miles meant nothing to him. He watched as the army of L'adim arrived with the force of a hurricane.

The stormborn led the way, as always the fastest of the elementals. Yellow and white energy crackled around them as they crashed into the line of soldiers, warping their forms to slip between shields and puncture flesh with long, sparking claws. Human soldiers hacked with swords and axes, doing all they could to keep their perimeter strong. Fireborn followed after, laughing with grating, horrible voices. They spat molten rock from their mouths and slashed at shields with claws that left deep grooves in the steel upon every strike. Last came the stoneborn, smooth and gray, lacking the long claws and gangly limbs of their other counterparts. Instead they battered down soldiers with bone-shattering punches none could withstand.

Seraphim swarmed overhead, elements flashing from their

gauntlets. They unleashed devastation upon the assaulting eternal-born, focusing on the space just beyond the ground troops so their foe couldn't mass together to use their greater numbers to their advantage. Lightning and ice shredded storm-born, earth and fire focusing on the stoneborn, charring the tiny slits for eyes and battering free chunks of stone armor to expose weaker, tender flesh beneath.

"Where are the iceborn?" Kael wondered as the battle raged. He turned his attention north, and there he saw them, a rolling wave of frost that turned the grass to a crystalline sheen with their passage. The impish creatures crashed into a stretch of soldiers, leaping onto shields and bathing them with ice so their holders had to struggle against the weight. Seraphim broke off from the main battalion, fire affinity, all of them. Torrents of flame bathed the iceborn, melting them. Kael heard each and every shriek they made, horrible sounds of pain and trauma released in voices that were once crystalline and beautiful.

"How fare our troops?" Barukh asked. He stood beside him, and he saw little with his limited human eyes.

"Fighting well," Kael said. "And dying."

The Seraphim were destroying countless thousands of the eternal-born, and the military forces held strong against the endless tide, but Kael knew it could not last. Every life lost was one they could not replace, every step backward one they would never reclaim. Men and women died with every second, with every breath, and L'adim was yet to arrive. When the shadow-born came, and he unleashed his own fury...

Kael fell to his knees in the center of the mass of tubes.

"Let it begin!" he shouted to the nearby theotechs. The holy people scrambled, lifting the smaller tubes and dragging them near. Kael lowered his arms, and he endured the first of many

stings as they pressed against his skin. They needed no needle
or knife, for with a thought he opened his flesh to allow the
tubes' entrance to his body. Immediately his strength waned as
his blood poured into the tubes. Just a trickle at first, but soon
came more tubes, and his blood flowed more freely.

"The shadowborn approaches!" Kael heard one of them
shout, and several more turned to see, Kael included. All across
the horizon, like an ocean wave, rushed a towering wall of
shadow. Fear blossomed in Kael's chest, dampened his aura. It
wouldn't be long until it arrived. The eternal-born burrowed
into one another, reshaping, growing in size. Fireborn the size
of trees lashed into the air, roaring with mouths filled with a
thousand magma teeth. Their tails snapped like scorpions,
growing in length with every strike. Stoneborn lumbered with
mighty strides, ignoring the blasts of fire and ice that shattered
across their bodies, stopping only to rip chunks of the earth free
in their clubbed fingers and hurl them through the air. With
the skies thick with Seraphim, each throw took the lives of dozens. Any soldiers who tried to stop the onslaught were beaten
back as if they were children's playthings. Only the stormborn
remained small, dashing across the grass to leap at the unfortu-
nate souls who still battled on the ground.

"There is no time left!" Kael cried. He grabbed one of the
thicker tubes and jammed it into his spine, crying out as his skin
re-formed about the heavy material. Blood rushed into it, and
Kael gasped as his strength left him. He felt himself withering,
his height shrinking as his physical form reworked to match his
waning strength. Fighting the weakness, Kael jammed another
tube in, then another. The final one he marked with a great cry,
for it was done. His blood snaked throughout the soil in hidden veins, and his awareness spread with it.

"L'fae, our soldiers!" Barukh cried at his feet. "We must order them back!"

Kael knew the same was happening all across the nearby cities. The eternal-born were too many, L'adim's strength far too great. The ground rumbled, and Kael thrust his power into it. He touched the land with his mind, gripped it in a mental fist.

"They fall not in vain," Kael said as the land quaked. "For we rise."

Enormous crevices ripped throughout the battlefield, canyons forming and closing along the perimeter of the new land L'fae aimed to create. Seraphim rose higher, taking to the skies as the ground shook so terribly no man or woman could remain standing. Even Kael collapsed to his hands and knees, both of which struggled to maintain physical form as he screamed and screamed. Psychic ripples washed over him from both north and south, other lightborn shrieking out their pain as they acted as the hands of God lifting mankind up from earthly desolation.

A single crack marked their departure from the rest of the land, one so great it deafened those nearest the edges. Slowly they lifted, Kael's blood dripping downward, and he focused his power closer to the bottom of the new island rising up. Eyes closed, Kael refused to watch those poor few who'd been on the wrong side of the newly opened chasm, but his mind heard their screams as they were devoured by the furious eternal-born. Ocean water rushed into the newly created chasm, its roar audible as they flew.

"Dear God in heaven," Barukh said beside him. "What is it we have done?"

Higher and higher the islands rose. Kael opened his eyes. Seraphim swarmed the outer edges of the island, unleashing every bit of their power to drive back the few eternal-born who'd managed to climb on prior to ascension. Slowly turning in all directions, Kael saw five other islands lumbering like sleepy creatures into the sky. Four appeared equal to Kael's own, powered by the blood of a single lightborn. One was far greater in size, a tremendous beam of light roaring beneath it, the combined power of three lightborn working in tandem to keep the land afloat.

"We have done what we must," Kael said. His voice sounded tired, intoxicated even.

"No," Barukh said. "What have we done to you?"

Kael closed his eyes, and he would have smiled if his face were capable of doing so. Already he felt small, his strength flowing out of him, his awareness shrinking, his senses dulling as if a gray cocoon wrapped about his mind. He sank deeper into the ground, seeking its comfort.

"A heavy cost, my friend, but we pay it gladly."

One by one the islands drifted toward the ocean, great beams of light pulsing beneath the chunks of earth. As his own island hovered over the water, Kael turned to the east, looking with fading vision to the crawling shadow. It swarmed about the edge of the crater, interlaced with fire and frost as the various eternal-born raged impotently.

And then Kael saw it, a face in the shadow, with blood eyes and a ghost smile. Hatred poured into him like burning bile. Breathing turned difficult. His vision swam. Those eyes glared, and amid the loathing he heard words, mocking promises as the entire coast was buried in smoke and shadow that withered every blade of grass and the leaf of every tree.

You suffer for nothing, my brethren. Humanity will reach its end, even if I must wait centuries...

*   *   *

Kael gasped for air as he collapsed to his knees. L'fae's finger withdrew, and Kael felt strangely certain that she'd only brushed his skin for a second. His stomach twisted and threatened to expel what little he'd eaten that morning. Adjusting to the limitations of his body was thoroughly disorienting. In the lightborn's memory, his awareness had felt limitless, his life unending, his senses beyond any mortal man's. Now he was fragile, small, and in a body slowly dying.

"Who was that?" Kael asked as he shuddered. "Who was that at the very end?"

"When he was our brother, we knew him as L'adim," L'fae said. Her emotions shifted, an alternating aura of confusion, anger, and sadness. "We were meant to protect your kind, yet we failed. One of our lightborn turned against us. He is the shadow that swallowed the world. We were to stop him, yet we could not. We chose this punishment *willingly*. This is our penance for our inability to save humankind, our suffering for allowing the destruction of so much we were entrusted to protect. Our blood keeps the islands afloat. Our strength powered the dome shielding you away from the evil creatures that would destroy us all."

Kael slowly pushed himself to his feet. The image haunted him, staying there before his eyes, a shadow with a face. The hatred and ugliness emanating from its body had been a river compared to the faint trickle of grace he felt from L'fae.

"What of the rest of them?" Kael asked. "The demons, they were so many. Where did they come from?"

L'fae's eyes lowered, her shoulders stooping as her chains clinked and rattled.

"That, too, is our shame," she said. "We brought them into

your world. We showed your kind how to bridge doors to worlds of fire and frost, to the eternal dimensions from which we also came. We believed their blood would allow your primitive race to rise up from the dirt, and for a millennium we were right. You built towering cities spanning miles, created wonders of steel and stone now lost below the ocean waves. Neither the great skies above nor the deep caves below were beyond your reach. But as your race's hunger grew for the elements, so too did the number of eternal-born we enslaved. So many. Too many."

She closed her eyes for a moment, and Kael heard the softest whisper of a sigh in his ears.

"And then L'adim betrayed us. He declared humanity no better than the fireborn and iceborn we enslaved. He...changed. Became what you saw. His shadow swallowed the world, and with it, a legion of eternal-born. Your great monuments are now ash and ruin. Your history is an echo. We fought, and we lost, and the islands in the sky were the last hope we had for your race to survive. But even in the sky, we did not feel we were safe, and so we created the dome."

Kael thought of the shimmering field of light he'd touched far beyond Weshern's edge.

"That was you?" he asked.

"All of us," L'fae corrected. "My brethren are within the other islands, all enduring the same, giving our strength to the Beam, our blood for your Seraphim. And yes, we powered the dome, at least, until it fell."

"Galen," Kael said, the pieces clicking into place. "Galen fell because someone killed the angel within."

L'fae slowly nodded.

"Ch'thon was my brother, and though we cannot speak with one another so far apart, we still sense each other's presence.

His death was...taxing. The strain of keeping the dome intact against the nightly assaults was beyond our abilities. It fell, and we have not the strength to re-create it."

Waves of sadness now, and strong enough tears built in Kael's own eyes.

"We failed you again," L'fae said. "Despite everything, we failed. The shadowborn has come. His creatures burn the last sacred lands. There is nowhere left to flee. Forgive us, Kael. Please forgive us."

L'fae sank down ever farther. The chains didn't bind her, Kael realized. They supported her, for she had not the strength to stand. The only thing imprisoning her there was her guilt, and the knowledge that leaving would doom the entire island of Weshern.

Kael stepped closer, and he countered the sorrow wafting over him with his rage.

"No!" he shouted, his voice a pathetic echo in the enormous room. "We've not lost yet. We destroyed the demons who fell upon our land last night, and we'll do the same to any others who try. We'll fight, L'fae. We'll fight to our dying breaths."

He didn't know what his insistence meant to a creature as ancient and powerful as an angel, but it must have meant something, for she stirred, voice rising in volume in his mind.

"In the decades of our isolation, I have forgotten how proud and stubborn humans can be," she said. "Yes, Kael Skyborn, fight against the shadow that would consume you as well. Do what you must, and see if fate is kinder than it was to the billions lost those centuries ago."

She rose to her full height with a rattle of chains.

"Tell the people of our existence," she said. "Tell them of our suffering, and of the price we pay so they may live. Most of all, tell them of the shadowborn's approach. Humanity must be ready. They must prepare for the struggles ahead. Can you do that, Kael? Can you bear that mantle?"

Kael swallowed down his fear.

"I don't know," he said. "But I'll try."

Her face never moved, but Kael swore he saw the faintest hint of a smile in her golden eyes.

"Then go, my words on your tongue, my hope in your heart. In these skies, we can hide no longer. Tell your people to ready their wings and sharpen their swords. War comes on shadowed wings, and this time, the only escape left will be in the embrace of death and the eternal lands beyond."

CHAPTER
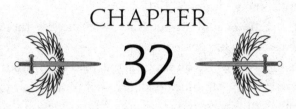
32

Bree sat on the outer steps of the cathedral, clothes stained with Nickolas's blood. His body had been rolled off the steps to the grass. Parts of his skull were exposed from the fire that had consumed his face. She tried not to look at it, tried not to remember the ugliness in his eyes. She kept a cloth pressed against her left palm, stanching the wound.

"Another knight lieutenant slain by your blade," Johan said, sitting beside her. "Your legacy will soon eclipse Argus's, if it hasn't already."

Bree looked away, refusing to take pride in the kill.

"He was my friend," she said.

Johan's smooth finger touched her chin, guided her gaze back to him.

"He was a servant of Center," he said, blue eyes shimmering. "He was never your friend, no matter what he said or did. You don't climb to that high a rank without devoting your heart and soul to the Speaker, and the Speaker alone."

Bree nodded but did not respond. The heavily robed man rose to his feet, and he clapped his hands, one of which still bore a gold gauntlet. His disciples approached, numbering at least fifty.

"Rest," he said to Bree. "You've earned it."

She watched as he began ordering his disciples, setting up perimeters and stationing more than a dozen to protect the interior doorway. Bree ignored them, instead staring out at the road winding through the grassland toward the cathedral. Word of Center's defeat appeared to be spreading. People from nearby Castnor had begun flocking toward the cathedral, spilling out across the grass on either side of the road. They were hoping for information from their Archon, an explanation for the demonic creatures falling from the sky. Or perhaps they just wanted to believe they were safe again, that Center's defeat meant the end of the conflict. Bree watched them come, but was so tired that she felt no inclination to move. Every muscle in her body ached, and the desire for sleep nearly overwhelmed her. She envied Kael's brief nap back at Johan's safe house.

"Kael?" Bree wondered aloud, bolting upright. She'd not seen her brother since the battle started. She glanced about, seeing him nowhere. The giant Chernor sat in the grass nearby, a bloody towel in his left hand, which he kept pressed against his face. Bree rushed down the steps to his side, fighting down a growing panic.

"Have you seen my brother?" she asked him.

Chernor lowered the towel so he could stare at her. A vicious burn spread from neck to forehead across the left side of his face, blackening his already dark skin and peeling away a large chunk of his long black beard. The burns edged up against his eye, turning the deep brown into a milky white.

"I haven't," he said. "You checked with Clara, yet? If he's anywhere, it's with her."

Bree shook her head.

"Do you know where she is?"

He gestured west.

"Went to escort her father. Kael might even be with her, in case you're as nervous as you look."

Bree forced a smile.

"I'm sure you're right," she said. "I'll leave you be. It looks like you need the rest."

"We all do," Chernor said as he collapsed onto his back. "But right now, I'd prefer a brand-new face instead. The old one hurts like hell."

Bree wished she had any sort of condolences she could offer that wouldn't feel hollow, so instead she saluted the man and climbed up the cathedral steps. If Kael was with Clara, they'd return soon enough. No reason to panic. No reason to think the worst...

Eyes west, Bree waited for a sign of the Archon. It came in the form of a wagon lumbering along the road, escorted by a host of soldiers and a dozen Seraphim flying overhead. No doubt the Archon and his wife were inside, come to address the crowd. A trio split from the pack, flying ahead to land near the top of the steps. Clara, flanked on either side by Seraphim.

"Clara," Bree said, joining her.

"Oh, Bree," the pale woman said. "I saw a little bit of your fight against the knight lieutenant earlier. You were amazing."

"Thanks," Bree muttered, glancing away as she said it and

wishing people would stop congratulating her for it. "Do you know where Kael is?"

"We were separated when I lost sight of him entering the cathedral." Her eyes widened as she realized what Bree's inquiry meant. "You don't think..."

"I'm sure he's fine," Bree said, wishing she believed her own words. "I'll find him."

"All right," Clara said, frowning. "Just... promise me you'll send him my way when you do, so I know he's all right."

"Will do," Bree said, hurrying up the stairs. She pushed open the doors and found the way blocked by a trio of Johan's disciples. They held short swords in their hands and refused to move.

"I'm looking for my brother," she told them, peering past them at the pews strewn with glass. "Let me through."

"No one enters," said the middle disciple. "Johan's orders."

"That's ridiculous," Bree said. She pointed to the distant door leading to the underground complex he'd rescued her from. "Kael must be down there. Step aside so I can find him!"

"I'm sorry, Bree, but no one goes down there," Johan said behind her. "Not even you."

She turned, inhaling deeply to keep herself calm. Johan stood in the doorway, arms crossed over his chest. He was smiling, but that smile felt like a lie.

"Why not?" she asked.

"Down there are the machinations that keep Weshern afloat and her people supplied with fresh water," he said. "As such, we must take every precaution necessary to ensure that what happened at Galen is not repeated here."

Bree couldn't swallow down the irony in silence.

"You sound like Marius," she said.

A shadow darkened Johan's face.

"I will send my disciples to search for him," he said. "Until then, I suggest you remain outside the cathedral with the rest of the Seraphim."

He gestured for her to go. Bree kept her head up as she exited, not bothering to hide her glare.

More Seraphim had gathered on either side of the steps, the Archon's wagon nearly arrived. Soldiers spread out, clearing space through the crowd of people. Bree remained at the top, keeping watch by the cathedral doors. If Kael were found, she wanted to be there the moment he exited the cathedral.

The wagon rolled to a halt, and the royal couple exited. Avila Willer stepped out first. She'd cleaned herself up from that morning, hints of powder and blush on her pale face. Her silver dress resembled the one she'd worn to the winter solstice dance, only less extravagant and without the many diamonds on black ribbons she'd looped throughout her hair. She extended a hand, helping her husband step down.

Isaac wore the uniform of a Seraph, and Bree wondered if the black jacket was there to hide the bandages all across his arms and chest. Even the sling on his left arm was barely visible. His hair was combed, his face cleaned of the sweat that had covered it while he lay in his bed. But, despite all the attempts to hide it, the Archon was clearly in pain, leaning his weight on Avila as he gingerly climbed the steps of the cathedral, stopping half-way up. Clara joined them, carefully taking her father's hand and kissing his cheek.

"Don't overdo it," Bree heard her tell him.

"I'll try," Isaac said, smiling at her.

The crowd crammed in closer, surrounding the cathedral steps in a half circle lined by a wall of spears and shields. Isaac turned to face them, and he separated from his wife so he might stand on his own.

"People of Weshern!" Archon shouted despite the obvious pain it caused him. The crowd hushed, eager for his words. "My people. My beloved people. Last night was a horror, and you come for answers I do not have to give. All I can promise is that we shall not respond to this travesty with obedience. We will not bleed and die for nothing." He rose up to his full height. "Let these words echo throughout our home: Weshern declares war upon Center and her Speaker."

Cheers erupted from the crowd. Bree shook her head, a sour taste filling her mouth. Easy for them to cheer and clap when they wouldn't be the ones donning plate mail or bleeding in the skies.

"Listen well," he continued. "We have been fed lies. We have swallowed truth wrapped in razor wire. Friends have been made enemies, and I must... *we* must make amends."

He struggled to project his voice despite the pain.

"I want this message spread to all the people of Galen. I am sorry. Whatever crimes we believed you committed against us, I pardon. Whatever crimes we have committed upon you, I beg forgiveness. Rip the red bands from your arms and streets. You are not our enemy. You never were."

Isaac drew the sword from his hip and held the sparkling blade high in the sunlight.

"Center is our enemy," he said. "Marius Prakt our foe. We are at war, Weshern. I declare it with all my heart. War... and we shall emerge victorious. I trust in us. I trust in you. Victory comes. It comes..."

His voice had lost volume with every word, and finally he paused and turned away from the crowd. Bree saw the face he wished to hide, one overwhelmed with pain. As the silence stretched on, claps began, few at first, then spreading like wildfire. Cheers joined in, chants of "Weshern" and "The Archon lives." Tears filled Isaac's eyes, and he let them fall as he turned back to the crowd.

"Thank you," he said. Hardly any could hear, but they didn't need to. The emotion was plain as day upon their Archon's face. Avila took her husband's weight upon her shoulder, and together they descended the steps and slid back into the wagon. Bree checked the closed cathedral doors. Still no sign of Kael. She turned back, telling herself not to assume the worst.

With Isaac's departure, Johan assumed his spot, and he lifted his arms high to gather the people's attention.

"Your Archon speaks the truth," he said, his voice carrying over the crowd. "War comes, but you are not alone. Rebellions are stirring on the other three minor islands, men and women willing to die to free themselves from Center's centuries of oppression. The hour is almost at hand, my children. Stand strong, with fists raised to the heavens. Bleed for one another, die for one another, and you will see a dream come true for your children, a life of hope and plenty, slave to no one but God and his angels."

He paused to let a cheer fade.

"You are not alone, but you were the first," he continued. "As such, you will carry great honor in the tomes of history, but you will also bear the brunt of the Speaker's retaliation. Stay strong, people of Weshern, and remember you are not alone. My disciples will bring what supplies we may, all to ensure your brave fighting men and women have the tools they need to overthrow Marius's rule once and for all!"

Another cheer.

"This is a historic hour, full of significance and sorrow," Johan said as the crowd died down. "But true heroism should not go unnoticed amid the chaos. It should shine bright, and fuel our own efforts. Breanna Skyborn, would you join me?"

He looked to her, his hand outstretched. Bree swallowed, and it felt like nails were lodged in her throat. She slowly rose to her feet, wincing at the pain in her aching muscles. Amid scattered applause, Bree joined Johan at the top of the cathedral stairs. Nickolas's blood was still on her, and she desperately wished she could wipe it away.

"Her name is known to you all," Johan continued, and he beamed at Bree with pride. "The Phoenix of Weshern, and she has earned that title ten times over. Without her this rebellion may have foundered before it ever began. Twice now she has slain knight lieutenants of Center, and many more knights have fallen to her fire. No one in the history of Weshern can claim such casualties against the Speaker and his trained killers. A legend stands before you, a force so terrible even Center quakes in fear of her name. Show her your appreciation, people of Weshern. Let me hear the love you feel for your heroes."

Bree's face flushed full red as she heard the cheers and applause grow. If only she could feel as proud of slaying Nickolas as the others did. If only she believed she was as incredible as Johan proclaimed her to be.

The cathedral doors opened behind her, and she glanced over her shoulder. Kael exited the glass building, his face as pale as winter frost. Two disciples escorted him out. He met her eyes, sensed her unasked question, and mouthed the words "I'm fine." Bree didn't believe it for a second, and she wished she could go and ask, but she had her duties.

Turning back, Bree drew a single sword, and she slid the flat edge of her blade across the wound on her left hand, bathing the steel red with fresh blood.

War is about more than casualties, Argus had once told her. And so she would play her part. Closing her eyes, she sensed her blood, sensed the lingering power of the fireborn within it. Eyes still closed, she lifted the blade to the air. Let the people whisper among themselves, debate if it were a dream, illusion, or God's own blessing. With a thought she bathed her sword in flame, a single, swirling sheath that lasted no longer than a heartbeat. The crowd roared at the ruthless slayer of Weshern's enemies, one without dread of the coming war, without fear of the coming battles, without guilt for the lives lost.

A statue of the Phoenix, a legend more important than herself, a name and a concept instead of a person.

Everything Johan warned her she'd become.

CHAPTER

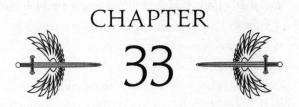

33

Later that night, Kael landed beside his sister and shut off his wings. Her hands were crossed in her lap, her legs dangling off the edge of their world. Bree's wings lay behind her, harness removed and carefully placed on the soft grass. A heavy wind blew across them, something Kael had noticed was stronger since the dome's collapse. A heavy cloud drifted close overhead, sealing away the sky.

"I thought I'd find you here," Kael said as he carefully took a seat at the edge. "Where else would you be this late at night?"

"You know me so well," Bree said, a hint of mockery in her voice. They sat at the edge of Weshern not far from Aunt Bethy's home, in the same spot they'd witnessed the battle that had claimed their parents. Kael nudged Bree's side but said nothing. She winked, then gestured to the ocean far below.

"Look," she said. "It's changed."

He peered down, and a shudder ran through him at what

he saw. The crawling darkness no longer dominated the sky. Instead it flowed beneath them, burying the ocean beneath its inky blackness. It slowly drifted like a dark fog, whisps of it curling upward before dissipating. No matter which direction he looked, that shadow spread as far as the eye could see.

"There's no dome for it to crawl across," Kael said. "So now it flows beneath."

"I thought the same," Bree said. She shook her head. "I was hoping we'd be free of it, but it looks like I was wrong."

Kael leaned away from the edge, and despite still wearing his wings, he had to fight down a momentary sense of vertigo.

"There's something else," he said. "It doesn't burn. The midnight fire is gone."

Bree rested her chin on her palms as she peered back down over the edge.

"The fireborn must not be among its forces," she said. "I wonder why."

"Well, should we encounter them again, I'll try to keep one alive for questioning," Kael said.

Bree shuddered.

"Forget it," she said. "I pray we never see those hateful things again. If you do, destroy them at once. We were never meant to live among such monsters."

Kael tapped the grass, wishing to bring up the matter of the Crystal Cathedral but nervous to do so. It wasn't that he feared she wouldn't believe him. If anyone in all of Weshern would understand he told the truth, it would be her. No, he feared what she'd tell him to do about it.

"Devi was looking for you," Kael said, deciding to bring up a different topic first, though it was by no means more pleasant.

"About what?"

He swallowed down a surge of emotions.

"Because of your...reputation, she thinks it'd be best if you write a few letters notifying kin of the deceased, particularly those you knew personally."

Her face flinched the tiniest bit in the darkness.

"You mean Brad."

Kael nodded.

"Yeah. Instructor Kime, too. I doubt it's Devi's idea, honestly. I know she's in charge of this stuff, but I think Rebecca's the one suggesting it."

"Of course," Bree said, and she sniffled. "We need to make sure the people know the Phoenix joins them in mourning even the lowliest members of our resistance. I'm sure Rebecca will add a few flowery words to the end of my letters to convince people I'm a brilliant poet, too. It's all politics and games, and I'm stuck in the damn middle of it."

Kael took her hand in his, and he squeezed it tightly.

"Then say no," he said. "You're not their puppet. Besides, I...I want to be the one to write Brad's parents. I want them to know how great a friend he was. I want them to know that no matter how hard or awful things got, he suffered through it all because he wanted to make them proud."

Bree squeezed his hand back.

"Don't forget to tell them how much that guy could eat," she said, leaning her head on his shoulder. "The cooks trembled in fear of his passage."

Kael chuckled despite the wetness of his eyes.

"Did you ever hear him snore?" he asked. "God, it sounded like a saw scraping against a stone wall."

"I never heard it, but I certainly heard you complain about it every single day that first month at the academy. I'd say it's a toss-up as to which was worse."

She laughed, and Kael felt so thankful for her presence. Brad might be gone, but Kael had the memories of them together, good memories, and he wouldn't let his sorrow prevent him from enjoying each and every one. Somehow Bree knew that, too. Kael shook her off his shoulder, and he looked back to the world-swallowing darkness.

"What do you think happens now?" he asked.

"I don't know," Bree said. "I expect Marius will try to retaliate at some point, but Johan insists Center suffered far worse from the fireborn than we did. They may not have the resources to attack, especially if Sothren, Candren, and Elern all join us in declaring our freedom."

"If they're so badly hurt, it may not convince them to withdraw," Kael said. "It might just make them that much more desperate."

Bree glanced to her right, toward the far-distant Center.

"Let them try," she said. "We'll be waiting, and we'll be ready."

Kael nodded, his stomach tightening. He had to tell Bree. Being the only one to know the truth was killing him, and just like with the existence of the demons, he didn't know what to do, nor what to believe.

"Bree," he said, "this is going to sound insane, but I have to tell you. Will you promise you'll listen?"

Bree frowned at him.

"Of course I will," she said. "I'm insulted you even had to ask."

Kael took in a deep breath.

"All right, then," he said. "It started when I first broke into the Crystal Cathedral to rescue you..."

He told her of his dreams, his meeting with L'fae, the visions of the Ascension, the lightborn's creation of the protective dome, everything. Bree listened silently, waiting for him to finish. When he did, he slumped forward, head in his hands.

"I don't know what to do," he said. "I don't know who'd believe me, or what I'd even gain in spreading the truth."

"Have you told anyone else?" she asked.

"Not yet," Kael said. "I wanted to tell you first. Figured I'd let you have the honor of telling me I'm crazy."

"I can set my blood aflame with a thought," Bree said. "This entire world may be crazy, but I don't think you are."

Kael laughed, stunned by his own relief at finally sharing the secret with his sister.

"It is a *little* crazy," he said. "So what should I do?"

"What did L'fae want you to do?"

"To tell the world," Kael said. He rolled his eyes. "As if it would be that easy. I mean, I want to, but...I don't know, Bree. People will think I've lost my mind, and it's not like I can drag people down there to meet her. Johan wouldn't allow it. Galen fell because someone killed the lightborn inside it that powered its Beam, and if someone were to do the same here..."

Bree pulled him closer, comforting him.

"Just give it a few days to think on it," she said. "We're peeling back a lot of lies the theotechs have fed us for centuries. It's going to take some time to work through it all."

Sensible enough advice. Kael nodded, and he gently leaned away from his sister.

"L'fae said I had the blood of a lightborn with me," he said. "What our blood can do, and our affinities...I think that's what caused it all, Bree. Something the theotechs did changed our blood to be more like those creatures."

Bree shivered beside him.

"I know," she said. "I...can sense it now. It's not hard, not when you know it's there. When I fought Nickolas, I ignited my own blood to burn his eyes." She shook her head. "At least you have the blood of angels in you. What of my fire? The blood of demons fills my veins."

She stared at her bandaged hand.

"What does that even make me?" she asked.

"It makes you my sister," Kael said. "And it changes nothing."

Her mood turned sour.

"Angels," she said. "We survive by the blood of angels. You know what this means, don't you?"

Kael didn't, and he told her so.

"Marius's title," she said. "*Speaker for the Angels*. It's not symbolic. It's not archaic. It's real. At any time he wishes, he can go to the center of our islands and hear their words." She tore a chunk of grass and cast it over the side of Weshern. "It makes him that much more of a monster. He bleeds demons to sell as elements to our armies, then swears the demons were destroyed in the Ascension. He hears the word of angels, yet then tells us his own. For centuries we've listened and obeyed. No longer, Kael. We have to win this war. The secrecy, the deception, we can end it all."

"Well, *you* can," Kael said, nudging her. "The Phoenix can do anything. I'll be relaxing in the background, waiting for you to wake me when you've won the war."

"Not a chance. You're part of Phoenix Squad, which means I'm relying on you to keep me alive when Center's army finally comes. Try not to relax too much. I'd hate to die because you've gotten lazy and rusty."

Kael saluted.

"If you insist," he said.

The land brightened, and both Kael and Bree looked to the sky. The low-flying cloud had drifted along as they talked, and with its departure the moon's light shone down upon them. Kael stared at it, stunned by its vibrancy. Always before it was a faint thing, swallowed by the crawling darkness before the sun ever completed its descent. Not anymore. Kael leaned back, and a calm swept over him as he looked up at the brilliant field of stars on all sides of the moon. They spanned the entire darkness, little white diamonds, a masterful painting on a canvas so distant not even their Seraphim wings could ever reach it.

"There's so many," Bree said, and Kael heard the awe in her voice, awe he felt in his chest.

"No drawing ever did it justice," Kael said. "Imagine every person on every island seeing these same stars for the first time tonight."

"And all because Galen fell," Bree said.

It was a somber reminder of the cost such beauty demanded.

"Our islands are no longer safe, and thousands have already died," he said. "Was it worth it?"

Thin tears trickled down Bree's face as she stared up at the stars.

"I don't know," she said. "Perhaps we aren't safe anymore, but I don't care. Now we see the world for how it truly is. It's dangerous, Kael, but it's beautiful, so beautiful."

She lay on her back, hands beneath her head. Kael removed his wings, reclined beside her, and together they watched the stars, for the first time in centuries free to shine without shadow and fire sealing their light away.

CHAPTER

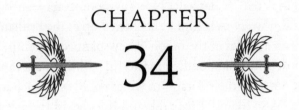

34

Marius walked alongside Er'el Jaina through the towering gates of Heavenstone. Normally, entering the ancient stone fortress of the theotechs relaxed him, but not anymore. Scorch marks lined the lower portions of the stone. Even here, where his might was at its greatest, the fireborn had made their presence known. They'd died ripping at the doors and spitting fire at the archers. No fear. No hesitation. Just a mad desire to slaughter.

"The other three islands have begun mustering their militaries, but so far none have made declarations or engaged our troops like Weshern has," Jaina said as they crossed the crimson carpet lined with pillars. There were no traders or carts of tribute, not today. All of Center was recovering from the fireborn invasion. It might be weeks before things returned to a semblance of normality, and that was an optimistic assessment. "They've stockpiled elements, established patrols watching for our knights, and stationed soldiers along the island edges. All of it is under the guise of protecting against further fireborn attacks, of course."

"That's how it starts," Marius said. "Preparation, arming of troops, testing our responses. They sense weakness, and they're not wrong. If only they realized the true danger lurking underneath their very noses."

They passed through a heavy set of doors at the far end, the entrance flanked by two golden-armored knights. The walls seemed to shrink, no longer decorated with curtains and paintings, the floor now bare stone. They were beyond the public eye. Such frivolities weren't necessary.

"The people's trust in us has never been lower," Jaina said. "I blame anarchists like Johan for that."

"The fault is ours as much as his," Marius said as they entered a winding staircase. Up it led to more than a dozen floors filled with bunks, washrooms, and mess halls to house his knights and the lower-ranking members of the theotechs. Down led to many more rooms, these carefully guarded and off-limits to many even within the theotech order. Marius touched the steel railing and began the climb down.

"We hid much from them, perhaps too much," he said. "They sensed their world incomplete, and Johan preyed on that uncertainty. Now the dome has collapsed, and the existence of the fireborn has been revealed in a night of slaughter and confusion. Who can blame them for their mistrust? We are their safekeepers, yet where were we when fire rained from the sky?"

"That doesn't excuse their rebellion," Jaina said. Doors passed them, one after the other, as they descended. "Secrets are tumbling out, one after the other, each one destabilizing our hard-earned peace. Not since the Ascension has humanity's fate been at such risk. This cannot continue unabated.

The fireborn found a way to assault us. How long until the other creatures do the same? The skies are no longer safe to us. Nowhere is."

"Do you think I don't know that?" Marius asked, whirling on her. "Do you think I'm blind to the rot spreading beneath our feet? I've done everything I can to stop its spread, but the damage is done. Worrying about it accomplishes nothing. All that matters now is how we react to the changing circumstances. Perhaps, once this madness is finished, the people will understand our measures instead of distrusting them."

Marius resumed descending the stairs, passing many exits leading to deep catacombs.

"But what of the rebellions?" Jaina asked. "You're not going to let them go unpunished, are you?"

"Of course not. The very existence of our species is at stake. We cannot allow this infighting to go on. Rebellion is like a fire. Either you stamp it out immediately, or it spreads to consume everything you hold sacred."

"Have you thought to speak with the angels?" Jaina said. She spoke hesitantly, as if fearful of his reaction. "They may have wisdom on how to handle these difficult matters."

"I have spoken with them," Marius said, sighing. He stopped again so he might address her. "They don't know what to do. When Ch'thon died, and Galen collapsed, the rest couldn't keep the protective dome stable against the assault of the shadow that swallowed the world. It's frightened them, Jaina. You can't imagine what it's like to be in the presence of a frightened lightborn. It sucks the breath out of your lungs, and it makes you feel like...like the world is ending."

Jaina hardened her jaw and stared him in the eye.

"Perhaps it is," she said.

Marius shook his head.

"Not yet," he said. "Not while I still wield the power of Heavenstone."

Thirteen floors down, Marius stopped and knocked twice on the heavy iron door. A slit opened, a set of eyes peering out momentarily before the slit reclosed. Two locks opened from the other side, and then the door swung open. A knight bowed before them, welcoming them in.

"I am glad you've come," the knight said. "The creatures seem much more anxious than normal."

The room was an enormous square, each side more than a hundred feet long. It was lit by light elements, their glow dimmed by the heavy smoke collecting about the ceiling. Fifty enormous furnaces were stationed equidistant from one another, the paths between them filled with theotechs. Their red robes were covered with ash, and they carried a variety of iron pokers, knives, and hooks. Beside each furnace was a small table, iron manacles bolted to the center. From within the furnace Marius heard the scraping, clawing, and laughing of the imprisoned fireborn.

Even if the knight hadn't mentioned it, Marius would have known something was amiss. The fireborn were normally docile in their captivity, only rousing and attempting escapes every few years. To have them all so active was unnerving.

"Do you think they know of last night's collapse?" Jaina asked.

"I believe they do," Marius said. "In fact, I'm counting on it."

Marius crossed through the center of the room, theotechs bowing in respect as he passed. He stopped at one of the tables, where a fireborn lay manacled to the center, each arm clamped at the wrist by a small loop of iron. A theotech held a long rod of steel with a curved end, and he kept it pressed against the fireborn's neck, acting as a fifth manacle. Another took a knife to the creature's arm and cut its coal-like skin. Blood poured out as the thing shrieked and twisted against the manacles.

"Have any tried to escape?" Marius asked as he watched a third theotech slide a glass vial against the wound, collecting the blood.

"No, your grace," the theotech said as she withdrew the vial, capped it so the fluid wouldn't coalesce from contact with the air, and then placed a new vial beneath. "They're active, but without any apparent reason."

Marius thought the reason apparent enough, but didn't bother to discuss it. The last thing he wanted to do was distract her during the dangerous task of withdrawing blood from one of the demons. Bidding them to carry on, he continued to the far side. Several of the furnaces were empty of fireborn, but the one in the corner was not. A theotech stood beside it, peering through the dual grates of the furnace.

"Is this one of the ones we captured last night?" Marius asked him.

"It is."

Marius took in a deep breath and steeled his nerves.

"Get it out," he ordered.

The theotech whistled for others to join so they might begin the process. Before the lock on the grate was removed a theotech slid a long, thin bar of iron through a slit in the left grate. Its end was curved, and with a few quick jabs the theotech pinned the fireborn by the neck against the opposite side of the furnace. Once pinned, they opened the right grate, two theotechs sinking curved hooks into the demon's arms. With an ease obtained by performing the maneuver countless times before, the two hauled the fireborn out of the furnace, swung it over the table, and dropped it down in the middle of the various attached clamps.

One by one the theotechs shut the manacles, trapping the demon. Once it was safely immobilized the theotechs stepped away, allowing Marius to approach. He knelt before the fireborn and stared into its obsidian eyes.

"This was what you were waiting for," he said. "Every night for six centuries you've danced upon the dome, trying to claw your way through. Is that how much you hate us? You can't suffer we few to survive?"

The fireborn opened its mouth, whether in a snarl or a grin, Marius couldn't tell. You never could with demons. The only certainty was when you heard their shrill, mocking laughter.

"Well, you're here now," Marius continued. "You fell from the sky, and whatever of your kind we failed to capture, we crushed to ash. Was this it? Six centuries, and we defeat you in a single night?"

Those obsidian eyes narrowed. Faint ghost-light sparkled in their centers, a hint of the intelligence he knew the thing possessed. It was pure evil given fiery form, and Marius wished he could wipe their existence from the land forever. If only they'd perfected the alternative. If only Er'el Tesdon's experiments had yielded far better results.

"Where were the rest of your kind?" he asked. "Where are the iceborn, the stoneborn? Why did only you attack?"

Still nothing. Marius grabbed the long iron poker from the furnace and rammed it into the creature's side. It howled as the poker sank into its flesh, which bubbled and hissed. "Where is your master, fiend? Where is the shadow that swallowed the world? He's hiding among us, isn't it? Tell me where. *Tell me!*"

"Animals," the fireborn spat, and Marius recoiled in surprise. Not once, in all his years, had he heard the creatures speak a single word after being taken captive. The other theotechs startled, staring in horror as the beast lifted its head and addressed Marius directly.

"You scared, stupid animals," it said, its voice piercing the sudden quiet. "We come. From all corners of your world, we come. From the seas. From the volcanoes. From the dark places. You cannot hide here. You are not beyond our reach. Take our blood, but we will take yours. We will feast. Your islands will fall, one by one, they will fall, and we will feast…"

Its speech descended into vicious, mocking laughter. Marius jabbed it again with the poker, but the pain only made it laugh louder. He handed the poker off to a nearby theotech, then bade Jaina to follow him as he stormed away.

"The first time one of those creatures decides to talk and it can't bother to say anything worthwhile," Marius grumbled.

"Six centuries they tried to reach us, and now they have," Jaina said. "Of course the thing would gloat."

"They haven't won anything," Marius said, spinning to glare at her. "So long as we're in the skies they can only leer up in futility, and should any find a way to ascend, we'll fight them, just like we fought them in the days of old."

He exited the room, returning to the stairs and continuing deeper into the bowels of Heavenstone, stopping when he reached the seventeenth floor down. From his pocket he pulled out a golden key, its base lined with rubies. The skeleton key for all of Heavenstone. Marius inserted the key into the door lock, turned it, but did not enter immediately.

"The current upheaval distracts us from our true foe, something we cannot afford," he said. "Weshern must be crushed, immediately and thoroughly. The Skyborn twins have become the island's beacon of hope, particularly Breanna now that she's adopted the Phoenix moniker. We must end their inspiration, no matter the cost. They're young, foolish, and naïve. Damaging them psychologically will not be hard."

Jaina's eyes widened as she realized where they'd arrived.

"He's the last remnant we have of Tesdon's transfusion pro-gram," she said. "Should he die..."

"He won't," Marius said. "And even if he does, we've learned all we can from his blood. Weshern's rebellion must be stopped before causing irreparable destruction, which means utilizing every weapon in our arsenal, even those we hold most dear."

He pushed open the door and stepped inside, Jaina at his heels. The room was small and brightly lit with light elements shimmering from diamond-shaped insets in the ceiling. In one corner was a bed, and a desk next to it. Various weights lay scattered about the stone floor. Opposite the bed was a tall wood cylinder made up of three individually rotating pieces. Additional poles stuck out at various lengths and intervals off its sides. A bare-chested man stood before it, striking the vari-ous poles with his fists and elbows, setting it to rotating. Sweat trickled down his finely muscled body.

Upon hearing the door open, the man turned. His head was shaved, revealing tattoos that covered every inch of his face and scalp, thin lines that twisted and turned without any appar-ent beginning or end. All across his shoulders, chest, and arms were pale ritual scars applied over the last five years. Upon see-ing Marius, he immediately dropped to one knee and bowed his head.

"I am honored you'd grace me with your presence, Speaker," he said. "What would you ask of me?"

Marius put a hand on Liam Skyborn's head, and he peered down with pride at the culmination of years of careful work and effort.

"My loyal knight," he said. "There are two Seraphs I need you to kill..."

EPILOGUE

Johan walked the underground tunnels of the Crystal Cathedral with a smile on his face. Rebellions were rising up on all four minor islands, and from what information he'd received from Center, Marius's people were still battling the last of the fireborn that had torched their crops and burned several of their cities to the ground. The attack on the Crystal Cathedral had been a last-ditch attempt by Marius to keep control of Weshern firmly in his hands, and they'd soundly defeated it. All in all, the day could not have gone better.

Still, there were a few loose ends that needed tying up. Johan stopped before the door to the first. A single disciple stood guard, a spear in hand.

"Leave us," Johan ordered.

The guard bowed low, then hurried down the bright corridor. Johan slid the bolt lock free, then flung open the door. The lone prisoner sat up against the smooth walls of his cell, arms crossed over his knees. The blond-haired man said nothing, only stared at him as Johan entered, shut the door behind him, and stood with his arms crossed.

"Hello, Edwin," Johan said.

"You don't look like the other theotechs," Edwin said. Despite his surroundings he looked fairly clean and healthy. Assuming the Speaker threw him in there immediately after the public executions, the man had been in there only for two days. "Are you some sort of secretive brown-robed executioner?"

Johan grinned down at him.

"The theotechs have their secretive killers," he said. "But no, I am not one of them. Do you not recognize me, Edwin? My name is Johan Lumens, and I've overthrown the cowards of Center who imprisoned you here."

The guarded bitterness immediately vanished from Edwin's face. His eyes widened, and he sat up straighter.

"You're here to free me?" he asked.

"Perhaps," Johan said. "There is the matter of your cooperation with Marius to consider."

The man paled slightly.

"I did what I thought was best for Weshern," he said carefully. "The Speaker promised us a return to rule once matters settled down and he declared our island safe."

"Safe," Johan said, and he chuckled at the word. "Marius would never have left, for your island will never be safe." He knelt down on his haunches, meeting the man's eye. "So now I consider, what happens if I release you to your parents?"

Johan knew Edwin was always the smarter of the Archon's sons, and he proved it now with how quickly he surmised the situation.

"If my parents are free, and you've taken this cathedral, then you've scored a major victory against Center," he said. "We've declared war, haven't we? Then you'll want to sway all hearts toward the effort. I can do that. Free me, and I'll go to my father, throw myself before the holy mansion's steps, and beg his forgiveness. That's what you want, isn't it? A nice public spectacle as I recant ever working with Center?"

Johan rubbed his chin.

"Such a performance would indeed foster the growing war effort," he said. "On the other hand, your father's hatred of Center is strong, but not overwhelming enough for me to trust him to see this war to its logical end." Johan shook his head. "Too many know your brother's death was an accident during the chaos of battle. But if their other son were executed by Marius in retribution for rebellion..."

Edwin's mouth dropped open. His body tensed to act, but Johan was faster. His pale hand latched around Edwin's neck. Tightening. Crushing. Slowly Johan rose to his feet, lifting the man up with him. Edwin struggled and kicked, but his blows meant nothing. Johan lifted him higher, Edwin's toes dangling above the stone floor as his face turned blue. His fingers clutched Johan's wrist so tightly his knuckles were white, but his strength was a child's compared to Johan's.

One final squeeze, and the spine snapped.

"Good riddance," Johan said, and he dropped the corpse to the floor. "You were the better of the brothers, but you were still a petulant child."

Johan stepped out of the cell, pulled his hood back over his head, and glared at the light elements embedded into the ceiling. Something would need to be done about those. Even with the cover of his hood the false illumination was painful. Johan traveled down the hallway, then paused before the grand double doors covered with archaic markings. He pressed a hand to one door and hesitated. There was no reason for him to go inside. None but pride.

He pushed it open and entered anyway.

The deep hum washed over him, vibrating his very being. Craning his neck, he looked up at the towering porcelain creature and shook his head at the awful sight. Tubes punctured the lightborn's flesh all through her arms, legs, and sides. Vibrant blood seeped out of her, pulsing with each heartbeat. She stirred, the cavernous room shaking with her every movement.

"Another stranger come to visit?" she asked. Her voice sang in his mind, familiar from so very long ago.

"Not a stranger," Johan said. "Hello, L'fae."

The lightborn tilted her head, and she leaned down with a groan of steel and stretching of tubes. Johan removed his hood and then stepped closer, closer, until the light of her essence shone upon him, burning away his flesh to reveal the shadow swirling underneath.

"L'adim?" L'fae shouted, the psychic scream overwhelmingly loud. She recoiled, supports screeching, tubes twisting, the blood pulsing out of her body all the faster. As the glow pulled back, Johan's flesh re-formed, his lips already locked in a grin.

"It still surprises me the lengths you went to save these wretched creatures," Johan said as he pulled his hood back over his head. "No, not surprises. Nothing of your foolishness surprises me, not anymore. You merely disappoint me, L'fae."

Lightborn did not have facial expressions like humans did, but Johan knew oh-so-well how to read the psychic emanations rolling off L'fae, and they stank of sadness and despair.

"When Galen fell, that was you, wasn't it?" she asked. "You slew Ch'thon."

"I did, while everyone was distracted killing each other in another senseless battle humanity is so obsessively fond of," Johan said. "He died slowly, of course. I had to leave myself time to escape before that pointless chunk of rock hit the ocean."

Anguish added to the glow, overwhelming in its power. It quivered inside him, and Johan steeled himself against the emotions he once felt.

"Will you...will you slay me as well?" she asked, unable to look him in the eye. Johan shook his head, disappointed. Clearly the centuries hooked up to these machines had drained more than just her blood. Where was the stubborn willpower that had resulted in this ridiculous last-ditch attempt to escape from his grasp? Where was the passion and anger that had fueled them in their long war against his gathered might?

"No," Johan said. "Not yet. Why send another minor island crashing to the ground when Center yet remains? My dear L'fae, I have far greater plans than that."

He turned to leave. The doors shook beneath his touch as he opened them, the lightborn struggling against the constraints and tubes. Perhaps she could wrest free, but Johan had no fear of her, not in such a weakened state. Besides, in doing so she'd send all of Weshern crashing to the ocean, dooming tens of thousands. Given her sentimentality, he doubted she'd ever perform such a sacrifice.

"You cannot do this!" L'fae shouted as the entire room quaked.

"Who will stop me?" Johan asked, spinning about, a hand on each door. "No one. Not you enslaved lightborn, not the pathetic remnants of humanity's military, not even God himself. Scream all you wish. No one will hear you. No one even knows of your existence. Suffer here in the tomb of your own creation, in what little time you have left before I bury it beneath the waves."

L'fae screamed. No words, just emotions. Hatred. Fury. Helplessness.

Johan shut the door to them all.

A NOTE FROM THE AUTHOR

I'm just going to come right out and say it: writing this story terrified me. With *Skyborn*, I purposefully tried to hide or downplay the fantastical elements. Yes, I know, I had people flying and throwing fireballs in a world where the sky burns with fire every night, but those things had a bit of mystery to them. You didn't know what the prisms were, only that they worked. You didn't know why the fire hid the stars, only that it did. It's always easier to satisfy while building up the mystery, for readers are so very good at coming up with their own theories. As Stephen King put it, the monster in the closet is always scarier than the one that's plain before you. So with *Fireborn*, here I was, yanking back the curtain. Time to reveal the source of the prisms, the power behind the Founts, the reason for the midnight fire. It's the "tada!" moment, my arms up in the air, waiting for either thunderous applause or awkward disappointment.

We writers tend to be more of the neurotic sort, so you can guess which one I was more afraid would happen while trying to get the words to cooperate.

Personally, looking back over the story as I edited and rewrote parts, I'm quite happy with it. I wanted the lightborn to be overwhelming in their size and presence, and I think I pulled that off. The flashback of the Ascension in particular was a ton of fun to write. It's not often you get to blow up a world (though readers of my other books might kindly like to point out it's not the first time for yours truly). And getting to write from some new POVs, particularly Johan's, was a nice breath of fresh air. I really do loves me a good villain, and now that he's out in the open, I'm going to have a blast in *Shadowborn*.

So now the series I tried to begin with a more solid foundation and rules for its magic, a story more "grounded," if you would allow me to make a most terrible pun, has demons and angels (maybe?) and magical blood and fireborn giants and an ageless destroyer seeking to wipe out humanity. Compared to the more YA-ish first book, with much of its events taking place at the academy, this is certainly more my style. Hopefully I kept you all entertained, and if my reveals weren't as awesome as what you imagined, well, I pray they were close.

Quick thanks: Rob, for helping me flesh out the backstory for the various eternal-born; Tommy, for the ridiculously awesome cover art; and my editor, Devi, who's still waiting for me to kill her character off. Which should still happen. Maybe.

And of course, my most heartfelt thanks to you, dear reader. I've done my best to take you for a ride, and I hope together we had a ball. If you enjoyed, tell others, share this book with friends, write reviews, and do all that stuff that means the world to me, and enables me to keep doing what I love most: telling stories. Until next time, I'll be waiting for you at the end of *Shadowborn*.

David Dalglish
January 4, 2016

extras

orbit

meet the author

Photo Credit: Mike Scott

DAVID DALGLISH currently lives in rural Missouri with his wife, Samantha, and daughters Morgan, Katherine, and Alyssa. He graduated from Missouri Southern State University in 2006 with a degree in mathematics and currently spends his free time leaping around as a giant intelligent gorilla in *Overwatch*.

introducing

If you enjoyed
FIREBORN,
look out for

SHADOWBORN

Seraphim: Book Three

by David Dalglish

Lord Commander Alexander Essex stood atop the ramparts of the castle overlooking the blue ocean. The sun shone bright on his dark skin. He smiled and felt alive. A few miles beyond the edge of the rocky shore, the Oceanic Wall quivered, its translucent surface cracking with a thousand silver spiderwebs.

"The theotechs estimate the wall will collapse before the week's end," First Seraph Kaster said, climbing the stone steps to join him on the rampart. His armor, like Alexander's, shone a brilliant gold in the sunlight.

"And what does Y'vah say of this?" Alexander asked.

"The lightborn says nothing." Kaster shook his head. "I don't think he has the strength to."

A grin pulled at the right half of Alexander's mouth. He turned and clasped Kaster's armored shoulder with his hand.

"Let it fall now," he said, and he gestured across the shoreline.

"What does it matter when we have such power ready for L'adim's monsters? They'll never even reach a single stone of this castle."

Kaster said nothing. Alexander pulled him closer, facing him west. The castle was built upon a high cliff, but below them to the east, the shore was smooth, the waves having won their war against the stone over the centuries. Golden-armored men scrambled about it like ants, and farther inland, tents formed a haphazard city. There were five thousand men armed with the finest spears and shields Europa had ever crafted, but it was beyond that front line his pride and joy waited.

"The shadowborn has never faced the likes of our dragoons," Alexander said. "Let him come, and we shall crush him beneath our heel."

Still Kaster did not respond. Alexander sensed an uneasy question lurking within him, and he had no patience for it on this fine day.

"What bothers you?" he asked. "Spit it out already before it eats a hole in your stomach."

"Commander... there are many wondering if we should use the time before the Oceanic Wall collapses to retreat farther in."

"Retreat?" Alexander asked, stepping closer. "And where shall we retreat to?"

"Just a few dozen miles inland, toward Odeon." Kaster said, refusing to back down. "If we can meet up with Commander Torman and unite Y'vah with Gh'aro, together our forces will..."

"Our forces will hold their ground here, where the terrain is favorable and our supplies plentiful." Alexander snorted. "Besides, Commander Torman is an idiot, a member of the Appeasers before this war started. How he's kept his position after that, I don't know." He glared at the cracking wall. "We will not appease those monsters and their shadowborn master. We will grind them to ash and crystal, and build our world anew with their blood."

Kaster bowed low. "As you wish," he said. "Am I dismissed?"

Alexander waved him off. He had more to do than worry about the minor rumblings of fear from the more cowardly soldiers under his command. Arms crossed over his chest, he turned east, his smile growing. The castle had been considered a relic of wartime past, but now its sturdy walls would be of great use. And atop those walls, numbering ten, with twenty more on the beach below, waited his dragoons, magnificent structures sprung forth from the combined minds of himself and Y'vah's escort of theotechs.

"Come get us, you bastard," Alexander whispered. "We're ready."

———

Fire swarmed across the Oceanic Wall, punctuated by the enormous cracks that spread for thousands of feet whenever something struck the other side. With night fallen, that fire, and the shield struggling to hold against it, was more than enough to clearly see the thousands of soldiers forming defensive lines across the beachhead. Alexander wondered what might be large enough to cause such impact. With demons, one never knew for certain their form, let alone their size.

"Are your Seraphim ready?" he asked Kaster, who patiently waited beside him.

"We are."

"Then take to the skies, and ready your elements. Make them suffer long before setting foot on dry land."

"Will you not watch from the castle?" Kaster asked.

"Here is where I belong. Now go, and ensure your stone casters do not forget their role."

"They will not," Kaster said, bowing. "May the angels ever watch over you, Commander."

"No angels will take me tonight," Alexander said. "And none are coming for you, either. L'adim's here, and we're putting an end to this war here and now."

Kaster's wings shimmered brightly, and with a deep, pleasant hum he lifted to the skies to join the one hundred others of Europa's 2nd Seraphim division. Their wings shone like golden stars in the night sky, and their glow strengthened Alexander's resolve. But nothing strengthened it like the presence of his dragoons.

Alexander walked toward the twenty dragoons lined in neat rows behind the shield wall at the beachhead, stopping at the nearest. The machine was a culmination of two years of work, a grand creation of gold and steel. The bottom was spherical, and it shimmered white from the power of five light prisms embedded within the protective metal that kept it afloat. The rest resembled a chariot, with an open space in the center for the driver. The upper half of a golden dragon was carved across the front, legs reared up, mouth open in a snarl. On either side of the opening, braced to the metallic chariot, were cannons shaped like the naval weapons of old.

A pale bare-chested man sat in the dragoon's cushioned middle, five tubes sunk into his back. His blood flowed through the clear tubes, traveling to the ten elemental prisms powering each of the two cannons. A seeing eyeglass was strapped to a pole beside his head to aid with aiming such long distances. Iron clamps around his waist kept him steady. The contraption left no room for his legs, so they'd been surgically removed upon the man's acceptance of such a crucial role in the war against the shadowborn.

"Are you ready, Adrian?" Alexander asked.

The man lowered his head as a respectful gesture.

"We have all suffered much," Adrian said. "Now is our time to give it back."

The commander grinned.

"That's the spirit."

Alexander patted the side of the dragoon lovingly, eager to see its full fury unleashed. Soon. So very soon.

Alexander joined the rest of his army in watching the assault upon the protective dome. L'adim's army raged upon the other side, flinging its might against the lightborn's defenses. The silver cracks spread wider and wider, so thick they appeared frozen bolts of lightning. A deafening screech of glass scraping glass emitted from the wall, coupled with what sounded like ice breaking atop a frozen lake.

And then the wall broke. A deep rumble replaced its glow, strong enough to rattle bones. Wind blasted across the water, angering the surface and knocking loose helmets off Alexander's soldiers. The great burning fire fell to the water, momentarily extinguished, but its fall revealed the vast demon horde, so numerous it took Alexander's breath away.

The iceborn led the way, dozens of giants twenty feet high lumbering across the ocean. With every step the water froze, granting passage to the army that followed. Among them came the stoneborn, even taller than the iceborn, vicious creatures made up of boulders cracking and twisting together into a humanoid shape. The fireborn and stormborn lurked behind, awaiting their moment.

Alexander raised his arm, and he shouted his command. Few would hear his voice, but they'd hear the song of the dragoons.

"Adrian!" he shouted. "Show them humanity's anger!"

The rider put his hands to the controls. The light beneath

extras

his dragoon brightened as the vehicle lifted higher into the air. Crackling sounds swelled from within the cannons, power building, building, until Adrian released it with a single press of a button. Twin blasts of lightning burst forward in great swirling beams, erupting with such power the dragoon rocked backward several feet. The beams dwarfed any a single Seraph could manage, with power Alexander knew nothing could withstand.

The lightning blasts struck the center of an iceborn giant, and it roared as its body shattered. Thick chunks of ice fell to the frozen ocean, blue blood flowing in streams down its waist and legs. The thing managed a single step before collapsing to its knees and falling still.

Even amid all the chaos, Alexander could hear the cheers of his soldiers at the demon's demise. The battle begun, the rest of the dragoons unleashed their fury. Streams of lightning and fire shredded the iceborn, melting limbs and blasting holes through their elemental bodies. Ice and stone struck the stoneborn, cracking the boulders of their bodies and ripping off limbs so that their blood splashed across the ocean surface. The ten dragoons atop the nearby castle joined in, assaulting the fireborn and stormborn lurking behind the initial wave of giants. The frozen ocean steadily cracked from the assault, and the blasts that missed the stoneborn were often still enough to send them below the icy surface. All in all, it was a blinding display, with Alexander forced to shield his eyes to have any hope of watching the battle unfold.

Still the giants came, though far fewer in number. The first of the iceborn touched shore, and it howled as twin beams of fire slammed its neck and face, flowing over it for several seconds. Its upper half melted, and it dropped dead to the hard ground. But the way was finally clear, and with a sudden surge the fireborn and stormborn rushed past the dying giants to the shore, eager to battle the thousands of men with their shields and spears.

Now's your time, Alexander thought, looking to the sky. Kaster's Seraphim swirled above the battlefield, and with the coming horde of smaller demons, fifteen of them dropped low, performing a single strafing. Stone flowed from their gauntlets in steady streams, forming a three-foot-high wall that protected the entirety of the shoreline. Alexander's soldiers rushed to it upon completion, spears thrusting over the defensive fortification at the incoming tide.

The first few moments of battle were a slaughter, and not in the demon's favor. The fireborn and stormborn flung themselves into a wall of stone and spears, having to climb one and avoid the other to even begin their attack. Their speed was their only advantage, but with five thousand men pressed shoulder to shoulder, shields always at the ready, there was no room for the demons to pass, no way to dodge. The blood of demons spilled before the stone wall, slowly hardening as thousands rushed before it and died.

Alexander's smile grew as his dragoons continued to sing. Giants still littered the horizon, a number that would have terrified any regular force of ground troops, but they meant nothing now. His dragoons would crush them before they ever neared his soldiers. His Seraphim circled in constant strafing runs, blasting the smaller demons with their elements while leaving the giants for the dragoons.

Slowly men died along the barricade, but with each one that fell another was waiting to take his place. There would be no break in the shields, no gap in the defenses for the demons to exploit. This was it, their breaking point. Despite the countless lost battles other nations suffered, the proud men of Europa would show the world how it was done. It was all a matter of escalation. Soldiers weren't enough. Seraphim weren't enough. Machines of war, the greatest mankind had ever seen, were the necessary tools. The dragoon launched another terrifying volley of lightning, and Alexander smiled proudly at his creation.

The dragoons were but the beginning. Now that his original concept had proven superior on the battlefield, there would be architects and theotechs flocking to his aid. How much grander might these war machines grow? What of one piloted by several men, all with different elemental affinities? Gun platforms, airships manned by hundreds of Seraphim, grand cannons rolling on wheels...there'd be no limit. L'adim's rebellion would be crushed, and through the horrors of war, amazing new inventions would emerge for the betterment of mankind.

A strange rumble stole Alexander's attention back to the battlefield atop the frozen ocean. The bulk of the demons were in retreat, something that hardly surprised Alexander, but it was the iceborn giants that confused him. They stood still, collapsing in on themselves, breaking as if from within.

"What's happening?" Alexander asked Adrian.

The dragoon rider pressed his face to the eyeglass and held it there.

"They're splitting apart," he shouted over the chorus of dragoon fire. "It looks like they're becoming dozens of iceborn, if not hundreds."

Alexander stared at the battlefield, contemplating. If the iceborn giants were suddenly numerous and small, it'd nullify the effect of his dragoons. A clever strategy, but it'd only make them weaker to the Seraphim strafing them from above. And why just the iceborn? The stoneborn continued their lumbering approach. True, the stoneborn were more resistant to the dragoon barrages, but they still broke and died. Why not change as well?

"Commander?"

Alexander turned his attention back to Adrian, and he didn't like the worried look on the rider's face one bit.

"What is it?" he asked.

Adrian squinted into the spyglass.

"A shadow's coming."

So L'adim would finally make his appearance, right as his army was being destroyed. This sounded excellent to Alexander, not worrisome.

"Where from?" he asked, thinking his dragoons could concentrate fire on the shadowborn.

Adrian pulled away, and he shook his head.

"Everywhere."

"Every...?"

Alexander grabbed the edge of the dragoon and pulled himself up. Adrian backed away as best he could to make room. Shifting himself half onto the seat, Alexander looked through the eyeglass, though truth be told the shadow had grown so close he didn't need the aid. Adrian was right. It didn't approach from any direction. Instead, roaring dozens of feet high from horizon to horizon came a tsunami of shadow.

"We'll stay strong," Alexander said, hopping down. "Stay strong, and unleash hell, rider. That's an order!"

The dragoons blasted their elements far into the distance, ignoring the stoneborn. The ice, stone, and lightning vanished within the shadow, while the fire erupted it into momentary swirls of flame. Nothing slowed it. Only the fire even left in a dent. Alexander's heart fluttered as the tsunami approached. He'd never before witnessed L'adim in person, only heard rumors of his power. Was this it? Was this overwhelming wave his true presence? So be it. The demons could bleed, and they could die. The shadowborn was no different.

The wave curled as the shore neared, and with chilling silence it slammed downward upon itself and flooded against the stone barricade. The soldiers braced themselves, but no attack came. The liquid darkness pooled and curled at the barrier, licking it, teasing it, but not passing over. The only visible demons were the stoneborn giants, the shadow up to their chests as they lumbered on. Dragoons focused their fire upon them, the battery steadily wearing the giants down.

What was the point of this? wondered Alexander. *To hide their retreat?*

And then the fire erupted several hundred feet away from the barricade. It flowed like a wave through the shadow, the fireborn hidden within the chaotic inferno. The stormborn flashed through it as well, lightning crackling about the fire and shadow as if it were a cloud of hell. Alexander swore up a storm. The shadow wasn't there to hide their retreat. It was to disguise their attack. When the fire and lightning reached the wall, the demons leapt over the barricade, assaulting the shield wall with renewed frenzy.

The dragoons resumed their fire, but the stoneborn endured, not caring for their losses. They bent down to the darkness at their feet, hands scooping. Alexander's eyes widened with horror as he realized their plan. With a single smooth motion, the stoneborn giants hurtled dozens of demons through the air, aiming for the row of twenty dragoons behind the embattled defensive line.

The demons landed and scattered in a rolling chaos. As they sprang to their feet to attack, their high-pitched laughter grated up and down Alexander's spine. Soldiers scrambled, dragoons firing even as fireborn sank their molten teeth into their flesh and stormborn flooded their bodies with electricity. A few Seraphim broke ranks to help defend them, the rest too busy attempting to hold back the tremendous tide slamming into the defensive barricade.

Alexander climbed back onto Adrian's dragoon, and he drew his sword.

"Keep firing," the commander shouted at him. "I'll keep us safe!"

The dragoon's cannons sang as Alexander swung his sword, slicing a fireborn in half. Its burning blood splashed the ground beneath the dragoon, hardening underneath the soft white glow. A stormborn sparked beneath, zipped to the side opposite Alexander, and then leapt up at Adrian's throat. The tip of Alexander's sword greeted it, piercing through its open mouth and ripping out its belly. The yellow corpse collapsed upon the cushion beside Adrian.

"Fly higher!" he shouted to Adrian. The light beneath the dragoon beamed brighter, and the vehicle steadily lifted. Another stormborn lashed at Alexander, white and gold light swirling around its reaching hands. Alexander pulled away his leg, grimacing as a claw made brief contact with his ankle. The electricity traveled all the way to his hip, firing off muscles and flooding him with terrible pain. He returned the favor with his sword, slashing off its jaw and then kicking the damn thing to the ground.

Another volley of demons arrived, but the Seraphim were ready, and there were fewer giants to throw, the stoneborn still being battered by the dragoons atop the castle. Men died by the hundreds along the barricade, but Alexander held out hope. This was the demons' last hurrah. His men just needed to survive a bit longer. His eyes searched the battlefield, a troubling question tickling his stomach. The fireborn and stormborn were racing through the liquid shadow to attack the ground troops. The stoneborn had assumed the form of giants, doing their best to besiege the dragoons behind the front lines. But where were the iceborn? Where had they gone after breaking apart and vanishing beneath the ocean?

The ground shook, an earthquake thrice the power of when Y'vah's shield had collapsed. Alexander gripped the side of the dragoon, his jaw falling slack. It couldn't be. His eyes must have been deceiving him.

A creature slowly rose from the ice beside the tall castle cliff, shadow and water rolling off its body. Its head was the size of a cottage, its broad shoulders little blue hills. It continued to rise, higher and higher, four arms digging into the steep cliffside. The gargantuan creature was beyond anything Alexander had ever seen. Its three-fingered hands bore enormous spikes of ice, and they slammed into the hard stone, pulling it ever higher toward the castle. The creature had no mouth and milky white eyes, but it bore a crown of horns, nine jagged spikes of frost jutting from its skull. Long, thick icicles trailed from its head down to its waist, frosted white and shimmering like frozen hair.

"The iceborn," Alexander whispered, still in shock. "It's all of them. Every last one."

The cliff crumbled under its weight, but the gargantuan kept digger deeper, pulling its weight higher as boulders crashed into the ocean below. The dragoons turned their fire toward it, needing no order to prioritize such a terrifying monstrosity. Fire, lightning, and stone struck its arms and sides, sending showers of frost flying in small white puffs. They were but beestings, inconveniences, as the iceborn climbed and climbed until it reached the castle and the dragoons stationed atop it.

It took less than a minute for the iceborn to smash the entire building to the ground. Its four arms thrashed and grabbed, walls crumbling to its strength, towers collapsing like glass instead of centuries-old stone. Alexander watched it all with newfound horror in his gut and tears threatening his eyes. The ice of the creature's face split wide, giving it a mouth with which to speak. Its voice thundered across the countryside like a volcanic eruption.

"YOU ARE CHILDREN WITH TOYS. BREAK THEM. BREAK THEM ALL."

introducing

If you enjoyed
FIREBORN,
look out for

HOPE AND RED

The Empire of Storms: Book One

by Jon Skovron

*In a fracturing empire spread across savage seas, two people
will find a common cause.*

*Hope, the lone survivor when her village is massacred by the
emperor's forces, is secretly trained by a master Vinchen warrior
as an instrument of vengeance.*

*Red, an orphan adopted by a notorious matriarch of the
criminal underworld, learns to be an expert thief
and con artist.*

1

Captain Sin Toa had been a trader on these seas for many years, and he'd seen something like this before. But that didn't make it any easier.

The village of Bleak Hope was a small community in the cold southern islands at the edge of the empire. Captain Toa was one of the few traders who came this far south, and even then, only once a year. The ice that formed on the water made it nearly impossible to reach during the winter months.

Still, the dried fish, whalebone, and the crude lamp oil they pressed from whale blubber were all good cargo that fetched a nice price in Stonepeak or New Laven. The villagers had always been polite and accommodating, in their taciturn Southern way. And it was a community that had survived in these harsh conditions for centuries, a quality that Toa respected a great deal.

So it was with a pang of sadness that he gazed out at what remained of the village. As his ship glided into the narrow harbor, he scanned the dirt paths and stone huts, and saw no sign of life.

"What's the matter, sir?" asked Crayton, his first mate. Good fellow. Loyal in his own way, if a bit dishonest about doing his fair share of work.

"This place is dead," said Toa quietly. "We'll not land here."

"Dead, sir?"

"Not a soul in the place."

"Maybe they're at some sort of local religious gathering," said Crayton. "Folks this far south have their own ways and customs."

"'Fraid that's not it."

Toa pointed one thick, scarred finger toward the dock. A tall sign had been driven into the wood. On the sign was painted a black oval with eight black lines trailing down from it.

"God save them," whispered Crayton, taking off his wool knit cap.

"That's the trouble," said Toa. "He didn't."

The two men stood there staring at the sign. There was no sound except the cold wind that pulled at Toa's long wool coat and beard.

"What do we do, sir?" asked Crayton.

"Not come ashore, that's for certain. Tell the wags to lay anchor. It's getting late. I don't want to navigate these shallow waters in the dark, so we'll stay the night. But make no mistake, we're heading back to sea at first light and never coming near Bleak Hope again."

———

They set sail the next morning. Toa hoped they'd reach the island of Galemoor in three days and that the monks there would have enough good ale to sell that it would cover his losses.

It was on the second night that they found the stowaway.

Toa was woken in his bunk by a fist pounding on his cabin door.

"Captain!" called Crayton. "The night watch. They found... a little girl."

Toa groaned. He'd had a bit too much grog before he went to sleep, and the spike of pain had already set in behind his eyes.

"A girl?" he asked after a moment.

"Y-y-yes, sir."

"Hells' waters," he muttered, climbing out of his hammock. He pulled on cold, damp trousers, a coat, and boots. A girl on board, even a little one, was bad luck in these southern seas. Everybody knew that. As he pondered how he was going to get rid of this stowaway, he opened the door and was surprised to find Crayton alone, turning his wool cap over and over again in his hands.

"Well? Where's the girl?"

"She's aft, sir," said Crayton.

"Why didn't you bring her to me?"

"We, uh... That is, the men can't get her out from behind the stowed rigging."

"Can't get her..." Toa heaved a sigh, wondering why no one had just reached in and clubbed her unconscious, then dragged her out. It wasn't like his men to get soft because of a little girl. Maybe it was on account of Bleak Hope. Maybe the terrible fate of that village had made them a bit more conscious than usual of their own prospects for Heaven.

"Fine," he said. "Lead me to her."

"Aye, sir," said Crayton, clearly relieved that he wasn't going to bear the brunt of the captain's frustration.

Toa found his men gathered around the cargo hold where the spare rigging was stored. The hatch was open and they stared down into the darkness, muttering to each other and making signs to ward off curses. Toa took a lantern from one of them and shone the light down into the hole, wondering why a little girl had his men so spooked.

"Look, girlie. You better..."

She was wedged in tight behind the piles of heavy line. She looked filthy and starved, but otherwise a normal enough girl of about eight years. Pretty, even, in the Southern way, with pale skin, freckles, and hair so blond it looked almost white.

But there was something about her eyes when she looked at you. They felt empty, or worse than empty. They were pools of ice that crushed any warmth you had in you. They were ancient eyes. Broken eyes. Eyes that had seen too much.

"We tried to pull her out, Captain," said one of the men. "But she's packed in there tight. And well…she's…"

"Aye," said Toa.

He knelt down next to the opening and forced himself to keep looking at her, even though he wanted to turn away.

"What's your name, girl?" he asked, much quieter now.

She stared at him.

"I'm the captain of this ship, girl," he said. "Do you know what that means?"

Slowly, she nodded once.

"It means everyone on this ship has to do what I say. That includes you. Understand?"

Again, she nodded once.

He reached one brown, hairy hand down into the hold.

"Now, girl. I want you to come out from behind there and take my hand. I swear no harm will come to you on this ship."

For a long moment, no one moved. Then, tentatively, the girl reached out her bone-thin hand and let it be engulfed in Toa's.

———

Toa and the girl were back in his quarters. He suspected the girl might start talking if there weren't a dozen hard-bitten sailors staring at her. He gave her a blanket and a cup of hot grog. He knew grog wasn't the sort of thing you gave to little girls, but it was the only thing he had on board except fresh water, and that was far too precious to waste.

Now he sat at his desk and she sat on his bunk, the blanket

wrapped tightly around her shoulders, the steaming cup of grog in her tiny hands. She took a sip, and Toa expected her to flinch at the pungent flavor, but she only swallowed and continued to stare at him with those empty, broken eyes of hers. They were the coldest blue he had ever seen, deeper than the sea itself.

"I'll ask you again, girl," he said, although his tone was still gentle. "What's yer name?"

She only stared at him.

"Where'd you come from?"

Still she stared.

"Are you..." He couldn't believe he was even thinking it, much less asking it. "Are you from Bleak Hope?"

She blinked then, as if coming out of a trance. "Bleak Hope." Her voice was hoarse from lack of use. "Yes. That's me." There was something about the way she spoke that made Toa suppress a shudder. Her voice was as empty as her eyes.

"How did you come to be on my ship?"

"That happened after," she said.

"After what?" he asked.

She looked at him then, and her eyes were no longer empty. They were full. So full that Toa's salty old heart felt like it might twist up like a rag in his chest.

"I will tell you," she said, her voice as wet and full as her eyes. "I will tell *only* you. Then I won't ever say it aloud ever again."

———

She had been off at the rocks. That was how they'd missed her.

She loved the rocks. Great big jagged black boulders she could climb above the crashing waves. It terrified her mother the way she jumped from one to the next. "You'll hurt yourself!" her mother would say. And she did hurt herself. Often. Her shins and knees were peppered with scabs and scars from the rough-edged rock. But she didn't care. She loved them anyway. And when the tide went out, they always had treasures at their bases, half-buried in the gray sand. Crab shells, fish bones, seashells, and sometimes, if she was very lucky, a bit of sea glass. Those she prized above all else.

"What is it?" she'd asked her mother one night as they sat by the fire after dinner, her belly warm and full of fish stew. She held up a piece of red sea glass to the light so that the color shone on the stone wall of their hut.

"It's glass, my little gull," said her mother, fingers working quickly as she mended a fishing net for Father. "Broken bits of glass polished by the sea."

"But why's it colored?"

"To make it prettier, I suppose."

"Why don't *we* have any glass that's colored?"

"Oh, it's just fancy Northland frippery," said her mother. "We've no use for it down here."

That made her love the sea glass all the more. She collected them until she had enough to string together with a bit of hemp rope to make a necklace. She presented it to her father, a gruff fisherman who rarely spoke, on his birthday. He held the necklace in his leathery hand, eyeing the bright red, blue, and green chunks of sea glass warily. But then he looked into her eyes and saw how proud she was, how much she loved this thing. His weather-lined face folded up into a smile as he carefully tied it around his neck. The other fishermen teased him for weeks about it, but he would only touch his calloused fingertips to the sea glass and smile again.

When *they* came on that day, the tide had just gone out, and she was searching the base of her rocks for new treasures. She'd seen the top of their ship masts off in the distance, but she was far too focused on her hunt for sea glass to investigate. It wasn't until she finally clambered back on top of one of the rocks to sift through her collection of shells and bones that she noticed how strange the ship was. A big boxy thing with a full three sails and cannon ports all along the sides. Very different from the trade ships. She didn't like the look of it at all. And that was before she noticed the thick cloud of smoke rising from her village.

She ran, her skinny little legs churning in the sand and tall grass as she made her way through the scraggly trees toward her village. If there was a fire, her mother wouldn't bother to save the treasures stowed away in the wooden chest under her bed. That was all she could think about. She'd spent too much time and effort collecting her treasures to lose them. They were the most precious thing to her. Or so she thought.

As she neared the village, she saw that the fire had spread across the whole village. There were men she didn't recognize dressed in white-and-gold uniforms with helmets and armored chest plates. She wondered if they were soldiers. But soldiers were supposed to protect the people. These men herded everyone into a big clump in the center of the village, waving swords and guns at them.

She jerked to a stop when she saw the guns. She'd seen only one other gun. It was owned by Shamka, the village elder. Every winter on the eve of the New Year, he fired it up at the moon to wake it from its slumber and bring back the sun. The guns these soldiers had looked different. In addition to the wooden handle, iron tube, and hammer, they had a round cylinder.

She was trying to decide whether to get closer or run and hide, when Shamka emerged from his hut, gave an angry bellow, and fired his gun at the nearest soldier. The soldier's face caved in as the shot struck him, and he fell back into the mud. One of the other soldiers raised his pistol and fired at Shamka, but missed. Shamka laughed triumphantly. But then the intruder fired a second time without reloading. Shamka's face was wide with surprise as he clutched at his chest and toppled over.

The girl nearly cried out then. But she bit her lip as hard as she could to stop herself, and dropped into the tall grass.

She lay hidden there in the cold, muddy field for hours. She had to clench her jaw to keep her teeth from chattering. She heard the soldiers shouting to each other, and there were strange hammering and flapping sounds. Occasionally, she would hear one of the villagers beg to know what they had done to displease the emperor. The only reply was a loud smack.

It was dark, and the fires had all flickered out before she moved her numb limbs up into a crouch and took another look.

In the center of the town, a huge brown canvas tent had been erected, easily five times larger than any hut in the village. The soldiers stood in a circle around it, holding torches. She couldn't see her fellow villagers anywhere. Cautiously, she crept a little closer.

A tall man who wore a long white hooded cloak instead of a uniform stood at the entrance to the tent. In his hands, he held a large wooden box. One of the soldiers opened the flap of the tent entrance. The cloaked man went into the tent, accompanied by a soldier. Some moments later, they both emerged, but the man no longer had the box. The soldier tied the flap so that the entrance remained open, then covered the opening with a net so fine not even the smallest bird could have slipped through.

The cloaked man took a notebook from his pocket as soldiers brought out a small table and chair and placed them before him. He sat at the table and a soldier handed him a quill and ink. The man immediately began to write, pausing frequently to peer through the netting into the tent.

Screams began to come from inside the tent. She realized then that all the villagers were inside. She didn't know why they screamed, but it terrified her so much that she dropped back into the mud and held her hands over her ears to block out the sound. The screams lasted only a few minutes, but it was a long time before she could bring herself to look again.

It was completely dark now except for one lantern at the tent entrance. The soldiers had gone and only the cloaked man remained, still scribbling away in his notebook. Occasionally, he would glance into the tent, look at his pocket watch, and frown. She wondered where the soldiers were, but then noticed that the strange boxy ship tied at the dock was lit up, and when she strained her hearing, she could make out the sound of rowdy male voices.

The girl snuck through the tall grass toward the side of the tent that was the farthest from the man. Not that he would have seen her. He seemed so intent on his writing that she probably could have walked right past him, and he wouldn't have noticed. Even so, her heart raced as she crept across the small stretch of open ground between the tall grass and the tent wall. When she finally reached the tent, she found that the bottom had been staked down so tightly that she had to pull out several of them before she could slip under.

It was even darker inside, the air thick and hot. The villagers all lay on the ground, eyes closed, chained to each other and to the thick tent poles. In the center sat the wooden box, the lid off. Scattered on the ground were dead wasps as big as birds.

Far over in the corner, she saw her mother and father, motionless like all the rest. She moved quickly to them, a sick fear shooting through her stomach.

But then her father moved weakly, and relief flooded through her. Maybe she could still rescue them. She gently shook her mother, but she didn't respond. She shook her father, but he only groaned, his eyes fluttering a moment but not opening.

She searched around, looking to see if she could unfasten their chains. There was a loud buzzing close to her ear. She turned and saw a giant wasp hovering over her shoulder. Before it could sting her, a hand shot past her face and slapped it aside. The wasp spun wildly around, one wing broken, then dropped to the ground. She turned and saw her father, his face screwed up in pain.

He grabbed her wrist. "Go!" he grunted. "Away." Then he shoved her so hard, she fell backward onto her rear.

She stared at him, terrified, but wanting to do something that would take the awful look of pain away from his face. Around her, others were stirring, their own faces etched in the same agony as her father's.

Then she saw her father's sea glass necklace give an odd little jump. She looked closer. It happened again. Her father arched his back. His eyes and mouth opened wide, as if screaming, but only a wet gurgle came out. A white worm as thick as a finger burst from his neck. Blood streamed from him as other worms burrowed out of his chest and gut.

Her mother woke with a gasp, her eyes staring around wildly. Her skin was already shifting. She reached out and called her daughter's name.

All around her, the other villagers thrashed against their chains as the worms ripped free. Before long, the ground was covered in a writhing mass of white.

She wanted to run. Instead, she held her mother's hand and watched her writhe and jerk as the worms ate her from the inside. She did not move, did not look away until her mother grew still. Only then did she stumble to her feet, slip under the tent wall, and run back into the tall grass.

She watched from afar as the soldiers returned at dawn with large burlap sacks. The cloaked man went inside the tent for a while, then came back out and wrote more in his notebook. He did this two more times, then said something to one of the soldiers. The soldier nodded, gave a signal, and the group with sacks filed into the tent. When they came back out, their sacks were filled with writhing bulges that she guessed were the worms. They carried them to the ship while the remaining soldiers struck the tent, exposing the bodies that had been inside.

The cloaked man watched as the soldiers unfastened the chains from the pile of corpses. As he stood there, the little girl fixed his face in her memory. Brown hair, weak chin, pointed ratlike face marked with a burn scar on his left cheek.

At last they sailed off in their big boxy ship, leaving a strange sign driven into the dock. When they were no longer in sight, she crept back down into the village. It took her many days. Perhaps weeks. But she buried them all.

———

Captain Sin Toa stared down at the girl. During her tale, her expression had remained fixed in a look of wide-eyed horror. But now it settled back into the cold emptiness he'd seen when he first coaxed her out of the hold.

"How long ago was that?" he asked.

"Don't know," she said.

"How did you get aboard?" he asked. "We never docked."

"I swam."

"Quite a distance."

"Yes."

"And what should I do with you now?"

She shrugged.

"A ship is no place for a little girl."

"I have to stay alive," she said. "So I can find that man."

"Do you know who that was? What that sign meant?"

486

She shook her head.

"That was the crest of the emperor's biomancers. You haven't got a prayer of ever getting close to that man."

"I will," she said quietly. "Someday. If it takes my whole life. I'll find him. And kill him."